Praise for

CARLA NEGGERS

"Neggers's engaging romantic mystery neatly blends fiction
with authentic detail."
— *Publishers Weekly* on *Tempting Fate*

"Carla Neggers is one of the most distinctive, talented writers of our genre."
—#1 *New York Times* bestselling author
Debbie Macomber

"When it comes to romance, adventure and suspense,
nobody delivers like Carla Neggers."
— *New York Times* bestselling author
Jayne Ann Krentz

"Neggers has created yet another well-matched pair of characters
and given them a crackerjack mystery to solve—
complete with a seriously creepy villain."
— *Romantic Times BOOKreviews* on *Abandon*

"Neggers keeps the reader guessing 'whodunit'
to the end of her intriguing novel."
— *Publishers Weekly* on *The Widow*

"A keen ear for dialogue and a sure hand with multidimensional
characterizations are Neggers' greatest gifts as a storyteller.... By turns
creepy and amusing, the story engages on several levels."
— *Romantic Times BOOKreviews* on *Breakwater*

TEMPTING FATE

CARLA NEGGERS

TEMPTING FATE

MIRA®

MIRA

ISBN-13: 978-0-7783-2586-4
ISBN-10:   0-7783-2586-5

TEMPTING FATE

First published by Berkley Books 1990

www.MIRABooks.com

Printed in U.S.A.

Dear Reader,

If you've ever been to Saratoga Springs in the foothills of the Adirondack Mountains, you know it's a great place to be. I've spent many days there enjoying its beautiful Victorian streets and sidewalk cafés, its colorful history, its incomparable mineral springs—and breakfast at the Saratoga racetrack in August is an experience not to be missed.

All these elements are the perfect backdrop for *Tempting Fate,* a favorite novel of mine that I'm delighted to see back in print—updated, even better than the original! I loved diving back into this story and revisiting its colorful cast of characters and the dangers they face. They've stayed with me from the moment they started percolating in my head on a pleasant stroll in downtown Saratoga, and I hope they stay with you, too.

Enjoy!

Carla

www.carlaneggers.com

One

Before she could change her mind, Dani Pembroke cut down a narrow side street in downtown Saratoga Springs, New York, and joined the line outside a small theater.

It was a beautiful August evening, the start of Saratoga's racing season, a tradition since 1863, when, just a month after the bloody Battle of Gettysburg, John "Old Smoke" Morrissey and Cornelius Vanderbilt had brought twenty-six horses to America's favorite spa for four days of racing. Dani loved the energy, the excitement, that she could feel in town. People jammed the pretty streets, the shops and restaurants were crowded and the sidewalk vendors were out in full force.

The Chandlers would have arrived by now, she thought.

My family.

Dani fought the urge to head up to the restored Victorian house they owned on North Broadway, Saratoga's "Millionaires' Row." She could see if the wraparound front porch had the hanging baskets of pink and white petunias and antique wicker furniture she remembered as a little girl. If the gardens still smelled of summer roses and lilies.

If the place still reminded her of her mother.

For twenty-five years—ever since she was nine years old—

Dani had avoided Saratoga in August. Her one searing memory was of watching her mother take off in a hot-air balloon, never to return.

More people fell into the line. The August factor at work, Dani thought. Usually the theater had to scramble for a crowd. But today, a hundred people would pack the house.

Then someone said, "It's twenty-five years this month that Lilli Chandler Pembroke disappeared," and Dani felt herself go cold. But she did nothing to draw attention to herself. The theater was showing a double feature of Nick Pembroke's masterpiece, *The Gamblers,* and its sequel thirty years later, *Casino.* The owners had gotten hold of the old posters. The one of *The Gamblers* showed a smiling, black-eyed Mattie Witt.

She's so beautiful, Dani thought, staring at her grandmother, a young woman in the picture—dazzling and mysterious with her midnight-black eyes and glossy black hair. Even then, before she'd become a star, her famous mystique was in place. Mattie Witt had made her last movie, given her last interview and abandoned Hollywood long before Dani was even born.

Her grandmother had also been long divorced from Nick Pembroke by the time her one and only grandchild was born. But as reckless as she was feeling, Dani didn't want to think about her grandfather, a talented, scoundrel Pembroke if there'd ever been one.

Her gaze shifted to the second poster, and her chest tightened at the image of her mother. It wasn't the original *Casino* poster. It was the one the studio had made after Nick Pembroke admitted that the unknown young blonde in the movie-stealing scene in the second act was his daughter-in-law, missing heiress Lilli Chandler Pembroke. He'd given her the part when he'd filmed *Casino* on location in Saratoga the previous August, days before she disappeared.

Her photograph captured not the mother Dani had known and

loved and lost, but the woman Lilli Chandler Pembroke had longed to become: vivacious, sexy, independent—someone else. She had a completely different look from Mattie Witt thirty years earlier. Lilli was all Chandler, slender, fair, patrician, pretty but not exotic. She'd believed her destiny was to be the proper heiress, always gracious and elegant, never taking a wrong—a daring—step.

Until her father-in-law had cast her in his comeback movie.

Lilli's searing performance had helped catapult *Casino* into the commercial and artistic success Nick Pembroke, who hadn't done much since Mattie Witt's defection from his life and work, had needed. Naturally he'd squandered it. No one had expected him to do anything else.

All Dani's instincts urged her to leap out of the line and keep going, keep walking.

Twenty-five years.

Blood pounded in her ears, but she didn't move.

She remembered herself at nine, waiting for her mother to come home. She'd sat on a wicker swing on the front porch of the Chandler cottage in her raspberry-smeared white dress, plucking a basket of petunias bald-headed until finally her white-faced father—Mattie Witt and Nick Pembroke's only son—had come for her. She made him put the raspberries she was saving for her mother into the refrigerator. They'd molded there, untouched.

Dani stayed in the line. She didn't look like the women on the posters. With her black eyes and short black hair, her strong features and straight, athletic figure—and her supposed recklessness—she was usually compared not to the southern Witts or the blue-blooded Chandlers but to three generations of Pembroke scoundrels. She'd seen the comparisons in the worried faces of her marketing consultants in New York. Through two days of nonstop strategy sessions, reports, brainstorming, even casual meals together, she'd sensed their unasked questions. Had she gone too far? Had she overextended herself? Was there any Chandler in her, or was she, after all, pure Pembroke? Not one Pembroke in the last hundred years had been worth a damn when it came to reliability, trustworthiness, commitment or responsibility.

When people did recognize a trace of her mother, of Chandler, in Dani—in her full, generous mouth or her occasional displays of graciousness—it was commented on with surprise, as if they must have imagined it. Even as a little girl, before her mother had disappeared, a New York gossip columnist had said, "Danielle Chandler Pembroke is not a child meant to have been born rich."

But she'd taken care of that.

Inside the theater she found a seat in the front near an exit. She'd seen both movies before, but never on the big screen. Never in public.

Sitting through *The Gamblers* was relatively easy. It was fun, romantic, like watching someone she didn't know, although she'd visited her grandmother in Greenwich Village just a few days ago. Mattie Witt was eighty-two now and still beautiful, still fiercely independent.

The film's rendition of Ulysses Pembroke's life—the murdered grandfather Nick had never known—painted him as a lovable rogue, a well-meaning scoundrel. It skipped his tragic end.

Dani almost left before *Casino* started.

She'd seen it just twice, both times on television at one o'clock in the morning. When it was released in the spring after her mother's disappearance, the adults around her all had agreed she should be spared. Nonetheless, Dani had felt the tension between the two sides of her family. Caught in the middle, her father had tried to mediate. Yes, his young wife should have—

could have—told her family that she'd taken the role in *Casino*. But no, his father hadn't been wrong to offer it to her, to let her be reckless this once, to let her put this one dream into action.

There had been no reconciliation, no understanding. Twenty-five years later, Eugene Chandler remained horrified and humiliated by what he regarded as his older daughter's betrayal, her underhandedness. He continued to believe that by encouraging Lilli to be something she wasn't, Nick Pembroke bore at least partial responsibility for her disappearance.

The story of *Casino* picked up where *The Gamblers* had left off. It painted a less romanticized, more realistic picture of Ulysses Pembroke, not shying away from how he'd gambled away his fortune at Saratoga's gaming tables and New York's stock market, how he'd wanted desperately to do the right thing but always came up short. In *Casino* he didn't get the girl, and he didn't ride off into the proverbial sunset. As in real life, he was shot dead by an anonymous sore loser outside Canfield Casino, now a Saratoga landmark. Three weeks later his wife gave birth to their son on the gleaming ballroom floor of the outrageous mansion he'd built near the Saratoga Race Course. Unable to find a buyer for her husband's eclectic, unaffordable estate, his widow had stripped it of anything she could sell to make a life for herself and her child.

The last scene in the movie showed her holding her baby as she gathered up the keys to every wrought-iron gate on the property. Ulysses had had two keys made for each gate, one of brass, one of gold. His widow sold off the gold keys.

It was a nice touch—an example of Ulysses Pembroke's profligacy. For years Dani had thought it pure fiction. She'd never seen hide nor hair of any gold keys.

Until a few weeks ago.

While rock climbing on the old Pembroke estate, she'd run across an old gate key on a narrow ledge. It turned out to be twenty-four-karat gold. And it matched exactly the brass key to the wrought-iron gate of the pavilion at the springs.

Dani had hung both keys on a gold chain. They'd attracted no comments whatever in New York. Her consultants apparently had been more interested in looking into her eyes for any sign she was going off the deep end.

She touched the keys as she watched the movie. In a performance as enriching as it was painful, the thirty-year-old heiress to the Chandler fortune managed to capture not only the soul of her character—a stunning, tragic singer in late Victorian America, a complex woman of torn loyalties and dreams she herself didn't dare acknowledge—but also of countless women like her. She bridged the gap between rich and poor, between educated and illiterate, between virgin and harlot.

Lilli Chandler Pembroke tore out her own heart and gave it to every woman in her audience.

To her own daughter.

Yet if millions of moviegoers had their image of the famous missing heiress forged by her one short, unforgettable scene in *Casino,* Dani's central vision of her mother was of her smiling and waving from the basket of a hot-air balloon.

She'd looked so happy.

As Dani had called up to the balloon as it lifted off with her promise to save her some raspberries, she'd never guessed—couldn't have imagined—that she'd never see her mother again.

It was late when the theater emptied, but Saratoga was a late-night town, and the sidewalks were still crowded. Dani cut through Congress Park, past stately Canfield Casino. She wouldn't have been surprised if she walked right over the spot where Ulysses Pembroke had been murdered.

On the other side of the park she crossed onto Union Avenue, a wide street lined with beautifully restored Victorian houses. The air was cool, fragrant with grass, pine and summer flowers. She passed the historic racetrack, quiet so late at night, its tall, pointed wrought-iron fences and red-and-white awnings silhouetted against the dark grounds.

Soon she came to the narrow, unpretentious driveway and discreet sign that marked the entrance to the Pembroke. Not long ago there'd been no sign, just the crumbling, pitted driveway. No more. Transforming Ulysses Pembroke's dilapidated house and grounds into an inn and spa had been Dani's biggest gamble. So far, it looked to pay off.

The biggest miracle, she thought, was that Nick hadn't sold the property to a mall developer years ago, never mind that she'd threatened everything short of murder if he did. Instead, she'd leased the land from him and revived Ulysses's long-defunct mineral springs, turning it into a profitable company that enabled her to buy out her grandfather. Of course, Nick liked to claim he'd never have sold out on her. Hadn't he hung on to the old place, let it be a drag on his finances, for decades? But Dani was unimpressed. Nick Pembroke was a gambler. This time he'd just gambled on her.

Walking up the driveway, she could smell the roses even before she passed the rose garden she'd restored, first on her own, with goatskin gloves and some books on roses, then later with a gardener and landscape architect. The garden was free and open to the public, as Ulysses Pembroke himself had intended when he'd first planted roses there over a hundred years ago.

Beyond the gardens the paved road veered to the right, onto the hillside where she could see the lights of the main house through the trees. It was as big and ugly and ostentatious—and amusing—as one would have expected of someone as grandiose as her great-great-grandfather. The outbuildings were just as unconventional: a sixteenth-century stable the legendary rascal had had shipped stone by stone from Ireland; a Vermont red barn for which he'd had no discernible use; a marble bathhouse with Roman columns. There were two guesthouses and more gardens—informal, formal, vegetable, flower, herb, perennial, annual. Dani had had everything gutted, renovated, spruced up, modernized, restored—whatever was necessary, she did.

Risky, maybe, but what was the worst that could happen? She could fulfill her Chandler grandfather's expectations and fall flat on her face.

She didn't follow the road up to the main buildings now. Instead she headed straight along a narrow dirt road, onto a wooden bridge. She could hear the brook below her tumbling over rocks. The dirt road curved sharply to the right and opened into a clearing. In the middle stood her gingerbread cottage. She'd had it painted pink, mauve and purple, planted its front yard with a wild-looking mix of flowers. The area bordered woods that led to the far edge of the estate and Pembroke Springs.

Dani went into the cottage through the front door and shook off the nostalgia that had gripped her since arriving back in Saratoga. She sorted through her mail. There were more cards from friends congratulating her on the opening of the Pembroke, and there were more requests for media interviews. Please, wouldn't she reconsider her aversion to reporters? Her marketing team had counseled that the judicious, well-rehearsed interview could be good for business. Dani had countered that business was fine.

On the bottom of the pile was the card from her aunt.

She'd been expecting it.

It was burgundy on cream—the Chandler racing colors—and addressed to Miss Danielle Chandler Pembroke, inviting her to the hundredth annual Chandler lawn party next Friday evening.

Dani was always invited. She just wasn't expected to attend. *Twenty-five years.*

She dropped the card into the trash and made herself a cup of chamomile tea, wondering if she should even bother going to bed. She knew she'd never sleep tonight.

* * *

"You and your kooky office."

Dani grinned up at Ira Bernstein from the overstuffed couch in her office at the Pembroke. She'd been at work since dawn; it was now just before noon. She had her feet up on a coffee table of cherrywood and green-tinted glass she'd picked up at a yard sale in the Adirondacks. She liked to think of it as art deco. Ira insisted it was junk.

"Heard you were up prowling the grounds again last night," he said. "Couldn't sleep?"

"I was up early."

"Stealing tomatoes, I understand."

He did know how to inch close to the line. He was a stocky, healthy-looking man in his mid-forties, with iron-gray corkscrew curls and an unfortunate tendency to undermine his brilliance as the Pembroke's manager with impertinence if not out-and-out insubordination. Eugene Chandler had personally fired him ten years ago from the staff of the Beverly Hills Chandler Hotel. Apparently Ira hadn't displayed proper deference toward her grandfather, the chairman of the board. Dani could just imagine. She'd plucked him from a managerial job at a mid-priced chain hotel in Istanbul. He'd instantly fallen in love with the Pembroke.

He was also one of the few people who knew about his boss's occasional bouts of insomnia. Thanks to Ira, Dani had nearly gotten her face knocked in when he'd set security on her a few weeks ago after a report of a prowler on the grounds. He considered the incident additional proof that he was damn good at his job: nothing slipped through Ira Bernstein's fingers.

"You can't beat a tomato fresh off the vine," Dani said. "Is there something you need from me?"

He smiled, clearly relishing how far he could push and still not have her go for his throat. "Just wanted to let you know that two reporters have been by looking for you."

"And you told them what?"

"That you'd been in a rotten mood for days—"

"Ira."

"Took their names and numbers and promised I'd give them to you. I made no promises about what you'd do. However, here you go." He dropped two scraps of paper on her table. "You can throw them away yourself."

"Did they want to discuss the Pembroke or the sordid details of my personal life?"

Ira grinned. "There are no sordid details of your personal life."

The man did grate.

When he didn't get a rise out of her, he continued. "Both want in-depth interviews covering your professional and personal life in whatever detail they can get." He waved a hand lightly. "They tried to bribe me for your dress size and brand of perfume, but I—"

"Are you like this with the guests?"

"I'm only cheeky with the people who sign my paychecks. A fatal flaw, I must admit. With guests I'm smooth as honey. Mind if I sit down?"

She motioned to a mission-style rocker she'd found in a dusty store off the beaten track in Maine. Ira groaned—she might have asked him to sit on a bed of nails. Her Pembroke office wasn't nearly as weird as he liked to pretend. It was an odd-shaped room with twelve-foot ceilings and double-hung windows, its decor reflecting her unorthodox executive style. In addition to her chintz-covered couch and rocker, and maybe art deco table, she had a Shaker jam cupboard, two caned side chairs, a truly ugly brass plant stand in the shape of a screaming eagle and a turn-of-the-century Baldwin player piano she'd found squirreled away in the far reaches of the main house before she'd begun renovations. Since the house had sat empty for so long, she hadn't been able to save all she'd have liked to, but what hadn't succumbed to rot—structurally, cosmetically or in furnishings, or to termites, mice or plain disuse—had remained untouched virtually since Ulysses Pembroke's day. Her architects had been delighted not to have to undo "improvements"— layers of paint, linoleum, wall-to-wall carpeting. Unfortunately that still hadn't made their job easy or cheap.

"How was New York?" Ira asked.

"Fine."

"None of my business, eh?" But his gray eyes had turned serious. "Look, Dani—"

"Out with it, Ira. What's on your mind?"

He sighed. "People talk—and I hear things."

"Such as?"

"Well, for starters, word's out that you're considering the purchase of a company in West Virginia that manufactures glass bottles."

Dani slipped her feet back into her shoes, purple flats that didn't go as well as she'd hoped with her straight cotton-knit dress, above the knee, ordered from a catalog and an entirely different shade of purple.

"Are you?" Ira asked.

"I wouldn't say I was considering. I was just inquiring."

"You don't know anything about making glass bottles. Dani—look, I'm no expert on the beverage business, but seeing how the fate of Pembroke Springs and this place are tied together, I've been doing some research. From what I can gather, glassmaking companies are a dying breed. They've all been bought out by the big guns. This outfit in West Virginia is tiny by comparison. You could lose a bundle."

"Now you sound like my bean counters."

She'd listened to them rail about her tight cash flow for two days in New York. She figured that was what bean counters were supposed to do. Since she was a Pembroke, she worried that her tolerance for risk was perhaps dangerously high and expected straight talk.

"Ira, Pembroke Springs uses a lot of glass bottles."

"I know, but that doesn't mean you have to manufacture your own. I understand you could save a ton of money if you switched to a stock bottle—"

She shook her head. "No."

"Why not?"

"Brand awareness is the name of the beverage game, Ira. People look for the Pembroke bottles. They're distinctive and they're attractive. A restaurant here in town uses our mineral-water bottles for vases on its tables. That's free promotion. They wouldn't use a bottle that some mouthwash company also uses."

"A restaurant sticks daisies into maybe ten Pembroke Springs bottles. Big deal."

"Pink roses," she corrected.

"Proprietary bottles are expensive."

"Yes, they are, but in the long haul, a private design—unique to us—more than pays for itself."

Ira scratched his head, not on firm ground when talking about Dani's mineral water and natural soda company. "Look," he said, "you know, I know—pretty soon everyone else will know—you're stretched thin. Getting the Pembroke ready has cost you. Now that it's opened, your cash-flow situation should improve, but before it does—"

"If I have to entertain cost-cutting measures, Ira, I will do so."

"Guess it's a good thing you pay yourself less than your housekeeping staff."

"That's an old rumor, Ira, and not true. I'm not personally extravagant, I'll admit. I don't mind making sacrifices in the long-term interests of my businesses. The Pembrokes have a long tradition of losing their shirts. Thank you, I'll pass."

"I'm sure your father and all the rest of them said the same thing," Ira pointed out.

"I won't compromise on quality. It's what we sell. The resort and water and natural soda businesses are highly competitive—the big guys swallow up the little guys all the time. I'm not Perrier or Coke or Club Med, and I can't pretend to be. But I'm not going to get stepped on."

Ira leaned forward. "Dani, it doesn't have to be this difficult. You took on a lot at once. You're practically a kid still. You've got a fortune tied up in equipment at the bottling plant—you've expanded into natural sodas and flavored mineral water at an incredible pace. The Pembroke is a valuable asset, but right now it burns cash."

"All to a good end."

"Ever the optimist. There is one more thing."

With Ira, there always was.

"There's a rumor floating around you're thinking of selling this place."

Dani stiffened. "Not true."

"I know, and ordinarily I wouldn't even bring it up, but, Dani, if people didn't smell blood—"

"Ira, I'm a Pembroke. There'll always be talk I'm on the verge of self-destructing. I've been listening to it ever since I told my grandfather he could give my Chandler trust to charity." Actually her words had been far more to the point, but this Ira Bernstein knew. "I'm not selling the Pembroke, I'm not switching to a stock bottle, I was only asking about the glass-making company. I am not going broke. Anything else?"

Ira shrugged, irreverent as ever. "You could admit you're lucky to have me. Am I not one of the few people you know in my line of work who'd put up with a boss who flies kites at lunch? Who just two weeks ago was caught by several guests rescuing one of her kites from the tippy-top of an oak tree and asked me—me—to lie to these guests and tell them that no, that wasn't the owner of the Pembroke but some stray kid?"

"You are, Ira," she said with a straight face, "one of a kind."

"But I've gone too far?"

She smiled. "You always do."

When he left, Dani found herself restless, unusually irritated by the false rumors, the constant battle to get people not to see her as a Pembroke or a Chandler, but simply to see *her*. Dani Pembroke.

"Most people look at this place and see disaster and folly. I see someone's dream."

Her mother's words, spoken in the overgrown Pembroke rose garden just days before she'd disappeared.

At nine, Dani had been confused. To her, dreams weren't real.

"Sometimes you can make them real," her mother had said. "Not all dreams, of course. Only the best ones. The ones you cherish most, the ones that come back to you again and again."

She'd stopped at a crumbling fountain. Her vivid blue eyes had mesmerized her small daughter with their intense yearning.

"It's far better to have tried to make your dreams come true and failed than never to have tried at all. Longing isn't enough."

But what of the people hurt in the process?

Fighting a sudden, searing sense of loneliness, Dani sneaked out through her private terrace so she wouldn't have to face Ira down the hall. She took one of the brick paths done in Saratoga's traditional herringbone pattern that snaked through the grounds. In a few minutes the main house was behind her. It was the jewel of the unique estate—lavish, overdone, oddly whimsical. The exterior was a maze of clapboards, shingles, brick, stone and stucco, with bay windows, towers, turrets, porches, balconies and gingerbread fretwork. Inside there wasn't one ordinary room.

Ulysses Pembroke's dream. And what had it cost him? What had it cost his family?

Dani made her way back to her cottage, where she quickly changed into a T-shirt, sweatpants and battered sneakers. No need for her full rock-climbing regalia. She rubbed on sunscreen, then headed through her meadow into the woods, bumping into some guests out for a nature walk or exercise run—and one enterprising couple picking wild blackberries. Seeing people enjoying the place lifted her spirits.

She bypassed the Pembroke Springs bottling plant. She could hear the clatter of bottles running through the expensive, automated equipment. The plant was operating at top capacity. Orders were up. Business was great. Why did people think she'd overextended?

Because you're a Pembroke. It's what Pembrokes do.

She came to the rocks. By standards farther north in the Adirondack Mountains, they weren't much as cliffs went. But they gave novices a taste of climbing, and kept her in shape, and a drop from top to bottom wasn't too terrifying to imagine, although no doubt it could be lethal. After circling a hemlock, Dani jumped off a smallish boulder on the far edge of the vertical rock, then went down to low-lying brush, so that the steepest part of the cliffs were above her. If she'd been doing a climb, it would be cheating. But she had other plans. She walked out on a flat rock and sat down, letting her legs dangle over the edge. Below, at the bottom of the cliffs, were hemlocks and oaks and a path that led around the rocks back up to the bottling plant.

Flipping onto her stomach, Dani worked her body down so that she was pretty much hanging from the flat rock by her arms. Inexpert, but it got the job done. Glancing down, she saw the narrow ledge directly below, where she'd found the gold key.

She counted to three and let go.

Keeping her body close to the rocks, but not so close she'd

smack her face, she dropped onto the ledge. It was just three feet wide, but she was small. She fit fine.

She squatted and groped in the dirt, moss, dead leaves and doomed seedlings for anything interesting, any clue as to how her key had ended up there. Finding it had been a pure accident. At first she'd thought it was just an old key. Only afterward had she realized what it was. This was her first opportunity to return to the ledge, and she took her time and examined every inch of it in case she'd missed something.

But she hadn't. There was nothing.

How had the key gotten there?

She imagined Ulysses and his practical wife arguing, imagined her urging him to concentrate on saving and investing instead of throwing his money into idiotic things like gold keys.

Dani could see her great-great-grandmother flinging the key off the cliffs.

Probably there was a more ordinary explanation. Or, at least, a less dramatic one.

Getting back up from the ledge without her gear proved easier than she'd anticipated. There were good handholds and toeholds, and she hoisted herself up in no time. But it was a warm afternoon, and she hadn't slept much last night. She was sweaty, and as she sat on a boulder to catch her breath, she could feel the ache in her legs.

"Miss Pembroke?"

Dani whirled around, immediately recognizing a young local reporter at the top of the cliffs. A camera dangling from her neck, she apologized for startling Dani and explained she'd been assigned to do an article on the Pembroke and Pembroke Springs.

"No one will talk to me," she said. "I just tried to interview the plant manager, but he said he can't talk to reporters, and I noticed you walking over here."

"He can't. It's nothing personal—mineral water is an extremely competitive business, and we have to watch ourselves."

"Oh. That's what he said." She licked her lips, looking awkward, which, Dani had come to discover, was unusual in a reporter. "Would you mind…I know this is short notice…could you answer a couple of questions? I've done my homework. I've read everything I can find on you, your family, the estate—I won't ask you questions you've been asked a million times before."

Dani squinted up at her. "I won't talk about my mother."

"Oh, I assumed that. You never have—and it's old news." She blushed. "I'm sorry—I didn't mean to sound callous."

"It's okay. What's your name?"

"Heather. Heather Carey."

"You could use a break?"

"I sure could. My boss says I'm not aggressive enough."

She wasn't, but sometimes aggression wasn't what got the story.

Dani knew she wasn't dressed for an interview. And she wasn't prepared. She hadn't gone over possible questions and answers with her staff. She hadn't gotten their advice, their consent.

Heather Carey had climbed down to the flat rock. She was small, thin, no more than twenty-five. "That's an interesting necklace."

Dani glanced down at the two keys. They were heavy for a necklace, and it had been stupid to wear them rock climbing. But how could she resist? "Have a seat."

"No kidding?"

"No kidding."

Clearly Heather Carey didn't believe her luck.

Ninety minutes later Dani arrived back at her cottage with no regrets. Before she showered—before she called her PR people and confessed what she'd done—she dug out a pen and a sheet of Pembroke Springs stationery.

Whistling, she jotted a quick note.

It may or may not have gotten Emily Post's stamp of approval, but it did graciously—even cheerfully—indicate her acceptance of the invitation to the annual Chandler lawn party.

Two

As he eased into the pilot's chair on the flybridge of his restored 1955 Richardson all-wood cabin cruiser, Zeke Cutler felt the fatigue and tension of the past three weeks subside. He was home again. Or as close to home as he expected he'd ever get.

Crescent-shaped San Diego Bay glistened in the late-day sun, and he had just enough left in his fifth of George Dickel to fill his glass. Which he did. Slowly. Savoring the sound of splashing Tennessee bourbon and the feel of the wind and the peace of being back on his boat. He had two weeks. Two weeks of fishing and sleeping and watching the waves and the sunset before he had to tackle his next job.

His last job he'd just have to put out of his mind. He'd spent two torturous weeks teaching a group of self-centered, greedy, unscrupulous executives how to stay out of trouble and, should reasonable means of prevention fail, how to get out of trouble. "Trouble" meaning anything from a simple street mugging to international terrorism. These particular individuals, however, reminded Zeke a bit too much of the last group of white-collar thugs he'd handed over to the police. He really did like being able to tell the good guys from the bad guys without looking too hard.

But life wasn't that simple.

Security consulting didn't used to be so complicated. Like everything else, it had gone high-tech, which had its points, except the bad guys had gone high-tech, too. They had high-tech security systems and high-tech communications systems and—his favorite—high-tech weaponry. Too much high-tech weaponry for Zeke's tastes.

He swirled the George Dickel around in his mouth and swallowed. He'd eaten green chili at a distinctly low-tech Mexican restaurant, and his stomach still burned. The bourbon and Southern California sun didn't help. He closed his eyes. For half a cent he'd dive into the bay.

"If I was a bad guy and wanted to kill you," Sam Lincoln Jones said nearby, "you'd be dead."

"Not unless you had a grenade launcher and fired off down on the dock." Zeke opened his eyes and grinned. "I saw you coming, Sam."

Sam grinned back at him. "Guess I'm not easy to miss."

That he wasn't. Sam was four inches shorter than Zeke's six-one, but, at two-twenty, thirty pounds heavier. They were both solid; seldom was either accused of being handsome. Many shades darker than Zeke, Sam had had his nose broken at least three times too many, but he liked to say Zeke had come into the world with a grim face. They'd both entered their profession through the back door, Sam with a doctorate in criminology and a yearning to get out of the ivory tower he'd worked so hard to get into, Zeke with a host of dead dreams and a yearning never to get caught up in a dream again. They'd met ten years ago over the corpse of a mutual friend. Together they'd found his killer.

"Don't know why this old tug hasn't sunk into the bay by now," Sam said.

"Because it's a classic, and like all classics just gets better with age. I'd offer you a drink, but I emptied the bottle. What's up?"

Sam withdrew a pale pink envelope from the back pocket of his tan linen pants. He had on a mango-colored polo shirt. Zeke felt underdressed in his cutoff shorts, and it was his damn boat.

Sam said, "Letter from home."

It would have come to their shared postal box in San Diego. Given their profession and peripatetic lifestyle, such things as home and office addresses made little sense. They took turns checking the box. They were independent specialists but worked together on and off. Most of their communications were handled by telephone and computer, with the occasional need for a fax machine or courier. Neither received many letters. Zeke had never received one from home. He'd left for good twenty years ago, at age eighteen. His parents and his only brother were dead, and there was hardly anybody he knew left in Cedar Springs, Tennessee. His hometown and the kid he'd been there were just a part of his dead dreams.

Sam discreetly knelt one knee on the polished mahogany bench in the sun and looked out at the bay. Zeke tore open the delicate envelope. Inside was a folded newspaper article and a single pink page, with Naomi Witt Hazen embossed in tiny script at the top. He tried not to react. Seeing her name, his hometown, was like having the fading shreds of a dream stay with you as you woke up, making you unsure of what was real and what wasn't.

It was like getting a letter from home when you'd almost talked yourself into believing you no longer had a home.

Like everyone else, Zeke made no claim to understand Naomi Witt Hazen. She always used all three of her names, as if she could be anything she wanted to be—a daughter, a wife, a widow, a Witt, a Hazen. An ordinary woman. Zeke only understood that he owed her. She'd helped save his soul if not his life.

He was glad she was still alive, although she could have been dead for all he'd have known. There was no one in Cedar Springs who'd have thought to tell him otherwise.

Tilting back in his pilot's chair, he read her letter first.

Dearest Zeke,
I know this letter will come as a surprise, and perhaps not altogether a pleasant one, but I don't know where else to turn. Please come home, Zeke. I need your help. I'll explain everything when you get here.
Yours truly,
Naomi Witt Hazen

Zeke refolded the letter and tucked it back into the envelope. "Guess I won't be spending my time off fishing."

"Anything I can do?" Sam asked. There was no urgency in his tone, no desire or need to help; he was just asking a question.

Zeke shook his head. He unfolded the newspaper article. The *Cedar Springs Democrat* had picked up a story on Pembroke Springs and the Pembroke, a new spa-inn, and their owner, Dani Pembroke. Mattie Witt's granddaughter. Mattie was Naomi's older sister. She hadn't stepped foot in her hometown in sixty years. Nonetheless, people there kept track of her.

Dani Pembroke was described as an entrepreneur and "former heiress." Apparently she'd thrown her inheritance into Eugene Chandler's face when he'd suggested she drop the Pembroke from her name after he'd fired her father as vice president of Chandler Hotels. She'd built her mineral water and natural soda business from scratch, without one nickel of Chandler money. Zeke was unimpressed. She'd had the famous name, she'd had access to a world-famous mineral spring through family, and she'd known she could go crawling back to her rich granddaddy if worst came to worst. There was no "from scratch" about what she'd done.

Why had Naomi sent him the article? It wasn't the first piece written about a Chandler or a Pembroke.

Then he looked more closely at Dani Pembroke's picture, past her black eyes and resemblance to Nick Pembroke that had first caught his attention. He focused on the two keys dangling from her slender neck. The caption said one was brass and one was gold. She'd found the gold one while rock climbing near the Pembroke Springs bottling plant.

Zeke swore under his breath.

"You going home?" Sam asked.

And here he'd been thinking he'd just come home. Zeke smiled sadly, staring at Dani Pembroke. "I reckon so."

Zeke flew to Nashville the next day, and by the time he got to Cedar Springs, Naomi Witt Hazen had a peach pie in the oven and sun tea poured in a tall clear glass.

"It's good to see you, Zeke." Her voice was melodic and genteel. "I knew you'd come."

He hadn't known himself. "I'm glad you knew."

In her inexpensive turquoise suit and walking shoes, Naomi looked even tinier than Zeke remembered. Her hair had gone from deep brunette to a soft, pure white, but it was curled the same as always, in a lady's do, short and neat. Although she never told anyone her age, everyone in Cedar Springs knew she was seven years younger than her famous sister Mattie. That made her seventy-five.

She had Zeke sit in the front parlor on the antique sofa her father had always insisted came from the Hermitage, the Nashville home of Andrew Jackson. Jackson Witt had been the richest man in Cedar Springs. He'd owned the woolen mill where Zeke's father and mother and brother had worked and had been a benefactor in his small town in the rolling hills east of Nashville. He'd died before the New South had made its big push into his corner of Tennessee. Cedar Springs was no longer the town in which Zeke had grown up. Farmland had been divided up into estate lots for huge brick houses, and old farmhouses and chicken coops bulldozed. Streetlights had gone in, as well as fast-food chains and discount department stores and vast supermarkets. Nobody shopped on the square anymore. West Main had been widened and built up, most of its houses converted into apartments and beauty shops and carpet stores and real estate offices. Naomi had once said her house, a beautiful Greek Revival but no longer the biggest and fanciest in town, would make a nice funeral parlor.

The oven buzzer sounded, and she started toward the kitchen.

"Let me help," Zeke said.

"No, no, you just sit here and let me wait on you."

He'd known that would be her answer. "You don't have to."

She smiled. "I know I don't have to. I want to."

Zeke didn't argue. In Naomi's world he was her guest and a man, and it was her responsibility—her pleasure, she'd say—to wait on him. She rushed off to the kitchen, playing the proper southern lady. Zeke knew better. Jackson Witt's younger daughter usually managed to do as she pleased, afterward working her actions into her belief system. Like her scandalous affair with Nicholas Pembroke, her sister's husband. It had lasted less than a summer but had cost her. It left her marriage to the vice president of Cedar Springs Woolen Mill and her reputation in her hometown in shambles. And it prompted her father to disown her, just as he'd disowned Mattie when she'd run off with Nick Pembroke more than twenty years earlier. Thenceforth, Jackson Witt maintained he had no daughters. Zeke had never liked nor understood the stern, uncompromising old man, but he'd never once heard Naomi complain about him, no matter how cruelly he'd treated her.

She returned from the kitchen with a blue willow plate of her steaming, incomparable peach pie. She'd put a fat scoop of vanilla ice cream on top. "I'm not having any," she said, handing him the plate. "I have to watch my sugar."

Knowing she wouldn't talk until he'd finished, Zeke downed the pie quickly, its filling juicy and as sweet as his best memories of growing up. A ceiling fan whirred, keeping the room remarkably cool. The parlor hadn't changed. It was dark and crowded, with small, framed oval photographs of Jackson Witt and his long-dead, delicate, prim wife hanging above the marble fireplace. There were other photographs, of elderly cousins, friends, mill executives, but none of the dazzling Mattie Witt or the filmmaker she and her sister both had loved. None of Mattie's only son, none of her long-missing daughter-in-law, none of her only granddaughter.

Zeke finished his pie and tried the sun tea, cool and smooth and, like the pie, tasting of the past.

"You're not an easy man to locate," Naomi said without criticism. "Is that by design?"

"Yes."

"I suppose in your profession discretion is a matter of life and death."

He smiled, or tried to. "It can be."

"Do you ever wish you hadn't left home?"

"No."

And he wanted to ask her, but didn't, if she'd ever wished she had left. After her affair with Nick, she'd returned to the house of her birth and childhood. Her husband had refused even to speak to her again, or to divorce her. She'd nursed her ailing father until his death from cancer. Through those eleven years, Jackson Witt had paid her a wage and referred to her as his live-in housekeeper. She'd even had to eat in the kitchen while he ate in the dining room. To Zeke's knowledge, Naomi had never complained nor given in to any temptation to try to drown the old bastard in the bathtub. She'd saved the meager salary he paid her and, after his death, bought the Witt house with her own money. Her first order of business had been to get rid of the rosewood bed in which her grandfather and father had died. She and Zeke dragged it down to the flea market and sold it to the first comer for thirty dollars. It was probably worth a hundred times that much, even then, but Naomi, determined, had told Zeke, "I won't be the third generation of Witts to die in that bed."

With her warm, dark eyes fastened on him, Naomi Witt Hazen suddenly looked old and sad. "Zeke, I know I could have told you everything in my letter, but I wanted to see you. You look well. Are you happy?"

He thought of the sunset sparkling on the blue waters of San Diego Bay. "Sure."

"You've never married."

"Wouldn't work in my profession."

"I've always thought you'd make a fine husband and father."

Not with the dead dreams he carried with him, not with the life he led. But Zeke didn't try to tell Naomi she was wrong. He liked having someone think those kinds of things about him; he could almost believe they could be true.

She twisted her fingers, gnarled with arthritis, in her lap and lowered her eyes. "Zeke, I—" She looked at him. "I need you to go to Saratoga Springs, New York."

Automatically he felt himself falling back on the training and discipline that had sustained him through years of dangerous work. He had expected something difficult and painful. Yet even with the article on Dani Pembroke, he'd talked himself out of believing it was Saratoga. He'd imagined Naomi telling him she'd developed colon cancer like her daddy and wanted him to see to her funeral, to selling the Witt house and its contents. But he'd seen the keys around Dani Pembroke's neck, and deep down he'd known what Naomi would ask.

"Go on," he said.

Naomi's cheeks reddened. "This is much more difficult than I'd anticipated. I— Zeke, I'm afraid there's something I've never told you."

That didn't surprise him. He'd always believed Naomi Witt had neglected to tell anybody—least of all him—a great number of things. He took another sip of iced tea and set the glass carefully on a coaster decorated with irises, the Tennessee state flower. "What do you want me to do?" he asked, needing to get this done.

"Zeke, before your brother died…"

But she stopped, biting her lip, and in her watery eyes—Zeke didn't know if the moistness was from tears or age—he could see not only loss and disappointment but also anger. For all she'd had done to her, for all the pain and anguish and betrayal she'd witnessed and perhaps even committed, Naomi, in Zeke's experience, had never expressed any anger over her lot. She would say anger was an unladylike emotion. Fits of temper weren't proper for a well-bred lady. And yet Zeke could see it bubbling to the surface, choking for air, for renewed life, even if she refused to acknowledge its presence.

She cleared her throat and looked away for a moment, then continued in a strong, controlled voice. "Before Joe died, he sent me a letter. I've never shown it to you—to anyone. It didn't say much. I can't tell you he knew he was going to die, I can't say there was any sign he was going to do any of the things people said he did." She paused, the moistness—the tears—filling her eyes. "He enclosed a picture. I should have shown it to you before now, Zeke, but I never have."

With a trembling hand she opened the frayed Bible on the marble end table beside the Andrew Jackson sofa and withdrew a color snapshot. She was breathing rapidly, and Zeke was afraid she might faint. He leaned forward, taking the snapshot from her so she wouldn't have to move.

It was one he'd never seen before, but he immediately recognized the place, the time, the two women.

Saratoga Springs, New York.

Twenty-five years ago.

Mattie Witt and her daughter-in-law, Lilli Chandler Pembroke.

Joe had taken their picture. They were in the basket of Mattie's hot-air balloon, just as it had started to float onto the evening winds. It had been Lilli's first time up. In her expression, frozen for all time, was that mix of fear and excitement Zeke remembered as she'd watched the huge balloon inflate. She'd wanted to go and didn't want to go. Joe had offered to serve as their chase team. But Mattie had told him no. She and Lilli would just ride the winds for a while and see what happened, and find their own way home.

Looking at Lilli's fearful, exuberant smile, her tawny hair caught in the wind, Zeke saw how young she'd been, and how unsure of herself. For Lilli Chandler Pembroke, going up in a balloon with her eccentric mother-in-law instead of playing the good little heiress at the Chandler lawn party had been a monumental act of rebellion. Mattie Witt stood beside her in the gondola, looking as tiny and independent and heart-stoppingly beautiful as Zeke remembered.

After her balloon ride, Mattie had told Joe that she couldn't go back to see her father before he died or the sister she'd left behind decades years earlier.

An hour later, he and Zeke were on the road back to Tennessee.

"I don't understand it," Joe had said as he and Zeke headed home in defeat. "I'd go through hell and back for you, and she won't even go home to see her only sister and dying daddy. I know he's not an easy man, but he's her father. I just don't get it."

That was Joe Cutler. He hadn't understood why people

couldn't get along. All they had to do was put their minds to it and it'd happen.

And he did go through hell for Zeke. He just hadn't come back.

Zeke saw the gold key hanging from Lilli's alabaster throat, remembered it. Even for a wealthy Chandler, it had seemed exotic and extravagant. Yet Joe had given it to her.

He made himself look up from the picture. "It doesn't have to be the same key."

"But it could be," Naomi said.

And if it was, the next question would be how it ended up on the Pembroke estate for Lilli's daughter to find all these years later. If it had anything to do with Lilli's disappearance. If Joe was involved, had known something—if he'd done something.

"I have to know the truth, Zeke."

He remained silent and still, hot liquid pain coursing through him. He had to repress his physical reaction and concentrate on the situation at hand. He had to be the cool, distanced professional. He had to ask himself the tough questions. Not just about his brother, but about Naomi herself. She was a woman he'd known and trusted all his life, but he forced himself to ask if the years of loneliness and abuse had finally driven her over the edge and he was being sucked along with her, just by being back in Cedar Springs, back under Jackson Witt's roof.

But there were never any saner eyes than the ones that held him to his seat.

There was more. He could tell. But he didn't prod her. Experience had taught him patience. Rush people and they could panic and make up things. Let them think. Choose their words. Hide what they wanted to hide. Sometimes it worked better if they had control. He could learn more about what was really at stake and what wasn't.

Naomi withdrew another envelope from her Bible, handed

it to Zeke. "Joe sent this to me with the picture. He asked me to hang on to it and not open it." She smoothed her skirt with her unnaturally bent fingers. "I didn't, until I saw the picture of Dani Pembroke wearing that gold key."

Her eyes were lowered, and Zeke pulled a yellowed sheet of typing paper from the envelope and unfolded it. There were four lines of type:

> *Don't underestimate me. The whole world will know Lilli Chandler Pembroke isn't the perfect heiress she pretends to be. But your secret is safe with me if you pay up tonight.*

Zeke didn't say a word. He didn't have to.

"I'm not asking you to be a hero," Naomi Witt Hazen said softly. "All I'm asking is for you to be that brave, levelheaded young man I once knew who so badly wanted to do some good in the world."

As if it were so easy. As if the kid Zeke Cutler had been— so filled with energy and optimism and determination—mattered anymore. He'd failed and changed in ways he didn't want to examine and maybe didn't want Naomi to know, although he could see she did.

She collapsed back against the soft cushion of her chair. In her look of fatigue and near despair was the impact of the years, of the losses she'd endured and the choices she'd made. "I believe in you, Ezekiel Cutler." She sounded worn down, as if that was the last belief she held and now even it was being challenged. "I believe in you even if you don't believe in yourself."

He couldn't meet her eye. He'd faced death as recently as six weeks ago and now couldn't look at the old woman who'd always been there for him.

"Will you go?" she asked.

Before he'd opened her letter in San Diego, he'd have said

he'd put the past behind him. Now, sitting in the dark Old South parlor, Zeke knew he'd only been sidestepping the past, one land mine at a time in a field of hundreds, always aware, somewhere in the recesses of his mind, that his next step could blow him and those around him—anyone left he cared about—to pieces.

He jumped up, unable to sit another second.

As he started across the threadbare Oriental rug, he saw in Naomi's face the fear that Zeke Cutler would fail her as so many others before him had.

"I need to think," he said.

And he walked into the entry and out the front door, onto the porch and into the heat and glare of a Tennessee summer afternoon.

In the shade of the oak trees Jackson Witt had planted almost a century ago, Zeke walked down West Main, where the memories were as pervasive and unavoidable as the summer heat. He could see himself and Joe, shirtless and barefoot, on their way home from swimming in the creek. As a boy, Zeke had never even noticed the heat. Now he could feel the humidity settling over him, could smell the exhaust that hung heavy in the oppressive air. He was aware of the constant hum of traffic on a street where dogs used to lie in the sun on warm mornings.

The memory came at him sideways, fast and silent, catching him defenseless.

It was a hot, still afternoon, like this one, twenty-five years ago.

Naomi's husband, Wesley Hazen, had dropped dead of a heart attack at his office at the woolen mill, on the same day his estranged wife had finally talked to her father—who for the previous ten years had maintained he had no daughters—into seeing the doctor about his stomach trouble. Doc Hiram referred him to a cancer specialist in Nashville. The old man refused to make an appointment. His father had been born in Cedar Springs and died there, and that was good enough for Jackson

Witt. How long was a man supposed to live? Joe Cutler had driven him to Doc Hiram's office on account of Jackson Witt's being too sick to drive himself and too stubborn to ride in a car with Naomi.

When he got back home, Joe told Zeke what had happened. Zeke was thirteen and knew that Jackson Witt wasn't the benevolent old man most people in Cedar Springs pretended he was. He had started Cedar Springs Woolen Mill to provide jobs for the impoverished people of his town, a market for its farmers' wool, opportunities for its children. Back then it was the biggest employer in town.

"So Mr. Witt's going to die?" Zeke asked.

"Not right away."

"What'll happen to Mrs. Hazen?"

"I expect she'll go on pretty much the way she's been going. Truth is, she'll be better off with him gone."

Joe was eighteen and worked the graveyard shift at the mill. He still lived at home, in their little one-bedroom, uninsulated house northeast of the square. He gave half his paycheck to their mother to help out, covered his own expenses and banked any left over. Someday, he'd told Zeke, he'd leave Cedar Springs, maybe go to California. He said he didn't plan to work the graveyard shift at Cedar Springs Woolen Mill the rest of his life. But right now his mother and Zeke needed him, and he'd stick around.

After taking Jackson Witt to the doctor's, Joe, who hadn't been to bed since getting off work at seven that morning, turned on the baseball game and sacked out on the couch. When Emmy Cutler came home from her shift at the mill, she got him up and called Zeke in from playing ball and told them Wesley Hazen was dead.

"He had a heart attack right at his desk." She looked tired, as she almost always did. She was a thin, dark-haired woman who'd once been pretty. "He went quick. Now, I want you boys to go into town and get a dress coat and tie. I'll iron your good white shirts. There'll be calling hours probably the day after tomorrow, and then the funeral. I want you both to go."

"Mother," Joe said, "we can't afford new coats."

"I've got some money put away. You take it and go on. Wes Hazen and Jackson Witt gave me a job when I needed one. I was a widow with two small boys, and I don't know what I'd've done without the mill. Don't matter what anybody else says about Mr. Hazen, we're going to pay our respects."

Joe was adamant. "If a clean shirt's good enough for church, it's good enough for Wes Hazen's funeral."

Emmy Cutler was equally adamant. "You listen to me, Joe Cutler. If I have to get in the car and drive to Nashville myself and buy you two coats, then that's what I'll do. By this time you boys ought to know when I mean business."

Zeke hadn't said anything, but he was used to their mother lumping him and Joe together. She went into her bedroom and came back with a bunch of twenties in a rubber band.

"I'll bring back the change," Joe said.

"There'd better not be much. I won't have people in this town saying I wasn't grateful for what Wesley Hazen did for me."

Joe's eyes darkened. "Like what? Work you half to death at sweatshop wages—"

"I won't have that kind of talk in my house. There's never been a Cutler too proud to work. Now, you take your brother and go. Zeke, make sure he goes to a decent store. I want you coming home with proper coats and ties."

Zeke nodded but made no promises, not where his brother was concerned. Joe didn't listen to him any more than he did anyone else. When it came to their mother's sense of right and wrong, however, Joe usually relented. They went to Dillard's, but Joe hunted up a couple of khaki coats on the clearance racks that looked good enough to him. Since they'd been instructed not to come back with much change, he bought their mother a bottle of perfume and a pretty scarf and took Zeke to the local diner for a piece of chess pie.

When they got back home, Joe gave their mother her change and her presents, then said he'd go to the bank in the morning and pay her back for his coat and tie. Emmy Cutler said he was impossible; then she hugged him.

Over five hundred people attended Wesley Hazen's funeral, and Joe muttered to Zeke that he'd bet nobody would have noticed if they hadn't worn a coat and tie. Their mother had on her new scarf. Zeke looked around and saw Naomi sitting in back with the lowest-paid workers from the mill. She had on a black suit and a black hat with a veil. Her face was very pale, and she looked tiny. She hadn't lived with Wesley since she'd run off with Nick Pembroke ten years earlier.

Her father was up front with the Hazen family and the mill management. He never looked back at Naomi.

"I'm going back to sit with Mrs. Hazen," Zeke whispered to his mother. Emmy Cutler looked pained; she didn't tell him yes, but she didn't tell him no, either. So Zeke sneaked to the back of the church. Naomi smiled at him. It was a sad, soft smile, but at that moment Zeke knew she didn't mind being an outcast. It was the only way she had of being who she wanted to be.

That night Joe Cutler announced over supper that he was heading to New York to find Mattie Witt and tell her that her daddy was dying. Zeke expected his mother to argue with him. From the look on his brother's face, he guessed Joe expected the same thing.

But Emmy Cutler surprised her two sons. Or maybe she just knew Joe. Dipping her spoon into a bowl of redeye gravy, she said, "You do what you think is right."

"Can I go, too?" Zeke asked.

His mother put the spoon back into the bowl. She hadn't gotten any gravy. Her eyes misted over. "That's up to your brother," she said.

"Won't you need him here?" Joe asked.

"I reckon it's time I started learning to do without you two boys. Now you go on and make up your own minds about what you need to do. I'll be fine." She folded her hands in front of her plate and looked at her sons. "I have just one request."

Joe nodded. "Yes, ma'am."

"You ask Naomi Hazen if she wants you to go."

"It's Mr. Witt who's sick—"

"And it's Mrs. Hazen who'll have to live with the consequences of what you do—whether her sister decides to come home or whether she doesn't."

So that evening Joe and Zeke walked over to West Main Street, and Naomi met them on the porch and she didn't say she wanted them to go to New York and she didn't say she didn't want them to go. Which was good enough for Joe. The next morning he and Zeke packed up his Chevy and headed north.

As he walked on the cracked sidewalks of his childhood, Zeke could hear Joe's laugh, and for the first time in years it sounded real and alive and immediate to him. It was as if his brother were there with him, not as the man he'd become—a man Zeke didn't know—but as the boy he'd been, another boy's big brother, idolized and imperfect.

He'd come to the West Main Street branch of the Cedar Springs Free Public Library. Jackson Witt's father had donated the land for the building not long after he'd helped the town establish a pure-water supply after an outbreak of typhoid fever in 1904. Jackson himself had left the library a hefty endowment. The dirt wasn't settled good over his grave when Naomi carted down the oil portrait he'd had painted of himself and donated it to the library, not, Zeke had always felt, out of generosity, but because she couldn't stand to keep it hanging in her house.

Inside, the library smelled as it always had, of musty books and polished wood. Zeke found himself glancing around for a gawky kid in jeans and dangling shirttail, looking to books as a way out of his poverty and isolation. Go for it, Joe had always told him. Do some good in the world.

He had wanted to.

"May I help you?" the middle-aged woman behind the oak desk asked. She sounded tentative. Zeke suddenly realized he must look even more tight-lipped and grim than usual. And hot. The air-conditioning was set a notch below sweltering.

He tried to smile. "Thank you, but I can find my way."

A hint of his old middle Tennessee accent had worked its way into his voice. The woman seemed somewhat reassured. He went to the local-history section, just across from Jackson Witt's portrait above the fireplace. On one shelf were a Bible signed by Andrew Jackson and a pair of boots reputedly worn by Davy Crockett. Below them, in a locked glass box, was the red-feathered hat Mattie Witt had worn in *The Gamblers*. Some newcomer to town had bought it on auction and donated it to the library. There was also a copy of two unauthorized biographies of her famous sister.

On the bottom shelf—Zeke had to kneel—was the flag, properly folded, that had draped Joe Cutler's coffin. Naomi had taken it after the funeral when Zeke didn't want it.

He rubbed his fingers over the coarse fabric.

Twenty years later, and he still missed his brother.

"We're not like other folks, brother. We never will be."

Even in Cedar Springs the Cutler brothers hadn't been like anybody else. They were a couple of country boys whose daddy had died when a tractor fell over on him when Zeke was a year old, and whose mama did the best she could, working overtime at the mill.

After Saratoga, Joe had enlisted in the army. After he shipped out to basic, their mother cut herself so badly on the card machine at the mill that she'd bled to death before Doc Hiram could get to her. He'd cried when he told Zeke, who'd just turned fifteen. Joe came home on emergency leave but went back, convinced the best way—the only way—he could help his younger brother was to stay in the army. Zeke went to live with a second cousin, and Joe wrote to him every week; every week Zeke wrote back, and Naomi Hazen and Doc Hiram were there for him, too, all through high school.

He'd failed them all. Joe, Naomi, Doc. And himself.

Two weeks after Zeke had started Vanderbilt on scholarship, Joe Cutler was killed in Beirut. He was just twenty-three years old.

On the shelf next to the flag was the slim volume that had come out after his death. Zeke picked it up. The book had won a Pulitzer Prize. It was the story of a solid southern boy who'd become a soldier with good intentions, then was "corrupted," transformed by a system and a world he didn't understand. The book explained how Joe Cutler had taken a stupid risk, disobeyed orders and got his men and himself killed. He hadn't lived up to his own expectations of heroism. His story was all the more searing and memorable for its banality, depicting an ordinary soldier who'd lost faith in his country, his men, himself.

Had that downward spiral started in Saratoga?

Quint Skinner, the man who wrote Joe's story, was himself an army veteran and had served with Joe, considered him a friend. Skinner had tried to interview Zeke at Vanderbilt. They'd ended up in a fistfight, and not long after Zeke quit Vanderbilt altogether.

Worse was giving up the dream he'd had of his brother, the dream of what he'd wanted to do for Joe when he came home, of repaying him for all he'd sacrificed. How he'd wanted them to be real brothers again. But maybe that was every brother's dead dream.

The book's presence on the library shelf next to the flag had to be Naomi's doing. She'd believed in Joe Cutler as much as Zeke had, and maybe she still did. But he could hear her say she also believed in truth and fairness.

On his way out, Zeke stopped at a big clay pot on the library steps and plucked a marigold, its orange color as deep and dark as the center of a Tennessee summer sunset. He wondered if somewhere beyond the subdivisions and fast-food chains two brothers were out on the creek fishing for their supper, waiting for the sun to go down so they could light their campfire and tell ghost stories and pretend they wanted to be men.

He climbed the steps onto Naomi's front porch. She was in a rocking chair, crocheting as she watched the cars go by. She glanced at him but didn't say a word.

He tossed the crumpled marigold blossom over the porch rail. His shirt had stuck to his back, and he picked up the picture and the envelope with the blackmail letter in it and tucked them into his back pocket.

"I shouldn't have written," Naomi said.

"You did the right thing." He tried to smile to reassure her but couldn't. "I don't know if there'll be anything there for me to find at this late date, but I'll go to Saratoga."

She started to say something, stopped, and finally just nodded as she slowly, almost painfully with her gnarled fingers, continued to crochet.

Three

━━━◦⟋⟍◦⟋⟍◦━━━

Mattie Witt could feel the high ozone levels of the summer city air in her sinuses as she sat on the front steps of her Greenwich Village town house. Her whole face ached, even her teeth. New York was so damn hot in August. She'd read that in the old days people from the southern end of Manhattan would come to Greenwich Village during the summer to escape yellow fever. At least that was no longer the case.

She neatened her skirt around her knees. Her long, loose broadcloth dress reminded her of long-ago summers in Tennessee, when the heat—there'd been no air conditioners and precious few fans—had never bothered her. The warm brick step ground into her bottom. She walked forty-five minutes every morning but at eighty-two didn't have the muscle tone she'd once had.

Across the street a woman chatting with the mailman spotted Mattie and waved. It was an effort, but Mattie waved back. Normally by late afternoon her front steps would be crowded with friends and neighbors, indulging in the time-honored Greenwich Village tradition of stoop-sitting. Today they seemed to sense her need to be alone and stayed away.

The woman went through her courtyard to the back entrance

of her building. The mailman continued on his way. In the many years since Mattie had left Hollywood and moved east, she had come to love the crooked tree-lined streets of Greenwich Village, with their brick town houses and lamplights and long history. She appreciated the variety of people there—artists, actors, writers, doctors, bankers, garbage collectors, drunks, nurses, students, secretaries—and the tradition of tolerance, independence and nonconformity. Everyone knew her, the aging movie star who'd introduced generations of Greenwich Village kids to the fun of kite flying. It was no big deal that she was a film legend. There were other legends in the neighborhood.

But in her heart, no matter what she did or where she went or how long she stayed away, home for Mattie would always be Cedar Springs, Tennessee.

She could feel the warm air on her face, the pressure of her inflamed sinuses.

Dani, Dani. What am I going to do?

Her granddaughter's sheer, stubborn, incorrigible Pembroke nature worried Mattie. Dani would have to find out where that damn key had come from, how it had gotten onto the rocks.

But perhaps she should.

One of Dani's friends in New York had stopped by with the article on her and Pembroke Springs and groaned as she'd handed it to Mattie. "Couldn't she have taken a shower first?" But overall it was a good piece. Dani was as unpretentious and as totally honest as ever. Maybe she wasn't as smooth and as prepared as she could have been, but her energy shone through every quote.

But those gate keys...

Feeling stiff and old, Mattie climbed slowly to her feet. She had to use the rail. She went back inside, where a ceiling fan, much like the one she remembered in her father's house in Cedar Springs, helped keep her front room cool. She'd pulled the drapes to keep out the hot sun. The room seemed dark, crowded, too much like the Witt front parlor on West Main Street a thousand miles—a thousand years—away. Mattie concentrated on the roses and Prussian blue of her decor, colors her father would never have chosen. She caught her breath before going upstairs.

In her small feminine bedroom she sat on the edge of her four-poster bed. A lace-curtained window overlooked the hidden garden behind her town house, where she spent many peaceful, solitary hours among her roses, hollyhocks, morning glories and asters. She had a good life here. Few regrets.

She opened the old Bible on her bedstand. Even before she could talk, her father had taught her his favorite psalms. She remembered them all. They were a part of her. On dark nights they'd come to her, sometimes in her mother's almost-forgotten voice, or Naomi's, even her father's. Never in the voice of the child she'd been. It was as if that girl had never existed.

With a trembling hand she set aside the obituary of her father from the *Cedar Springs Democrat* that Joe Cutler had sent her, and the letter she'd received from his commanding officer telling her of Joe's death three years later, because Joe had asked him to. That was before Quint Skinner, that snake, had written his book.

She came to the photograph Joe had taken of Lilli and herself going up in the balloon that warm, clear August night. "I thought you'd want it," he'd written.

Mattie switched on her clock radio, just to have something to listen to. Frank Sinatra was singing.

"There's nothing romantic between Nick and me," Lilli had assured her mother-in-law during their balloon ride over Saratoga. "I'm not infatuated with him or anything like that—it's just that no one understands me the way he does."

Mattie had known exactly how Lilli felt, and she'd tried so

hard to explain. "Darling, it's not that Nick understands you—it's that he's willing to let you be whoever you want to be. He demands it. He's a rare man in that he has no expectations of you whatever."

On the flip side, Nick had no expectations of himself, either. For a woman who'd based her goals and ideas on the expectations of others—parents, husband, society—being exposed to Nicholas Pembroke's talent and vision and enthusiasm for life, his love of freedom without responsibility, could be an enormously liberating and intoxicating experience. But there were costs. Always there were costs.

For Mattie, those costs had been her home and family. To be free, she'd had to leave them behind all those years ago. There had been no opportunity for compromise, no possible middle ground. Yet even after six decades, the pull of home and family on her remained strong. Every day something would catch her off guard and trigger a memory of her stern father, of her dark-eyed little sister, of the people and oak-lined streets of Cedar Springs. Mattie didn't regret her choices. She treasured her independence, her good years with Nick, their son, the work she'd done, the life she'd made for herself in New York. She'd had time to put the costs of her freedom into perspective.

Had Lilli discovered, too late, what those costs would be for herself?

Frank Sinatra stopped singing.

Mattie stared at the photograph. At Lilli's smile. At the gold key hanging from her neck. Joe had given it to her.

How had it ended up on the Pembroke estate for Dani to find so many years later?

"Nicholas Pembroke is an extraordinary man," Mattie had told Lilli. "I'd be a liar if I tried to tell you otherwise. The good Lord only knows where I'd be if he hadn't decided to go fishing in Tennessee way back when. But, Lilli, Nick can't save himself, much less anyone else. Darling, I know what it is to want to be free."

"At my age you were already a legend."

Mattie had tried to explain. Her acting had had its rewards, but fame was a strange thing. Mattie wasn't famous to herself, but to other people—people she didn't even know. She couldn't get inside their heads. Back at the height of her fame, she'd disguised herself and sneaked into a theater playing one of her films, but still couldn't get inside the minds of those strangers watching her and be a part of her own fame. And Mattie had realized she was only herself. She wasn't what other people thought of her.

Lilli had shaken her head, as if at her own shattered dreams. "I'm thirty, and I've done nothing at all with my life."

Which wasn't true. Lilli Chandler Pembroke had given as much of herself to her daughter and husband as any woman could be asked to give. She was a tireless volunteer, a wonderful sister, a devoted daughter. She managed a large apartment in New York and a house in the country, and had taken over as Chandler hostess admirably since her mother's death. But she'd wanted more. And who was Mattie to tell her she couldn't have it?

Aching and tired, more depressed than she'd felt in years, Mattie replaced the photograph in her Bible. She'd never shown it to anyone, not even Dani. Few people knew about Joe and Zeke Cutler's trip to Saratoga that summer. Certainly not her granddaughter. Mattie hadn't told her. Nor had she ever sat Dani down and explained about the little sister she'd left behind in Tennessee, the half-crazy father who'd died a long, tortured death. About her own ambivalent feelings about her hometown and her childhood there.

Dani would be surprised and hurt. She thought her grandmother had no secrets from her.

The problem was, she had too many.

Four

With her bare feet propped up on the teak umbrella table in the garden behind her gingerbread cottage, Dani regarded Sara Chandler Stone with reasonably good humor. "Tell me, Sara, have you ever been on Pembroke property before?"

Her aunt didn't answer. So far she hadn't said much. She'd slipped into the garden while Dani was enjoying a bottle of Pembroke Springs Mineral Water after a late-afternoon stint of weed pulling. She'd offered Sara a bottle. Sara had refused politely. She was a tall, slender woman, with tawny hair cut into a classic bob and pretty, rich blue eyes and a slightly uptilted chin. She'd just come from the races and had on a raspberry-flowered dress, very feminine, with raspberry heels and a long raspberry scarf tied around her straw hat. Dani herself had on gym shorts and a T-shirt. But her aunt—her mother's younger sister—was the quintessential Chandler heiress, everything her niece made no attempt to be, couldn't have been even if she'd tried.

"I received your note." Sara was as icily polite as only a Chandler could be. "You really are coming tomorrow?"

"I really am."

"Well, that's wonderful, of course. We're delighted. I only

hope—" She smiled, cool and gracious. "You do understand how much the hundredth anniversary of the running of the Chandler Stakes means to Father."

"And seeing how Mother ruined the seventy-fifth by so inconveniently disappearing, I'd better not make a scene."

Sara reddened, inhaling sharply. "I didn't mean that."

Dani felt a stab of guilt, having forgotten—or simply not consciously reminded herself—that hers wasn't the only loss, that her aunt had lost a sister. She dropped her feet to the stone terrace, warm in the afternoon sun. "I know you didn't. Don't you want to sit down?"

"I can't stay—we have a dinner party this evening. I just wanted to be sure that the note was in fact from you, that it wasn't some sort of cruel practical joke. This is such a sudden change of heart on your part—although of course we welcome it—and I know you're very busy." She paused, looking around at the cracked marble birdbath that stood in the midst of the myrtle, at the hundreds of marigolds Dani had planted. There were perennials, flowering shrubs and trees, herbs, more annuals, all enclosed by a tall Victorian wrought-iron fence. "I saw the article on you."

Dani winced, taking another sip of her mineral water. The bottle was a handsome proprietary design of evergreen-colored glass, with a distinctive long slender neck and an ornate P engraved on one side. The label was a design Dani particularly loved: a red kite floating above a pine grove. Eugene Chandler—her grandfather, Sara's father—considered her use of Pembroke for her profitable, visible company just one more example of his only grandchild's thumbing her nose at him.

"I didn't mention you or Grandfather," she said. "Or my mother."

"You didn't have to. Any article on you will dredge us up no matter what you say or don't say. Having all that…history come out now is painful."

Dani refused to feel guilty. The interview had been on the spur of the moment, and she wasn't supposed to do anything on the spur of the moment. She had too many responsibilities. She was half Chandler. She had a missing mother. Even Ira Bernstein had offered his two cents, threatening to take up a collection to buy her new sneakers. Her sneakers hadn't even been in the photograph of her. "The holes," he'd said, "were implied by the rest of your 'outfit.'"

There was no pleasing anyone anymore.

"It's not as if our 'history' isn't already on people's minds," Dani said. "It's the hundredth anniversary of the Chandler Stakes, the twenty-fifth of my mother's disappearance—people will talk, even if we don't."

Sara straightened. "I'm not a fool. I might not run a company, but that doesn't mean—" She stopped abruptly, replacing the demure stance, the stiff, polite smile with the look of a well-bred Chandler. "Let's not argue. Father's delighted you're coming tomorrow—Roger is, too." Her smile broadened at the mention of Roger Stone, her husband, and seemed genuine. "So am I."

Dani almost believed her.

After her aunt left, Dani didn't return to her flower beds, but propped her feet back up on her umbrella table and contemplated the blue sky, felt the cool afternoon breeze against her skin. Something must not be quite right in her head, she thought. Otherwise she'd have told her aunt that she'd changed her mind and wouldn't be attending the annual Chandler lawn party tomorrow night after all.

"Dani, you back here?"

She recognized Kate Murtagh's voice even as her six-foot-tall, blond, gorgeous friend barreled through the gate at the far end of the garden. Kate marched up to the stone terrace. She had on an inexpensive chambray dress, her long hair held back with a jade-and-rose-colored scarf; she didn't even have to work at looking stunning.

"Do I take it from your auntie's stiff-upper-lip exit that the rumors are true and you're going tomorrow?"

Dani shrugged. It didn't surprise her there were rumors or that Kate Murtagh had heard them. She was one of Saratoga's most sought-after caterers. She'd even landed the Chandler lawn party for the first time, in spite of her long friendship with Dani.

"It's going to be all over the gossip columns, you know," Kate said. She was clearly on one of her tears. "Are you prepared for that kind of publicity?"

"People will say what they say."

"Oh, indeed they will. In my opinion—" not that Dani had asked "—things have gotten too quiet between you and your grandfather. You'd rather have him fighting with you than not paying any attention at all."

Dani deliberately didn't answer. Everyone, including her friends, seemed to have a theory about her relationship with her mother's family.

Kate sighed. "What're you going to wear to this shindig?"

"Is that the real reason you're here?"

"You know you can't be trusted to pick out a party dress on your own."

Dani laughed but was already on her feet, leading Kate through the back door into her cottage's small, charming kitchen. As always, her friend had to take a minute to shudder. "I have nightmares about this kitchen."

"You just have unrealistically high standards."

"Like a fully functional stove and a refrigerator that postdates Donna Reed?"

"Picky, picky."

"And counters," Kate added.

"The kitchens at the inn are state-of-the-art—"

"So?"

Dani pushed through the dining room, hoping to circumvent one of Kate's lectures on how she should scrimp a little more on her companies and a little less on herself.

"I don't know how you live like this," Kate grumbled, following Dani upstairs.

She'd kept the small back bedroom she'd used during stays there as a child, leaving the larger front bedroom for Mattie's increasingly rare visits. Its leaded-glass windows and view of the garden made up for its size and meager furnishings. Dani had cleared out the junk and old furniture that had gathered over the years, then painted the walls a fresh white. She'd added an antique chestnut bureau and a cherry bed she'd covered with a flower-garden quilt and an old woolen blanket from a mill in Mattie's hometown in Tennessee.

Kate immediately went to the closet, giving an exaggerated groan when she opened the door. "Is this it? Don't you have stuff in other closets in the house?"

"No."

"What about your apartment in New York?"

The biggest closet in her three-room apartment was half the size of her one here. Kate had never been to her apartment. She hated New York.

"It's bursting with gowns and furs," Dani said, straight-faced. "I have entire drawers filled with diamonds, sapphires, silk scarves—one whole closet just for shoes."

Kate scowled over her shoulder. "Very funny."

With a brave sigh, she plunged into the closet. Dani flopped down on her bed, convinced that Kate, with her unerring sense of style, would come up with something. She could turn heads in a five-dollar flea-market rag.

There wasn't a sound from inside the closet.

Finally Kate emerged with static hair and a grim look. "It's bad," she said.

"Sometimes I wish I were as rich as people think I am."

"You could have been. It was your idea to tell your grandfather to shove your Chandler trust up his rear end."

"I wasn't that blunt."

"Doesn't make any difference. The way the Pembroke's going and with mineral water and natural sodas all the rage, you'll be rolling in money before too long. Which will no doubt drive you crazy, and you'll buy some moribund company to gobble up your cash."

"Have you been talking to Ira?"

"You always need a challenge in front of you. Worse thing for a Pembroke is to have everything he or she wants." She waved a hand. "Anyway, money isn't the reason you don't have anything to wear tomorrow. Much as you'd like to pretend otherwise, you're no pauper. The only reason you don't have anything to wear is because you won't buy anything. When's the last time you wore an evening gown?"

"The works?"

"Yeah, the works. Floor-length, jewels, hair done, heels, gloves."

"I don't do gloves."

"Come on. When?"

Dani sighed. She remembered. Oh, Lord, did she remember. "Five years ago. On December sixteenth, to be exact."

Kate stared at her, annoyed.

"No, I'm serious. It was Beethoven's birthday. I had a date."

"Well, then, no wonder you remember." Her sarcasm was a none-too-subtle slam on Dani's notoriously inactive love life. "Where did you go?"

"To a charity ball, of all things. Unfortunately I didn't get the details on where it was and who was throwing it. I almost croaked when this guy drove right up to the New York Chandler."

"Granddaddy and Aunt Sara were there?"

"Bejeweled and not expecting me."

"They kick you out?"

"That would have been too crass. They were sickeningly gracious. Turned out my date—unbeknownst to me—worked for Chandler Hotels. He was new in town, brought in from Hawaii, and was unaware of my relationship with that side of my family. Thought I was his ticket to the top. Little did he know."

"So that's why you now have guys submit their résumés before you'll go out with them."

Dani shot her friend a look. "The man was a heel, Kate."

"Yeah, well, heels do exist." She got back to the point. "But you did wear an honest-to-God evening gown?"

"Black velvet with sequins. Low-cut. Very expensive. Even my grandfather approved."

Kate looked as if she was trying to picture it. "Still have it?"

"Somewhere. I keep it around as another reminder of what being a Chandler and a Pembroke's all about."

Ever pragmatic, Kate said, "Well, velvet's too heavy for August anyway. Why don't you go into town and buy something. Little dresses are always in. Come on, Dani. You know clothes. You just don't like to spend money on anything you might wear for fun. And—as you well know—you wear little dresses all the time. Just make it short and close-fitting and over forty dollars and you'll be a hit. You've got a flat stomach and great legs."

Dani frowned. "I don't have time for a full-fledged shopping trip before tomorrow. Isn't there something in there I could dress up?"

"No."

"You could have hesitated."

"Look." Kate wasn't about to give up. "Why not rent a dress. People do it around here in August all the time."

Dani jumped off the bed. "I must have been crazy to accept that invitation, but I refuse to back down now, just on account of not having anything to wear. Don't you have something you could lend me?"

"You'd look like a little kid dressing up in her mother's clothes." Kate winced at her faux pas, as if Lilli Chandler Pembroke had disappeared yesterday and not twenty-five years ago and all Dani's wounds were still raw. It was a reaction Dani often received, even from her best friends. "I'm sorry—I know tomorrow won't be easy for you."

"Forget it. Actually, you've just given me an idea. I knew I could count on you. See Ira before you leave for a bottle of champagne. Your choice. You and your people will deserve to celebrate after pulling off tomorrow night."

"Thanks," Kate said. "Believe me, we'll need to unwind. Your auntie's a great big pain in the butt, if you'll pardon my saying so—but she's ever so sweet. Kills you with a look and twenty polite demands, if you know what I mean."

"A Chandler lady never raises her voice."

"No wonder you don't fit in with that crowd."

"Shouldn't you be julienning zucchini or something?"

But Kate's expression suddenly turned serious. "Dani, are you sure you know what you're doing?"

She smiled. "No."

"Look—"

"It's okay, Kate. I don't know exactly why I'm going this year. It's true my grandfather and I have maintained an undeclared cease-fire in the last few years—mainly by each pretending the other doesn't exist. But it's August in Saratoga, and I'm here. I can't ignore that I'm half Chandler." She paused. "Neither can my grandfather."

Kate stared at her for a few seconds, then threw up her hands. "Go for a little dress. You'll look great."

Not long after Kate left, Dani headed to her attic and pulled the string attached to the naked seventy-five-watt bulb at the top of the steep stairs. The air was hot and musty, the rough wood floors crowded with old kites and abandoned projects, college textbooks on subjects she barely remembered taking and a thousand-piece puzzle of a castle in Germany she and Mattie had put together one rainy July weekend. There was a vase she'd made in the first grade from an old liquid-detergent bottle for Mother's Day; she had no idea how it had landed in Saratoga.

It was an attic of memories, but most attics were.

Pushing past overflowing cardboard boxes, she knelt on the dusty floor in front of a huge old Saratoga trunk. It had belonged to her great-great-grandmother, the intrepid Louisa Caldwell Pembroke. She'd been a survivor. Just twenty when she'd married Ulysses, she'd never been a real part of the extravagance— the notorious capitalistic excesses—of Saratoga in the last decade of the nineteenth century. But she'd fallen in love with a gambler, had known Diamond Jim Brady, the onetime bellhop who'd become a millionaire, and Lillian Russell, the voluptuous singer whose cocker spaniel Mooksie had a collar made of diamonds and gold. Louisa had been in Saratoga when Joseph Pulitzer sent Elizabeth Cochrane—"Nellie Bly"—to the upstate spa to write her famous exposés for his New York newspaper. One had been on Ulysses Pembroke's oddball, moneyeating estate.

The Saratoga trunk was now a valuable antique. Train conductors had despised their curved lids because they made stacking them difficult.

Dani threw open the trunk. On top was the frayed, motheaten fox stole Mattie Witt had worn in *The Gamblers*. It'd probably sell for a fortune. Gently pushing it aside, Dani dug through layers of dresses, scarves, old shoes, gloves, crushed hats. Things from Mattie, things from her mother. She felt the tears on her cheeks and angrily brushed them away. She had no business crying. The past was the past. She'd carved out a niche for herself separate from the self-destructive Pembrokes, the celebrated Mattie Witt, the lost Lilli Chandler Pembroke. She'd moved forward with her life and had learned to live in the present.

She'd learned to stay out of attics.

Refusing to knuckle under to self-pity, she got on with her task.

Deep in the trunk, she found the dress.

It was red and sleek and perfect. Mattie had worn it in *Tiger's Eye,* the movie that had transformed her from an overnight sensation into a star.

Dani dug even deeper and produced the ostrich plume.

Rolling back on her heels, she held it up to the dim light. I must be out of my mind. Dyed red to match the dress, it was an integral part of Mattie's glamorous look. Dani had never in her life worn a feather in her hair.

It's my Pembroke genes. I don't know what the hell I'm doing.

And she couldn't stop herself.

The plume was squashed from having been stuffed in the trunk, but otherwise in good shape.

Would anyone at the Chandler lawn party recognize it?

Oh, yes.

In her unforgettable scene in *Casino,* Lilli Chandler Pembroke had worn Mattie's ostrich plume. Nick had said she'd meant it as a tribute to her mother-in-law, a symbol of independence and freedom to Lilli and to millions of women.

Maybe Kate was right, Dani thought, and she ought to dust off her checkbook and go to town and buy a dress.

If no one else recognized the dress Mattie Witt had worn in one of her most famous roles, the feather she and Lilli both had worn, the Chandlers certainly would. And they'd know—as perhaps Dani meant them to know—that it was yet another of her attempts to force them to confront their image of who she was. To remind them she'd always fight that image. To show them she was determined, and would remain determined, to be herself.

She closed the lid of the trunk and rose stiffly, then pulled the string on the lightbulb and carried the dress and ostrich plume downstairs. She got a hanger from her closet, shook the dress out and hung it on a curtain rod in the bedroom window. Perhaps the clear light of day would make her change her mind.

It'd have to be cleaned. And she'd have to buy shoes. Preferably red. No. Definitely red.

She could wear her gold key with it. Maybe the scarred old brass one, too.

Eyeing it, she debated. Had the clear light of day helped her change her mind?

Nah. It was a great dress.

As far as Zeke could tell, the Pembroke "experience" could be anything from quiet, healthy luxury with a nutty twist to something approaching marine boot camp.

He didn't care. He just wanted his experience to be brief.

He'd been put in a small room on the third floor with twelve-foot ceilings, a window seat, rose-flowered wallpaper and a jewel-colored crazy quilt on a brass queen-size bed. There was a marble-topped dresser and a needlepoint-cushioned chair he didn't think he was supposed to sit on.

There was no beer in the tiny refrigerator, just a six-pack of Pembroke Springs Natural Orange Soda. He opened up a bottle. It was clear glass with a pale green label featuring a kite floating above a stand of birches. What kites and birches had to do with natural soda Zeke didn't even want to speculate. He took a sip. It wasn't as syrupy as regular orange soda, but it was still soda.

He examined a brochure. If he wanted to, he could take hang gliding lessons, climb rocks or show up on the front lawn at the crack of dawn for a hot-air balloon ride. There were quilting bees on the "north porch." Nature walks. Kite-making and kite-flying lessons. Tubing expeditions on the Batten Kill. "Hands-on workshops" in the many flower, herb and vegetable gardens. Zeke took them to be weeding sessions. He could soak in mud if he wanted to. Get scrubbed, clipped, polished, deep cleaned and massaged. He could jog. Ride a bike. Climb a mountain. Tour Saratoga. Go to the races. Shop. Take in a concert at the Saratoga Performing Arts Center, a lecture at Skidmore College.

He could, if he chose, pick wild blueberries and make his own jam.

Only a Pembroke could get people to pay good money to do something they could do for free. Did Dani Pembroke have her guests do their own sheets as well? Beat them against rocks like in the old days?

Quite a place, the Pembroke.

He called Sam Lincoln Jones in San Diego. "Sam, if you've got some time on your hands, mind doing me a favor?"

"Been figuring you'd call."

"Always a step ahead. Could you check out what Nick Pembroke's up to these days? I think he's still alive."

"I'll look him up and let you know. Where are you?"

Zeke told him.

Naturally Sam had heard of the place. He chuckled. "Going to sign up for croquet?"

After he hung up, Zeke headed into the bathroom, which was small but cozy. The fluffy white towels were monogrammed with the same ornate P that was engraved on his soda bottle. On the back of the john was a basket of glycerin soaps, bath gels, bath salts, lotions, shampoos. He turned the water on in the tub, which was up on legs. Homey. Feeling reckless, he dumped an envelope of bath salts into the hot water and watched them dissolve.

Croquet and jam making, he thought.

He just couldn't wait to meet Dani Pembroke.

Five

Tucking her box of brand-new red shoes under one arm, Dani headed up to her bedroom, exhausted. She swore she'd rather scale Pikes Peak than go shopping for shoes. She'd tried downtown Saratoga first, where one could find handmade jewelry, fine wines, expensive antiques, art supplies, adorable children's outfits, fancy toys, homemade pastries and chocolates, fresh pasta, health food, Victoriana, nice clothes. Everything, it seemed, but a pair of size-six shoes that matched Mattie Witt's red ostrich plume. She'd finally had to drive south of town to a shoe outlet. The red was an exact match, but the heels were three inches high. Fortunately she'd only have to wear them a few hours.

Presumably it would have been simpler just to buy a new dress. Or to wear her all-purpose black pumps. But, in for a penny, in for a pound.

A long, relaxing bath, however, was in order.

Her only bathroom was downstairs, which meant fetching her robe from upstairs. In renovating the main house, she and her architects had become quite clever at finding places for bathrooms where there were no obvious places. Space wasn't the problem at the cottage; the problem was getting around to the job. An upstairs bath just wasn't a pressing need.

She stopped hard at her bedroom door, clutching the shoe box. Holding her breath, she stared, frozen, at the mess.

Someone had removed all the drawers from her bureau, dumped them out on the floor and tossed them aside. Her underwear, her nightgowns, her socks, her T-shirts—the entire contents of her bureau were scattered and thrown everywhere. Her mattress was torn halfway off the bed frame, blankets and sheets in a heap under the window. The curtains billowed in a strong afternoon breeze. She could hear birds twittering in her garden.

Her heart pounded. *Mattie's dress...*

It was there, in a ball beside Dani's bed.

Clothes and shoes spilled from her ransacked closet. The antique shaker box she used for jewelry was turned over, empty, on top of her bureau.

Slowly and carefully, intensely aware of what she was doing, she withdrew one of her red high heels from its shoe box and held it by the toe, its lethal three-inch heel pointed out.

"Hello?"

Despite her constricted throat, her voice sounded eerily calm in the silent house. She could hear the faint laugh of Pembroke guests in the distance.

Naturally there was no answer.

What a stupid thing to say, she thought. She'd been mugged once in New York. A decidedly unpleasant experience. But it had happened outside, on a street far from her own familiar neighborhood, and it had been quick. Give me your money. Okay, here you go. The mugger leaves, you call the police. Nothing they can do. You go home, open a bottle of wine, call some friends, complain about New York's crime rate. Scary and nothing you'd want to repeat, but different—very different—from having someone walk into your home and go through your personal belongings.

Very different, she thought, from having to guess, heart thumping, whether or not the thief was still around.

"Look, I don't want any trouble." She sounded controlled but not belligerent, at least to her own ears. "If you're still here, wait just a second and I'll go down into the kitchen and you can leave. Okay?"

Still no response.

But she did as she said. She set the shoe box on the floor, took her one high heel with her and made sure her footsteps were loud on the stairs. She started to run when she hit the living room, but made herself stop in the kitchen. Should she keep running? But what if the thief was lurking in the garden? What if he followed her?

She turned on the radio so the burglar would know she'd kept her word. She was in the kitchen. She'd give him a chance to get out the front door.

Should I call Ira? The police?

So they could come and scrape her off the floor after the thief had figured out she'd tried to trick him?

Most likely the burglar had taken off already. Or was outside waiting to make his escape. Surely if he were inside, he'd have made his presence known by now.

Dani switched off the radio and listened past the sound of blood pounding in her ears and the blue jays chasing off the sparrows in her garden.

"Okay." She tried to project her voice without yelling. "I'm coming back upstairs."

If he was in the garden, he'd hear her and make good his escape. Which was just fine with her. If he was hiding in the living room, he could sneak out while she was upstairs. If he was in the kitchen—

Swallowing hard, she resisted the urge to look around. If

he was stuffed in the broom closet, best to give him a chance to leave quietly.

What if the bastard was upstairs?

He wasn't. Of all her choices, going back up to her bedroom scared her the least. She'd just come from there, and nothing had happened.

She debated taking one of the knives she'd ordered from a company that advertised during a late-night television show she watched when she was suffering through a bout of insomnia. Kate hated the knives. "You get what you pay for," she'd said.

Never mind, she thought. She had her shoe.

She repeated her words in the living room, again on the stairs, again on the landing, and one last time as she approached her bedroom door. Whoever had trashed the bedroom had to have gone by now. She was just being dramatic.

But she heard a sound behind her. A movement.

"No, wait—"

She started to turn around—to plead, yell, jab with her high heel—but before she could do anything, she felt a hard push against her back, propelling her up and across the room like a missile. Her shoe went flying, and she was hurtling so fast her feet barely touched the floor; she couldn't control them or where she was going. Arms outstretched to brace her fall, she tripped on the edge of her mattress and fell over a pulled-out drawer, landed atop another, banged her shins and elbows and wrenched her hand. She hurt so much she didn't think to do anything but utter a loud, vicious curse.

Behind her she heard heavy footsteps pounding down the stairs. *Now* her intruder was taking off. Obviously he hadn't believed she'd keep her promise.

Groaning, aching, Dani sat a moment amidst her scattered underwear, trying to calm her wild breathing and assure herself she'd live. She wasn't hurt that badly.

Clearly the garden would have been a better choice.

The front door slammed shut, startling her. A fresh wave of adrenaline flowed through her system. Okay. At least he was gone.

She raced into Mattie's room and looked out the window but saw no one. How could her intruder disappear that fast?

Unless he hadn't.

Trying to ignore her bruises and scrapes and the throbbing in her left knee, Dani grabbed the poker from the fireplace in Mattie's room and checked everywhere, starting with the two bedrooms and the closets upstairs. She climbed up to the attic and checked it. She went downstairs and checked under the couch and in the closets and in every nook and cranny in the kitchen and pantry. She even went down to the basement and checked behind the furnace.

Nothing.

Back upstairs, her palms sweaty, her body aching, she sorted through the mess in her bedroom for what was missing. Twenty dollars in odd bills. Her canning jar of emergency change. Her sterling-silver earrings, her turquoise bracelet, a jade pin, the fetish necklace her father had sent from Arizona saying it was handmade, but for all she knew had been mass-produced in Taiwan.

Then she remembered the one piece of jewelry that she really did care about: the gold key she'd found on the cliffs.

"The bastard!"

The matching brass key was gone, too. Any relief she'd felt at not having been killed quickly transformed itself into anger. She started to pick up a drawer and throw it, but remembered her chestnut bureau was an antique and set the drawer back down.

She was furious.

This felt better than being scared.

Her thief must have seen the article on her in the paper or

any of the recent publicity on the hundredth running of the Chandler Stakes. Like too many before him, he must have figured someone with a name and a family history like hers would have tons of valuables and disposable cash. That he'd been wrong was at least a small consolation.

But her keys—she'd definitely miss them.

She headed painfully back downstairs and started to call Ira, but hung up before she finished dialing. What good would calling the police or even Pembroke security do at this point? Unfortunately Saratoga in August was a stomping ground for petty thieves. Hers hadn't gotten away with much that anyone else would care about. And, in retrospect, he hadn't really tried to hurt her. He'd just been too stupid to make his getaway when he'd had the chance. Besides which, he was probably long gone by now. He had only to cut through the woods to the bottling plant or mingle with the crowds in the rose gardens and he'd be home free. She couldn't even provide a decent description of the son of a bitch.

She also didn't need that kind of publicity.

But she'd have to tell Ira a thief was skulking about the premises. As Pembroke manager, he needed to know such things. She'd tell him…later.

First she doctored the worst scrape on her shin with a dab of antibacterial goo, then put two 7.7-ounce bottles of Pembroke Springs Mineral Water into an ice bucket, filled it with ice, got out a tall glass and went out to the terrace.

Her garden was bathed in cool afternoon shade, a hummingbird darting among the hollyhocks. Dani opened a bottle of mineral water, took a sip and poured the rest in her glass. Her wrist ached. So did her elbows. Her shin plain hurt.

Setting her bottle on the umbrella table, she pulled out a chair so she could sit and think and regain her composure before she did anything.

Something moved in the garden to her left.

Adrenaline pumped through her bloodstream with such velocity that she ached even more. She flew around, hoping she was overreacting, that it was just a bird or a squirrel.

It wasn't.

A man materialized from behind the dogwood. Dani reached for her empty Pembroke Springs bottle. He was strongly built, around six feet, striking but not exactly handsome. He had very alert dark eyes and a small scar under his left eye.

He looked capable of coming at a woman half his size from behind and giving her a good shove.

"Afternoon," he said. "I didn't think the cottage was occupied."

Nice try. Her fingers curled around the cool neck of her green bottle. "Who are you?"

"I'd be happy to tell you if you'll think twice about throwing that bottle at me."

But Dani had grown up in New York City and knew better than to think twice or give anyone a chance to explain something like pitching her across her own bedroom.

She whipped the bottle as hard as she could, aiming for the man's head. Before it could strike its mark, she spun around and bolted for her kitchen.

Behind her, she heard a distinct curse as the bottle hit its target or came close.

She grabbed her car keys off their hook in the kitchen and, while she was at it, the eight-inch cast-iron frying pan soaking in the sink. Water spilled out over her legs, stinging her scraped shins. She raced through the dining room and into the living room, surprised at how clearly she was thinking. She'd get to her car, head for the main house, alert security. Ira would say she should have called him or the police in the first place....

She scooted out the front door, bounded down the brick walk with her frying pan and came to the gravel driveway where she kept her very used car parked.

The man from the garden was leaning against the door on the driver's side, looking unhurt and in amazingly good humor.

Dani raised the frying pan.

"Throw that thing at me," he said amiably, "and I'll duck. You'll break a window. Won't accomplish much. Besides, I'm harmless."

She kept the frying pan raised high. "You don't look harmless."

He smiled. "I consider that a gift."

What kind of man was he? She lowered the frying pan a fraction of an inch. She thought he noticed. But it was heavy, and her wrist hurt. "Who are you, and what were you doing in my garden?"

"I didn't mean to startle you." He hadn't moved off her car and didn't seem particularly worried that she might decide to bonk him on the head after all. It didn't appear her bottle had struck home. "My name's Zeke Cutler. I would have taken more care if I'd realized the cottage was occupied and you'd just been robbed."

She almost dropped the frying pan. "How do you know I was just robbed?"

"A woman throwing bottles and arming herself with an iron skillet is usually a dead giveaway." But his smile and the touch of humor in his dark, dark eyes gave way to a frown and a squint, a serious expression of determination and self-assurance. He seemed to know of what he spoke. "So are bruised wrists, skinned elbows, scraped shins."

"You're very observant."

"However," he said, the humor flickering back to his eyes, "if you're Dani Pembroke, and I take it you are, you could have gotten banged up fetching a kite down from a tree or climbing rocks."

She straightened, suddenly acutely aware of the position in

which this man had found her. Bruised, scared, robbed. "Are you a reporter? Can't you guys leave me alone? Look, I haven't admitted anything—"

"I'm not a reporter." Zeke Cutler pulled himself from her car. His eyes never left her. He was, she thought, one intensely controlled man. "Do you want to tell me what happened?"

"Why would I do that?"

"Did you get a good look at the man who attacked you?"

She refused to answer. What if this was an act and he was the one who'd attacked her? What if he really was a reporter?

"You didn't call the police," he said.

"What makes you so sure?"

His expression was unreadable now, any humor gone. "It's an educated guess."

"Well, Mr. Cutler, I appreciate your concern, but if you don't mind, I'd like you off my property. Under the circumstances, you're making me nervous. I'm sure you understand."

"Suit yourself."

Without further argument, he started down the driveway. His running shoes scrunched on the gravel. Dani made herself notice his clothes: jeans and dark blue pullover. Black sport watch. No socks. He looked clean enough. And he moved with a speed, grace and economy that struck her as inordinately sexy and not entirely unexpected. It suddenly occurred to her that he could be a lost guest from the Pembroke. But he didn't seem the type to stay at a spa-inn, nor, certainly, the type to get lost.

He seemed more the type who could have pitched her across her room and lied about it.

She waited until he was out of sight. Then she returned to her cottage, pried the frying pan from her grip and picked up the phone again.

This time she didn't stop dialing until she'd finished. But it wasn't Ira she called, or the police, or Pembroke security, or any of her friends, or, God knew, her father or grandfathers or her sweet aunt Sara. She called the one person she could always call when she found her house ransacked and a strange man in her garden, and that was her grandmother, Mattie Witt.

Dani Pembroke wasn't what Zeke had expected.

He entered the rose garden, figuring that if *he'd* just robbed Dani Pembroke, it was where he'd head. But as he stepped through the iron gate, memories—dreams that were dead and done with—assaulted him. He pictured how the garden had looked twenty-five years ago, with Mattie Witt sitting in its overgrown midst, wearing her orange flight suit as she'd worked on the basket of her hot-air balloon.

He'd been a fool to let the past determine his actions. He couldn't afford to make that kind of mistake again.

But there was a lot of Mattie in her granddaughter, in her dark good looks, her independence. And with her zest for a fight—an iron skillet, for pete's sake—a flash of Nicholas Pembroke.

Instinctively Zeke knew all those qualities were what Dani wanted people to see in her. She wouldn't want them to see the mystery and vulnerability he'd detected behind her direct manner, the parts of her she held back, the parts that would remind people of her gentle, sensitive, lost mother. Her eyes, as black as Lilli's had been blue, said she had secrets and knew you knew she had them but wasn't going to tell you what they were anyway.

There was a lack of self-pity about the owner of Pembroke Springs that Zeke could admire.

And, given the circumstances, a hotheadedness that worried him.

The rose garden covered two acres and was, in his view, the best part of the estate. There were fountains, gazebos, marble statuary, stone benches, low iron fences and dozens of beautiful, perfectly pruned rosebushes. Their fragrance filled the afternoon air.

He noticed a discreet plaque dedicating the rosebushes to the memory of Lilli Chandler Pembroke. His throat tightened. He needed distance. Control. Squinting against the bright sun, he scanned the crowd meandering along the brick walks. He'd come to do a job. Time to get on with it.

He went utterly motionless.

Quint Skinner.

There was no mistaking the bull-like physique, the cropped red-blond hair, the scarred face. Skinner had served with Joe Cutler. After he got out of the army, he'd become a journalist and hooked up with his old unit, discovering that morale was low and Joe's sense of pride and honor had deteriorated. He'd seen Joe's men die. And he'd seen Joe die.

Joe Cutler: One Soldier's Rise and Fall was Quint's book. He hadn't done much since.

What the hell was he doing in Saratoga?

Tucked between two teenage girls, Skinner edged out of the rose garden. A small pack was slung over one massive shoulder. Zeke would bet he'd find Dani Pembroke's belongings in that pack. But there was nothing he could do. Not right now—not that made sense. Pulitzer Prize winner or not, Quint Skinner was perfectly capable of ransacking a woman's bedroom and smacking her around. He was also capable of using a couple of innocent girls to get his ass out of a sling with Zeke.

And it occurred to Zeke that Dani Pembroke just might not appreciate his efforts. The media would pounce on a confrontation between Quint Skinner and Joe Cutler's brother in the Pembroke rose gardens. Zeke had already noted that Dani hadn't reacted to his name. Seemed she had no idea who he was. What all hadn't Mattie told her?

He let Quint go. For now.

It was teatime at the Pembroke. Wild-blueberry muffins, fresh fruit and Earl Grey tea were being served on the veranda. Zeke headed on up. Afterward maybe he'd try to scare up a fifth of George Dickel in this Yankee town.

If he was lucky, in due time he'd bump into Quint Skinner on neutral turf. If not, he'd just have to hunt him down and have a little chat.

Ira Bernstein was not pleased to learn a burglar had been prowling the Pembroke grounds. He was even less pleased to find out over an hour after the fact. "Why didn't you call me?" he screamed at Dani.

She leaned back against the couch in her office. Now that the crisis was over, she was aching and tired; even thinking was an effort. And talking to Mattie hadn't helped. Instead of offering her usual love, wisdom and concern, she had been shocked and withdrawn, which led Dani to worry something was wrong with her grandmother. But Mattie had denied that Dani had caught her at a bad time, assured her she was well—and then urged her not to call the police, because she didn't need the added publicity.

Since when had Mattie worried about publicity?

When Dani didn't answer, Ira paced, hands thrust in his pants pockets, hair wild. "You don't have any description?"

"No." She paused. "Not of the burglar. But there was another man… I was wondering if you've seen him around. Dark hair, dark eyes, maybe six feet tall. Looks really fit. Very controlled." And sexy, she thought, but judiciously left out that assessment. "He says his name's Zeke Cutler. Ring any bells?"

It hadn't with Mattie, but Ira stopped pacing and hesitated.

"What?" Dani prodded.

He looked at her. "You won't fly off the handle?"

"Ira."

"He's a guest."

Hell's bells, she thought. Just her luck. She decided not to tell Ira she'd thrown a bottle at him. "Go on."

"He arrived this afternoon—"

"He had a reservation?"

"Not exactly. Apparently he called in a favor and got the room of a former client or the daughter of a former client—something like that."

"A client? Who is he, what's he do?"

"He's a security consultant. From what I understand, he's very good at what he does."

Dani could feel her face redden. What in blue blazes had she gotten herself into?

"Anyway," Ira went on, "I believe he's having tea on the veranda—"

She was on her feet and out the door, leaving Ira Bernstein to do what he would about her burglar. A professional white knight. What next?

Her head throbbed, and her antibacterial goo hadn't done a thing to stop her scraped shin from hurting. But she pounded down the wood-paneled hall, past the library, through the ballroom and out to the veranda, which looked out onto a formal garden and a small fishpond.

Zeke Cutler was there, alone.

"Tell me, Dani Pembroke," he said, rocking back in his rattan chair. "What's the difference between a wild blueberry and the regular kind?"

She inhaled, remembering he was a guest. "Wild blueberries are wild, for one thing. They're smaller, and many people think they're more flavorful than cultivated blueberries."

"Ah."

"Mr. Cutler—"

"Zeke."

The rhythms of his southern accent and his subtle but unmistakable humor softened the hard edges of his voice. But his eyes, she noticed, remained alert and intense, taking in everything. She became aware of the spots of blood on her T-shirt, the ratty socks she'd quickly pulled on before heading up to the main house, her crummy sneakers, her short, messy hair. She usually dressed up when she was in a spot where she could run into guests.

"I understand you're staying here at the Pembroke."

"That's right."

"What brings you to Saratoga?"

He shrugged, his eyes never leaving her. "Curiosity."

That could mean anything, and she suspected he knew it. "My manager tells me you're a professional white knight."

He gave a short laugh. "I've never thought of it quite like that."

"You're not looking at a potential client, in case the thought crossed your mind."

The dark eyes narrowed. Suddenly self-conscious, Dani ran one hand through the pink geraniums in a marble urn, looking for a wilted blossom. There wasn't one, so she snapped off one that was still healthy.

"Was your being in my garden a coincidence?" she asked.

"I didn't rob you."

A man of few but well-chosen words. Dani didn't know what to make of him. "If you think you saw an opening to get yourself hired to protect me or some such thing, you're wrong."

There was a distinct gleam of amusement in his eyes. "Honey, I'd rather protect a pack of pit bulls." But the humor vanished; he became, once again, calm and steady, utterly in control. "I'm not in Saratoga on business, if that's what you're getting at. You want to tell me what happened at your cottage?"

"No, I don't."

"You surprised your thief, didn't you? He pushed you from behind—I take it you didn't see him. Did he get away with anything of value?"

"Nothing much." She wished she hadn't come out here. She imagined Zeke Cutler was very good at what he did.

"Did he snatch your gold key?"

Dani controlled her surprise. So Zeke Cutler had read the article on her. Was that why he'd come to Saratoga, to the Pembroke? Had he robbed her after all? Or had he staged the burglary to get her to hire him? She saw that her hand was shaking and pulled it away from the geraniums; she clenched it at her side so he wouldn't see.

"That's not your concern," she said.

"I suppose it isn't."

"If I find out you are a leech," she said, "I'll have you thrown off my property."

He stretched out his long legs. "Fair enough."

"Meanwhile—" she managed a gracious smile that would have done any Chandler proud "—enjoy your stay at the Pembroke."

Having survived tea and being called a professional white knight, Zeke headed into town for something real to eat. Dinner at the Pembroke had included flowers. His waiter had promised they were edible. Zeke had passed. Besides which, he had an appointment to keep.

Roger Stone was waiting for him on the terrace at a hopping restaurant just off Broadway that did, indeed, serve hamburgers. A good-looking man in his mid-forties, Roger had taken over as vice president of Chandler Hotels after his brother-in-law—Dani Pembroke's father—was caught with his hand in the cookie jar. He was now president and chief executive officer; Zeke had checked. Roger rose, and the two men shook hands.

"It's good to see you," Roger said, as if they'd seen each other since the summer his wife's sister had disappeared, which they hadn't.

"Sorry I'm late."

"I'd begun to wonder if you'd gotten my message."

It had come to Zeke's room at the Pembroke, before he found himself ducking Dani Pembroke's mineral water bottle. "Word travels fast. How'd you hear I was in town?"

Roger shrugged evasively. He was fair and tall and fit, with angular features, pale blue eyes and impeccable taste in everything. His suit, Zeke noticed, was custom tailored. He himself had put on a fresh shirt but had left on his jeans. "A friend arrived at the airport the same time you did. It's a small airport. And half the fun of coming to Saratoga is keeping track of who else is here." Roger had already ordered a bottle of wine; he poured Zeke a glass. "But I suppose if you'd wanted to keep a low profile, I'd never have found out you were here."

True, Zeke thought.

"Does that mean you're not here on business?" Roger asked.

Zeke smiled. "Just here for health, history and horses, as the saying goes."

"But you're staying at my niece's hotel…or whatever she calls that place of hers."

"It seemed as good a place as any."

Zeke tried his wine. It was, of course, an excellent choice. A waiter took his order for a hamburger. Roger wasn't eating. "Sara and I have a dinner party later this evening."

Sara, Sara. Zeke wondered what she looked like now, if she was happy. Had she regretted picking Roger, one of her own kind, over Joe? Even twenty-five years ago, from what Zeke could gather the couple of times he'd met him, Roger Stone had been wealthy and polished, an Ivy Leaguer, everything Joe Cutler wasn't. Joe had known it and hadn't cared. He'd never understood things like social class and the gulf between the Cutlers of Cedar Springs, Tennessee, and the Chandlers of New York City, Kentucky and Saratoga.

"Zeke, I…" Roger paused, exhaling, not meeting Zeke's eyes. "I'm sorry about your brother. He had such promise." He winced, looking embarrassed. "I'm sorry. That sounds patronizing, and I don't mean to patronize."

"It's okay. And thanks. Why did you ask me here?"

He smiled thinly. "I'd heard you were one to cut to the heart of things. It's a delicate matter. About Danielle, in fact."

Danielle. Zeke could see her shining black eyes, the fear behind them. But if Roger was looking for a reaction, he didn't get one.

"Frankly, Sara and I are worried about her—something we dare not let her realize. She's independent to a pathological degree, in my opinion. But we do care about her."

"Worried in what way?"

"I'm not sure—we could be overreacting. Rumors have been circulating all summer that she's overextended herself, but I see no real evidence of that myself. And she's coming tomorrow night." He said it as if Zeke would automatically know what tomorrow night was, which he did. "She hasn't attended since her mother…well, you know."

"Anything else?"

He shrugged. "Nothing specific. We just don't want anything to happen to her."

A sentiment, Zeke had a feeling, that would just irritate the hell out of Dani Pembroke. His hamburger arrived, without flowers. He poured on the ketchup and dug in. "You're worried she's going to prove herself a true Pembroke and let everything she's accomplished go up in smoke."

"As a matter of fact, yes, that is what worries us. Zeke, Danielle's as reckless as any Pembroke's ever been. Her risks just aren't at the poker table. We're afraid—Sara and I, and Eugene as well—that she's going to self-destruct."

"What's that got to do with me?"

A faint sheen of color rose in Roger's pale cheeks. "I'd like you to keep an eye on her."

Zeke tried not to laugh. What would Roger do if he knew his niece had come after him with an iron skillet only a few hours ago? Obviously her sweet, caring uncle had no idea she'd surprised a burglar. "That's not what I do."

"The pay would be substantial."

"I don't care about the pay, Roger. I don't babysit heiresses."

"Oh, she's hardly an heiress any longer. She saw to that herself years ago. Zeke, please reconsider."

"The Chandlers must have all kinds of security people at their disposal. Hire one of them."

Zeke swallowed another bite of hamburger, drank some wine and considered what Roger Stone really wanted from him. A sense of why Zeke was in Saratoga? If Dani was up to something, about to bring more embarrassment on the Chandlers?

"Why don't you talk to your niece yourself?" Zeke suggested.

Roger laughed, incredulous. "Obviously you don't know Dani. She doesn't want anything from her mother's side of the family—she'd be furious if she knew we were worried, knew I was talking to you. That I was willing to hire you on her behalf. The point is, she has enough on her plate."

"Is she in any danger?"

"As far as I know, only from herself."

"I'm sorry I can't help, Roger, but that's just not my gig."

The CEO of Chandler Hotels sighed, nodding. "You're right, of course. I guess we're just feeling helpless, given Danielle's lack of affection for us all." He stared into his wineglass, then looked at Zeke. "Oh, by the way—did you know Quint Skinner is in town?"

Bingo, Zeke thought. This was why Roger had asked for this little tête-à-tête. Quint Skinner and Zeke Cutler in Saratoga at the same time was more coincidence than Roger could swallow—though it didn't concern him, except that he was Dani's uncle. It was more than Zeke could swallow, too, even if he hadn't seen Skinner in the rose garden that afternoon.

"No, I didn't. Small world, I guess."

Roger's blue eyes narrowed. "He's not the reason you're here?"

"Not at all." Zeke gave the rich man across the table one of his easy smiles. "I'm on vacation."

He could see Roger didn't believe him. "Well, thank you for letting me air my concerns. You're sure you won't reconsider?"

"Dani Pembroke's not my problem."

Six

$\multimap \circledcirc \circledcirc \multimap$

John Pembroke lay on his back, stark naked, debating whether to answer the door. The knocking had woken him up. It was noon—he'd checked his Timex—and he'd been sound asleep. No one ever visited him.

There was another knock.

A reporter? He hoped not, but it was Friday. Tonight was the annual Chandler lawn party and the twenty-fifth anniversary of Lilli's disappearance. John wished he could sleep the whole damn day.

His two window air conditioners—one in his small bedroom, one in his all-purpose room—rattled and groaned trying to keep up with the blistering Tucson summer heat. He'd heard the temperature was supposed to climb to a hundred-fifteen today. Might as well be living in hell.

He rubbed one hand across the grizzled gray hairs of his chest, trying to wake up. He'd been dreaming about swimming in the ice-cold stream out behind his nutty mother's gingerbread cottage, as he had summers as a boy. But he'd never go back, hadn't since Lilli disappeared. Saratoga was nothing but memories for him. Even Lilli had become just another memory. You couldn't touch a memory, he'd discovered. You couldn't live one.

Except once in a while.

Like just now, when he'd opened his eyes, thinking he was in the maple bed in his and Lilli's old room at the Chandler cottage on North Broadway. He'd heard her breathing beside him. He'd rolled over, knowing she was there. So certain. He'd wanted to hold her, to make love to her.

There was yet another knock.

"I'm coming!"

He heaved himself out of bed and pulled on a pair of wrinkled elastic-waist shorts. He'd developed the habit of working late, often past dawn, and sleeping well into the afternoon. In summer he missed the worst of the blazing heat. And the desert night sky, he'd discovered, was incomparable. He'd head up into the mountains and stare at the sparkling stars and endless dark and imagine Lilli's spirit in union once more with him, imagine what their life together might have become.

Hell of a romantic he was.

He'd tell her, as he hadn't often enough in their too-short time together, how much he loved her.

Rubbing his face with his palms, he could feel the rough stubble of a couple of days' growth of beard. He seldom shaved every day. His neighbors initially had thought he was a do-gooder or gentrifier come to restore one of the street's old adobe houses and sell it at a profit. Now they pretty much figured he was just an old reprobate. He'd once asked the family next door, eight people crowded into an apartment not much bigger than his place, their advice on identifying and killing—unless there was a damn good reason why he shouldn't—a giant spider that had taken over his bathroom. Turned out it was just an ordinary desert spider. Nothing to worry about. They'd thought his naïveté and terror great fun and gave him a beer and had Carlos, the baby of the family, go back with him to liberate his bathroom. Meanwhile, of course, the spider had vanished. Now John never took a leak without wondering where the damn thing had gone.

He went through his all-purpose room to the front door. When he'd fallen into bed early that morning, he'd left out the books, photographs, articles and two hundred pages of the manuscript for the biography he was writing of his notorious great-grandfather, Ulysses Pembroke. Dani had commissioned him. John had no idea what she planned to do with it. He hadn't asked. He knew damn well she hadn't given him the job out of a sense of charity. He'd used up his daughter's goodwill a long, long time ago.

He pulled open the door, the dry heat hitting him as if he'd pulled open a furnace running full blast against a subzero chill. "Yeah, what's up?"

A kid, no more than eighteen, in shorts, T-shirt and sandals, stood red-faced on the landing. He looked parched. John felt a wave of guilt at having kept the poor bastard waiting in the scorching heat. It *was* hot, even for Tucson in August.

"Mr. Pembroke?" the kid asked tentatively.

John stiffened, immediately thinking of Dani. Something had happened to her. Then he thought of Nick: his father was dead. Ninety years old and finally gone to the great beyond. Or Mattie. But he wasn't ready to say goodbye to his mother yet. He tried to will away the habit of thinking the worst, but couldn't. The worst had happened often enough.

"Yes," he said sharply, trying to control his fear.

The kid took a step back, no doubt wondering if he'd come to the wrong place. John supposed he looked like hell. Although still lean and rawboned, his black eyes as alert as ever, he'd lost weight, both fat and muscle, and his skin had begun to sag on his neck and elbows. He was fast becoming an old man with flabby knees. Lately his grooming amounted to daily teeth cleaning and a weekly shower. Part of his routine came from conviction: the desert wasn't a place to be profligate with water.

Part came from not giving a damn. Twenty-five years ago he'd never have answered the door unshaven, gray hair sticking out, in nothing but a pair of wrinkled turquoise shorts.

"I'm from Tucker's Office Supply," the kid said. "A fax came for you."

John had never received a fax here. He didn't own a telephone or a computer. He'd given up on as much technology as he could since Eugene Chandler had given him the boot.

"Delivery was included," the kid said.

"So I don't owe you anything?"

He shook his head. The air was so hot and dry his sweat evaporated instantly. Or maybe John had left him out there so long he'd stopped sweating. Dehydration and hyperthermia were constant threats in summertime Arizona.

John took the offered envelope. "Wait a second."

He went back into the cooler gloom of his adobe, walking right over the scattered books and papers in his bare feet, and dug in his small refrigerator for a bottle of Pembroke Springs Natural Orange Soda. Dani had sent him a case—and the bill. His daughter was a barracuda. He handed the soda to the kid, who looked relieved. John heard the fizz of the bottle opening as he shut his door. His good deed for the day. Didn't want the kid croaking on his drive back to the two-bit office-supply store where he worked.

The fax had been sent from Beverly Hills:

Dear John,
What kind of damn fool would live in the desert with no phone? Dani's been robbed. She's okay, but I'm not. Call me: I have a phone.
Nick

Not, John observed dispassionately, "Love, Dad," or even the conventional "Your father." Just Nick. Like they were old pals, which they weren't. Of course, they weren't much as father and son, either.

John laid the slippery fax on the counter and got out a Dos Equis, then heated up a leftover quesadilla and lit a cigarette. He'd learned to smoke the night he'd lost his first thousand in a poker game. He hadn't had a thousand to lose, and gambling had seemed a hell of a way to get rid of his money. Smoking hadn't helped. He'd known it wouldn't, but he'd needed something to try to assuage his guilt and self-hate, although why he'd thought a cigarette would do the trick he still couldn't figure out. Now he smoked whenever he felt particularly guilty or rotten. Usually all someone had to do was mention his daughter.

He sat on the tattered couch he'd picked up from the Salvation Army fifteen years ago. He'd always thought he'd have it recovered but never had. He reread his father's fax. A fax machine wouldn't intimidate that old geezer. Nicholas Pembroke was the most selfish and egotistical and totally unreliable man John had ever known, but endearingly honest about his failings, and direct, and unafraid—to a fault—of taking risks. John, on the other hand, seldom told anyone what was on his mind and had learned to avoid risk. To him his gambling wasn't taking risks. It was avoiding them. Popular media opinion declared that his Pembroke genes—a penchant for gambling and adventure and self-destruction—had led to his downfall. He disagreed. He'd been all over the world, gambling, writing the odd travel article, doing as he damn well pleased. But it was a life he'd chosen not for its risk but for its safety. Staying on at Chandler Hotels and being the only parent to his only child would have required greater courage. Staring in the mirror every morning and wondering if he'd driven Lilli off all those years ago. Wondering if he'd helped make her feel trapped and unhappy. If he'd pushed her into making her deal with his father to act in *Casino* on the sly.

Give him a hot poker game any day.

He stubbed out his cigarette. He hadn't seen Nick in months. Despite their many differences, the one thing he and Nick did share—this mismatched father and son—was a deep affection for Dani. Daughter and granddaughter, she was the one person they both loved without condition.

And whom both had failed without reason.

John smoked another cigarette and drank another beer. In his gut he knew what Nick was going to ask him to do.

Twenty-five years ago tonight Lilli had disappeared.

How could Nick ask?

"Damn," John whispered, smashing his cigarette into an ashtray. He'd only smoked half of it. The other half he'd save for another day.

The minute he'd finished reading his father's fax, he'd known what he would do.

He dressed in khaki pants and a white cotton shirt he didn't bother tucking in and his ratty, once-white tennis shoes. All in all, he still looked like a desert rat, brown and wizened, squinty-eyed, a pathetic shadow of the proud, determined man he'd once been. When he got to Saratoga—he knew he'd go—some jackass would take his picture and put it in the paper. Dani wouldn't be mortified. She'd say, "Yeah, that's my father, the crook."

She'd always been one to embrace reality.

After tossing a few things into a battered overnight bag, John headed out into the dry, blistering heat to the convenience store on the corner. He didn't have a car, either. He used the pay phone to call his father collect. Nick accepted the charges. He always did. Dani paid his phone bill.

"You packed?" Nick asked in his famous gravelly voice.

"Yeah. You?"

"I'd drop dead before the plane got halfway to Chicago. No

great loss to you and my charming ex-wife, of course, but I'm uninsured. You'd have to bury me. Think of the expense."

John ignored his father's morbid humor. "Tell me what's going on."

"Mattie called."

John was more amazed than surprised that his parents continued to tell each other most everything after fifty years apart. Their fights—which they preferred to call "quarrels"—had become the stuff of legend. But each knew exactly what the other was.

"Dani called her after being robbed?" John speculated.

"Naturally. Apparently the son of a bitch was still in the house when she got there. Pushed her around a little, but she's not seriously hurt."

"Thank God."

"Yeah. Happened yesterday afternoon. With all the publicity she's had lately, people think she's rolling in money. Probably some bastard finally decided to have a look-see."

"But you don't think so," John said.

"Hell, I don't know. Mattie's got a bee in her bonnet over the whole thing. You know that gold key Dani found? It was stolen along with some other stuff."

"So?"

His father didn't answer immediately, and John waited. He knew better than to interrupt one of Nick's dramatic pauses. He'd come to the point only after he'd built the tension to a suitable climax or John yelled at him to get on with it. Nicholas Pembroke's success as a filmmaker, John had come to believe, stemmed not from any particular artistic or technical genius, but from an innate talent for zeroing in on the essence of drama. He simply knew how to wring every drop of emotion out of a scene.

"So if Mattie's right, Lilli was wearing the key the night she disappeared."

John shut his eyes and felt the perspiration sticking his shirt to his back and the tightness in his eyes from the low humidity and insufficient sleep. He could see the Pembroke cliffs on a bright, clear Saratoga August afternoon.

Lilli.

"There's another little gem," Nick said.

John was losing patience. "This call's costing you money—"

"It's costing Dani. The little shark will demand a written explanation, I'm sure." Nick inhaled and coughed, suddenly sounding old. "Zeke Cutler is in Saratoga, John."

Exhaling slowly, John retained his self-control. He knew what his father was talking about. Zeke and Joe Cutler had been in Saratoga twenty-five years ago to tell Mattie her father was dying. They'd left the night Lilli disappeared. As far as John knew, the police had never questioned them. There had seemed to be no reason to. But John had read the book on Joe Cutler. The man who'd died in Beirut and the boy who'd come to Saratoga earlier had seemed like two different people, but who knew?

"Why?" he asked his father.

"Mattie doesn't know. Apparently Dani found him in her garden after the burglary—she only mentioned him in passing when she talked to Mattie. John, Mattie's never told her about the Cutler boys. You know she hates talking about Cedar Springs."

And Dani idolized her grandmother, trusted her and believed in her as she couldn't believe in anyone else, including her own father.

"Do you have a plane ticket?" Nick asked.

"I'll get one."

"If you need money, I can try and peel some off Dani."

"I don't need money." His daughter wasn't nearly as generous with her father as her grandfather, on the grounds, she claimed, that Nick was unreformable and too old to leave to the streets.

"John…"

He swallowed. "I'll do my best."

"That's all I've ever asked of you."

If only, John thought, either of them had asked as much of himself.

In his one-bedroom apartment on the ground floor of a pink stucco building on one of Beverly Hills's less exclusive streets, Nicholas Pembroke settled into the leather chair he'd had sent to him in California from his grandfather's peculiar estate—it seemed like a lifetime ago. Over sixty years. He'd left New York for good after his mother's death. His father had died when Nick was five. Barely remembered him. He was named Ulysses Jr., but he'd tried hard not to be like his own father—that was a sentiment Nick understood. His own son, likewise, had never wanted to be like him.

"I have only one request to make of you," his mother said to him on her deathbed. "Promise me you won't make the same mistakes your grandfather did. Don't let your good intentions be responsible for trapping anyone else, for inflicting pain on anyone else, especially those you love."

He'd promised. He'd adored his mother, had been shattered by her illness and premature death. And he'd always been very good at making promises. He just wasn't very good at keeping them.

He'd leave the chair to Dani in his will.

He couldn't be thinking about death now. He had to concentrate on the present.

And decide whether he should try to get hold of John at the Tucson airport and tell him the rest.

All of it.

He laid his head back and closed his eyes. His chair had seemed larger in recent years, but he'd finally admitted it was the same size: he had shrunk. He was ancient, for the love of God. He might yet live to a hundred. And what did he have to show for his long life? An unforgiving ex-wife. A son he'd failed. A granddaughter who treated him like a charity case. Hell, he was a charity case. And a few well-regarded movies— *The Gamblers*, *Tiger's Eye*, *Casino*. He'd lived too long and had too many forgettable movies, too many dry years and too much bad press to be admired the way people admired Mattie Witt.

Yeah, well, what was a reputation? Glorified gossip. Not the sort of thing in which one took great comfort a month before one's ninetieth birthday.

And he had his mistakes to show, too.

Using his cane, he rose slowly. Twenty years ago the cane had been a dapper affectation, but now it was an unfortunate necessity. He was thin and stooped, and sometimes when he looked in the mirror, he wondered who the hell that scrawny old fart was looking back at him. His black hair had turned completely white, and what was left of it was so thin he seldom had to comb it. His eyes, veined and weak, had a tendency to bulge. He hadn't asked the doctors why. Didn't want to know. His crepey skin sagged on his brittle bones. He supposed he ought to be grateful he still had all his faculties: he could recall every asinine thing he'd done and said in the past century.

And yet there were times, especially on quiet, warm nights, when he yearned to be, if only for a moment, the irresistible cocky young man he'd been decades ago, when he'd stumbled upon Mattie on the banks of the Cumberland River.

"God willing, you'll live a long life," she'd told him many times, and she'd never meant it kindly.

He crept into the kitchen, pulled open his refrigerator and found a bottle of Pembroke Springs Mineral Water. Dani sent him a case every couple of months. With a shaking hand, he un-screwed the cap and drank straight from the bottle, the cold, ef-fervescent water dribbling down the sides of his chin. It tasted as it always had, from the first day he'd tried it as a boy almost a century ago: clean and crystal clear, slightly earthy, as if he were taking in a little of the Adirondack Mountains with every sip. Maybe he could blame his longevity on a boyhood spent drinking this stuff.

He set the empty bottle on the counter and belched.

Consequences, he thought. He'd always hated facing conse-quences.

If you make a promise to your dying mother you break time and time again, you stand to endure a lifetime of guilt. If you screw another woman while you're married to someone else—someone who's a part of your soul—you stand to lose her. If you spirit a sad, tortured young woman away from her abusive father and husband for a summer of freedom, you stand to set into mo-tion a series of events over which you and she have no control.

Nick sagged against the refrigerator, trying not to remember Joe Cutler. If Joe hadn't come north to fetch Mattie back to Cedar Springs to see her dying father…if he'd understood that Mattie could never go back…

Unlike her younger sister, Naomi Witt Hazen, whom Nick, too, had loved. "I'll go back home and do what I have to do," she'd told him after the heat of their long-ago summer affair had expired and they'd known they'd gone as far as they ever would together. "But my father and husband will never have the same hold over me as they once did. I'm free."

Nick banged his cane against the refrigerator and wished the memories—a century of them—would just go away. Some-times he'd rather be a drooling old man in a nursing home.

He should have known twenty-five years ago one was never finished with a blackmailer.

If Saint Mattie hadn't told Dani about the Cutler boys' trip to Saratoga the summer her mother went missing, Nick hadn't told anyone about the nasty, pathetic blackmail letters he'd received while filming *Casino*. Someone—he'd never known who—had found out about his secret deal with Lilli to let her play the minor role of the singer. He'd never expected that one scene, his daughter-in-law's one performance, would take over the movie the way it had, to set its tone, deepen its meaning, make itself not just accessible to its audience, but a part of them. But he'd promised her he would keep her identity a secret. If she wanted the world—her family—to know, she could be the one to tell them. It was one promise he'd kept, until it became moot when *Casino* was previewed and a critic recognized Lilli Chandler Pembroke. Nick admitted everything.

But he'd never mentioned the blackmail.

The scheme had been pitiful, inept. A few hundred dollars here, a thousand there. He'd received a letter threatening to expose Lilli's role if he didn't pay up. So he'd paid up. He hadn't told Lilli what was going on; she'd had enough on her mind. And a couple of days before her disappearance, the blackmail had stopped.

He supposed he should have gone to the police, at least after Lilli disappeared. But he'd wanted to protect her, wanted to keep the notoriety and nastiness, the cheapness, of blackmail from being tied to her. The blackmailer had never threatened her— the letters had never even hinted that any harm would come to her—and had been directed to Nick, not to Lilli. As far as he knew, she had no idea he was being blackmailed over her role in *Casino*.

As far as he knew.

What if she had known? What if she had been blackmailed herself? She'd had a hell of a lot more money than Nick ever did.

And what if the blackmailer had been Joe Cutler? Or his then thirteen-year-old brother, Zeke? Or both of them?

The doorbell was ringing. Nick couldn't have said for how long. As he shuffled back to the front room, he considered that the one thing—the only thing—he could reliably do these days was to die. Just drop dead like an old dog. And yet his death would accomplish nothing.

He would still have sent his son to Saratoga without all the facts.

When he opened the door, a strongly built black man nodded to him. "Mr. Pembroke? Sorry to bother you. My name's Sam Lincoln Jones. I'm an independent security consultant."

"You work with Zeke Cutler," Nick said. Over the years he'd kept track of Joe Cutler's little brother.

Jones hid any surprise. "I'd like to talk with you, if I may."

"About what?"

"About what you've been up to lately."

Nick grinned. "Nice try, my friend. Zeke Cutler sent you to find out what I know about a certain gold key my daughter-in-law was wearing the night she disappeared."

"Which is?"

"Not a damn thing."

John hitched a ride to the Tucson airport from a skinny kid who'd stopped in the convenience store and mentioned he was headed in that direction and paid for his ticket to Albany, New York, with the emergency traveler's checks he kept on hand. With elderly parents, he felt compelled to have airfare available at all times—something that would only disgust Nick and Mattie, who apparently thought they'd never die. Or didn't give a damn if they did. John had given up on ever truly understanding his famous mother and father.

In Albany he'd rent a car or get a cab for the thirty-mile drive to Saratoga Springs. After that, he didn't know what he'd do.

He had no trouble getting a flight east and, slinging his beat-up old bag onto his shoulder, he boarded the plane.

Saratoga, he thought. It had been so long.

Did the gold key mean Lilli had been on the rocks on the Pembroke estate the night she disappeared? Was it stolen to keep that from coming out?

John suddenly felt colder than he'd felt in weeks.

Don't jump ahead. One step at a time.

Settling back in his seat, he shut his eyes and tried not to think about how different he was from the corporate executive he'd once been, from the optimistic boy determined not to repeat the mistakes the Pembroke men always seemed to make. Who'd wanted desperately to be something other than Nicholas Pembroke and Mattie Witt's son. He'd loved being the cog in the wheel at Chandler Hotels his wife had accused him of being. He'd loved that anonymity.

Oh, Lilli…

He hadn't made the same mistakes as the Pembroke scoundrels who'd come before him. He'd made his own mistakes, more egregious, more unforgivable.

Dani, however, was different.

She had to be.

And this time John was determined not to fail her.

Seven

~~~~~~~~~~~~~~~~

Dani spent most of Friday with her nose to the grindstone. Work helped keep her mind off her ransacked bedroom, her stolen things, her scrapes and bruises. She was more upset than she'd first realized over losing her two gate keys. Ulysses's gold keys—made famous in *The Gamblers*—had always seemed just another of the legends surrounding him. Now one had surfaced, and it was gone.

Losing it was preferable to being killed, Dani thought, but she still wished she had it.

And work kept her mind off what day it was. That tonight was the annual Chandler lawn party.

She'd had her dress cleaned, and carted it and the ostrich plume and her red shoes up to the Pembroke salon, located in the estate's former bathhouse, for some pampering and advice. It was getting close to seven. Time to put herself together.

She passed Zeke Cutler sitting on a stone bench in the shade of a sugar maple. He had his arms hooked on the back of the bench and his legs stretched out, his ankles crossed. He looked relaxed, confident.

"Afternoon, Ms. Pembroke," he said in an exaggerated southern drawl, designed, no doubt, to undermine her sense of professionalism.

She didn't let it, although she'd changed from her business clothes into shorts and a Saratoga T-shirt and had Mattie's dress hanging over her arm in its plastic cleaner's bag. She nodded briskly. "Mr. Cutler."

"Nice day."

That it was. Dry, clear, warm. But, of course, it would be. In its hundred-year history, the Chandler lawn party had enjoyed remarkably good weather. Someone had once figured out that it would have rained on the historic party the few Augusts that the Saratoga racing season had been canceled, in the early 1900s and during World War II.

"Have you been keeping busy?" she asked, trying to treat him as she would any other guest, regardless of his profession or how they'd met. What questions she still had about him. How physically attractive she found him.

"More or less. Right now I'm debating between tubing down the Batten Kill and weeding tomatoes. Which do you think?"

His sarcasm—or humor—was nearly, but not quite, undetectable. Dani said coolly, "It doesn't seem to me you're seriously considering either one."

He almost smiled. "Maybe I should take a mud bath?"

"You'd find it refreshing, I'm sure."

Dropping one hand, he picked up a bottle of Pembroke Springs Mineral Water he had beside him on the bench. "Nice package. I tried your orange soda—haven't worked up the nerve to try this stuff yet." He unscrewed the top. "I usually get my water from the tap."

"It's not the same."

"That's what scares me." He took a sip and paused a moment, seeming to contemplate the taste. "I suppose it could grow on you."

For some reason, Dani wasn't offended. "It's milder than a lot of the mineral waters around here. My grandmother—"

"Mattie Witt."

She nodded but noticed the slight darkening of Zeke Cutler's already dark eyes. "She knows—or used to know—the properties of a hundred different springs in the region, which ones would bind you up, which ones would unbind you, which were more suited to bathing. She claims there's a spring that'll cure virtually any intestinal ailment. She's not as rabid as she used to be—I understand she used to pump my father full of various waters when he was a boy."

"That was after she retired from Hollywood?"

"Oh, yes."

Zeke Cutler drank more of his water, and this time Dani felt he was contemplating her. His eyes darkened even more, and she couldn't tell what he was thinking. The effect on her was more unnerving than she would ever want to admit. "Tell me," he said, "do you take such a personal interest in all your guests or only the ones you've assaulted with iron skillets?"

The humor was back in his eyes. It softened them, made them a little less intense. Dani felt a rush of warmth and might have fled without answering, pretending she hadn't heard him. But she said, "I'm keeping my eye on you, Zeke Cutler."

He raised his bottle to her. "Ditto."

The rush of warmth turned hot, and she got out of there, heading along a brick walk in the sun, which was nowhere near as broiling as she was.

Magda Roskov, who presided over the salon, and who was even tinier than her boss, shook her head in despair when she saw Dani. "But you give me just an hour! I need at least a week to work on you."

Dani had thought an hour was a lot. "Well, just help me figure out how to get this feather to stay in my hair."

Magda inspected the red ostrich plume. "This has possibilities."

Coming from her, that was a major vote of confidence.

She worked on Dani for her allotted hour, lecturing her on leg waxing, manicures, pedicures, the right cosmetics. She signed her up for an herbal facial next week and insisted on setting Dani's hair in pin curls. Magda examined her cuts and bruises with clinical objectivity and sighed loudly. "You want to climb rocks, you suffer the consequences." Dani didn't tell her she'd surprised a burglar.

The results—the pin curls, the dramatic makeup, the perfectly placed feather—were, she had to admit, far superior to anything she could have accomplished on her own. If not transformed, Dani felt downright glamorous. She wondered if Zeke Cutler would have been so sarcastic and controlled if he'd caught her in the garden looking like this.

Dangerous thinking. She had to stop it.

"Well," Magda said, appraising her handiwork, "you'll do."

It was the best Dani would ever get from her by way of a compliment.

"You will put on your shoes?"

Dani grinned. She'd kept on her beat-up sneakers. "When I get there. Those three-inch heels are killers."

"If you'd practice wearing them—"

"Bye, Magda. Thanks for everything."

Watching Dani glide past him in a sexy retro dress, ratty sneakers and an ostrich feather in her shining dark hair, Zeke concluded the woman was pretty muddy on the subject of how heiresses were supposed to act.

He'd rejected tubing on the Batten Kill, weeding tomatoes and anything else the Pembroke had to offer early on a Friday evening, and he'd dumped the rest of his designer water in the grass.

Ms. Danielle Chandler Pembroke, he observed, really wasn't very big.

He didn't know why her feather didn't fall off. "Got that thing stuck on with Krazy Glue?"

She whirled around, startled, a pair of red high heels in hand. Zeke ducked. First a mineral water bottle, then an iron skillet, now shoes.

"In another life," he said, "you'd be a knife thrower."

"I'm sorry." She lowered her shoes. "I'm a little on edge."

"Heard you were going to the Chandler party tonight."

She nodded, biting her lower lip, painted as red as her dress. Zeke suspected that she was hell on men. Ira Bernstein had told him the sure way to get shot out of the saddle with his boss was to send her a dozen roses and tell her you existed to make her happy. "She doesn't want anyone to feel responsible for her happiness—her mother's legacy." Ira, of course, hadn't intended to tell Zeke anything; it had just happened. Besides being an expert on weaponry and such, he prided himself on his ability to eke information out of people.

"Yes, I am," Ira's boss said.

"Alone?"

She looked annoyed. "I don't see that my personal life is any of your business."

"I don't see that it is, either. I suppose a date would detract from the impact of your grand entrance."

Her black eyes zeroed in on him; he could tell she was miffed. "I'm not planning a grand entrance—"

"Ha. You have Nick Pembroke's and Mattie Witt's flare for drama. That's her dress, isn't it? And the feather your mother wore in *Casino?*"

"You seem to know an awful lot about me, Mr. Cutler."

"Honey, a lot of people know an awful lot about you, so that's no big deal." He was on his feet. "Come on, I'll give you a ride."

"I really don't think—"

"I'm harmless," he said.

"So you told me yesterday afternoon. And as I said then, you don't look harmless."

He shrugged. "Given my business, I suppose that's just as well. My car's in the Pembroke lot."

"I have no intention of driving anywhere with you."

"Sure you do." He glanced down at her, noticing that the luscious red of her lips only made her skin seem paler and her eyes blacker. "It'll save you having to park your car and risk spoiling your entrance."

Her mouth snapped shut. "I was planning on walking."

"And risk getting caught by the paparazzi in holey yellow sneakers?"

"Mr. Cutler—"

"You've got to stop that mister business."

"I'm not going to hire you."

"Fine, but will you let me drive you to your granddaddy's mansion?"

"It's a cottage."

"Where I come from," he said, "it's a mansion."

And he wondered if someday he'd tell her where he came from, or if she'd find out on her own, if Mattie would tell her, or someone else who knew about Joe and him and the ugly possibilities of their trip to Saratoga twenty-five years ago. But he couldn't think about that now. He had to concentrate on the present, on the job he'd come to do. As he'd told Roger Stone last night, Dani Pembroke wasn't his problem.

They headed together down the brick walk, and when the walk divided, one way going toward her cottage, the other toward the main house and the parking lot, she stayed with him. Zeke made no comment. When they came to his rented car, a nondescript midsize sedan, he unlocked the passenger door, opening it for her. Minding her feather, she slid in.

"Don't get any ideas," she said, pulling the door shut herself.

Her cheeks, he noticed, had gained some color.

She played tour guide on the drive up Union Avenue and Broadway, pointing out where the gargantuan United States Hotel had once stood—"It was built in 1874 and occupied seven acres"—and the Grand Union and Congress Hall, where the wealthy and famous of that earlier time had played. The massive hotels were all gone, burned or torn down.

"The Adelphi survived," she said, gesturing to a Victorian hotel in the middle of Broadway. "It's small by the standards of nineteenth-century Saratoga—it's been completely restored in keeping with the era. I love having wine in the courtyard with friends."

Zeke tried to imagine having a quiet glass of wine with her, amid flowers and greenery, with no agenda. But, with practiced skill, he shoved the image aside. He wasn't a dreamer. Not anymore.

He drove straight up Broadway, through the light where the wide, busy street became North Broadway, quiet, residential, lined with Victorian mansions. He pulled up in front of the cream-colored Italianate that a Chandler had built. A couple hundred people had gathered on the side lawn. From what Zeke could see, they were dressed for a good time among their fellow rich. He could hear the soft strains of a jazz trio.

"To think," Dani muttered, "I could be picking beetles off my rosebushes."

The mystery and vulnerability that he'd detected in her that afternoon were there once again, playing at the edges of her eyes, at the corners of her frown. The smart comeback he had ready slid right out of his mind.

She already had her yellow sneakers off and was slipping on her red high heels. Her black eyes, liquid and maybe a little afraid, fastened on him. "Thank you for the ride."

"Knock 'em dead, angel."

Her smile was full of mischief and pain as she climbed out of his car, teetering a moment on her too-high heels. Then she started down the sidewalk in her saucy vintage dress and ostrich plume, a slim, fit, dark-eyed, dark-haired woman who didn't look anything at all like the tall, fair, proper, ever-gracious Chandlers.

Zeke had never seen anyone look more alone.

"Yikes," Kate Murtagh said. "Your checkbook must be as moth-eaten as that dress."

She planted a tray of skewered tortellini, drenched in a spicy-smelling sauce, onto a server's outstretched arms. Dani felt a touch of relief at Kate's blunt words; she was among friends again. She wished she knew what had gotten into her to accept Zeke Cutler's ride. Of course, she wished she knew what had gotten into her even to be here tonight.

"You're just mad because I didn't take your advice."

"Aaron," Kate said to one of her cohorts, a paunchy man arranging nasturtiums on a pasta salad, "make sure the shades are up when this crowd gets a load of this outfit. Everybody may drop dead, and we won't have to serve dinner."

Dani laughed, trying to stay out of the way as servers flowed in and out. "Do I look that bad?"

"You amaze me sometimes. Can't you look in the mirror and tell you look terrific? A little bizarre maybe, but terrific. Honestly, Dani, I've never met anyone as gorgeous as you are who has no idea—maybe who doesn't want to have any idea..." Kate glared at her, as if Dani had done something particularly annoying. "You could have your pick of men."

"Maybe it's lousy pickings."

"And maybe you're just too afraid to let anyone care about you."

"How can you deliver a lecture while serving two hundred?"

Kate grinned, unembarrassed. "Talent. Where'd you get the shoes?"

"I bought them."

"Mark the calendar, Aaron."

The teasing loosened the tightness in Dani's stomach, not just from having to face the Chandlers and the crowd, but from having spent fifteen minutes in a car with her mysterious guest.

"Kate, I need a favor. A guy's been following me around."

"Who?"

"His name's Zeke Cutler. He's some kind of professional white knight—he's staying at the Pembroke."

Kate wiped her hands on her oversize apron. "Is he here?"

"I don't know. He drove me over—"

"Oh-ho."

Dani felt her cheeks burn. "It's not what you think. I just thought with your sources you could find out more about him."

"The name's familiar, but I don't know why. I'll see what I can find out." A woman who missed nothing, she indicated Dani's bruised wrist with a curt nod. "He do that?"

"I don't think so."

"Dani, what—"

"It's a long story, and I know you're busy. Later, okay?"

"You're damn right later."

A server raced over for more tortellini, and while Kate got to work, Dani made her exit. Soon, she thought, she'd tell Kate about the burglary, about finding Zeke in her garden, about Mattie's reaction. But first she had to concentrate on tonight.

Memory took her back through the house. She hadn't been there since Mattie came to take her back to New York while the search for her mother continued. Nothing in the big, elegant house seemed to have changed.

Outside, the breeze held the fragrance, still familiar to her, of the Chandler flower gardens, and she remembered the girl she'd been, so feisty and determined and free, willing to take on her grandfather or the whole world, it didn't matter. She'd had a mother who'd loved her and a father who'd been honest, and she'd adored them both, at nine not seeing them as flawed human beings, and never feeling alone. But that was then.

She rounded the curved front porch with its baskets of pink-and-white petunias, heard someone whisper her name, and people began looking in her direction. In seconds a hush had come over the two hundred Chandler guests.

Dani hesitated, her resolve wavering. She knew these people. They'd been her mother's friends. They'd helped look for her—they'd joined search parties and talked to the police and called everyone they knew for any possible tips, any hints about Lilli's state of mind, where she might have gone. What might have happened to her. In the ensuing years they'd cooperated with the scores of private detectives Eugene Chandler had enlisted to find his missing daughter.

And all the while Dani had avoided them, had avoided Saratoga Springs in August. For twenty-five years the prestigious Chandler Stakes and Lilli Chandler Pembroke's disappearance had been inexorably linked, not just for Dani, but for her mother's family and friends as well.

Looking at them, elegantly dressed, uncertain of what they should do, Dani wondered if they secretly resented her mother for not having vanished at a more opportune time, then realized how horribly unfair she was being.

But she understood their shock as they gaped at her. She could feel herself becoming not the good-humored, risk-taking child of Pembroke scoundrels, not herself, but the image of what they wanted her to be.

It was as if, for a brief, stunned moment, lovely, lost Lilli Chandler Pembroke had finally come home.

Only she hadn't. Dani had always known, even at nine, that she couldn't—didn't want to, ever—take her mother's place.

She thought of Zeke Cutler. Was this enough of a grand entrance for him? It was far more than she'd bargained for. But this was her own doing, and her response was her choice. She pictured Kate Murtagh in the kitchen with the shades up, howling with laugher because she'd told Dani so.

Dani made herself smile. There was really nothing else to do. "Hi, everybody," she said. "Good to see you all."

Their relief was palpable. She wasn't going to make a scene. They could have another glass of champagne and a bit of caviar before dinner and not have to think about Lilli's disappearance or John Pembroke's embezzling from his own father-in-law or Dani's having walked away from her Chandler trust.

She swept a glass of champagne from a passing tray as Sara Chandler Stone came up beside her. "Danielle," she said, taking her niece by the hand and kissing her lightly on the cheek, "I'm so glad you came tonight. It's been far too long."

Dani almost believed her. "I'm glad I came, too."

Her aunt smiled, playing the perfect Chandler hostess to the hilt. Her perfume was light and elegant, the same scent her older sister had worn, and probably their mother before them. She wore a simple, stunning coral dress, with diamond studs at her ears and a sprinkle of diamonds in her hair.

She was staring at Dani. "That feather…in your hair…"

"It's the one Mother wore in *Casino*. It's meant as a tribute, Sara. Nothing more."

"Of course," Sara mumbled. But she looked shocked, and grief-stricken.

"I didn't mean to upset you."

Sara carefully restored her hostess face. First the charming smile, then the rich, bright eyes; her cosmetics, Dani noticed, were expertly applied. She bet Sara hadn't needed a Magda to do her up.

"Oh, don't be silly. I was just surprised, that's all. I think it's a wonderful idea. Lilli would have been delighted. Here, let me introduce you to some of my friends. You haven't seen Father yet, I take it. He should be out soon. He doesn't move as fast as he used to."

While Sara chattered on, Dani followed her around, surprising her with how many people on the lawns, among the beautiful gardens, her niece already knew. Their lives, hers and Dani's, were concentric circles within a larger circle, never touching.

People were gracious and interested, asking about the Pembroke and Pembroke Springs. No one mentioned Lilli or commented on the ostrich plume. Dani invited everyone she spoke to up to her newly opened spa-inn for high tea; many said they'd already sneaked a peek at her rose gardens.

Finally Sara excused herself. "I'll let you mingle now—I need to check with the kitchen."

Dani wondered how Kate liked being called "the kitchen," and smiled to herself, sipping her champagne near a stone statue of Demeter she'd tried to dress when she was six or seven. She realized, suddenly and with a rush of relief that surprised her, that she was no longer a frightened nine-year-old waiting for her mother to come and share her raspberries.

"You could have chosen a different dress," Eugene Chandler said beside her. "Mattie's, isn't it?"

Dani tried not to let her grandfather's cold tone undermine her surge of confidence. "Yes—I'm surprised you recognized it."

"It was a credible guess." He wasn't very convincing, but he'd never admit to remembering what Mattie Witt had worn in a movie more than fifty years old. As for the ostrich plume, he'd claimed never to have seen *Casino* and his older daughter's searing performance. "I assume it was a deliberate choice on your part."

It was an accusation, not a question, but Dani refused to let him get to her, which was exactly what he was trying to do. "No need to spend money on a new dress when I've got a perfectly good one in the attic. How are you, Grandfather?"

Tilting his head back slightly, he inhaled through his nose. Even at eighty-two he was straight-backed and still possessed an uncanny knack for irritating her. His bearing and arrogance—his pride, he'd say—had seen him through scandal and loss. But clearly he'd aged. He was the only surviving child of Ambrose Chandler and his very young third wife, Beatrix, who'd lost their three older children to diphtheria when Eugene was just a baby. Now he was an old man with parchment-thin skin and brown spots on his hands, arms and face. His blue eyes had clouded, and his lips had a purplish cast to them. Dani might have felt sympathy for him, for the man had endured pain and anguish—the early death of the wife he'd adored, the years of not knowing what had happened to his firstborn child, the embarrassment of having his son-in-law steal from his family's firm and the lack of a close relationship with his only grandchild.

But if tragedy ennobled some and embittered others, it seemed to have had no effect whatsoever on Eugene Chandler. His daughter was missing, so he just didn't talk about her. His son-in-law was a reprobate, so he ignored him. His granddaughter had thrown her inheritance in his face after his cruel, offhand remark about dropping the Pembroke from her name, so he went right on as if nothing had happened between them and he'd said nothing wrong.

But they'd never gotten along. As a child, even before her mother had disappeared, he'd shut down her lemonade stand because "Chandler ladies" weren't supposed to be entrepreneurs. He'd refused to let her climb trees where anyone might see her, he'd called her incorrigible and had pointed out every flaw in what she wore, what she said, what she did. It was as if from the moment he saw her black hair and black eyes he'd been looking for the Witt and Pembroke in her, and had tried at every turn to stamp them out. He'd never, it seemed to her, looked for the person she was: neither Chandler nor Witt nor Pembroke, but only herself.

"You know, Danielle," he said softly, "you're much harder on us than we deserve."

His words caught her off guard. "I'm not trying to be hard on anyone."

But he walked away, proud and in control. Fortunately one of Kate's helpers stuck a tray of tiny spanakopita triangles under Dani's nose, keeping her from chasing down her grandfather for an explanation for his remark, or to apologize, guiltily, for behavior that had become automatic over the years. "Kate said for me to tell you she's hit the jackpot. I'm not sure what that means."

Dani was: Kate had found out something on Zeke Cutler. But before she could sneak off to the kitchen, Roger Stone appeared beside her, handsomely dressed, the corners of his eyes crinkling when he smiled. Dani had always liked him, even if her unconventional executive style would give him ulcers and he'd seemed a little too eager to step into her father's shoes after Eugene Chandler had fired him from Chandler Hotels, refusing to involve the authorities in the misdeeds of his own son-in-law.

"It's been forever, Dani." Roger took both her hands and whistled as he gave her a quick, appreciative once-over. "Don't you look smashing."

"Thank you. I hope I haven't caused any trouble for you and Sara tonight by coming. I just wanted to see folks." And she realized it was true—she'd *wanted* to be here.

His blue eyes warmed with understanding. "It's not you—it never has been."

"It's my mother."

"You don't have a sister, so perhaps it's difficult for you to understand, but Sara has deep feelings about your mother. Lilli disappeared less than a year after their mother died—it was a double shock, quite devastating. Tonight's always difficult for Sara, that's all. It's a reminder of what she's lost."

"So am I."

Roger studied her a moment, not a man to pretend or deny, and finally he nodded, without elaborating or minimizing.

Dani suddenly felt chilled. She'd almost rather have her aunt's flawless, if phony, good cheer. "I suppose it's the same for Grandfather."

But Roger studied her, seeing much more, she suspected, than she wanted him to see. She sensed no condemnation, only a desire to understand. "It's not such a bad thing, you know, to remind them of Lilli. They don't want to forget her. They—" He stopped, frowning in concern as his eyes fell to her bruised arm. So far no one else had noticed the effects of yesterday afternoon's festivities at her cottage. "Dani—what on earth happened to you?"

"Oh, I stumbled on a burglar yesterday."

"At the inn?"

"No, at my cottage. He didn't get away with much."

"But you're okay?"

His concern made her feel uncomfortable, awkward. "Yes, I'm fine. It was a good lesson in locking my doors."

"What did the police say?"

"Nothing. I didn't call them."

Roger paused, assessing her response. "That was good thinking, I suppose. You just don't need that kind of publicity right now."

"None of us do," she said curtly.

"I wasn't thinking about us."

"I'm sorry, I didn't mean—"

"But you did, Dani," he said, not harshly. "It's time to get rid of that chip on your shoulder. Your grandfather needs you. You're his only grandchild. Sara needs you, too. We have no children of our own. She—" He broke off, annoyed. "Dani, can't you see? We all care about you."

Unable to think of anything to say, she swallowed and bit her lip, and Roger sucked in another breath and hurled himself back among his guests, leaving her to wonder if it wouldn't be easier on all of them if they didn't care. She about them, they about her.

Life, she thought, could be so damn complicated.

Zeke melted into a small crowd of onlookers who hadn't been invited to the hundredth annual Chandler lawn party. They'd gathered on North Broadway to watch the comings and goings of the rich and elegant.

With her red feather, Dani was easy to pick out.

It wasn't as easy to pick out Sara Chandler Stone, but Zeke did. She would be forty-seven now. Four years older than Joe would have been if he had lived. Eighteen months after her sister's disappearance, she had married Roger Stone. Joe was a soldier by then. Zeke wondered if his brother had ever stopped loving Sara Chandler, or if he really ever had. Joe had been so young twenty-five years ago.

Zeke watched Sara greet a guest with a hug and a kiss and a smile, and it was easy to forget that she and the hothead with the iron skillet were from the same family. But they were. That was something Zeke needed to remember.

There was no point in sticking around. He wasn't even sure why he had this long.

But as he turned, he felt the hair rise on the back of his neck, almost as if by instinct.

Quint Skinner came up beside him. "Evening, Zeke."

"Quint."

"Heard you were in town. Working?"

Zeke shook his head. "You?"

"Nope. I was passing by and thought I recognized you." He narrowed his small blue eyes and scrutinized Zeke, his soldier's training apparent in his steady, steely gaze. "I don't want any trouble."

His tone was amiable, but Zeke wasn't fooled. Despite his Pulitzer Prize, Quint was a man of physical action, threats, intimidation. He'd never seemed entirely comfortable with his role as a celebrated writer. Zeke's experience in protection and security wouldn't impress him. Quint would still think he could beat him senseless. And very likely he could.

"See you around," he said, starting down the wide brick sidewalk.

"Hey, Skinner."

The soldier-turned-writer looked back, the evening sun catching his broad red face. He wore a khaki suit cut a size too small for his muscular frame, probably just to remind people he wasn't just a smarmy journalist but a man who'd killed people.

Zeke's gaze was direct and unintimidated. "Didn't know you liked roses."

There was no indication of surprise in the intense, beady eyes. Quint put a hand the size of a butt ham into the palm of his other hand and cracked his knuckles one by one. Just itching to knock out a few of Zeke's teeth. "I'll go where I want to go, and I'll do what I want to do. You just stay out of my way."

Zeke said nothing more. Quint had no gift for melting into a crowd, and Zeke was able to watch him all the way down North Broadway. If Skinner had robbed Dani, why? Had he made the connection between the gold key and the night Dani's mother had disappeared? Between the gold key and Joe Cutler?

And the blackmail note, Zeke thought. Where did that little gem fit in?

Lots of questions. He just wished he had a few answers.

Dinner was served on long tables covered in pink linen and decorated—Kate Murtagh style—with simple milk-glass vases of asters and baby's breath. Sara had Dani sit next to her grandfather at the end of the table, where a portly man was expounding on the yearling sales and the state of Saratoga's thoroughbred-racing tradition.

Someone commented that the revival of Pembroke Springs and the opening of the Pembroke would be good for the town, and Dani felt her grandfather stiffen next to her. He didn't look at her, but she knew he disapproved of her having gone into business for herself against his wishes and against his advice, a different sort of embarrassment for him than her mother's disappearance and her father's embezzling.

But he didn't say anything, and the conversation drifted to other, more innocuous topics. Someone asked how long she'd been in Saratoga. Someone else asked where her date was, the unsubtle implication being that she'd been seen arriving with Zeke.

"One of my guests dropped me off," she explained.

Her grandfather's clouded, watery eyes fastened on her, his irritation apparent, she was sure, only to her. Getting a ride from a male guest—even having paying guests—would grate on him. Mentioning it at his dinner party would be, in his mind, rude, a deliberate act to embarrass him.

Dani lasted through the main course, then excused herself and ducked into the kitchen.

Thankfully, no one followed her. The racing talk and flower-scented breeze, and just being there, reminded her of the nine-year-old who'd waited and waited and waited for her mother to come home.

Trying to squash the flood of memories, she stopped at the counter, where Kate was sifting confectioner's sugar onto a plate of her incomparable brownies.

"Rough night, eh? Well, if you'd wanted to avoid the nonsense," she said without sympathy, "you could have stayed in here with me and watched the show from the kitchen. I'd even have let you help—except you in a black skirt and white top carrying a tray of stuffed mushrooms would probably kill your grandfather. Though I don't know why you in that dress hasn't killed him."

"Maybe he was anticipating something worse."

Kate looked remarkably calm despite being in the midst of serving two hundred. "I suppose it's possible."

But there was something in her eyes. "Kate?"

She set down her sifter. "We have to talk."

"Okay. Tomorrow—"

"Now. Dani, have you ever heard of a book called *Joe Cutler: One Soldier's Rise and Fall?*"

Dani shook her head.

"Joe Cutler is—was—this Zeke character's older brother. I knew there was something familiar about his name. I asked Aaron, and he remembered." Aaron also taught history at the local high school. "Joe was pretty messed up."

"You've read the book?"

She nodded. "A few years ago. It's got nothing to do with Zeke being in town so far as I can see." Her intelligent eyes focused on Dani. "Except for one thing—he and his brother grew up in Cedar Springs, Tennessee."

And there it was. A connection. Cedar Springs and Mattie. But her grandmother hadn't returned to her hometown since she had left for Hollywood at nineteen, long before Zeke was even born.

"What's he up to?" she asked.

"Beats me," Kate said, "but you need to watch yourself with this guy."

Dani snatched a brownie. "I will."

"If Cutler's responsible in any way for that bruise on your arm—" Kate waved her spatula "—you let him know he'll have to answer to me."

Impossible to tell if the woman was serious. And yet, beneath her bantering tone was a concern for Dani, something she never wanted to take for granted.

She went down a darkened hall and through the antique-filled drawing room where the oil portrait of her mother at sixteen still hung above the mantel. She seemed so sophisticated, yet demure, the perfect young heiress. The artist had failed—or, given who was paying the bill, perhaps simply had known better than to try—to catch the glint in her eye, the determined set to her jaw that hinted at a seething soul. Lilli Chandler had been privileged and beautiful at sixteen. At thirty, privilege and beauty hadn't been enough to satisfy her.

"I've tried to take that portrait down," Eugene Chandler said from a Queen Anne chair, startling Dani. "I thought it would be easier on all of us, Sara in particular. She always adored your mother. But she insisted it should stay."

Dinner must have broken up for the more informal dessert, or he, too, had made good his escape. "Look, if I in any way—"

He cut her off, or hadn't heard her. "You know, right or wrong, that's how I remember Lilli—as a lovely, devoted sixteen-year-old girl who might never really have existed…" He trailed off as he sighed, sounding tired and old. When he continued, his voice was almost inaudible. "That's the most difficult part. She's gone, and I never knew her. My own daughter."

"I'm sorry—"

"No. I am."

Dani took a step toward him. "Are you all right?"

He smiled sadly. "No, I'm not."

She'd never seen him so depressed. Even when it had become clear that something had happened and her mother had disappeared, he'd shown only anger, determination, raging worry. Never real, quiet, reflective sadness. "Should I get Sara?"

"You should go on, Danielle."

As she moved closer, he looked away. He was not a man given to touching, the quick kiss, the tender hug. And he'd come not to expect such affection from his only granddaughter. "I'm not sure I should leave you—"

"I prefer to be alone," he said, not gently.

"If you're sure."

"I'm sure." His clouded eyes met hers, just for an instant. "I've never known what to say to you nor you to me. So go on, Danielle. Carry on. You always have, you know."

Would he like her better if she fell on her face? If she had to crawl on her knees to him in desperation? But it wasn't the time for accusation or asking him to be something he wasn't. How could she ask him to accept her when she couldn't accept him?

Suddenly she was nine again, running from the grandfather she'd never been able to please.

She kicked off her high heels on the porch and scooped them up in one hand, walking through the cool, soft grass to the sidewalk. She'd left her sneakers in Zeke's car. It didn't matter—she'd walk home barefoot. She wanted off North Broadway, away from the Chandlers and back to her own little cottage where she'd learned to keep the memories at bay.

"Your feather's drooping."

Zeke fell in beside her, dark, solid, taking her in with an efficient glance that told her nothing of what he was thinking. In the darkness the shadows of the trees and streetlights played on his face, making his expression even more impossible to read.

"What're you doing here?" she asked.

"Just hanging out."

Dani didn't believe him. "You don't strike me as the type to just 'hang out.'"

He shrugged. "Know me so well, do you?"

"Mr. Cutler—"

"You've really got to stop that. The name's Zeke, as in Ezekiel James Cutler. Only bad guys call me Mr. Cutler. How come you're leaving early?"

"No reason."

He slowed his pace, eyeing her. "You're not a very good liar, are you?"

She wished she hadn't noticed the humor playing at the edges of his voice and in his eyes. She didn't answer, instead thinking about what Kate had told her about him. She'd hoped she'd have a chance to think, to talk to Mattie, before confronting him again.

"Why don't I give you a ride home," he said, "and you can tell me what's on your mind."

They'd come to his car. He unlocked the passenger door and swung it open. He looked very tough and very controlled, and Dani suddenly wondered what kind of woman a professional white knight went for, what kind he attracted.

"I prefer to walk," she said.

"Kind of a long way to walk in bare feet."

"You could give me my sneakers back."

He smiled. "I could."

They were at an impasse, his will against hers. Her high heels dangling from one hand, she wiggled her toes on the cool, rough sidewalk and became aware—too aware—of the fit of her dress and the aching of her bruises and just how tired she was.

"I'll ask you again. Was your being in my garden yesterday afternoon a coincidence?"

He stood back from the door, leaving it open. "Dani, you

know I didn't rob you or—" he touched her wrist "—do that to you." His eyes, dark and serious, held hers. "But I don't often believe in coincidences."

Dani knew there were other ways to get home without Zeke Cutler's help. She could call the Pembroke for a ride, or call a friend, or a taxi. She could even go back and ask her aunt or grandfather if their driver could take her home.

She could fight one Ezekiel James Cutler for her sneakers.

But without a word, she slid onto the passenger seat of his rented car. She wanted to know more about this man. *Had* to know more about him. It wasn't just the burglary, his profession, his being from Cedar Springs, Tennessee. It was also her reaction to him, the strange, unsettling feeling that she was meant to find him in her garden one of these days. And how could she explain the rushes of warmth when she was around him? She was wary, and annoyed that he was clearly holding back on her, but, she had to admit, she was also intrigued.

"If I'd been your crook," Zeke said, climbing in behind the steering wheel, "I'd have gone after you when you tried to nail me with that bottle of mineral water."

"You did go after me."

He glanced at her, turning the key in the ignition. "Honey," he said in an exaggerated drawl, "that wasn't going after you."

There it was again, not just a rush of warmth but a flood. Dani shifted in her seat, reaching down onto the floor for her sneakers. She slipped them on and didn't bother tying the laces.

"Tell me, would you have thrown the skillet or just bonked me on the head with it?"

"I don't know. I guess it would have depended on what you did. I'm not a trained white knight. I have to operate on instinct—like when I walked into my room and saw it had been trashed. Since I don't carry a weapon, I used what was at hand."

"Which was?"

She hesitated, then held up one red shoe as she had yesterday.

Zeke grimaced.

"It worked out," Dani said, not defensively.

Without comment he pulled into the street and started down North Broadway toward the main commercial center of town. He seemed to give his driving his total concentration. Dani noticed the dark hairs on his forearms, the muscles, the tanned skin. His long fingers. For no reason she could fathom, she found herself wondering if he dreamed. Was he ever haunted by the past? Did he ever lie awake nights asking what might have been? She thought of the book Kate had told her about. Easy to guess that his brother probably hadn't come to a happy end.

Had Mattie known Joe Cutler? Did she know Zeke? Was that why she'd responded the way she had when Dani had told her about the burglary?

He turned down Circular Street, and Dani had the feeling he was letting her make the next move, giving her a little time to pull herself together.

Finally she decided just to get on with it. "I want you to leave the Pembroke."

He glanced at her. "Why?"

"Because you haven't told me the truth."

Following the traffic onto Union Avenue, he didn't argue or protest, but kept his eyes on the road.

"You have until tomorrow morning," she said.

"Dani, you can't throw me out."

She breathed deeply. "Yes, I can."

"It'd end up in the papers." He slowed for a traffic light, then came to a stop. "Enough reporters are on your case without you going toe-to-toe with an internationally recognized security specialist such as myself."

There was a note of self-deprecation in his tone, of humor,

but it was buried underneath the seriousness. Dani felt her mouth go dry. She should have found another way home.

The light changed, and he continued a short way past the racetrack and turned smoothly onto the Pembroke driveway. "A photographer caught you tonight, feather and all. Someone could easily have seen you get into my car. Imagine what a heyday the gossips would have if they found out that you'd given me the boot."

"Are you threatening to tell them?"

"No."

They passed the rose garden, the fragrance permeating the cool night air, easing Dani's confusion and nervousness. Zeke bore left at the fork in the road, onto the dirt road and over the narrow bridge. She could hear the trickle of the stream, smell its coldness.

"Why are you here?" she asked softly.

"I have my reasons."

Which, his tone said, were none of her affair. "Do they have anything to do with the business you're in?"

He didn't answer, sliding his rented car to a stop at the end of the flagstone path that led to the front door of her cottage. "Do Hansel and Gretel show up every now and then?"

"Are you implying I'm a wicked witch?"

His expression was impenetrable in the darkness. Probably he wanted it that way. "Maybe not wicked."

Dani bit the inside corner of her mouth, feeling unusually awkward, deeply aware—physically aware—of the man sitting next to her.

It would be so easy to back down, so easy to trust him. But she had no basis for trust, and she'd never been very good at backing down. "You have until tomorrow morning. I'll speak to Ira."

She could feel Zeke's eyes on her. He seemed capable of seeing things people wouldn't want him to see, of penetrating not only thoughts, but souls. In his business, such sensitivity—such probing—could be an asset. He asked quietly, "Do you like living out here all alone?"

"I did until yesterday afternoon."

"You know, you should lock your doors. It's often an effective deterrent."

His tone was professional, neither critical nor patronizing, but Dani hated being told what to do. "How do you know my doors weren't locked?"

"I tried them."

"When?"

"This morning. I wandered off on my own during a guided nature walk."

She placed her hand on the door latch, her heart pounding. She could be gone in a matter of seconds. Was she crazy to be alone with a man she didn't know—a man who apparently knew more about her than she did him? He was from Mattie's hometown. He was staying at the Pembroke on the twenty-fifth anniversary of her mother's disappearance. He was an internationally known security consultant. Dani was torn by curiosity, but she felt she had no choice. She had no reason to trust him. It wasn't, right now, a risk she was prepared to take.

"I want you off my property."

"So you've said."

"Are you going to go quietly?"

A flash of sexy smile. "Honey, I don't go anywhere quietly unless I so choose. And that's probably the only thing you and I have in common."

"Oh, no," she said coolly, deciding on gut instinct to take him on then and there. "That's not all we have in common, and you know it. You see, Zeke, upstairs, in my bedroom, I have a blanket on my bed. It's dark green, pure wool, quite old. My grand-

mother gave it to me. She took it with her when she left home."
In the darkness, through the opened windows, she could hear the
crickets and tree toads, the breeze soughing in the woods and
meadow. "It was made in a woolen mill in Cedar Springs, Tennessee."

Zeke didn't move a muscle or say a word.

"My grandmother's hometown," Dani said in a near whisper. "And yours."

She was off like a shot, racing up the walk and through her
front door, slamming it behind her. Her wrist ached. So did her
scraped shins and her feet from standing so long in her three-
inch heels. But she hunted up her car keys and locked all her
doors. Front, back, side. She hadn't bothered last night. What
more was there for her thief to get?

She didn't lock her windows. She'd suffocate.

And she didn't call Mattie right away, although she was
tempted. She wanted to think first. Get her perspective on tonight, on Zeke Cutler of Cedar Springs, Tennessee.

Groaning, pushing him out of her mind, she ran into her
kitchen and got out the half bushel of peaches she'd been meaning to freeze for days. They were going soft. She filled her biggest
pot with water and put it on the stove. When it was hot, she'd
scald the peach skins to make them easier to peel. Or so the theory
went. No matter what she did, the peel always seemed to stick.

As she worked, she considered, and finally admitted, what
really had gotten to her tonight.

Zeke's confidence, his striking looks and his unexpected
humor, cloaked as it was in his middle-Tennessee accent, had
made her aware of the void in her own life. Riding next to him,
she'd felt alone and needy—and that was unacceptable. It
wasn't that he gave two figs about her or she'd ever want him
to. He could have arranged the burglary yesterday just to un-
nerve her and get her to hire him. Given what she'd seen so far

of the man, such underhandedness seemed out of character, but that wasn't the point.

The point was that something about him, or tonight, had made her feel empty. She'd found herself wanting closeness. Wanting love and romance and companionship.

And she remembered something her father had told her years ago, in a static-riddled phone call from some fleabag hotel in some hellish corner of the world. "The love of your life," he'd said, "is the person who makes you forget what all your standards and preconceived notions about love and romance even were."

If such a man existed, Dani hadn't met him yet. And the last thing she needed now was to mess up her life with pointless longing. Loneliness was not a choice she planned to make for herself.

And it was silly to let a dark-eyed security consultant stir up her deepest doubts about herself.

She grabbed fistfuls of peaches and dropped them into the pot, although the water wasn't yet scalding hot. But she was impatient, anxious to get moving on something, anything.

"Oh, God," she whispered.

It wasn't just Zeke Cutler.

She watched the peaches bob to the surface of the water.

Had her mother ever peeled peaches? Had she ever made her own peach jam or known the satisfaction of pulling a peach cobbler from the oven in the dead of winter knowing it was made from fruit she'd frozen herself?

Dani couldn't remember. Or she just didn't know.

Twenty-five years tonight.

What happened to you, Mama? Are you alive? Are you dead? Why did you leave me?

She dropped in more peaches, burning her fingers. She knew she might as well peel peaches until dawn, do up the whole lot of them, because there was no way she'd get any sleep tonight.

Eight

Zeke drove back into Saratoga too fast for his own comfort. It wasn't the speed in and of itself that bothered him. It was how much he'd let Dani distract him. She could easily worm her way under his skin and bore a hole deep inside him before he'd ever realized he'd let down his armor.

Maybe she already had.

He slid his car to a stop across the street from the Chandler cottage on North Broadway. Kate Murtagh herself was hefting a folded table into a pickup truck, the evening's festivities now another Saratoga memory. Zeke wasn't sure what he was doing here. Waiting for answers to fall out of the sky?

Dani had gone after her burglar with a three-inch red high heel.

Definitely a hothead.

But she was also courageous and determined, and even now he could see her liquid black eyes shining in the darkness.

He could hear Kate speaking to her crew. "You sure we have everything? We leave so much as a gum wrapper out here, and Auntie Sara will have us back cleaning the place with a toothbrush."

Auntie Sara.

Had Roger told his wife that Joe Cutler's little brother was in town?

"Hell, Naomi," he whispered to himself, "I should have just pretended I never got your letter."

But he had never been any good at pretending, and he was here.

Kate spotted him and marched over, boldly poking her head in through the passenger window. "So you're Zeke Cutler," she said.

He smiled. "I know who you are, too."

"I'm Dani's friend is who I am. You drove her home?"

"I did. She arrived safe and sound."

"You didn't put that bruise on her arm?"

"I did not."

Kate's brow furrowed, and she looked tired. It must have been a long night for her. "I hope not, seeing how she got in your car with you. But you listen here, Mr. Cutler—I'm on the case. I may slice carrots and whip up crème fraîche for a living, but this is my town, and I've got friends here." She patted the car door. "I'll have my eye on you."

Didn't these women know he was licensed to carry a gun? Zeke stared out at Dani's tall, attractive friend. "I can see why you and Ms. Pembroke are friends. You both eat nails for breakfast."

"You hold that thought," she said and marched back to her pickup.

In another moment, Sara Chandler Stone took her place in the passenger window. "It's been a long time, Zeke." Her voice was quiet and ladylike, more so than it had been twenty-five years ago.

He nodded. "Yes."

She smiled, a cool, sad smile that didn't reach her deep blue eyes. "Welcome to Saratoga."

"Nice town."

"Will you be at the Chandler Stakes tomorrow?"

"Maybe."

Color rose in her cheeks, which looked even paler in the harsh artificial glare of the streetlights. "Even at thirteen you were laconic." She touched a hand to her hair, still perfectly in place, and he saw the manicured nails, not too long, not too radically colored. "I'd like to talk to you—not tonight. In the morning?"

"Sara—"

"I'll be at the track for breakfast."

She darted away as quickly and unexpectedly as a hummingbird, and it seemed to Zeke that she had become everything she'd dreaded becoming.

Maybe she should have run off with Joe and saved them both.

Zeke turned around in the entrance to Skidmore College up the street, then went back down Broadway through town, following the same route he had with Dani. He didn't have a plan—he was still just punting—but he knew what he had to do, at least for tonight.

He parked his car in the Pembroke's guest lot, wondering if come morning Dani would have it towed. But he'd take that risk. There was a part of him that was looking forward to having her try to toss his ass off her property—the part, he thought, that he had to keep under a very tight lid.

He followed a brick path through the darkness. In the distance he could hear an owl's hoot. Nearby, the purr of tree toads. The grounds were quiet, the jam makers and rock climbers gone to bed or to town to party. Leaving the walk, he found his way across gardens and lawns and down the hillside to the pink, mauve and purple cottage at the edge of the woods.

He sat under a pine tree in a small meadow of wildflowers that looked as though they'd been planted there intentionally.

He had a good view of the side entrance, a reasonable view of the front and an excellent view of the side-garden entrance, but none whatsoever of its rear gate. Fortunately, it squeaked. And every window in the place was open. If somebody got in, he'd hear Dani yell. Provided she wasn't too stubborn to yell.

One day he'd discuss her attitude with Sam Lincoln Jones. Sam liked to analyze people's attitudes. He said it helped him think he was making use of his education.

Until then Zeke would just do some thinking and keep an eye on things, in case Quint Skinner made a return visit.

Just before dawn, her last peach safely in the freezer, Dani gave up on trying to sleep. She kept seeing her mother waving to her from the basket of Mattie's hot-air balloon and feeling herself catapulting across her own bedroom, feeling the terror of not knowing who'd pushed her, who'd burglarized her house.

And she kept seeing Zeke's dark eyes and thinking about what great shoulders and thighs he had. He was the kind of man who could make a woman melt.

Could make *her* melt.

She'd tried listening to the tree toads. Sometimes yoga helped, or a hot bath, or hot milk. But she knew nothing would work tonight. She threw on a sweatshirt and jeans and headed outside with a simple multicolored flat kite made of nonconductive plastic, slipping quietly into her meadow. The sounds and smells of the night and the cool, damp grass on her bare feet, between her toes, eased her tension.

She estimated the wind speed at five or six miles per hour. Fine for kite flying.

With the wind at her back, she tossed the kite into the air a few times, until finally she felt it pulling and let out some line. It rose above the usual ground-air turbulence, higher, higher. Then it was soaring.

She let out more line, grinning, not thinking about her mother, her loneliness, not even hearing the tree toads.

The sun peeked over the treetops in streaks of orange and red, edged with pale pink. In its center her kite was a bold dot of color.

Staring at the dawn, she suddenly could see her mother with more clarity than she'd been able to see her in years. Her generous mouth, her blue saucer eyes, her smile. She could smell her mother's French perfume and hear her laugh, not her delicate Chandler-lady laugh, but the throaty, exuberant laugh of the woman she'd wanted to become. It was as if she were telling her daughter not to hold back, not to let anything or anyone stand in her way, but to dare to go after what she wanted.

But I have, she thought. She had the springs, the Pembroke, her friends.

She didn't have intimacy. There was no lover in her life. Zeke should have been the last man to remind her of the absence of romance in her life, but he had. Yet her mother had had a husband and a child, and they hadn't been enough.

Her kite continued to gain altitude, riding the wind from Dani's fingertips.

She could hear herself now as a little girl, promising to keep her mother's secret. She'd never tell anyone, she'd said, sincere, frightened as her mother towered over her, so beautiful, so frightened herself.

The memory was so vivid, Dani might have been back on that cold, dreary December afternoon when she'd visited her dying grandmother—her mother's mother. Claire Chandler had withered from an elegant society matron into a skeleton wrapped in sagging yellowed skin. Yet she retained her commanding presence, receiving her only grandchild in the cavernous living room of her New York apartment. She'd had her thinning hair fixed and wore a green silk robe, embroidered in red and gold at the sleeves, the one she wore every Christmas, not just this one, her last. It was way too big for her.

Dani remembered the strength in her grandmother's voice when she'd called her young granddaughter to her side. Christmas carols had played softly on the stereo. "The First Noel" and "Joy to the World." A huge Christmas tree, strung with hundreds of tiny white lights, awaited decorating. Big white boxes, brought in from storage, were filled with ornaments of handblown glass, painted toy soldiers, fragile angels, silver snowflakes. Dani was permitted only to hang the wooden ornaments. She'd eyed the nativity set carefully arranged on a polished antique table. She wanted desperately to play with the beautiful Madonna and the little baby Jesus, and the sheep and the Wise Men, but even touching the English porcelain figures was forbidden. Also off-limits was the New England village set up on another table, with its steepled white church, colonial houses and old-fashioned carolers. Ordinarily Dani would have pressed her case, but her mother had asked her to be especially nice that afternoon.

Dani had dug into the pocket of her wool blazer and produced a paper snowflake. "I made it myself—it's origami. You can hang it on your tree if you want."

Even now, she could remember her grandmother's trembling, bony hand as she'd taken the origami snowflake. "Thank you, dear. It's lovely. You're such a thoughtful child."

The snowflake, Dani had known, would end up in one of the scrapbooks her grandmother kept, put up on a shelf to be preserved for Dani's own children. Her parents had stuck dozens of her origami snowflakes on windows, the refrigerator, hung them on the tree. But that was their style, not Claire Chandler's, and Dani had made the snowflake for her because she loved her, not because she wanted praise and recognition.

"And how was school today, Danielle?" her grandmother had asked, regal even in illness.

"Good. All the kids call me Dani."

"Why would they do that?"

"Because I asked them to," Dani had said without fanfare. "Danielle's such a prissy name."

"Now, wherever did you get such a notion? Danielle's a perfectly lovely name."

"Mattie said it sounds kind of prissy—"

"Mattie? Danielle, where are your manners?" Claire had coughed, her skin going from yellow to red to white in the course of a couple of minutes. "Next you'll be calling us all by our first names."

"Oh, I'd never do that. It's just that Mattie hates to be called Grandmother."

"Well, she is one, even if she'd rather not admit it. We all get old. We all die."

And Dani had asked her, "Are you going to die?"

Her grandmother's sickly blue eyes had widened for a moment, then softened. "Yes, dear, I'm going to die—sooner, I'm afraid, rather than later. Please don't be sad. I've led a full, wonderful life, even in the relatively few years I've had on this earth. I wish only that we'd had more time together." She'd smiled gently even as Dani's eyes brimmed with tears. "You're a remarkable child. I should have told you that more often. I should have told my own daughters that more often. It's not always easy… One does one's best."

A maid had brought a tray of hot cider and gingerbread cookies, and Claire Chandler had permitted Dani to play with the New England village, although the nativity set was still forbidden, on the grounds that playing with religious figures was improper. Claire's only requirement had been that Dani gather up all the pieces and play with them on the carpet next to the couch, close to her grandmother.

By the time her mother arrived to pick Dani up, Claire had

fallen asleep. Dani had leaned over and kissed her grandmother's sunken cheek, something she'd never done on her own before. "Goodbye, Dani," her grandmother had said, and she seemed to try to smile.

On the elevator down to the lobby, Dani had noticed that her mother was crying. "Did Grandmother die?"

"No—no, not yet."

When the elevator's polished brass doors opened, her mother had rushed out, sobbing. "I'm not going to end up like my mother, I swear I'm not."

Left to follow, Dani had joined her mother on the street. The temperature had dropped, and the wind had picked up; a light snow was falling. Her mother had taken Dani's hand and began walking briskly in the opposite direction of their building.

"Where are we going?" Dani had asked, the wind stinging her cheeks.

"The subway station," her mother said tightly.

Dani had made no response. She often rode the subway with Mattie, who would spout off about the virtues of public transportation and conserving the world's resources, but never with her mother.

Lilli had stopped abruptly. "You look cold." Then she'd pulled off her pale gray cashmere scarf and wrapped it around Dani's neck for added warmth, tucking one edge up over her mouth and nose.

They'd taken the subway to Greenwich Village, her mother acting so much as if it was a grand adventure that Dani got caught up in her excitement. "Are we going to see Mattie?" she'd asked.

"No, she's gone ballooning in New Mexico."

That had sounded fun to Dani, but even her father didn't like the idea of her getting into a hot-air balloon with his mother. "Can we go to New Mexico?"

"Maybe during your winter vacation, after—" Her mother's eyes had clouded, her shoulders sagging. "One day we'll go."

They'd walked to a section of Greenwich Village where even Mattie, who had few rules, hadn't permitted Dani to wander on her own. Lilli had plunged down two concrete steps to a heavy, dirty door, its black paint chipped. She'd peeled off a black leather glove and knocked. There was one window, blackened with soot and covered with iron bars, and a sign over the door that said the Flamingo.

A voice yelled for them to come inside.

Even now, so many years later, Dani could smell the smoke inside that dark bar. It had been decorated—of course—with plastic flamingos and fake palm branches. In the dim light, she'd seen her mother's smile falter.

A black-haired man had greeted her from behind the bar. "You the lady who called?"

Lilli had nodded, looking faintly disapproving, the way she did when giving in to Dani and buying hot pretzels from a street vendor. "You're Mr. Garcia."

He was a Cuban exile, he explained. He had played jazz for the tourists in Havana before Castro. A picture of John F. Kennedy hung above the cash register. One of Fidel Castro hung behind the bar; it was struck with darts. Licking her lips, Lilli slid a hundred-dollar bill across the worn bar. Until that moment Dani hadn't been sure her mother even knew how to write a check; she'd always seemed to pay for things just by nodding. Mattie had insisted Dani learn how to handle money.

"The place is all yours," Mr. Garcia had said, a sweep of his chubby arm taking in all of the small, empty bar.

Lilli had removed her coat and hat, then helped Dani with the complicated clasps of the dress coat she'd worn for her visit with her grandmother. Her hair had crackled with static electricity as she pulled off the cashmere scarf.

"I'm going to sing some songs," her mother had told her. "You can sit up at the table by yourself and be my audience. How's that?"

"Can I have a Coke?"

Lilli smiled. "And pretzels."

She'd given Mr. Garcia more money, and he'd brought a tall glass of soda and a bowl of pretzels to Dani, who'd sat alertly at a rickety round table, aware that this wasn't like sitting on Mattie's front stoop discussing baseball and politics with anybody who happened by. This, she'd thought at age eight, was really scary.

Underneath her coat, her mother had been wearing a slinky black dress. She put on a pair of strappy black high heels that she'd had squished down in her handbag. Dani had never seen the dress or the shoes before.

Mr. Garcia had turned on the microphone and a hot, blinding stage light that at first made Lilli blink and look frightened. "Dani?" she called. "Dani, you're still here, aren't you, sweetheart?"

"Yep," Dani called back.

Her mother had smiled tentatively.

"Remember," Mr. Garcia had yelled. "If you stink, you got thirty minutes. If I can stand it, an hour."

Munching on pretzels, Dani had watched, stupefied, as her mother had transformed herself—and the tacky Greenwich Village nightclub—with her singing and dancing. Once she got started, she'd never checked on Dani, and the only reason she'd stopped was because Mr. Garcia turned off the stage light. "I gotta open up the place," he'd said apologetically. "Besides, you shouldn't overdo. Wreck your voice."

Her dress had been soaked with perspiration, and her hair had stuck to her forehead and the back of her neck. Dani had never seen her mother so hot, even after a summer tennis game. "How long?"

"Over an hour."

"Then I—"

"You've got talent, lady."

"You mean it? I wasn't awful?"

"You weren't awful. Come back another day. You want, you can sing for the crowd."

"But I couldn't."

"Nobody'd recognize you—not my customers, anyway."

"You don't—"

He'd shaken his head, again reading her mind. "I don't know your name, but I can see you're white bread. The kid wanted avocado on her tuna fish."

"Danielle!"

It was as if Lilli had just remembered she'd brought her daughter along. She'd rushed from the stage and found Dani merrily eating Hershey's Kisses, a stack of crumpled silver papers piled beside her, along with a half-eaten tuna sandwich, two empty soda glasses and the empty pretzel bowl.

"Are you finished, Mama?"

"Yes, we'll go home right away before Dad misses us. Good gracious, you're going to have to learn self-control. Did you like my singing?"

"I liked the fast songs the best."

"You would. We'll have to tell Dad you already ate. He—" Lilli had tilted her head back, chewing on one corner of her mouth as she gazed down at her daughter. "Dani, you mustn't tell anyone about this afternoon. People wouldn't understand. One day I'll explain, but right now I'm trusting you, sweetie. Promise me this will be our secret."

"I promise." It had never occurred to her not to.

That evening, Dani had thrown up her afternoon's indulgences. Her father canceled their walk to see the Christmas tree at Rockefeller Center and, unable to believe there could be so much food in one child, wanted to call the doctor. Her mother had persuaded him to wait until morning. By then, of course, Dani was fine.

On their next visit to the Flamingo, Lilli had packed a picnic for Dani and restricted her to one soda. Mr. Garcia slipped her goodies while her mother had sung and danced in her strappy high heels.

After two months, Mr. Garcia had figured out the identity of the lady in the black dress. Dani had heard him raise his fee to two hundred dollars.

"That's as much as I'll pay," Lilli had said, firm. "Even if you broke your promise and told everyone, who'd believe you? Eugene Chandler's daughter singing in a down-and-out Cuban bar? Paying to sing? It's just too ridiculous."

In fact, when she'd disappeared that August, Eduardo Garcia came forward with his unusual story about the missing heiress. The police had questioned him intensely, but he never changed his story: from that December afternoon a week before Claire Chandler died through the following July, Lilli Chandler Pembroke had practiced her make-believe nightclub act once a week or so at the Flamingo.

"Just ask the kid," he'd told the police.

Finally they did.

Confused and frightened, Dani had told them she knew nothing about her mother's singing and had never heard of a place called the Flamingo.

So long ago, she thought as she started to reel in her kite, little by little.

As slack occurred, she took in some line and let the kite restabilize itself. Then when more slack occurred, she took in a little more line. It was her favorite kite, and she didn't want to lose it. And she'd promised Ira no more climbing trees. But she wasn't about to call one of the grounds crew to rescue her kite like some little kid.

It was still high above the trees, steady against the wind.

"Why do you like to sing, Mama?"

She could see her mother's smile. "You know how Mattie says she feels when she's in a balloon? That's how I feel when I'm singing. Absolutely free."

When she felt fresh slack in her line, Dani didn't reel it in. Instead she slipped the jackknife she always carried kite flying out of her jeans pocket and, with one quick movement, cut the braided nylon line.

She walked away, her kite free to sail the winds.

Zeke finally left his post when Dani stumbled back to her cottage. He was tired. He'd watched her kite sail out of sight, and he'd seen her tears. They glistened on her pale cheeks, not tears of self-pity, he felt, but of loneliness and regret. The kind of tears that only came at dawn.

He needed a shower, a few hours' sleep and breakfast at a place that didn't remind him of his own loneliness and regret.

But first he called California. The phone rang just once before Sam Lincoln Jones picked up. "You awake?" Zeke asked.

"I am now."

"Any luck?"

"I took a spin out to Beverly Hills and talked to Nick Pembroke. I won't say he talked to me, but I'm not into intimidating old men. If he'd been fifty years younger, me and the old codger might have gone a few rounds."

"What's he like these days?"

"Same as always, I expect. For starters, he's as pigheaded as they come."

Zeke thought of Nick Pembroke's granddaughter pounding into her purple cottage after she'd told him to pack up and hit the road. "Must be a strong gene."

"Met Dani, have you? I'll bet they're a pair. Nick's also arrogant, brilliant and probably the most charming old buzzard I've ever met." Sam paused. "And he's scared, Zeke."

"Dani?"

"Yep. Heard she'd been robbed. Thinks she should have kept her mouth shut about that gold key. Most people thought Nick just made up the part in *Casino* about his grandmother selling off gold gate keys."

"So he feels Dani was asking for trouble mentioning it."

"It's already valuable because it's gold, but it's even more valuable because Ulysses Pembroke had it made. A consequence of Nick turning his granddaddy into one of the great rakes of American history."

But, Zeke wondered, could it be even more valuable—to the right person—because Lilli Chandler Pembroke had been wearing it the night she disappeared?

"Does Nick still gamble?"

"Not as much as he used to. He's broke. Dani pays his rent, keeps him in food and heart medicine. She doesn't strike me as the type who'd pay his gambling debts for him."

Hardly. And Sam hadn't even met her.

"There's something else," he said.

"Go on."

"It's just instinct, but I'd say old Nicky was holding back on me."

"Something important?"

"I'd say so."

Zeke sighed, imagining the possibilities.

"Like I say," Sam went on, "fifty years younger, and me and him would have gone a few rounds. I also took the liberty of checking up on the other living Pembroke scoundrel."

Dani's father. Four years after his wife had disappeared, John Pembroke had put the Chandler family back on the front pages with another scandal. Eugene Chandler had refused to press charges against his son-in-law for embezzlement—wouldn't even publicly admit John had stolen from Chandler Hotels—but had quietly tossed his daughter's husband out on his ear. From what Zeke knew, John Pembroke had taken to gambling as even Nick never had, scrounging good games the world over, while he did the occasional cheeky travel piece. He couldn't have been around much for his daughter.

"What's he up to these days?" Zeke asked.

"Lives in a crummy apartment in Tucson. Word is his daughter's hired him to write a biography of Ulysses, probably just charity by another name. Anyway, he doesn't have a phone, but I contacted a friend out that way, and she did some checking. Seems our man left town this afternoon."

Zeke kicked off his shoes. His pretty lace curtains billowed in the cool breeze, and his room filled with the fresh smells of early morning. "Find out where he's headed?"

"East. Booked a flight to Albany."

"Hell."

"Say the word," his partner and friend told him in a low voice, "and I'll be there."

"I know. Thanks. I've got another favor, though, if you have time."

"I'm listening."

Zeke shut his eyes, which burned with fatigue and too many questions, too many memories. He could see Dani cutting her kite free. What had she been thinking about? Did she know her father was en route to Saratoga—or already there?

"Check out what Quint Skinner's into these days."

There was a silence on the California end of the line.

"He's in Saratoga," Zeke said.

Sam breathed out. "Fun times."

"Lots of work to do, Sam."

"Yeah. I'll be in touch."

After he hung up, Zeke went into the cozy bathroom, where he was reminded the claw-foot tub didn't have a showerhead. He tore open a package of bath salts and took a sniff. He wasn't picky, so long as he didn't come out smelling like a lingerie shop.

Instead, he thought, remembering her beside him in his car, he'd come out smelling like the woman who owned the Pembroke.

Lowering himself into the cute little tub, the scalding water swirling around him, he considered that there were probably worse fates.

Nine

⤜⟲⟳⤛

Breakfast at the track was an August Saratoga tradition that Zeke might have found quaint if he'd been more awake. For a modest amount of money, one could enjoy a champagne breakfast in the clubhouse and watch expensive thoroughbreds work out on the picturesque track, said to be the most beautiful in the country. Up and at it before he was ready to be up and at it, Zeke had walked down from the Pembroke. He'd avoided the front desk, lest Dani had spoken to her staff about having given him the boot.

Sara Chandler Stone was on the upper level, at a white-covered table overlooking the track. The atmosphere was relaxed and cordial, with a touch of elegance that was part of the upstate resort's appeal. Zeke was underdressed as usual. Most everyone seemed finished with their breakfast.

"Am I late?" Zeke asked, sitting across from Sara.

"It's no problem." She was as poised and still as a mannequin, her porcelain face hidden under the wide brim of her straw hat. She wore an attractive, feminine dress, silky and expensive, an easy way to remind people who was a Chandler here and who wasn't. "I try to come to breakfast at the track once a season. My family has benefited a great deal from our connection with Saratoga racing. I enjoy giving something back."

"It's a dirty job," Zeke said, "but somebody's got to do it."

Her smile didn't falter. "I wouldn't expect you to understand."

He smiled back. "Touché, Mrs. Stone."

"Would you care for a glass of champagne?"

She already had a glass, and she didn't appear to have drunk anything else or eaten anything at all. Zeke shook his head and flagged a waiter, who promptly filled his coffee cup and took his order for eggs.

Sara stared down at onlookers gathered along the white fence to watch the horses warm up on the track. "Will you be at the Chandler Stakes this afternoon?"

"Probably."

"It's a large field of horses this year. The weather's beautiful. It'll be a grand day." Her smile was gone now, her porcelain skin without color. "Father's looking forward to today."

"Well, it's the hundredth running of the Chandler."

"And if it's as thrilling as everyone seems to think it will be, it could help put the seventy-fifth out of his mind." She sipped her champagne; it couldn't have been her first glass, Zeke thought. "None of us attended. We were all out looking for Lilli."

Zeke willed away his fatigue, the old, dead dreams that had haunted him through his few hours of sleep. "It must have been horrible. I'm sorry, Sara."

She waved a hand. "Oh, it was a long time ago. Wounds heal."

"Not all wounds. Not knowing what happened to your sister has to be hard."

"Yes." Her voice had dropped to a near whisper. "To be honest, Zeke, I've come to hate the entire Chandler Stakes weekend. I only keep up with the traditions because of Father and Roger. If it were up to me, I doubt I'd ever come back to Saratoga. But Roger loves racing season, and it seems to be a solace for Father." She swallowed more champagne, her eyes turned back down to the track. "When I'm here, all I can do is think of Lilli."

Downing his coffee, Zeke hoped Sara hadn't asked to see him just to cry on his sleeve. That occasionally happened in his business. He hated to be hard-hearted, but he had to maintain objectivity. Professionalism. Strict neutrality. But this, he reminded himself, wasn't business.

His breakfast arrived, and Sara motioned for the waiter—it was a slight, delicate gesture—to bring her more champagne. Then she turned back to Zeke, and he saw the fear slip into her eyes as she asked in a quiet, slightly hoarse voice, "Why are you here?"

"I'm on vacation."

Her reaction—her sudden, sweet, angry smile—caught him off guard. "You're a closemouthed son of a bitch, Zeke Cutler, just like your brother was."

"Even worse."

The anger and sweetness vanished, and so did her smile. She tilted her head back so that the shadows moved onto her face and he no longer could see her eyes under the brim of her hat. "Did he hate me?"

"No."

"But he wanted to," she said.

Zeke didn't answer. It wasn't his place—now, no one's—to speak for his brother.

"I'm sorry." But she didn't sound sorry, only wrapped in self-pity. "It can't be easy for you to talk about him. Zeke, I know this is probably hard for you to believe, but I really did care about your brother. Joe and I together…" She licked her lips. "It never would have worked. You must know that."

Maybe he did. But he wasn't sure Joe had. He'd been eighteen and still believed love could conquer anything, even the differences between Sara Chandler and himself.

She worked at a sapphire ring on her left hand, hesitant, way out of her rich woman's league. "You're staying at the Pembroke?"

"Yes."

"What do you think of our Danielle?"

"That she'd hate to be called your or anyone else's Danielle."

Sara smiled, smug and cool. "Oh, yes, you're right about that. This August is especially difficult, I think, for all of us. We're all in the limelight even more than usual—with the Chandler centennial. Danielle's little projects, the twenty-fifth anniversary of Lilli's having left." She caught herself, biting down on her lower lip; Zeke lost her eyes again under the brim of her hat. "I almost always say she left. It's just a habit with me. Not knowing what happened to her is a terrible burden—I'm not sure anyone really understands. I like to think my sister made a deliberate choice about her life. I used to think it would be easier if she'd died rather than abandoned all of us, but now…" She lifted her shoulders and tucked a stray strand of hair somewhere up under her hat. Her nails were pale pink, short, perfectly manicured. "It seems to me just up and leaving would have been an act of tremendous courage for a woman like her."

"How so?" Zeke asked as he sat forward, wanting to get Sara's perspective on her older sister's state of mind before she disappeared. It was so easy to discount Sara as having much perspective on anything. But even if she was wrong about Lilli, hearing what she had to say could be instructive. Twenty-five years ago, she seemed to have nothing in common with her older sister. Now Sara had become everything people had always thought Lilli had always been.

"Lilli felt more trapped by her circumstances than I ever did. She married fairly young. By the time Nick cast her in *Casino*, she had a husband, a child, unbelievable expectations placed on her. Perhaps she decided the only way she could change her life was to chuck it all and leave. Become someone else."

"Is that what you believe happened?"

Sara's shoulders sagged. She'd changed more than Zeke had anticipated. At twenty-two, she'd been dynamic and restless, grieving for a mother she'd lost too young and anxious to set the world on fire. Only she hadn't. That wasn't necessarily a failure in Zeke's view, unless she thought it was. Either way, he'd left behind enough plans and dreams of his own not to judge.

"I only wish I knew," she whispered, then blushed. "I'm sorry, Zeke—I realize I keep saying that, but I didn't mean for you to have to listen to me whine. I just wanted to say hello. I don't know, I thought you might have come to Saratoga because of Lilli, Joe, me, its being twenty-five years." But when he didn't respond, irritation flashed in her very blue eyes, undermining her gracious, sweet heiress act. She pulled a napkin from her lap and set it neatly beside her champagne glass. "You're not going to tell me anything, are you?"

"Sara, there's nothing to tell you."

That wasn't true, of course.

She gave him a cool smile. "Well, then. I hope you have a wonderful stay in Saratoga. It's been good seeing you, Zeke. Now if you'll excuse me, I have a great deal to do before the Chandler this afternoon."

She was on her feet. Zeke watched as she quickly—automatically—took stock of who was around her, who was paying attention.

"Wait," he said calmly.

She looked at him, expectant.

"There's something I've always wondered. Did you just use Joe to get Roger to notice you?"

It wasn't what she'd wanted Zeke to ask. She hesitated, then said quietly, "I hope you go straight to hell when you die, Zeke Cutler."

Then she was gone, stiffing him with the bill.

Zeke flagged the waiter for more coffee, noticing he didn't jump as fast as when Sara had been there, but he did come, and the coffee was hot, the weather was nice. Zeke sat back, watching the horses and thinking.

After about thirty seconds he realized he didn't have a whole hell of a lot to think about besides Dani's black eyes. He'd been in town almost two days and so far didn't know anything. Time to throw a stick of dynamite into the mix and stir things up.

But first, another cup of coffee.

The telephone woke her.

Fumbling for the receiver, Dani almost fell on the floor before she realized she wasn't upstairs in her bedroom. She'd crashed on the couch in the living room after her kite flying. She stumbled to her feet. Her eyelids felt swollen, and her bruises and scrapes hurt, but the damn phone was still ringing. She headed to the kitchen, shuddering when she remembered she hadn't locked the back door when she'd come in. But there were no robbers in the kitchen, no dark-eyed men on white horses. Just a bucket of peach skins and peach pits for the compost pile.

She grabbed the wall phone, but before she could grunt a hello, Ira Bernstein said, "You'd better get up here."

His words—his serious tone—instantly woke her up. "What's wrong?"

"One of the guest rooms has been ransacked. Totally tossed to hell and back."

"Was anyone hurt?"

"Not that I know of."

"Have you called the police?"

"Not yet. I, um, thought we should talk first."

Cutler, she thought. He had to be involved somehow. "I'll be there in ten minutes."

She ran into the bathroom and splashed cold water on her face and brushed her teeth, raked her fingers through her hair, grimaced at her reflection in the mirror. What a mess. She hadn't gotten off all of Magda's makeup; mascara was smudged under her eyes. And she looked as though she'd spent the night peeling peaches and flying kites.

She decided against fresh clothes and instead put on her sneakers and headed out in her jeans. She tore through her garden and out the back gate, moving fast over the familiar ground.

Ira was waiting for her in room 304. It was one of her favorites. She'd found the crazy quilt in a dusty antique shop in Vermont and had repaired it herself.

"Housekeeping came in to make up the bed," Ira said, "and found it like this. Efficient bastard."

Indeed. A duffel had been dumped out, its contents scattered. Dani noticed jeans, canvas pants, dark shirts. White-knight clothes. "This is Zeke Cutler's room, isn't it?"

Ira nodded. "Dani—" He sighed, running one hand through his corkscrew curls. "Look, I didn't call the police because I don't know what's going on around here. This guy shows up. Your cottage is broken into. He drives you to the Chandler party last night. He comes in this morning at the crack of dawn. Leaves. Now we find his room tossed."

"That about sums it up." Dani balled her hands into fists, trying to maintain some semblance of calm even as she fought to get a decent breath. The small room suddenly seemed oppressive and airless. "I don't know what's going on, either, Ira."

"If you want me to, I can handle this. I'll leave you out altogether. But if this is personal—if I'm going to tread somewhere you don't want me to tread…" He paused, his cockiness and irreverence nowhere in evidence. "You just tell me what you want me to do."

Any residual sleepiness or fatigue vanished as Dani straightened, looking around the ransacked room. The mattress was off the bed, drawers dumped, linens heaped, bath crystals and salts and powders emptied. What had Zeke brought down on her head?

"You've called our own security people?"

"On their way."

"Good. Let them deal with the police. I'll deal with Zeke myself."

Ira looked dubious. "You're sure?"

"No." She forced herself to meet Ira's eye, to smile. "But it'll be okay. Thanks, Ira."

Before he could stop her, she left, heading back across the grounds to her cottage, where she showered and changed. Fifteen minutes later, she was on her way into Saratoga. She found a parking space in a public lot and walked over to the library, where, after some digging, she checked out a copy of *Joe Cutler: One Soldier's Rise and Fall.*

Then she walked to Kate Murtagh's small yellow Victorian house, on a pretty street off—well off—Union Avenue. Dani went around back and knocked on the door, because it was August in Saratoga and if Kate wasn't catering some event, she was in her kitchen. She yelled that the door was open, and Dani went in.

The kitchen was bright, airy, functional and spotless, with open shelves, pots hanging from cast-iron hooks, stacks of pure white cotton towels and aprons, white cabinets and miles of countertop. Kate was decorating petits fours at her butcher-block table.

"Egad, Dani," Kate said, putting down her frosting bowl, "you look like the whirling dervish. What's up?"

"I need to know if you've found anything else out about Zeke Cutler."

"Aha." She wiped her hands on her apron and gestured to a chair across from her, but Dani didn't sit down. "Well, for starters, you didn't tell me the man's a stud. I saw him with my own two eyes, and he— Hey, are you blushing?"

"It's hot in here. Where did you see him?"

"Outside your grampy's place last night. Told him not to pester you or he'd have me to deal with. Didn't seem to bother him much. But as you can imagine, I've plumbed my sources for any information I can on the man."

"And?"

"And I've come up with precious little beyond what I've already told you."

"But you have something," Dani said.

Kate sighed. "Yeah, but what about you? Are you going to tell me what's going on?"

"I will, Kate—you know that. But right now I just don't have time to go into all the boring details."

"I can't imagine that any details about you and our white hat would be boring. But before you whirl out of here, I will tell you what remarkably little I know." She frowned at Dani. "Will you please eat a petit four or something and calm down?"

Realizing she'd been pacing, Dani did grab an unfrosted petit four and pop it in her mouth, but she didn't even begin to calm down. She needed to find Zeke and get some answers. Maybe she'd wring his neck while she was at it. She wouldn't think about his dark eyes and strong thighs. She'd just kick his sneaky butt out of her life. He had invaded her territory, her life, and she'd bet everything she owned he hadn't begun to tell her what he was doing in Saratoga. And it wasn't the kind of risky gamble three generations of Pembrokes had lost their shirts on. It was a sure bet.

"Have you talked to Mattie?" Kate asked quietly.

Dani shook her head. "Not yet."

"Are you going to?"

She felt the weight of the book on Joe Cutler in her bag. She already suspected that Mattie—her own grandmother, the one person she'd always trusted and believed in without question—hadn't told her the truth when she'd given no indication she knew Zeke. Maybe she hadn't lied outright. But she'd held back, and that Dani found disturbing.

"As soon as I know more," she said. "Zeke could just be using me to get to Mattie—for what reason I can't imagine, except that she's a reclusive, world-famous movie star." She tried to control her impatience. "Look, Kate, I know I owe you an explanation, but—"

"But you're going to start spitting blood if I don't talk."

"I'll tell you everything, I promise."

"Yeah, yeah. Meanwhile, would you like to know where our white hat's sitting at the Chandler this afternoon?"

The weather at the Saratoga Course was dry, clear and warm, perfect for watching skinny-legged racehorses run around in circles. Zeke had borrowed a private box on the clubhouse balcony. By the sixth race of the afternoon, he'd drunk one large, lukewarm beer, watched all the people he cared to watch and decided that horse racing had to be more exciting if you knew what was going on. He didn't. The people around him, however, clearly did. They seemed to be having a grand time for themselves.

The track's shaded grounds were jam-packed, the fifty thousand or so who'd come to see the Chandler Stakes running the gamut from shabby pickpockets to the superrich in their straw hats and panamas. Zeke had already checked out the Chandler box. Sara and Roger were there with old Eugene and a few guests. He was quite sure none of them had seen him. He was good at not being seen when he didn't want to be seen.

He had a decent view from his seat, but the backstretch was still a blur, and everything happened so fast that by the time he figured out which horse was which, the race was over. Most of the people around him had come prepared with binoculars and well-marked programs. Strategically placed monitors and an announcer helped make up for what Zeke couldn't see or understand, but the truth was, he didn't care which horse won any particular race. He was there for the atmosphere, for a sense of what drew people here year after year. It wasn't just the racing, which was supposedly impressive. It was more—in his opinion, at least—the history of the place, its continuity, its sense of its own past. The graceful iron fences, wooden grandstand and clubhouse, the red-and-white awnings, the flowers and trees and fountains and ultragreen grass, the well-dressed crowd—they all provided a tangible link with a bit of America's colorful past. Television couldn't capture that feeling. Neither, Zeke had to admit, could it fully capture the breathtaking beauty, the awesome power and speed, of a dozen thoroughbreds thundering around one of the world's great tracks.

He sipped his second beer. Since the average race lasted less than two minutes, most of the afternoon, technically, was between races. In his next life, Zeke thought, he'd run a racetrack concession stand.

Then he spotted Dani threading her way up the aisle, and the afternoon suddenly got a lot more interesting.

She had on a simple short white dress and no hat, and a pair of binoculars hung from her neck.

She looked even sexier than she had last night in Mattie's sleek dress.

As she moved closer, Zeke saw that she was also on a tear, hanging by her fingernails. Irritated about something and getting more irritated the more she thought about it.

She dropped into the seat beside him, a jumble of nerves, determination and energy. He could smell the clean fresh scent of the same soap in his room at the Pembroke. The bruise on her wrist had turned to a splotch of red, purple, blue and yellow. Her shins still looked sore. She sat for a few seconds without saying a word.

Finally Zeke said, "Afternoon, Ms. Pembroke."

She cut her black eyes at him. "Mr. Cutler."

Her tone was frigid, and she inhaled through her nose, one angry woman. Zeke took another sip of beer. "I'm just one among tens of thousands here. How'd you find me?"

"I looked for your shining armor."

For a no-nonsense entrepreneur, she was good at sarcasm. "Well, it couldn't have been that difficult—the guy I borrowed this little box from is fairly high profile."

"Someone you rescued from the jaws of death."

"You don't sound impressed."

Those eyes were on him again, telling him she'd just as soon go for his throat as sit there and talk. But there was fear there, too. She'd had her world turned upside down before, and now it must have seemed to her it was happening again. And maybe it was. He suddenly wished he'd told Sam to take the first eastbound plane he could get. With his ability to zero in on a person's insecurities, fears, strengths, the sources of his or her anger and frustrations, Sam would know what to say to a scared, angry, hotheaded ex-heiress. Zeke sure as hell didn't. Likely enough, whatever he said would only irritate her more, or, worse, suck her deeper into whatever was going on.

She stared down at the empty track. It was, of course, between races. "Who's your pick for the Chandler?"

"Dani," Zeke said carefully, "you didn't come here to talk horses."

"I'd stay away from the favorite. The Chandler's done its fair share over the past hundred years in helping Saratoga earn its reputation as the 'graveyard of favorites.'"

But underneath her rigidity and distance, Zeke sensed just how upset and vulnerable Dani was. He could see her twenty-five years ago, a nine-year-old waiting for her mother to come home, trying to make sense of what was going on around her.

Zeke became very still, blotting out the sounds and commotion of the milling crowd. He didn't take his eyes off her. "Tell me why you're here," he said.

"The Chandler and the Kentucky Derby are both one-and-a-quarter-mile races for three-year-olds. Since the Chandler's run in the summer instead of the spring, the horses are a few months older, more experienced. Many experts think that added maturity makes the Chandler a better race."

Zeke decided to go along with her, play her game, for now. "What do you think?"

"I don't care about the Chandler." She turned to him, her face white and her eyes huge and aching. It wasn't easy for her to be there. "I never have."

"I'm not much on racing myself. The horses are just names and numbers to me. I haven't placed a single bet. Still, it makes for a pleasant afternoon."

"You're just the opposite of Nick—my grandfather. He'd come to the track and not watch a single race, just sit in front of the monitors as close to the betting window as he could get." Her tone was neither affectionate nor bitter, simply matter-of-fact. But her skin was still pale, and Zeke could feel her emotion like a hot, dangerous breeze. "I want you off my property by six o'clock."

But something had changed since last night. There was more at stake now. She hadn't just found his car in the Pembroke lot and decided to hunt him up and personally give him the boot. "That's all?" he asked, dubious.

She said tightly, "Yes."

"Dani, you're not telling me everything."

She shot him a look. "And you've told me everything?"

Among her very high standards, Zeke suspected, was a profound distaste for people who neglected to tell her everything she thought she had a right to know. And he hadn't even begun.

She looked down at the track, still quiet. With her angular Pembroke features, she cut a handsome profile, but Zeke could see the fatigue, the shadows under her beautiful, dark eyes, the straight, uncompromising line of her mouth. He thought of the woman with tears on her cheeks as she cut her kite loose at dawn. How to figure Dani Pembroke?

"Your lifestyle's caught up with you," she said without looking at him.

Zeke felt himself tense. "What do you mean?"

"I mean—" and now she threw the full force of her black eyes on him "—that your room at the Pembroke has been turned upside down."

Falling back on his training and experience, Zeke let his muscles relax, kept his face impassive. "Was anyone hurt?"

"Not that I know of." In the bright sun, her eyes had narrowed to two black slits. "None of the other rooms were touched. It wasn't a random act of violence. It was deliberate. Whoever got into room 304 was specifically looking for your room—or for you."

"And you think that someone was maybe the same person who knocked you three ways from Sunday—"

"I think there's a high probability of a connection."

No doubt she was right, not that Zeke had any intention of telling her so. This wasn't her territory. She bottled water and made people feel good for a living. She didn't deal with the likes of Quint Skinner, who, Zeke had no doubts whatsoever, had tossed his room. It was a message. *You're not the big shot you think you are. I can reach you.* Or just Skinner's way of trying to find out what Zeke was really doing in Saratoga.

"So you think this break-in was aimed at me personally and not at you or your company?" he asked calmly.

"You're the expert." She gave him a look that made him realize how she'd succeeded in the competitive beverage and hotel businesses, how she'd gone on with her life after her mother's disappearance, her father's embezzlement, her war with the Chandler half of her family. Dani Pembroke was a survivor. She added smoothly, "After you're off my property."

He'd tackle that one later.

She jumped up, turned to him, her black eyes challenging. "I'm going to find out what you're doing in Saratoga."

Before he could decide whether or not to grab her and level with her, she was off, her small size helping her speed through the crowd. If he was to have a prayer of catching up with her, he'd have had to leap over seats and generally make a scene. He'd done that sort of thing before, gun in hand, even. But right now he wasn't sure what good it would do.

He made himself settle back in his seat. He sipped his warm beer and listened to the people around him, the idle chatter, the laughter.

And he reminded himself of his mission in Saratoga.

He was to find out if the gold key Lilli Chandler Pembroke had worn the night she disappeared was the same gold key in the recent photograph of her daughter twenty-five years later. He was to find out if the blackmail letter Joe had given to Naomi had anything to do with Lilli's disappearance.

If his brother had died knowing what had happened to the missing Chandler heiress. If he'd been a part of it.

That, Zeke thought, was his mission in Saratoga.

* * *

As she made her way through the packed clubhouse, Dani tried to blot out the sights and sounds and smells of the track, whose history and traditions were as personal to her as a family picnic. She remembered her mother's blond hair shining in the bright afternoon sun and her gentle smile as she'd held her young daughter's hand walking down the steep aisle.

Dani found a reasonably short line at a concession stand and bought herself a lemonade, then permitted herself a peek back toward Zeke's box before she moved on. She couldn't see him. He was a man, she thought, who defied prediction. He got under her skin more than anyone in recent memory had. He was careful and controlled, undoubtedly good at winning his clients' trust. But she wasn't a client, and his reasons for being in Saratoga, she was now certain, had nothing to do with business. They were personal.

Had they brought on the ransacking of her bedroom Thursday afternoon? His room that morning?

She gulped her lemonade, suddenly feeling thirsty and exhausted. Not for a second did she believe Zeke would leave the Pembroke of his own accord. He'd push her as far as he could and make her throw him out. Probably even enjoy going toe-to-toe with her. Would she toss him? Or was she bluffing? She could argue, she thought, that having him stay where she could keep an eye on him wasn't a bad idea.

She looked around her, not having paid attention to where she was going, and found herself face-to-face with Eugene Chandler. Before she could say a word, he took her by the elbow and pulled her aside. For a man in his eighties, her grandfather's grip was like a leghold steel trap.

Her grandfather was highly proficient at concealing his emotions, and Dani had to look closely to see the telltale signs that he was angry and upset: deep breaths through the nose, tightly clenched jaw, extra-straight back, extra-quiet voice, extra-piercing blue eyes.

She pulled her arm free, or maybe he just let her go. "Is something—"

"I wish you'd warned us that your father was in town," he said.

She felt blood rush to her face. "He is?"

Eugene Chandler's legendary control faltered. "Yes, I spoke to him myself a few minutes ago. Didn't you know?"

Dani shook her head. *Pop's in Saratoga. What next?*

"Danielle?"

"I'm fine." But she wasn't fine. She had a professional security consultant from Mattie's hometown skulking around, and now her father, whom she hadn't seen in months, had turned up.

"Perhaps you should sit down," her grandfather said softly.

"I'm okay," she said, anxious to make her exit, to find her father and grill him. "Thanks."

"Danielle…" He sighed. "Never mind. Go find your father. It's good to see you."

She wished she knew if he was being sincere or if he was just saying what he thought he was supposed to say. Either way, at least she'd know for sure where she stood with him. She tossed her empty lemonade cup into a trash bin and looked back, saw her grandfather join her aunt and uncle returning to the Chandler box.

She didn't linger. She wanted to find her reprobate of a father and make him tell her what he was doing in Saratoga.

Not for a moment did she believe it was another coincidence.

Altogether, John Pembroke was glad his trip east had cleaned him out or he might have put a few bucks on a homely bay with fifteen-to-one odds. There was no intelligent reason for his pick. A hundred years ago his great-grandfather had entered a homely bay in the first Chandler Stakes and won. So it seemed a fitting tribute, if not good betting, to wager on a similar horse at the Chandler centennial. But John hated the idea of crawling to his daughter for money.

He yawned, shaking off his jet lag and night on a lumpy cot at a trainer friend's crummy cottage. He'd entertained the idea of trotting up to the Pembroke and asking for a room, just to see what Dani would do. Show him to a park bench? Offer him a room for twice the cost? But John knew what she'd have done. She'd have let him stay with her. He was, after all, she would say, her father.

And wasn't that the damn thing about it?

But he hadn't gone up to the Pembroke, not so much because of Dani, but because of the memories. Right now, just being back in Saratoga, at the track, at the Chandler Stakes, was enough torture. Everywhere he looked he saw a reminder of Lilli, of all he'd lost, of how badly he'd failed her and his daughter. It was painful having one's shortcomings before him at every turn. He didn't expect anyone's sympathy, least of all his own. He'd earned his misery.

A crowd had gathered at his stretch of white fence, where a skittish chestnut was being led onto the track, its brightly clad jockey a popular favorite. He waved and smiled, knowing how to play to his audience. Then, when his gleaming thoroughbred touched the dirt, he turned his attention to his job, and the fifty thousand people watching him might not have been there. John was suitably impressed.

He stuck a cigarette in his mouth but didn't light it.

"I thought you quit."

Turning, he grinned at his daughter, as small and pretty as ever. "Hello, sweet pea."

"Don't 'sweet pea' me, Pop. What're you doing here? How come you didn't tell me you were coming?" She stopped herself, her hands balled into tight fists at her sides. "Never mind. Obviously we can't talk here. You, me, the Chandler Stakes—reporters would fall all over themselves if they saw us together. Where are you staying?"

"Don't trouble yourself about me."

"I'm not. I just want to be able to find you in case you try to wriggle out of telling me what you're up to."

"You sound just like Mattie in the old days when she'd yell at Nick for being such a heel. He used to say he'd never met a more unforgiving woman. Still says it."

"The Pembroke men," Dani said with a grudging smile, "don't make forgiving easy."

"True."

"You're welcome to stay with me at the cottage."

He grinned. "Can't leave your old man to the elements or you just want to keep tabs on me?"

But he noticed the dark circles under her eyes and the bruises and scrapes on her arms and legs, and his heart lurched.

"Pop," she said, "we need to talk. Meet me up at the cottage after the race."

He nodded, wishing and regretting and wanting so much to see his daughter smile—really smile—and to hear her laugh as she had when he'd scoop her up as a tiny black-haired toddler and toss her in the air. In those days, he had always counted on himself to catch her.

"I mean it, Pop. If you try to sneak out on me, I'll call the law on you if I have to."

"For what?"

"I'll make something up."

She darted into the crowd that was settling down now for the start of the Chandler. John held his position against the fence, watching his daughter. He'd heard rumors just in his short time in town that she was on the verge of self-destructing. That she'd rather end up broke and discredited like her father and paternal grandfather than rich and respected like her mother's father. That she'd rather, in the end, be a Pembroke than a Chandler. John didn't believe the rumors. All her life his only child had struggled simply to be herself. It was a struggle he understood, even if he'd been defeated by it, and even if she'd never believe he could know how she felt.

He turned back to the track and placed his forearms on the wide, flat top of the fence. The horses were taking their places at the starting gate. Amazingly, he hadn't even picked up a program.

But it wouldn't have mattered.

He wasn't there. He was at the track of another era, not twenty-five years ago when Lilli disappeared or even thirty years ago when they'd been so happy together, but all the way back to his first summer in Saratoga when he was thirteen years old. His mother had "retired" from Hollywood by then and moved him to Greenwich Village. He'd come to love the hustle and excitement of Manhattan, even as he longed for the dry, sunny days of Beverly Hills and his father's kidney-shaped swimming pool.

"Don't worry about being stuck in New York forever," Nick would counsel him during their weekly telephone calls. "Your mother will come crawling back to me soon enough."

John had known his mother would never return to California. At first, eager New York hostesses had invited her to all their society dinners and benefits. Mattie, who preferred flying kites in Central Park or wrapping herself in a tattered afghan by the fire and reading murder mysteries, refused—politely—any and all invitations. The twisted result was that she became even more of a legend. Her unconventionality in retirement coupled with her still-extraordinary beauty and the continued popularity of the fifteen movies she'd made had ensured her place not only in film history, but in the imaginations of ordinary people. To John, the Mattie Witt of film legend was unreal to him. The Mattie Witt he knew wasn't so glamorous and young, but spoke in a lingering southern accent, had had her hair cut off the moment she'd hit the streets of New York, seldom put on makeup or followed fashion. One of her favorite outfits was an orange flight suit, which she'd wear anywhere. John would remember seeing pictures of his mother in sequined evening gowns and gobs of makeup, her lips painted red and her hair done up and diamonds glittering at her neck, and would collapse in a fit of laughter, so different was she after she'd quit Hollywood.

For their trip to Saratoga that muggy August day, she'd collected her convertible—bright red with a cream interior—from the garage and had John drag out her old upholstered valise, which she'd stuffed full. He'd packed it in the back of the car, along with two boxes of glass bottles.

"What're the bottles for?" he'd asked.

"I'm going to fill them with mineral water and give them to friends as gifts. Here." She thrust a shoe box at him. "These are my labels. We'll ink them in during the evening and on rainy days."

It had sounded horrid to John.

His eccentric mother had put on her driving gloves and wore a lemon-yellow Chanel suit as she drove with the top down, the bottles rattling in the back. Her eyes had seemed blacker and huger than ever.

"Where will we stay?" John had asked.

"At the estate your great-grandfather built."

That sounded exciting to John. He'd never been there, and he'd imagined all sorts of things—maids, silk sheets, fresh-cut flowers, tennis courts, an indoor swimming pool.

"Remember he was a gambler who came to a bad end," Mattie added.

"But in *The Gamblers*—"

"That movie is more fiction than fact. The real Ulysses Pembroke was shot dead over a poker game and left his pregnant wife penniless. He could have done something worthwhile with his life. He was extraordinarily bright—and yes, I'm sure, quite charming." She glanced at her son with her dark, so knowing eyes. "Very much like your father, I imagine. And you, if you're not careful."

When they arrived in Saratoga, John had been hugely disappointed with the Pembroke estate. It was overgrown and spooky, a testament to his great-grandfather's wasted life. Locked and boarded up, the main house was just too daunting, and Mattie and John dusted up the gingerbread cottage and moved in for their stay. As he'd explored the grounds, he'd found countless indications of what the property must have been like in its day— leggy rosebushes, giant hedges, perennials surviving against all odds, a slate tennis court covered with brown rotting leaves, cracked marble and stone statuary and fountains, an abandoned croquet ball. He'd cleared decades of fallen leaves, twigs, moss and mud from a mineral spring near the main house, among the few original Saratoga springs not already bought up and preserved by the state, and tried its bubbling water. The taste was absolutely hideous. He'd thought he'd been poisoned.

"Mother, Mother!" He'd raced into the kitchen, where Mattie was frowning over a table full of kerosene lamps. The cottage had no electricity. Breathless, he'd told her, "Mother, we can't give that water to people! It's poison!"

"My dear, it's not poison, but I intend to give only a very small quantity of water from that particular spring. It's quite strong and really more suited to bathing. No, the water I intend to give away is from the springs on the other side of the woods. Its waters are far tastier."

All in all, John hadn't been impressed with Ulysses Pembroke and, gradually, had come to admit his own father wasn't much better. Cut from the same cloth, his mother liked to say. John, however, had been determined to be different. He'd do something positive with his life.

Tired of the Pembrokes, he'd asked if he could investigate the track.

Mattie had scrutinized him with a care and closeness that was unusual for her. Her child-rearing philosophy was laissez-faire, sometimes bordering on neglect—which she considered quite healthy. "Since you're too young to gamble, I suppose it's all right."

Small for his age, John had managed to slip onto the grounds unnoticed and soon found himself at the paddocks, staring up at the shiniest, most beautiful horse he'd ever seen. A girl a couple of years younger than he came up to him. Her neatly curled blond hair was parted in the middle and held off her face with mother-of-pearl barrettes, and she wore a blue-flowered dress and navy buckled shoes.

"I don't know you," she'd said.

"Well, I don't know you, either."

She'd laughed. "Everybody knows me."

He couldn't tell if she meant to sound snobby or if she really thought everybody knew her. "Well, everybody knows my mother and father. My mother's a movie star, and my father's a famous movie director—and my great-grandfather was a train robber. I'm staying at his estate."

"I know all the estates in Saratoga." Her blue eyes had glistened as she took up the challenge. "You don't have one."

"The Pembroke—"

"Oh, that. It's all boarded up. Father says it has rats."

John had felt his first sting of real humiliation. "We just keep it that way so no one bothers the treasure."

From her expression, he knew he had her interest, but her father, tall, fair and imposing, showed up and, with just a look, managed to scold her for running off by herself. "Lilli, I've warned you to stay away from the stable boys."

"He's not a stable boy. His mother's a movie star and—"

"A movie star?" Eugene Chandler had turned and appraised John with such frank distaste he could still feel his cheeks burning decades later. He'd felt shabby in his jeans, in contrast to the rich man's handsome gray suit. "You're Mattie Witt and Nicholas Pembroke's boy. Well, run along. You've no business here."

Mattie had been unsympathetic to her son's dejection. Why on earth should he care what the Chandlers thought of him? She was truly and honestly mystified. Only much, much later did John come to understand that his mother's fierce independence hadn't come naturally to her, that she'd had to fight and sacrifice—and suffer—for her treasured freedom.

That lonely summer, he'd only understood how much he'd wanted the Chandlers to approve of him. For the rest of that first August in Saratoga, he'd explored the Pembroke estate and Saratoga's library and all its museums and streets, not just for a sense of the Pembroke past, of their abused energy and promise, but for a peek at his own destiny.

He knew he'd be different. He had to be.

Ten years later he and Lilli were married. Eugene grew fond of his son-in-law. "I swear, John," he would say, "sometimes I forget you're even a Pembroke."

He'd lived to be reminded.

Now, so many years later, John ran his hand through his thinning gray hair and wiped the sweat from his brow, pushing aside thoughts of what might have been. He had to focus on what was. His wife had disappeared ten years into their marriage, and he'd become a bum and a wanderer and no kind of father to their only daughter.

Looking around him, he realized he'd missed the hundredth running of the Chandler Stakes. He glanced at the scoreboard. The homely bay had won. If he'd bet just fifty bucks…

"Look at yourself," he whispered. "What's become of you?"

He pulled himself away from the fence and almost ran straight into a brick wall of a man. He started to apologize, then the fellow said, "John Pembroke," as if he were a ghost.

John squinted. "Who are you?"

The man smiled, not a particularly friendly smile. "I take it you don't recognize me. I'm not surprised. It's been a while."

But John only needed a minute, a chance to pull himself back out of his memories and self-recrimination. He was good at faces, and he'd read the book on Joe Cutler, and had heard his younger brother had quit college and gone into security work.

"Zeke Cutler," he said. "You and your brother came to my office looking for my mother."

They'd refused to tell him why, and he'd sent them packing. A couple of country boys from Cedar Springs, Tennessee. Mattie didn't need them pestering her. She'd never mentioned if the two brothers from her hometown had found her, and he'd never mentioned he'd seen them. Mattie was entitled to her discomfort with her past. John had enough with his.

He looked at the man Zeke Cutler had become. It couldn't be easy being Joe Cutler's little brother. "What do you want with me?"

"I thought," Zeke said in his calm, efficient way, "you might want to walk up to the Pembroke with me."

Given his daughter's disposition, John decided having a security and protection consultant at his side was a pretty good idea. Besides, he wanted to talk to Zeke, find out if they were in Saratoga Springs for similar reasons.

Scratching his head, John appraised Cutler's impressive physique and hoped to hell they were on the same side. Slaying dragons had never been his long suit.

"This way," Zeke said.

"Yes," John said, stupidly irritated at being treated like a stranger. "I know the way."

Ten

Dani didn't relax until she was on her pine-scented driveway. When she reached her cottage, she paced in the garden, debating all the different reasons her father could be in town that didn't have to do with her, her missing keys or Zeke Cutler.

"You should learn to relax."

She whirled around at the sound of her father's voice. He walked through the gate, looking as devil-may-care as ever. "Pop," she said. "How can I relax with—"

But she stopped midsentence when Zeke followed her father into the garden.

Her father walked past her to the kitchen door. "Sit down before you run out of gas, Dani. I'm going to get something to eat. Then you can skewer me, okay?"

He disappeared into the kitchen, and Zeke came onto the stone terrace, moving with that surprising grace and economy. "We walked up together from the track," he said. "Your father's an interesting man. He told me he used to play spy in the rose garden when he was a kid."

"I don't understand him."

"Oh, I think you do. Maybe too well."

"Are you packed yet?"

"Haven't even seen the damage. Think I should sue the Pembroke?"

The humor danced at the back of his eyes and played at the corners of his mouth. He had a way of making her think things and notice things—about him, about herself—that she'd prefer not to think or notice.

When she got rid of him and her father, she'd call Mattie and insist they have a heart-to-heart talk about the Cutler brothers of Cedar Springs, Tennessee.

Her father emerged from the kitchen with a peach, a paring knife and a paper towel. "You know, you don't have much over me in lifestyle. I scoured the entire kitchen for a napkin and had to settle for a paper towel."

"I only have cloth napkins."

"La-di-da." He plopped down at her umbrella table and ate a slice of peach off the end of the paring knife. He'd lost weight in the months since Dani had last seen him. He had a gaunt look that made her wonder if he shared her affliction of insomnia. His clothes seemed even more threadbare than usual. "Place looks good. First time your mother and I took you up here after you could talk, you said you'd paint the cottage purple. You were just a little tot. How the hell old are you now?"

"Thirty-four."

He shuddered. "I must be getting old. Well, kid, it's good to see you. Going to have a seat, or are you planning to give me the third degree standing up?"

Zeke appeared to be observing the proceedings between father and daughter with great amusement. He'd already taken a seat at the table.

Still keyed up, Dani brushed crumbs off the table.

"You'll give yourself ulcers," John said.

She shot him a look. "Why are you here?"

"In Saratoga?" He lifted his bony shoulders in a shrug that

was not convincingly innocent. He'd always been a notoriously rotten bluffer, in life and in poker. "It's blistering hot this time of year in Arizona."

Weak, Dani thought. Very weak. "You could afford a plane ticket?"

"I'm here."

"It was hot in Arizona last summer and the summer before."

"The truth is," her father said, "the thought of coming here used to scare me to death. I had enough reminders of your mother in my life. Lately, though…" He leaned back and stared up at the clear, beautiful blue sky. "I don't know. Reporters have been pestering me for a quote about Lilli, the Chandler Stakes, even that gold key you found. I suppose it's all been working on me. I woke up the other morning and thought, my God, it really has been twenty-five years." He set his paring knife down on the table. "So I booked a flight and here I am."

"Nice try, Pop," Dani said.

He ignored her. "This place—" Squinting, he looked around the transformed garden, then waved one hand, as if to take in all of his great-grandfather's property. "It isn't what it used to be. It's changed. Everything around here's changed. I don't feel as if I'm stepping back into my past."

He was lying. Dani knew it, and so, she felt, did Zeke. It wouldn't have surprised her if her father had already told Zeke the real reason why he was in Saratoga. He had always found it easier to talk to anyone but his own daughter. They were so different. For years she'd struggled to embrace the past—to remember her mother in every detail, to relive every moment of their too-short time together. All her father wanted was to run as far as he could from the past. Yet now here he was in Saratoga, immersed in it.

But Dani didn't press the point. "Did Mattie send you?"

"I haven't talked to her in a couple of weeks."

"Then she called Nick about the burglary, and he sent you."

John sighed, but it couldn't have been a surprise to him that she understood the peculiar dynamics between him and his parents—and where and how she fit into their jumbled worlds. "They're worried," he said.

"Nobody needs to worry about me."

"But they do. We're your family, Dani."

Quietly, without a word, Zeke retreated to the kitchen. Dani appreciated the gesture. But she was still determined that he leave the Pembroke.

She changed the subject. "Grandfather said he spoke to you."

They both knew she was referring to her Chandler grandfather, not to Nick. "Yes, he was cordial. Of course. He invited me to join him for dinner tonight. I refused, but he knew I would." He grinned, his dark eyes sparkling. "Haven't had dinner with the old fart in over twenty years. He'd slip me a batch of poisoned mushrooms and bury me in the backyard with that dead mole you found when you were six or seven."

Dani laughed, surprising herself—and, she could see, her father. She'd carried the mole on a spatula she'd fetched from the kitchen and showed it to her grandparents at tea. They'd been apoplectic. Her mother had quietly maneuvered her out to the garden, where they'd had a proper burial. Lilli had cried. Dani, who'd adored small fuzzy animals, had wanted to find the culprit who'd killed the poor ugly little thing.

"When did you get in?" she asked, less confrontational.

"Early this morning."

"Where did you sleep?"

"Didn't."

"Pop, why didn't you knock on my door? You know I'll always take you in—" She broke off, thinking her life—and maybe his, too—would be easier if she didn't love him. It was that way with Pembrokes and their fathers. "Mattie's room is free."

"If it's all the same to you," John said, "I'll just find something in town. I stayed with a trainer friend last night, but he's having company tonight."

"You don't know Saratoga in August anymore. It's me or the gutter."

He made a face. Since her mother's disappearance, she and her father under the same roof hadn't been a winning combination. "Not much choice, then, is there?"

She looked at him. "Nope."

"Well, you might not be welcoming me with open arms, but at least you haven't told me you hope I fall into a well and drown. Not, I understand, that the thought hasn't crossed your mind."

She started to argue with him but realized he was just trying to jerk her string to keep her from asking questions—demanding answers—about what was really at stake. Zeke came out of the kitchen with her last beer but didn't sit down. Dani looked from him to her father and back again. "You two know each other," she said, and it came out an accusation.

Neither man answered right away. A squirrel ran up the crab-apple tree at the edge of the garden, and a breeze cooled the suddenly very warm late-afternoon air.

Finally her father got up, threw his peach pit over the fence, stretched and yawned. "I'm beat—really, this trip's taken everything out of me. I don't travel the way I used to. Why don't you two go to some nice, quiet place for dinner, and I'll take a walk and get some sleep. We'll have plenty of time to talk."

"Pop—"

"Sounds fine to me," Zeke said.

Her father planted a quick kiss on her cheek. "Good to see you, kid."

It was two against one, and her father was adept at getting himself out of a tight spot. And he was fast. He was out the garden gate before Dani had figured out a good counterargument and worked up the energy to make it.

She was intensely aware that she was alone in her garden, again, with Zeke.

"I'll walk back to the inn with you and see that you check out," she said stiffly.

"That line's wearing thin, Dani. I think we should do as your father suggests and head to town and a nice, quiet restaurant for dinner."

"Why should I do that?"

"Because," he said, "we need to talk."

Zeke turned down Dani's offer to cook on the grounds that he'd seen her kitchen, but agreed to ride with her in her car to town. She was a good driver. Even as distracted as she was, she concentrated on what she was doing. She found a parking space on Broadway in front of an attractive downtown restaurant with sidewalk tables that were tempting on such a beautiful day. But Dani led the way to a table inside, where it was quieter, pleasantly informal. A waitress brought them a small, steaming loaf of bread and dots of herbed butter.

"Is this all right?" Dani asked.

"It's fine."

She ordered a glass of the house red wine, and he did the same, watching her make a show out of examining the menu. She probably knew every item on it and had already decided what she wanted, but he figured she needed something to do besides look at him. He had no problem at all looking at her.

Their wine arrived. Dani immediately took a big drink of hers, then held on to the glass. "You don't mind having a blocked view of the entrance?"

It was an obstructed view, not blocked, but he didn't argue the point. "No, do you?"

She shrugged. "I'm just trying to figure out what kinds of things security consultants know, what they look out for. If I were to hire you, what would you tell me?"

Oh, sweetheart, he thought, *if you only knew.*

But he tried his wine and decided to take her question relatively seriously, even if it was intended to distract him. "I would teach you the basics of personal safety."

"Which are?"

"First you have to know what personal safety is. To my way of thinking, it's providing yourself with a stable environment in which you can pursue the activities and lifestyle you enjoy with limited fear of harm."

"Does that mean you'd make me stop rock climbing?"

He shook his head. "That's an activity you enjoy. I'm talking about ensuring yourself the kind of environment in which you can do your rock climbing, or whatever else you do for fun, without fear of intrusion."

"You mean like burglars and kidnappers and such?"

"I mean," he said, not especially appreciating her cheeky tone, "that an ounce of prevention is worth a pound of cure."

She drank more of her wine; he noticed that her eyes were as black as Mattie's and maybe even more dazzling. "Give me some examples."

"I encourage common sense and reasonable precautions—"

"For rich girls?"

"And boys. And men and women. And the poor, the middle-class, the downtrodden. I give the same basic instructions to everyone, regardless of gender, position or wealth. I encourage common sense and reasonable precautions," he repeated.

Their waitress returned and took their order, a cold pasta salad for Dani, lasagna for Zeke. He tore off a piece of bread and buttered it, then took a bite with a swallow of wine. He wondered if she was deliberately provoking him or if she just had a knack for it.

"An egalitarian bodyguard," she said.

He decided it was deliberate.

"What kind of precautions?" she asked.

"The usual. Make sure someone always knows your plans, change your routine periodically, don't draw undue attention to yourself."

"And people don't think that's too restrictive?"

"Some have more trouble with certain suggestions than others. One executive I worked with hated telling anyone his plans, another enjoyed flaunting his notoriety. And there are always those who are married to their routines. It's a balancing act. I don't encourage recklessness or paranoia."

"I see." She took a piece of bread but skipped the butter. "What do you advise when something bad does happen?"

Her voice had softened, lost its bantering edge, and Zeke yearned to reach across the table and take her hand, but he held back. Kept his distance. It wasn't just necessary, it was the right thing to do. Or so he told himself.

"Again, common sense," he said, focusing on her question, his answer. "If attacked, it's important to remain calm and to be assertive—to find a balance between seeming too weak or too superior to an attacker, or to becoming dehumanized. I suggest my clients give up money and valuables on demand, without question. In general, it's best not to resist unless in immediate mortal danger—but that's in general. Every situation is particular, needs its own reading."

"What if you do choose to fight?"

"Do so with the sole purpose of getting away. Don't worry about apprehending or defeating an attacker. Your safety should be your only concern. If you do use violence, use it only as a last resort, with authority, and never halfheartedly." His voice, he realized, was quiet, intense, controlled. It was the voice that often convinced people he meant business. Dani, however, didn't look convinced or intimidated, only slightly dubious, as if he just might be pulling her leg. "Again, the purpose of any violence is to debilitate your attacker long enough to make your escape."

"And you give your clients tips on appropriate types of violence?"

"I do."

Their dinners arrived, Zeke's lasagna hot and delicately flavored, a nice counter to his concession-stand fare. Before Dani could ask him how to poke a guy's eyeballs out with her car keys, he said, "I saw the book on my brother on your kitchen counter."

Her face paled just a little. "Kate told me about it."

He nodded.

"I haven't read it yet. Should I not bother?"

"If you're asking me if I believe what Quint Skinner wrote about my brother, all I can tell you is that his accuracy has never been challenged."

She stabbed a twist of red pasta with her fork. "Accuracy and truth aren't always the same thing. Anyway, I only got the book out because I wanted to know more about you." She quickly added, "About what your appearance in Saratoga has to do with me."

"Dani—"

"I'm sorry about your brother."

"He's been gone a long time."

"Does that matter?"

He shook his head, hearing Joe's laugh. "No, it doesn't."

"A lot of people think I should be over my mother's disappearance by now," Dani went on softly, "but you never get over something like that. You carry on, and you live your life, enjoy it, but that loss stays with you. Maybe it would be wrong if it didn't."

In the candlelight he saw the faint lines at the corners of her eyes and the places where her lipstick had worn off, and the slowly fading bruise on her wrist. He reached across the table and touched his thumb to her lower lip. She didn't look at him.

"You're not what I expected to find in Saratoga," he said.

Her eyes reached his, and he saw her swallow, but she didn't speak. And he knew what he had to do. Reaching into his back pocket, he withdrew the photograph of Mattie Witt and Lilli Chandler Pembroke in their red-and-white balloon twenty-five years ago.

He handed it to Dani. "My brother sent this to your grandmother's younger sister in Tennessee before he died. It's why I'm here."

Dani stared at her mother's beautiful smile and the gold gate key hanging from her neck. "Zeke…"

He rose, his meal barely touched. "I'm sorry. Take your time. Get your head around this. Talk to your family." He gave her a hint of a smile. "You know where to find me."

"Room 304," she said quietly.

But she was pale and sat frozen in her seat, and Zeke threw down some money on the table and headed out, overhearing people chatting about wine, fresh pasta and horses.

Dani found her father lying on the double bed in the second upstairs bedroom, smoking a cigarette on the soft, worn quilt. He looked wide awake. "It's unsafe to smoke in bed, you know," Dani told him.

"No chance of me falling asleep, I assure you." He sat up, ashes falling down his front, and tossed the half-smoked cigarette in a nearly empty glass of water. "I've stunk up the place, haven't I? If it's any consolation, I don't smoke nearly as much as I used to. It's— Dani…what's wrong?"

She knew she must look awful—pale, drawn, as if she'd

been seeing ghosts, which, in a way, she had. She could have stared all night at the picture Zeke had given her. She'd tucked the picture in her handbag and paid for dinner, and she'd debated running after Zeke and asking him to have that talk now. To get him to tell her everything he knew about her mother, the key. About her grandmother.

She wanted, too, his reassuring presence.

A dangerous man on so many levels, she thought.

She'd gone instead to find her father.

"Nothing's wrong," she told him. "What were you thinking about just now?"

He shrugged, looking awkward. "Myself, your mother. You."

"I guess we could have made things easier on ourselves and each other over the years."

"I guess we could have." He settled back against the pillows, looking older than Dani remembered. He'd always seemed so vibrant, such a devil-may-care scoundrel. "When your mother and I married, I was so thrilled at having extricated myself from the force of Mattie and Nick's legend—even that old cretin Ulysses's—that I never…" He exhaled, shaking his head. "I should have been more sensitive to your mother's need to rebel, perhaps to become something of a legend herself."

"What could you have done?"

"Listened."

"Did she ever try to talk to you?"

He didn't answer at once. Then slowly he shook his head. "What good would it have done? That summer she disappeared—it was just eight months after her mother had died, and I blamed her unhappiness, her restlessness, on Claire's death. I wanted to give her time to grieve, give her space. She didn't talk to me about her troubles, and I didn't ask." He stretched out his bony legs; Dani saw that he had a small hole in the toe of his sock. "So she went to Nick."

"You never guessed he'd put her in *Casino?*"

"I had no idea. None. He said he did it because she was good, but I think he understood her need to go beyond what her mother had done with her life, to take a risk."

"Nick thinks everyone has a capacity for risk. Pop, we can't blame her for her choices or her desires. She had a variety of pressures on her. She did her best." Dani's voice cracked, but she pressed on. "So did we."

John looked at his daughter. "Do you believe that?"

"It's been a long time coming, but, yes, I believe it."

"I wish I knew what happened to her."

"I know, Pop."

He nodded, patting her hand. "I know you do, kid. I like to think an answer—any answer—would be better than not knowing. But it's been so long. Eugene hasn't hired one of his private detectives in years. And we've carried on, you and I." He swung his legs over the edge of the bed. "For a while after the embezzlement and my first experiments with gambling and globe-trotting, I wondered if she might come back. I thought I was becoming more of the kind of man she wanted. A rakehell, a real Pembroke."

"But she didn't come back," Dani said, aware of the twittering of birds in the meadow outside and the sudden chill in the air.

Her father shook his head. "No."

She squeezed his hand, remembering how they used to walk everywhere together in New York, before Eugene Chandler caught him stealing money from him. There was no getting around it; her father had let her grow up without him. And, if she were somehow, miraculously, still alive, so had her mother.

"Pop," she said hoarsely, "I need to show you something."

She handed him the picture Zeke had given her and watched his hand tremble as hers had a short time ago.

"You knew about the key, didn't you?" she asked.

"Dani…"

"It's the same one I found on the rocks—it matches the key to the pavilion at the springs. I think whoever robbed me was after those keys."

Her father's face had paled, grayed, aged; she felt guilty. "Dani, don't do this to yourself."

"And this morning Zeke's room at the inn was tossed—searched, I think, for this photograph. It's why he's here. Pop, his brother had this picture. How? And how did the key end up on the rocks?" She was talking rapidly now, firing off questions, not stopping even to breathe. "How did Mother get it? Who took the picture? How did Joe Cutler get his hands on it?"

He caught her by the wrists and held up her arms so that she had to breathe, and she felt like a little kid in the middle of a tantrum. She tried not to cry. She tried so hard, but still felt the tears hot on her cheeks.

"It's okay, kid."

She fell against her father's chest, bonier than she remembered, smelling of smoke and stale sweat, and he stroked her hair, telling her to shush.

It was too much.

She pulled herself away. "I'm going to find out."

A pained expression crossed his face. "I know."

"Mattie recognized the key?"

He nodded.

"Did she say—"

"I didn't talk to her."

"But Nick did," Dani said, knowing how the three of them—no, she thought, the four of them—operated. Mattie and Nick, their only son, their only granddaughter.

"He didn't tell me anything. Or, I should say, he didn't tell me everything he knows."

She straightened. "I'll call Mattie first, then Nick."

"It won't do any good," her father said, "unless they feel like talking."

"I don't care—"

"Get some rest, Dani. Call them in the morning."

"Pop, the other day when I was robbed, I called Mattie, and she acted strange. She must have remembered the key, but she didn't tell me. And Joe Cutler and Zeke..." Dani ran a hand through her hair, trying to keep the threads of her scattering thoughts together. "They're both from Mattie's hometown."

"Cedar Springs," John said.

Dani stared at him. "You knew?"

"They came north that summer." He wasn't looking at her. "They stopped at my office in New York to find out where Mattie was, and I told them. But I thought Saratoga was too far for them to bother to go, and she never mentioned them to me—for years I assumed they didn't connect."

"You never asked her?"

He shook his head, tapping out another cigarette from a crumpled pack. "Mattie doesn't like to be reminded of Cedar Springs. And Lilli was gone by then. I just didn't think about it."

Dani picked up the photograph from the bed where her father had dropped it. "So Joe Cutler could have taken this himself. He could have—"

But she stopped, unwilling—terrified—of speculating further.

She knew why Zeke was in Saratoga now, today.

He was there to find out if his brother had had anything to do with her mother's disappearance.

"Take a hot bath," her father said. "Let all this settle a bit before you get too far ahead of yourself."

"Pop, if you find out anything," she said, "if you know anything—"

"I'll tell you."

"You promise?"

He tucked his cigarette in his mouth and struck a match, lighting it, polluting the air. Exhaling smoke, he said, "I promise."

She wondered—and expected he did, too—if that promise was as empty as all the others he'd made to her over the years. Or maybe it didn't even matter anymore. Maybe it was just enough that he wanted to keep his promises.

Smoke or no smoke, she kissed him good-night.

"This Cutler character—you're all right with him?"

She smiled. "You bet."

By the time she settled into her hot tub, scented water swirling around her, Dani realized she had no intention of kicking Zeke out of the inn. It wasn't a question of surrendering, although he clearly wasn't going to leave unless he wanted to leave. He'd vacate his room, perhaps, but he wouldn't necessarily vacate the premises. Dani preferred knowing where he was.

She opened Quint Skinner's book to page one and began to read.

Zeke sat on the porch swing of the small Cape Cod house Quint had rented in a middle-class neighborhood about two miles from the center of Saratoga Springs. It was painted sunny yellow and had an herb wreath on the front door and a painted wooden goose tacked up under the porch light. Charming. It was dark out, and the swing creaked. Zeke had been there almost an hour, trying not to think about Dani, thinking about her anyway. She was a woman who could make a man dream again.

He heard a car door shut.

"What the hell are you doing here?"

"I like the herb wreath," Zeke said. "The goose is a nice touch, too."

The Pulitzer Prize–winning ex-soldier climbed the steps and didn't put his gun away until he'd made sure Zeke saw it. It was a Smith & Wesson .38 that fit nicely into the shoulder holster under Skinner's silk jacket.

Zeke gave the swing another little push with his feet. "You have that thing when you robbed Dani Pembroke?"

"Go home, Zeke."

"It amazes me how a man of your limited mental capacity could win a Pulitzer Prize. Of course, that's the only thing you've ever done, isn't it? Tell me, were you tempted to blow Dani away when she came after you with her red high heel?"

Quint leaned against the railing and bent one knee, deliberately casual. There was enough light from the street and nearby houses that Zeke could make out his squinted eyes and blunt, shrapnel-scarred face, and he felt a wave of strong, mixed emotions—anger, envy, compassion. Quint had been with Joe when he died. He'd seen men die because of Joe. He'd served with Joe, had admired him. And he'd watched him transform from a kid from a small southern town who knew right from wrong into, in the end, a man who had betrayed his comrades and himself. In a way, it wasn't Quint Skinner who'd made Joe Cutler, but Joe Cutler who'd made Quint Skinner. The passion and pain of Quint's writing seemed incongruous with the big, red-faced man before Zeke now, a man who'd push a hundred-ten-pound woman across her own bedroom. But that was part of the power and the appeal of *Joe Cutler: One Soldier's Rise and Fall*. It captured the emotions of men too many thought weren't supposed to have any emotions at all.

"What do you want?" Skinner asked.

Windows were opened up and down the street for the

summer's night, and Zeke could hear televisions, dogs barking, the cry of a baby. "You stole the two gate keys, didn't you?"

Quint crossed his arms on his massive chest. "I don't know what you're talking about."

"And you tossed my room this morning. Find anything interesting?"

But he knew Quint wouldn't answer, so he got up from the swing, stretching. He needed sleep. With Pembroke security no doubt on the alert and John Pembroke staying at the little purple cottage, Zeke figured he could skip keeping watch on Dani tonight.

He stood close enough to Quint to see the bulge of his shoulder holster even in the dark. "Did Joe show you the picture of Lilli and Mattie in the hot-air balloon before he died?" His voice was just over a whisper.

Quint's eyes disappeared in the thick, scarred flesh around them. "Joe didn't show me anything."

"Here's what I think," Zeke said. "I think you're in Saratoga to find out what happened to Lilli and pin it on my brother so you can revive your career."

"My career doesn't need reviving. But you go ahead and think what you want to think."

"I'll do that."

He started off the porch, got halfway down when Quint grabbed his arm and pulled him around. His fingers dug in deep, in a grip that probably would have broken Dani's arm. Zeke didn't flinch. He met Quint's gaze dead-on.

"You think you're tough," Quint said in a low voice. "You think you've seen action doing the work you do, but you haven't seen anything. Nothing like what your brother saw." He hissed his words, saliva spraying from his mouth. "You can't make up for Joe. You can't go through what he went through and prove you wouldn't become what he became."

He released Zeke and spun around and made the front door in two long steps. The herb wreath wobbled when he slammed the door shut behind him.

Zeke shook his arm where Quint had had it in his iron grip. He walked out to the sidewalk and headed up the street to where he'd parked his car. The air was cool; he could smell freshly cut grass. Some kid had left his bike in the middle of the sidewalk. He climbed into his car and sat a minute behind the wheel, not moving. He'd underestimated Quint. Not physically. He'd have held his own on that score. But he'd let himself forget Quint's incisiveness.

"You can't make up for Joe."

He stuck the key in the ignition, turned it and pulled out into the neighborhood street, trying not to notice that his hands were shaking.

John Pembroke pushed his way through brush and low-hanging branches on the narrow path from the Pembroke Springs bottling plant through the woods to the steep rock outcropping where Dani had found the gold key.

It was almost dawn, and he'd had to get out of that cottage.

The memories.

The questions.

Lilli.

The estate his great-grandfather had built had changed and yet stayed the same. His daughter obviously had a peculiar talent, a knack for embracing the past without letting it dominate the present or determine her future. But John had half hoped—had told Dani himself—that everything would be so different, so changed, that being there would be easy.

Such was not the case.

"Oh, Lilli," he whispered. "Lilli, Lilli."

He didn't know if Dani had been asleep or not. Didn't stop

in her room to tell her where he was going or leave a note. He just went. His sneakers were soaked with dew and mud, and his face was scratched where switches and branches had slapped him. As a boy, he'd known every inch of these woods.

The path ended. He saw clouds rolling in from the west, encircling the moon. His breath came in ragged gasps. He was too damn old for this nonsense. Pounding through the woods at the crack of dawn. What did he think he was doing?

He hung his toes over the edge of a massive boulder and stared twenty, thirty, fifty hundred feet—whatever it was—down to the trees and rocks below.

His throat caught. *Lilli...*

Compared to Tucson, it was cold out, and damp.

He didn't know how long he stood there. When he finally turned back, he was shivering and crying and the sky had lightened, a light drizzle falling.

Walking along the path, he could feel the wind of forty years ago in his face as he'd played Zorro in these same woods. He loved to check out Ulysses's long-abandoned bottling plant. The old goat had sold mineral water throughout the country, then had tried to capitalize on the new soda market by drawing off and selling the carbonic acid that gave the water its natural sparkling quality. But he'd tired of the enterprise, and the plant fell into bankruptcy, which, given his tendency to overdo everything, had probably saved his springs from extinction. Had saved them for Dani.

John could feel his strength and exuberance, and all the optimism of being a kid and having his life ahead of him, believing still that he could make his dreams come true.

He'd been so confident. A true Pembroke.

He stumbled through a muddy spot and then realized he'd veered off the path. Up ahead, he recognized one of the lamps on the bottling-plant grounds. Keeping his eyes on it, he pushed forward through ferns and undergrowth, never minding the path. If he was right, he'd come out near the pavilion in the clearing just beyond the plant. He could easily pick up the main path back to Dani's cottage from there.

Feeling foolish, he brushed away his tears with the backs of his hands.

He heard a rustling sound behind him. A squirrel? He doubted his daughter would tolerate bears in her woods.

There it was again.

Pressing ahead, he could see the Doric columns of the pavilion. They anchored a Victorian wrought-iron fence, crawling with morning glories and roses that enclosed stone benches and an old marble fountain. Lilli's gold key, John remembered, had been a copy of the key to its gate. He wished he could have seen both keys before they were stolen.

He pictured his wife's exuberant smile as she stood next to his nutty mother in the basket of her balloon. He'd call Mattie in a few hours. Talk to his mother as he'd never talked to her before.

The rustling was right behind him now.

He started to turn and felt himself falling, and then felt the slicing pain.

Eleven

~~~~~~~~~~~~~~~~~~~

Someone knocked on Zeke's door just after seven, waking him. He'd collapsed atop the crazy quilt around one. Pembroke housekeeping had unransacked his room. He wished they hadn't. He might have been able to tell what Quint had been after. Did he know about the blackmail note as well?

"Hang on," he called, rolling off the bed. He pulled on his jeans and shook off the last vestiges of sleep. "Who is it?"

"Ira Bernstein."

So Dani wasn't bluffing about kicking him out. Zeke opened up. "Look—" He stopped instantly, taking in the Pembroke manager's pale face and shaken look. "What's wrong?"

"Dani's father has been found unconscious out near the bottling plant. He's being transported to the hospital by ambulance now."

"Does she know?"

Ira shook his head. "I thought you…"

He thought Zeke could tell her. "Do you know what happened to him?"

"He appears to have stumbled and fallen. He wasn't on the path."

"What's his condition?"

"I don't know."

"Give me three minutes."

"I'll wait out here."

Zeke nodded and shut the door. Outside his window the clouds and dawn drizzle had vanished, leaving in their wake a beautiful blue sky. Guests were already up and at it. He could see a half-dozen doing stretches on the lawn.

He dialed Sam in San Diego. "This thing's getting even uglier."

It was still night on the West Coast, but Sam was clear-headed. "One thing I've learned, the past is never past."

"Find out anything about our boy Quint?"

"He's broke and out of work."

Zeke appreciated Sam's matter-of-fact tone. Sam had never met Quint or Joe and wasn't one to judge people. "I need your help," Zeke said.

"I'll tuck a toothbrush in my backpack and be on my way."

"Thanks."

"What for?"

"He's asleep," Zeke said, as he and Dani stood next to her father's hospital bed.

Dani shook her head, her small, trim body rigid with tension and fear, neither of which, Zeke knew, she would acknowledge. He and Ira had found her throwing things around her kitchen and holding back tears even as she'd cursed her father to the rafters for sneaking out on her. She took the news about her father—Zeke told her the basics, and Ira supplied the details, what few there were—without a word. Ira had stayed at the Pembroke. Zeke had driven her to the hospital. She'd wanted to drive herself, but he'd prevailed.

"He's faking it," she said. She leaned over her father. "Pop, I know you're not asleep."

He didn't answer. He'd just come from the emergency room. His eyes were shut, and there was a grayish cast to his skin, except for the purple and red spots that seemed to seep from the edges of his bandaged head. He'd needed stitches on his forehead and had a bloodied nose where he'd hit a tree when he'd fallen. But Zeke was more interested in the lump at the back of his head. How had it gotten there if he'd pitched forward face-first? If the rain had continued, if he'd tripped before getting to the edge of the woods, if the night watchman hadn't checked the grounds before going off shift…John Pembroke could have been in worse shape than he was now.

"He shouldn't have been out there." Dani stared down at him, managing to look both irritated and terrified. "Pop, you should have gotten some sleep. People do need to sleep, you know."

Zeke touched her arm. "Dani, maybe we should wait outside."

"He's awake, Zeke. He just doesn't want to face me."

Under the circumstances, Zeke wasn't sure he would, either. Her father had no health insurance, but Dani had said she'd sign what she had to sign, write a check, hock the Pembroke—the hospital should concentrate on giving him the care he needed and let her worry about the tab.

Her black eyes were huge and mesmerizing, reminding him of Mattie and Naomi. And their difficult father, for they were Witt eyes. She pulled her arm free. "I give up. I'm going to get some coffee. Pop, no more games when I get back. Stitches or no stitches. I swear I'll dump a glass of ice water on you if you keep this up."

When she was safely down the hall, Zeke said, "She's gone."

John opened his eyes and managed a weak grin. "I knew she wouldn't have the patience to wait me out. Think she'd dump ice water on me?"

Zeke grinned. "I wouldn't doubt her."

"Probably just what I need. I feel like death warmed over." He cleared his throat, adjusting his position in the hospital bed, trying to pull himself up. "How close is my daughter to spinning out of control?"

"Her willpower keeps her under wraps. She's scared, John."

"Yeah. So am I."

Zeke waited for more, but John looked blankly out the window at the hospital parking lot.

Finally Zeke said, "You didn't trip."

John's dark, hurting eyes focused on Zeke, and he said hoarsely, "No."

"Are you up to telling me what happened?"

"Some jackass bonked me on the back of the head."

"Did you get a look at him?"

John snorted. "Before or after I saw stars?"

Zeke straightened, resisting the urge to press and press hard for information. He couldn't tell if the man lacked the energy and focus to explain what had happened due to his injuries, or simply refused to tell Zeke—a stranger with his own agenda—anything.

"Look," Zeke said, "I have no intention of meddling where I'm neither wanted nor needed. You and your daughter can handle your own problems if that's what you want. I'll stay out of your way."

John grabbed his wrist. "No, Zeke."

Zeke was silent, waiting.

"I went out to the rocks where Dani found the gold key. Someone either followed me or more likely was out there, too. If it had been Dani instead of me…" He inhaled, and the terror that had been in his daughter's eyes now was in his. "Maybe she'd have been killed, maybe not."

"I'll go out there and have a look."

"This is your business. You know you won't find anything."

John Pembroke was a gambler and an embezzler and something of a reprobate, but he wasn't a stupid man. Zeke acknowledged the truth of his words. And the hard knot in the pit of his own stomach. He had to pull back. He was getting too close to the Pembrokes and their reckless, personable ways.

The former vice president of Chandler Hotels struggled to sit up. "Get in her way, Zeke," he said, wincing in pain. "Get in her way and stay in it."

Kate Murtagh eyed Zeke from behind an enormous stainless-steel bowl of potato salad in her immaculate kitchen. Her backyard, he'd noticed, was nothing but herb and vegetable gardens. Dressed in overalls, her blond hair tied back with a purple bandanna, she looked gorgeous as she snipped chives with the largest pair of scissors he'd ever seen.

"I know she was here," Zeke said.

"How?"

"Eyewitness."

"What sneak—" She stopped herself, her glower deepening as she realized she'd been had. "You just make a wild guess that she'd come here."

"She didn't take her car, and she wouldn't have waited for a taxi and risked being inundated by reporters who'd heard scoundrel John Pembroke was in Saratoga for the first time since his wife's disappearance. So wherever she went had to be within reasonable walking distance of the hospital. I looked you up in the phone book, checked my chamber of commerce map and voilà."

"So clever. How come you didn't just track her down on the streets like a runaway dog?"

"She had a head start." He'd come out of John's room and found her gone. He hadn't been surprised. She'd already known her father wasn't going to cooperate.

Kate shrugged. "You had wheels."

"She didn't have to look you up."

"Must annoy you having a woman who sells water for a living give you the slip." But Kate set down her scissors, for which Zeke was grateful, and wiped her hands on her plain white apron. She could have been a butcher or a model for *Vogue*. "Is she in bad trouble?"

"That's what I want to find out."

"Word is you can be trusted."

"People either trust me or they don't."

"My father's a Vietnam-combat vet." She stuck the end of a skinny chive in her mouth, her blue eyes riveted on him. "He wouldn't talk to anyone after he came home, couldn't hold down a job for the first few years he was back. I don't think he slept a night through for years. He knows a lot of guys who have their names on the Wall. In my eyes, he was a hero, and he's the best man I've ever known." She threw her chewed chive into a paper bag of potato peels and eggshells. "I'd better be right about you, Cutler."

Zeke said nothing.

"Get out your chamber of commerce map."

He did.

She pointed out the Amtrak station. "Dani's on her way to New York. If you hurry, you'll catch her."

An hour down the Hudson River on the four-hour train ride to New York, Dani made her way to the dining car for coffee. She ordered a large, black. She'd already tried sleeping and had found she couldn't.

She located a quiet spot, sipped her coffee and called Nick on her cell phone.

"Hello? Hello, is someone there?"

"Quit pretending you can't hear me. It's me—Dani. Your

granddaughter. The one you and Mattie have been holding back on for years and years."

"Who? What's that? Who is this?"

"Knock it off, Granddad. You're nowhere near as deaf as you're trying to pretend."

"Dani—is that you?"

"Pop's been injured. Smacked on the head from behind."

Nick was silent.

Her tone softened. "He's going to be okay."

"And you?"

"I'm fine." But she could hear the fatigue in her voice. "Nick, I've read the book on Joe Cutler. He was from Mattie's hometown. Did you know him?"

"How would I know him? He wasn't born when I met your grandmother."

"But he was born when you had your affair with her sister."

He didn't respond.

"It's just a short paragraph in the book. It says Joe worked at the mill Mattie's father owned and became friends with her 'estranged' sister, Naomi Witt Hazen, who'd had an affair with you years after you and Mattie divorced." Dani hesitated. "I'm not judging you. I just want to know…"

"I was fishing near her home," Nick said softly. "I found Naomi floating on her back in the Cumberland River in the same spot where I'd met Mattie. She was just letting the current carry her. I got her ashore. She was covered with bruises, her eyes were as flat and dead as any I've ever seen and…" He sighed. "I took her away. It was so long after Mattie."

"But she went back?"

"Cedar Springs is Naomi's home. She'll die there."

Dani had known Mattie had a sister, but Naomi had never been real to her. She'd been portrayed—albeit passively—as an estranged sister who'd wanted nothing to do with her famous sister and her family. Now the reality seemed so much more complicated. Dani had a great-aunt she'd never met in a small Tennessee town, the same town where the Cutler brothers were from.

"Joe Cutler's younger brother is in Saratoga," she said.

"Go on."

She told her grandfather everything. When she finished, he didn't say a word.

Dani panicked. "Granddad?"

"I haven't kicked off yet," he said in his sarcastic, gravelly voice.

"I just want answers. Is there anything you can tell me that would help?"

"No."

"Is that the truth—"

"Dani…" He gave a small, fake cough. "Ouch…I'm having chest pains."

"Then call a doctor," she said and hung up on him. But she immediately felt guilty and called him back. "I'm sorry, Granddad."

"Just take care of yourself, urchin."

Of course, he sounded fine.

As she made her way back through the train, she spotted Zeke munching on a bag of peanuts in a window seat. The seat next to him was empty. Dani wasn't surprised. Even when he was in a good mood, the man had a grim look about him that didn't invite company.

She leaned over the aisle seat. "All that salt's not good for you."

"I'm from the South," he said. "We're immune to salt."

"Did Kate tell you where I was?"

He smiled innocently but didn't seem to try too hard to be convincing. "Just taking a trip to the Big Apple."

"I won't have you bird-dogging my every move."

His look cut her short. It was dark and serious and bored right through to her soul. "Dani, you don't have to do this alone."

"That's my decision."

He popped a handful of peanuts into his mouth. "Fine. I'll just see you at Mattie's."

Now she was surprised.

His smile seemed genuine, if not innocent. "You're not as difficult to predict as you think you are."

"My coffee's getting cold."

"Then sit down and drink it."

It was her turn to smile. "You aren't as tough as you think you are."

He laughed. "There goes my reputation."

"How's my father?"

"In pain but on the mend. And worried."

She nodded and sat beside him, not because her coffee was getting cold but because she really didn't want to be alone—which unnerved her probably as much as anything else that had happened in the past few days.

"I read the book on your brother," she said.

"I figured as much."

"Zeke…"

He looked at her. "Talk to Mattie first."

Twelve

❧❧❧

Nick didn't bother to pack. These days even picking up an empty suitcase was an effort. But Mattie would have something he could wear. If not, he'd buy what he needed. He was feeling quite flush, having called a Hollywood memorabilia collector he knew. "What would you give me for the dress Mattie Witt wore the same day she arrived in Hollywood?" he asked.

The collector was at his front door within the hour, cash in hand.

Having a reclusive film legend for an ex-wife had its uses.

Now he wouldn't have to beg Mattie or Dani for the money for a plane ticket east. He had his own money. He couldn't believe he hadn't hocked that dress years ago. He wasn't sentimental.

He settled back in the cab, on his way to LAX.

His eyes burned. He knew he was taking a physical risk and might not accomplish a thing beyond hastening his own death by going to New York and then Saratoga. But he couldn't stand to have Dani hate him. He was ninety years old, and nothing he'd accomplished—the movies he'd made, the awards he'd won, the place he'd earned in film history—meant more to him than that spitfire of a granddaughter back East. Didn't she know that?

Yeah, he thought. She knew it. But she was still furious with him.

He'd take the first flight he could get. He'd sit down with Mattie and talk. Tell her everything. Even about the blackmail. Then, if she didn't kill him, he'd take the train up along the Hudson River to Saratoga Springs, just as he and his mother had done so long, long ago, when the world had been a different place and Ulysses Pembroke's black-haired grandson had been filled with dreams.

Both his parents had died young, and Nick, just a kid himself, had fled west to sunny California and fast proved he had a knack for directing movies. But it was a fishing trip to Tennessee that had changed his life.

He'd chosen Tennessee because it was warm and crisscrossed with streams and rivers, and because it was far, far from the social whirl of show business. Lean, dark and charming, Nick had discovered the possibilities of being the grandson of a murdered gambler and a director with growing power. Women had flocked to him. He'd needed a rest.

Determined to be off by himself, he'd told no one his destination. He wanted to be utterly alone and try to remember the man he'd meant to become.

On his third day of fishing east of Nashville on the snaking, slow-moving Cumberland River, he'd startled a dark-haired girl bent over on the riverbank, absolutely still and silent as she'd stared into the water. So complete was her surprise that she'd slipped on the muddy riverbank and slid, without making a sound, all the way into the Cumberland, her blue cotton dress billowing out around her.

Nick had paddled furiously to get to her, then leaped from his canoe into the water. He'd meant to rescue her, but she came up dripping wet and fighting mad, a rock in one hand. She was small and slim and had the most dynamic black eyes he'd ever seen. Her dark hair was yanked back in a severe braid, with wisps, damp from the humidity and the river, escaping all around her hairline.

She'd raised her rock with the clear intention of striking him. "You get away from me."

"Easy there." Nick'd had no desire to return to California with stitches in his head. "I'm sorry—I didn't mean to startle you."

"You're not sorry. You're laughing."

"No!"

But he was, because he'd never seen anyone so beautiful look so mad and so ridiculous. And here they were in the middle of nowhere, not a soul in sight.

"My name's Nick Pembroke," he'd said, studying her for any sign of recognition.

There was none. Apparently she'd never seen any of his films. Nick wasn't insulted. He'd bitten his tongue trying not to laugh lest she knock him on the head with her rock after all.

"I fail to see what's so funny." She hadn't given him a chance to respond, but plunged ahead in her educated Tennessee drawl. "I have been coming out to this river for years and years, and I have never had anyone sneak up on me and scare me half to death."

"I didn't mean to. I was just fishing. What's your name?"

She'd eyed him dubiously, then said politely, "Mattie Witt."

"Pleased to meet you, Miss Witt."

He'd extended his hand, but she didn't take it. Regal even when soaked through to the skin, Mattie had looked very young, and although she was slender, her wet dress clung to some flattering curves. Nick had struggled to keep his gaze from resting too long on the outline of her breasts against the thin, wet fabric. But her eyes, expressive and yet secretive, had enchanted him.

"I saw your last movie at the picture show on the square," she'd said, catching him by surprise.

So she had heard of him, Nick had thought. The picture show.
The square. He couldn't imagine anywhere more remote than
wherever the devil she came from. But his heart was pounding,
and he'd felt as if he'd come all the way from New York to California to Tennessee just to meet dark-eyed Mattie Witt.

"I should let you get back to your fishing," she'd said. "I'll
have to tell my father I slipped from the riverbank out of pure
clumsiness. He wouldn't be pleased to know I was speaking to
a Hollywood movie director."

"Why should he care?"

"It isn't proper. And Hollywood is the devil's playground."

But there was a glint in her eye, perceptible to the observant
Nicholas Pembroke, that suggested to him that she didn't lose
sleep over what was proper and what wasn't or where the devil
played. She'd waded back to the riverbank and climbed gracefully from the water. On dry land, she looked even tinier and yet
surprisingly sexy, an intriguing blend of strength and vulnerability.

"This looks like a good place to fish," Nick had called after
her, feeling a surge of panic that he might never see her again.
"I'll probably be out here every morning."

"Well, sir, you just be careful and mind the snakes."

Snakes?

He'd wondered if she was too naive—too much of a damn
hick—to have gotten his message, but she was back the next
morning, in the same spot where he'd startled her.

"What are you doing?" he'd asked when he again found her
staring into the Cumberland.

"Oh—studying the changes in the river. I've been coming out
here since I was a small child. Some things about it have stayed
the same. Some have changed. Did you catch any fish yesterday?"

"Yes, but I released them."

"Why on earth would you do that?"

"Didn't feel like cleaning and eating them. I like to fish for the sport. If I played tennis, I wouldn't fillet and fry up every opponent who lost to me."

"But those would be human beings. These are fish."

Smiling, Nick had realized there was more to Mattie than big eyes and a fondness for movies, more to his attraction to her than simple lust. "My motive is the same whether I'm fishing or playing tennis—sport, not subsistence."

She didn't get it. He'd asked her where she was from. "Cedar Springs," she'd said. "It's a small town a few miles from here."

The next day she'd brought a picnic lunch in a wicker hamper—enough for two, she'd said, because eating in front of someone was rude. There was fried chicken and pimento cheese and a bag of cold biscuits, with two fat slices of caramel-iced prune cake for dessert. "My mother died a while back," she'd said matter-of-factly, as if her loss wasn't worth considering in comparison to what others suffered. "I cook for my father and younger sister. Naomi's just eleven. I'm eighteen. Where are you from?"

He couldn't get over how beautiful she was, even nibbling on a chicken leg. Her smile dazzled. "I was born in Saratoga Springs and grew up in New York City. Now I live in Beverly Hills."

"My father might care for Yankees even less than he does Hollywood people."

"Well, I'm not a Yankee anymore."

She'd laughed. "Once a Yankee, always a Yankee."

"Are you…" He cleared his throat, exercising caution. "Are you in school?"

"I finished high school last month. I'm to go to a two-year college in Cedar Springs in the fall and study to be a schoolteacher, unless I get married. Father never would let me work and have a family."

Again Nick had sensed an independence beneath the refined surface of Mattie Witt that he'd doubted her father, from the sound of him, would have noticed or, if he had, approved of.

"Do you have any prospects?" Nick had asked.

"For a husband, you mean?" Her dark eyes had sparkled, teasing him, perhaps herself. "Father has prospects for me, I don't."

"What does he do for a living?"

"He owns the Cedar Springs Woolen Mill."

"Would he—do you suppose I could meet him?"

Nick had thought he must have gone mad. Another three days and he'd be back in Beverly Hills planning another movie. Mattie and her black, bottomless eyes would be just a pleasant memory.

Mattie had invited him to dinner the following evening at the Witt home on West Main Street in Cedar Springs. It was a town out of a William Faulkner novel. The house was Greek Revival, shaded by oaks, pecans, magnolias; there were pots of geraniums on the porch.

Jackson Witt was a short, domineering, surprisingly muscular man who read from the Bible before and after dinner. There was no liquor, and Naomi—Mattie's little sister, a slim, tiny girl—wasn't allowed to speak at the dinner table unless she was directly addressed by an elder. All through dinner Nick could hear the grandfather clock ticking in the front parlor. It was the most oppressive sound he'd ever encountered. Mattie, for whom this life was normal, would catch his eye and smile. Her world—wherever it was—wasn't in that house on West Main. It was as if nothing her father said or did could touch her where she really lived.

"My daughter has informed me you're from California," Jackson Witt had said after dinner, while Mattie helped the maid—who hadn't spoken another word to him—clear the table and prepare coffee. "I trust you have no part of the movie industry."

Nick had coughed to cover his discomfort. Hadn't Mattie warned him?

"Hollywood is corrupting the children and young people of this great country. For next to nothing they can see behavior and clothing not tolerated in polite company." He'd fastened his gleaming black eyes on his guest; the clock had seemed to tick ever louder. "These Hollywood stars aren't proper examples for our children. Their immoral acts are played up in newspapers and magazines all across the country. Divorces, wild parties, illicit liaisons, extravagant spending. It seems there's a new scandal every day."

In the Witt household, Nick had already gathered, anything undertaken purely for pleasure was considered suspect, an opening for the devil.

"In my view," Jackson Witt went on, apparently assuming his guest agreed with his every word and that "his view" was the only right one, "these people have betrayed the public trust. They should be called to account. They are corrupt. As a business leader in this community, I strive to hold myself and my family to a higher standard."

"I can see that," Nick had said and tried to smile. He'd just wanted to get out of there. Forget Mattie and her beautiful black eyes. Her fanatical daddy was her headache.

"We're simple people in Cedar Springs. Yet even out here we can't escape the sins and sinners of the movie screen."

Since one of those sinners was sitting in his living room, Nick couldn't argue with the man.

When his older daughter had reappeared with a silver tray of coffee and something she called chess pie, Jackson Witt had changed the subject. The moral corruption of American society wasn't a topic for discussion in front of ladies, at least according to his scheme of the world. Nick'd had a feeling Mattie could argue circles around her father. He'd also have bet the old buzzard didn't know she and her little sister had been to the picture show on the square.

"I understand you're an engineer," Witt had said.

Nick nearly choked on his pie, which was smooth and ultra-sweet. He'd looked at Mattie, but she'd shown no sign of embarrassment. Her hand wasn't even trembling as she'd handed over a china cup and saucer. There was an intense, compelling serenity about her, and Nick had found himself wondering how it would translate on-screen.

"I would say so," he'd replied with a smile.

"Mattie tells me your daddy's in the hydroelectric business," Jackson Witt said.

"My father's dead, I'm afraid."

Witt nodded thoughtfully. "He's gone to a better life then."

That was what Nick believed, too, but the way Witt said it had made his skin crawl. He'd sipped his coffee, then set it and his empty pie plate back on the tray. "He wasn't in the power business."

"Oh, he wasn't. May I ask what his business was?"

Mattie gave no indication she was anything but fascinated by Nick's every word. He'd bet she knew just what his father's business had been. Sensing her seething soul, Nick wanted to jump up and grab her, shake her until she promised she would get out of this nuthouse.

"Gambling," he said, suddenly feeling reckless and malicious. "Like his father before him. A penchant for gambling runs in the family."

Witt had remained rigidly seated in his high-backed chair. "You said your name was Pembroke."

"That's right, Nicholas Pembroke."

The older man's eyes became tiny pieces of black coal, fierce and intense. "Your grandfather was Ulysses Pembroke." Jackson Witt's voice was high and hoarse with indignation. Without looking at his daughter, he'd said, "Mattie, this man has misrepresented himself to you. Please leave the room."

She'd obeyed silently, but moved with such grace and steadiness that Nick instinctively knew she'd hoped this confrontation would happen—her secret Hollywood friend would shock and horrify her father and perhaps even help set her free someday.

"Ulysses Pembroke was a thief and a profligate," Witt said, "and you are his grandson."

"Yep." Nick was on his feet. "And I make movies for a living."

He'd left before Jackson Witt could throw him out.

The next morning Nick had returned to the bend in the river, assuming Mattie wouldn't be within miles. He'd behaved badly, no matter that her father was a rigid fanatic who justified his cruelty to his daughter through a corruption of his religious principles. Nevertheless, Nick had felt he had no right to judge another man's beliefs. But he'd thought of the lost dark-eyed girl he'd met on the Cumberland. What kind of life could Mattie and her younger sister hope to have with such a father?

The canoe had rocked silently in the water, insects humming nearby. His life back in California suddenly had seemed enormously empty. He made movies. He bedded women. He went to parties. Every day was something new, and yet the same. To what end? Where would he be in another ten years? Another thirty?

"Nicholas."

Her voice was so soft and melodic he'd thought he must have imagined it. He'd opened his eyes but hadn't wanted to look, to have his hopes dashed.

Mattie had stood on the riverbank in a simple yellow broadcloth dress, a battered upholstered valise banging against her knees. Her dark hair was brushed out, hanging down her back, catching the morning sun. Nick had never seen eyes so huge and black.

"I want to go to California with you," she'd said calmly. "Some of the best people I know are in Cedar Springs, but I can't stay here."

Nick hadn't been able to speak. Jackson Witt would have the law after him. He'd be arrested before he could get to the train station in Nashville.

"I have money," she'd said.

"Mattie." Nick had been so overcome he'd feared he'd pitch headfirst from the canoe. "Mattie, you can't."

Her knuckles had whitened on the handle of the valise. "I can and I will."

"Your father—"

"I have no father."

"You don't mean that."

"He does. He disowned me this morning when I told him what I mean to do." She'd spoken without drama or self-pity. "He won't change his mind."

"But your sister…"

Her eyes had gone flat with unarticulated pain. "Naomi has her own life to live."

"What is it you mean to do?"

She hadn't hesitated. "I mean to become someone else."

They'd married on the train west.

Mattie had made her debut the following year in *The Gamblers*. Based on a romanticized version of Ulysses Pembroke's life, it was a film that launched her career, secured Nick's reputation as a director and turned his grandfather into one of the great American rakes.

Mattie had continued to work hard. She was popular with her

colleagues. Invariably gracious, she never spoke ill of anyone and engendered remarkably little envy. Her one failing—if it could be called that—was a profound reluctance to speak to reporters. She was a private person and never discussed her past with anyone, but her reticence had only added to her aura of mystery.

Shortly before starting work on *Tiger's Eye,* her second movie, Nick had brought up the touchy subject of her sister, something he'd usually avoided. "Why don't we have her out here for a visit."

"She won't come."

"Sure she will. Come on, Mattie, your dad can't stay mad forever."

"He isn't mad. He's disowned me completely. It's as if I never existed. Naomi—" Mattie's eyes had shone with tears, but not one spilled. "I asked her to come with me. I begged her to get away from him before he destroyed her, but she wouldn't. Nick, am I a bad person for having left her?"

She'd always seemed so sure of herself that her uncertainty had caught Nick by surprise. "No—no, Mattie, no. You had to leave."

"I could have stayed. I could have found a way to make a life for myself. Naomi stayed. She doesn't remember Mother as well as I do. Mother had her peculiarities, but she wasn't as rigid as Father. They were happy together in their own way. Father will never be happy with Naomi or me." She looked away from Nick; she still hadn't cried. "I know there's nothing I can do, but still I think about my sister every day."

Nick had offered to go to Cedar Springs and have it out with Jackson Witt, cart Naomi off himself. The kid would be better off living with her big sister in California than with that sour old bastard in Tennessee. But, claiming it would be useless to apply force, that Naomi knew the invitation to California stood,

Mattie had refused Nick's offer to intervene. Eventually she could no longer bear to talk about Cedar Springs and the father and sister she'd left behind.

After she and Nick had a son, the gossip pages carried pictures of the happy Pembroke family. Given Jackson Witt's lurid interest in Hollywood's goings-on, Nick had assumed his father-in-law had known he had a grandson. There was no note of congratulations, no softening of the old man's hard heart, nothing from the much-missed little sister. Nick had felt like crying every time his wife returned empty-handed and white-faced from the postbox in the weeks after their son's birth.

Their relationship was honest and fulfilling, and he had remained faithful to her for four full years. The temptations came on a daily basis. Not long after Mattie had arrived in California, she'd laughingly told Nick she'd learned most of the stories about her husband's sexual adventures were true, but she'd claimed to believe in the transforming power of love and expected that meeting her—marrying her, having a child together—had changed Nick forever. And it had. But it hadn't changed his wandering eye.

His first affair occurred on an August trip to Saratoga Springs while Mattie stayed in their Beverly Hills home to play with their baby and take unnecessary singing lessons. She'd never have to sing in any of her films. Being back in Saratoga had proved more than Nick could handle. The money flowed, and the temptations abounded. He'd lost a bundle, and as he'd driven past the abandoned estate he still owned, he remembered his promise to his mother. No gambling, no turning out like his father and grandfather.

Guilt had undercut his elation at winning at the track, and yet that night, unable to stop himself, he went to a private lakehouse gambling parlor. An attractive woman in her forties taught him poker, then invited him back to her room. He said yes.

Mattie found out through a mutual acquaintance. There was always someone, Nick had discovered, willing to bear bad news. He'd admitted everything. At first it was unclear whether the zest for gambling he'd just revealed bothered her more than his infidelity, but then she'd let him know in no uncertain terms that in her view, gambling and infidelity were part and parcel of the same basic corruption. Nick had tried to explain that he had no intention of self-destructing like his grandfather, that the woman had been nothing at all like her, just a stupid fling, he couldn't even remember her name. That only seemed to enrage her more.

"I had no idea monogamy meant so much to you," he'd said, stung by her anger.

"Does it mean nothing to you?"

As far as his heart was concerned, he was uncompromisingly monogamous. Mattie was the only woman he truly loved.

She'd left him after his second meaningless affair, but came back. After the third she stayed away six months. They'd begun to argue. Less the polite, repressed daughter of Jackson Witt, Mattie had learned to hold her own in a good fight. After her husband's fourth affair, she'd moved out for good. She finished the movie she was working on, announced her "retirement" and headed to New York. She and Nick were divorced. Mattie was thirty years old. Everybody—especially Nick—had believed she'd come back to Hollywood once she cooled down.

She never did.

Nick had accused her of being as hard-hearted and unforgiving as her father, igniting another of their by then legendary fights. And yet, even as she'd bought a town house in Greenwich Village and enrolled their son in school, he'd remained hopelessly and forever in love with her. He'd look back on his repeated affairs in despairing wonder. None of the women he'd slept with meant anything to him, nor he to them. So why had he indulged in affairs?

"I hope you find what you want in life," Mattie had told him in one of her more charitable moments.

Too late, he had.

What he wanted—all he wanted—was the dark-eyed girl he'd found gazing at the Cumberland on a warm, quiet Tennessee morning.

But as his cab arrived at the busy Los Angeles airport, Nick pulled himself out of the past. He couldn't undo his mistakes. What he could do, he thought, was to try to save his son and his granddaughter from them.

Thirteen

A lively discussion of the ailing Yankees had been going on for the past hour on Mattie's front stoop. She was right in the midst of it, fiddling with one of her handmade kites as she maintained that pitching was to blame for the team's latest ills. Not that she knew a thing about baseball. From argument over the years, however, she'd learned that a cry for more pitching was generally a creditable position to take.

She only half listened to the debate. A cab had turned down her street and slowed in front of her town house.

Before it came to a full stop, Dani jumped out.

Mattie quietly asked everyone on her front stoop to leave.

They complied. Nick had called a little while ago. She knew their son was now in the hospital in Saratoga.

A dark-haired man who had to be Zeke Cutler climbed out of the cab after Dani. He looked like his father, whom Mattie had known as a little boy. And like Joe. Naomi must have sent him, she thought.

Their eyes met. He was definitely a Cutler, and Zeke was the only Cutler left.

He came up onto the sidewalk. "It's good to see you, Miss Witt," he said.

"Hello, Zeke."

Dani stiffened visibly. "So you do know him."

Zeke looked at her, and Mattie instantly felt his attraction to his granddaughter. "I'll leave you two alone to talk," he said.

To talk, Mattie thought. Of course. She'd have to tell Dani everything.

"No. Don't leave." Mattie set her kite down. "This concerns you, too, Zeke. Come inside. Both of you."

Her front room was cool, the ceiling fan whirring, and she served fresh-squeezed lemonade she'd bought from a small grocery around the corner and a few butter cookies she pulled from the freezer and let thaw on a plate. Zeke sat on the couch. Dani sat across from him. There was one other chair, but it was uncomfortable, and Mattie had no intention of going through this ordeal on an uncomfortable chair. She sat next to Zeke on the couch.

"How's John?" she asked.

There was a moment's silence as Dani and Zeke exchanged glances, obviously debating who was supposed to answer. Finally Zeke said, "He's doing fine."

"It was an accident?"

"He told the doctors he tripped and fell."

Mattie suspected he'd told Zeke more. But Dani blurted, "Which isn't true."

"I see," Mattie said, setting down her lemonade glass, untouched. "John doesn't know anything of what I'm about to tell you. I didn't want him to have to be in the position of holding back from his own daughter...." She inhaled deeply through her nose, just wanting this done. "I thought this information was no one's business but my own."

Dani didn't say a word. That concerned Mattie, since her granddaughter had always been one to speak her mind.

"Zeke and his brother, Joe, came to see me in Saratoga about a week before Lilli disappeared. I gave them an old tent and let them camp out on the grounds—they chose a spot near the bottling plant, which of course was abandoned in those days." She looked at Zeke. "You were what, thirteen or fourteen?"

"Thirteen."

"And Joe was eighteen. I remember that."

The room was so silent. She wished she'd turned on the radio in the kitchen or even had a grandfather clock, although she'd refused to have one in her house since leaving Cedar Springs. A ticking clock always reminded her of her father's oppressive home. But the silence now was awful.

"He thought you were something," Zeke said gently.

Mattie smiled, appreciating his gesture. "I'm afraid I wasn't the glamorous movie star he expected to find. I dressed in Nick's old clothes half the time, I said and did as I pleased—and I wasn't as young as the woman he'd seen in the movies. Then again, maybe he wasn't expecting Mattie Witt the film star. Maybe he was expecting Jackson Witt's older daughter, I don't know. But what he got was me." She waved a hand. "Well, none of that matters. Joe was a tolerant young man."

"Why did he come see you?" Dani asked.

"I'm getting to that. I want…" She swallowed, twisting her hands together in her lap. "I want to tell everything. Not long after Joe and Zeke arrived, Lilli came up to the cottage while they were there. I introduced them. There was an instant rapport between Joe and Lilli—nothing romantic. Lilli was confused about what her life was supposed to be, what she wanted it to be. When her mother died, her whole world came apart. She didn't know if she wanted to be what she'd seemed destined to be. Joe understood. He helped her get some distance from herself and her problems—he encouraged her to see not just the obligations and responsibilities and restrictions of her life, but also its joys and meaning."

Mattie paused. Dani stared at the fireplace, her eyes shining. Zeke watched her, and Mattie wondered if he knew how close her granddaughter was to crying. She hid her vulnerabilities so well. But so did her grandmother.

"Did he know about *Casino?*" Dani asked without looking at her.

"Yes."

"Did you?" she asked, her dark eyes on Zeke.

Mattie looked at him, too, and he answered, "No."

"When Joe found the gold key out at the pavilion near the old bottling plant," Mattie went on, "he decided to give it to Lilli. He could have kept it for himself, but he didn't think that was right."

"And she wore it ballooning with you," Dani said.

"That's right. She had it with her when we landed. Our trip took longer than she'd anticipated. We got a ride to the Pembroke estate, and I offered to drive her back to North Broadway, but she insisted on walking. She was already late. Why fret about a few more minutes?" Mattie's voice cracked, and she had to fight off tears herself. It wasn't easy. "I never saw her again."

Dani's hands, she noticed, were twisted together, shaking. Beside her on the couch, Zeke impassively sipped his iced lemonade. Yet Mattie sensed his anguish.

She forced herself to continue. "Before I realized she'd disappeared, I felt quite smug. I'd thought Lilli needed to give her father a good jolt, remind her family not to take her for granted. I remember every detail of that night. I took a bath and put on baggy jeans and one of Nick's old sweaters—it came to my knees. It was cool, and I lit a fire." She sighed. "Then Joe knocked on my door."

"What time was that?" Dani asked.

Still no eye contact, Mattie said, "Around ten o'clock."

"We'd decided to leave Saratoga," Zeke added.

"Why?"

"Because Joe said so."

Mattie shot him a look, sensing there was more. Her heart pounded. Did Zeke know something she didn't? But he didn't continue, and she had to get this next part done. "I knew he'd come to tell me why he'd traveled a thousand miles to see me. There had to be a reason." She shut her eyes, feeling the tears hot against her lids. "He told me my father was dying of cancer. He'd been to see Doc Hiram—I knew him when he was a little boy—and he said the cancer was all through him. So I asked Joe—" Her voice broke, and she didn't think she'd be able to go on.

Zeke placed his hand over hers. He didn't squeeze or pat, just left it there. "You asked Joe if your father had sent him."

She nodded, blinking back tears. She hadn't cried because of her father in years. Decades. Even before she'd left Cedar Springs, she hadn't permitted him to make her cry. "He hadn't. He was an old man and dying, and still as far as he was concerned, I had never been his daughter. It wasn't even as if I'd died at eighteen. It was as if I'd never lived at all. I was a stranger to him."

"Your sister sent him?" Dani asked. Her voice was carefully controlled. She hadn't moved. If she did, Mattie thought, she'd shoot up like a too tightly coiled spring.

"No. No, Naomi didn't send him. It was Joe's idea to come. He said he owed Naomi because she'd been a friend to him and Zeke, encouraged Zeke in his studies. He—Joe said his brother wanted to become a doctor."

Dani's eyes met Zeke's, just for an instant. Then they were back on the fireplace.

"Naomi had my address here in New York," Mattie said. But she didn't care to explain the rest, how she'd tried through the years to get her sister to join her, first in California, then in New

York. Her letters home were returned unopened, presumably but not necessarily by their father, and then Mattie heard her sister had married Wesley Hazen, a vice president at the mill, and finally gave up. A few years later Nick went to Tennessee, and he and Naomi had had their affair, and Mattie had tried one more letter. Naomi had sent back a postcard. *You can relax now, Mattie,* she'd written. *I'm free.*

"She told Zeke he was wasting his time because I'd never return to Cedar Springs." The tears had vanished, and Mattie sniffled, removing her hand from under Zeke's. She went on in a strong, clear voice. "She was right. As I stood there talking to Joe, I knew that if I didn't go home soon, I'd never see my father again. That chance would be gone forever. At first I didn't know what to do. For years when I'd think of home, it seemed as if nothing should have changed since I'd left. If I went back, I'd still be eighteen, Naomi would be eleven, and our father would still be strong and unyielding. But he was dying, and I knew I'd never be able to step back into Cedar Springs—into my childhood—as it had been. Everything had changed after all. Time hadn't stopped. I'd left home at eighteen and had never gone back."

Dani, she saw, was staring at her with her wide, black eyes as if seeing her for the first time.

Mattie didn't have it in her heart to feel guilty. "I thought leaving home would make everything perfect, and of course it didn't. But it made living possible."

She paused, again aware of the silence. Even in the distance—and here they were in the city—she couldn't hear the wail of a siren or the honking of cabs.

"I know I must sound heartless—I don't expect anyone to understand. But Cedar Springs is quicksand for me. If I'd gone back to see my dying father, I'd never have extricated myself again. I'd have suffocated. So I told Joe to say hello to Naomi for me, to tell her I'd missed her. And I told him to tell my father—if he'd listen—that I'd never judged him. That I'd always loved him in my own way. And I did. And do." She didn't know if Dani or even if Zeke beside her heard her last words. She added, "I wrote and I tried to call, but the letters were returned and he refused to take my calls."

"Joe wanted to make things right between you and your father and Naomi," Zeke said. "He just couldn't understand what had gone wrong and stayed wrong between you. It didn't make any sense to him that a father would disown two daughters. Do you wish we'd never come?"

She shook her head. "No. Never. Joe wrote to me after he enlisted. He sent me a copy of my father's obituary—and the photograph of Lilli and me in the balloon." It was her turn to touch Zeke's hand. "I came to care about him a great deal. I'm sorry about what happened to him."

Zeke nodded but said nothing.

Dani jumped to her feet, almost didn't land before she started to pace. "So you know about Quint Skinner's book?"

"I read it in one sitting at the New York Public Library when it came out. I refused to have such a book in my house."

"Did you believe what it said about Joe?"

"It doesn't matter what I or anyone else believes. It only matters what Joe was. To me, he was a friend."

But that answer didn't satisfy Dani, and she continued to pace, her arms crossed tightly over her chest. Zeke stretched out his long legs, watching her without comment. Her volatility didn't seem to bother him in the least.

"And until this week I'd never even heard of him."

Mattie leaned back against the soft cushions of the couch. "Darling, I was in my forties when you were born," she said, hearing the rhythms of her southern upbringing in her voice. "In my fifties when Lilli disappeared and Joe was killed. I'm eighty-two now. I've had many years to develop the habit of not talking about certain parts of my life. I don't like to think of myself as keeping secrets, but simply as keeping my silence."

"Maybe," Dani said, "if you'd told someone about Joe Cutler twenty-five years ago, before he was killed—" But she stopped herself. "I'm going to do everything I can to get to the bottom of whatever's going on. I don't run away from my problems."

Mattie was stung by her granddaughter's anger, but she understood it. She said quietly, "Be glad you've never faced a problem that left you no choice but to run."

Without replying, Dani banged out of her grandmother's town house.

Zeke stayed put. "Are you all right?" he asked.

Mattie nodded. "I knew I'd have to face this day at some point. It's better off behind us."

"You told her everything you know?"

"Yes." She studied him, sitting so stolidly beside her in the cool, dim room. "But there's more, isn't there?"

He was on his feet.

"Zeke—"

Stopping in the doorway, he turned to her. "I'm also used to keeping my silence. You'll be okay here?"

"I always have been."

She let him go to her granddaughter, which, she thought, was as it should be.

Now that he knew he'd live, John was chafing to get out of bed. It was late afternoon, and two nurses had just finished picking and poking at him. He was sitting up cursing the entire medical profession when his father-in-law strode into his hospital room.

"What," John said, "no roses?"

Eugene Chandler sniffed. "The police say it's a wonder you were found. You could have died out there."

"Well, the Pembroke luck will kick in at the oddest times. Never when I'm calling a bluff, of course. I haven't called a bluff in ten years but my opponent's holding a straight flush."

"I've never been more wrong about anyone in my life than I was about you. You're every bit your father's son."

John shrugged. "Some things in life are just givens. Roger's done a better job for Chandler Hotels than I ever could."

"Perhaps."

And John saw—or, more accurately, let himself see—the disappointment in Eugene's eyes, and he remembered the affection they'd had for each other, even after Lilli had disappeared. They'd seen in the other what they'd wanted to see in themselves. Overlooking Eugene's rigidity, John instead had focused on his father-in-law's pride and sense of honor and duty. Eugene had seen in him an engaging personality and determination and energy, the same qualities that so frustrated him in Dani. With his own daughters, he'd believed their hopes and dreams would be determined for them simply by having been born Chandler women, rich and privileged, their roles set for them.

Eugene ran a trembling hand through his thin white hair. "John...what's going on?"

"I fell in the woods."

"You know what I'm talking about. One thing after another's been happening. Danielle's cottage is robbed. She decides to join us on Friday and turns up at the track yesterday. You're here. I also understand a private security consultant has been seen with her."

"Zeke Cutler."

There was a flicker of recognition. John let it pass. No doubt the legions of Eugene's private detectives had checked out the Cutler brothers. Eugene did like to play his cards close to his vest. He said scathingly, "Next it'll be Mattie and Nick."

"Nah. They're getting too old to tramp over the countryside."

"I wouldn't place a wager on that if I were you."

John grinned. "You know, Eugene, I've never met anyone more capable than you of slicing someone into ribbons without getting a drop of blood on his hands."

Color rose in his pale, dry cheeks. "I didn't mean to be insulting—"

"Yeah, you did."

Eugene clamped his mouth shut.

"You're worried about Dani," John said. The levity had gone from his tone, and he realized his head was throbbing.

"It would be a tragedy if…" He lifted his bony shoulders, letting John finish his thought. He'd already been caught once at being slyly derogatory.

"If she ended up like me and Nick, you mean."

Eugene pursed his lips. "It's not just recent events that have us—Sara and Roger and me—worried, although clearly they do. We are also deeply concerned that Danielle has overextended herself in business. Naturally we know nothing of the particulars of her affairs, but we've heard talk."

"You could advise her," John said.

His father-in-law smirked, incredulous. "And get my advice shoved right back down my throat? Thank you, no. If Danielle wants my advice, she can ask for it. I'd be glad to help her in any way I'm able."

"Does she know that?"

"If she doesn't, she's more stubborn and idiotic than even I think." Surprisingly, there was no condemnation in his tone. But John had never understood his father-in-law's relationship with Dani. It had been a complicated mess since the word go. Eugene straightened, inhaling through his nose. "Well, I just wanted to see how you were doing. If there's anything I can do—"

"Thanks, and no, there isn't, except to be a friend to my daughter."

He looked away. "She doesn't make that very easy, I'm afraid." Then he added formally, "A speedy recovery to you, John."

When his father-in-law retreated, stiff-backed as ever, John found himself pitying the repressed old fart. He and Lilli—and Dani—could have been a part of a happy old age for Eugene Chandler. But he'd made one mistake too many with his granddaughter, and Lilli had been gone a long time, and John couldn't even remember how to tie a tie, it'd been so many years.

Then a well-dressed, solidly built man walked into his room. "Hello, Mr. Pembroke," he said, putting out his hand. "I'm Sam Lincoln Jones. Zeke Cutler asked me to look in on you."

John shook the man's hand. There seemed to be no other choice. "To look in on me," he said, "or to watch me?"

Jones smiled. "Either way, I'm here."

Fourteen

Dani had her freezer door open, her tiny galley kitchen enough to keep Kate Murtagh awake nights. But it was charming and functional, just like the rest of her small apartment in the large prewar building across from her grandmother.

There was no food whatsoever in the freezer, just a near-empty pint of ice cream and some pathetic-looking ice cubes. She was suddenly hungry, still shaking from the ordeal with Mattie. She'd never seen her grandmother so subdued, so unsettled.

Zeke came in behind her. He had caught up with her in the courtyard and followed her up the elevator, but she'd dashed ahead of him into her apartment, leaving the door open. Part of her wanted to be alone, and another part wanted him there.

He peeked into the freezer. "Grim."

"I haven't been around much. I was down last week, but I ate out—I had wall-to-wall meetings." She shut the freezer and said hopefully, "But I have cans."

"Let me," Zeke said and smiled. "I'm good with cans. Take a break, Dani. You've had a lot thrown at you today."

"I'm fine."

"I know. But take a break anyway."

She smiled back at him. "Are you telling me what to do?"

"Wouldn't dream of it. I'm just offering to fix us something to eat, and it just so happens there isn't room for two in your kitchen."

"There is—"

"Not the way I cook. And since I am cooking—" He took her by the shoulders and maneuvered her out of his way.

Still feeling his strong hands on her, Dani went through the small living room—it had just enough space for bookshelves, a television and an overstuffed chair—and down a short hall to the bathroom. It wasn't an elegant apartment. She kept furnishings comfortable and simple: antique quilts on the bed, hand-woven cotton rugs on the hardwood floors, a blue-painted country pine table in what passed for a dining area. Whatever bent toward elegance she had was served by the Pembroke.

She splashed her face with cold water at the pedestal sink. Water dripping, she stared at her reflection. She looked bleary-eyed and stressed out. "Ingrate," she told herself. What right did she have to judge Mattie? Even to pretend to judge Mattie? She regretted her anger. She could yell at Nick and her father—they yelled right back. But she couldn't yell at Mattie. She was different. Always had been.

She dried her face, dabbed on lipstick and headed back to the kitchen.

It was disconcerting to see Zeke there. This was her space, and she wasn't used to having a man like him there. Or, these days, a man at all. He'd pulled out a bag of dried pasta, an onion, cans of tuna, tomatoes and tomato sauce, jars of herbs. He had a pot of water coming to a boil on her little gas stove and half the onion cooking in a frying pan and was rummaging in drawers. In a moment he emerged victorious with her handheld can opener. He said, "Everything's up to date in the Pembroke kitchen, I see."

"Space is a premium."

"Yes, I've noticed."

He opened the three cans, drained the tuna and the tomatoes into the sink, checked the onion. "You wouldn't have a bottle of wine squirreled away here somewhere, would you?"

She pointed to the wooden wine rack on top of the refrigerator, and he pulled down a bottle of chardonnay she'd forgotten she had. He went back to the same drawer where he'd produced the can opener and got out her corkscrew. Dani quickly set the table while he opened the wine.

She sat down and looked at the pigeon outside her casement window. "I have a lot of questions."

"It's your nature."

"And you think you know my nature, do you?"

"In my business," he said, filling her wineglass at the table, "you have to learn to size up people fast. Not the nuances of who they are, just the bare bones. You're honest and open by nature and very direct—some would say blunt. You make a lot of demands on yourself and the people closest to you, even if you're incredibly tolerant in general and—again in general—a lot of fun to be around."

She looked at him, dubious. "You figured all that out just since Thursday."

"Yep."

"No way. You've just been talking to Kate."

The humor in his dark eyes made her want to smile, in spite of everything. "Nope."

"Ira."

Zeke filled his wineglass. "Well, he is indiscreet, but no, I've just been observing you."

Dani tried her wine, which was smooth and very dry. "My father." From Zeke's look, she knew she was right. "He just thinks I'm hard on him. Any other daughter would have let him rot. Me, I put him up for the night, and he repays me by sneaking off at the crack of dawn—"

"He says he shouldn't have to check in with his own daughter. He's not in junior high."

She snorted. "He might as well be."

"You see? You've got that hard-nosed Witt streak."

Sipping her wine, Dani studied the man dumping pasta into the boiling water. Could she size up the bare bones of Zeke's character? He had a sense of his own limits. A sense of duty and honor. A sense of humor. But those were guesses. There was so much about him she didn't know. So much she wanted to know.

"You know my great-aunt," she said.

He nodded, giving the pasta a quick stir. He'd already dumped the tuna and tomatoes and tomato sauce into the frying pan with the onion; she'd missed that. He stirred the sauce, too. "I've known Naomi Hazen all my life."

She was real to him, a person. "I hardly even knew she existed—and I didn't know about the affair she and Nick had."

"It happened even before you were born. If you were Mattie, is it something you'd tell your only grandchild?"

"That's a fair point," Dani conceded. She watched Zeke take a dish towel by the ends and lift the bubbling pot, then empty the pasta into a colander in the sink. She lost his face in the steam. She asked, "What's Cedar Springs like?"

He set the empty pot on the stove, not answering.

"I don't mean to pry…"

"No, it's okay." He walked over to the table and picked up the two plates, taking them back to the counter. With a slotted spoon he scooped out the spirals of pasta onto the plates. "I just don't think about Cedar Springs every day, and I haven't lived there in a long time. I guess it's pretty much an ordinary middle Tennessee town. It's got oak-lined streets, magnolias, dogwoods, a slew of churches, good people, bad people. It's changed since your grandmother was a kid. I barely recognize it these days myself."

"Is the house Mattie grew up in still standing?"

He spooned sauce over the pasta and brought the plates over to the table, setting one in front of Dani. "I suppose I should have picked a few flowers on my way in."

She smiled. "Not around here. Too many stray dogs."

Sitting opposite her, the pigeons fluttering at the window, he drank more wine. "Yes, the Witt house is still standing. It used to be the fanciest house in Cedar Springs, and Jackson Witt was about as rich a man as any of us could imagine. But he wasn't rich at all. Well off, but not rich—not by Chandler standards." He shrugged. "I reckon the Witt house hasn't changed a bit since he built it."

His southern accent had become more noticeable, whether deliberately or unconsciously Dani didn't know. She tried to picture an oak-lined street and a fine old southern house, but she knew the image in her mind was mixed up with fantasy and stereotypes and probably wasn't accurate at all. She'd never even been to Tennessee. "Mattie's never told me much about her childhood."

"I don't blame her," Zeke said.

"I don't, either—"

"Yeah, you do."

It wasn't an accusation but a simple statement of fact.

She tried the pasta. It was surprisingly good. "I'm trying not to."

"Mattie and Naomi had a tough childhood. They had money, which a lot of people in those days didn't, but their mother died when Mattie was eight and Naomi just a tot, and their father wasn't fit to raise two little girls by himself. He was a complicated, difficult man. But the Witts did a lot for Cedar Springs. They started the woolen mill to give people work, planted trees, paved streets, donated land for a public library, kept their church going."

"Then he wasn't a total bastard," Dani said.

Zeke shook his head. "Maybe it would have been easier if he had been. Dani, Jackson Witt was the most unforgiving man I've ever known. He was deeply religious, but he missed or plain didn't get the lessons on forgiveness. His expectations of other people—especially his own children—were unrealistic. He demanded Mattie and Naomi fit his ideal of feminine perfection—subservient, obedient, soft-spoken, religious, industrious within very proscribed limits of acceptable work."

Dani shuddered, trying to imagine her grandmother living under such conditions.

"He forbade them to wear pants or cosmetics or fix their hair in ways he considered inappropriate, never mind offensive. They couldn't dance, play games, ride bicycles, read popular novels. He despised movies. Anything they did for fun was done behind his back. They were supposed to be an example to the rest of the town, proof of his own holiness, I suppose. It's one thing to live a puritanical life out of choice and conviction, to teach your personal values and principles to your children. But he crossed the line into psychological abuse."

"You're a lot younger than Mattie and Naomi. How do you know all this stuff?"

"Everyone in Cedar Springs knew."

"So if they were to have lives of their own, they had either to believe in their father's rules or break them."

Zeke nodded. "There was no middle ground."

"But it still must have been hard for Mattie to leave."

"With the particular kind of abuse her father dished out," Zeke said, staring into his wine, "she had to have suffered enormous guilt. Add to that leaving a little sister behind. Naomi was just eleven when Mattie took off with Nick. It's been rumored around town for years that she tried to get Naomi to go with her, but she wouldn't leave. Anyway, Naomi found her own way out from under her father's thumb."

"Nick again," Dani said.

Drinking his wine, Zeke studied Dani over the rim of his glass. She felt warm under his gaze, but not uncomfortable. That surprised her. He said, "Naomi married the vice president at the mill. He was a widower, considerably older than she, and about as hard to live with as her father. Rumor has it he beat her. I'm not sure if she knew that going in or not. Probably. She's always been remarkably clear-eyed about people. Her affair with Nick—it lasted barely a summer—allowed her to be free and still stay in Cedar Springs."

Dani shook her head. "I don't get it."

"Once her father and husband had disowned her, they also relinquished any control over her. By breaking their rules, Naomi could live on her own terms. She couldn't have left the way Mattie did. She loved Cedar Springs, belonged there."

"Mattie's never talked to me about her. And I mean never."

"Maybe she couldn't," Zeke said. He set down his wineglass. "Don't judge her, Dani. Naomi never has." He smiled warmly, sadly. "You should go to Cedar Springs one day. It's a pretty town. Naomi will serve you peach pie, and you'll never guess she ran off with a rake of a Hollywood director and her sister's ex-husband while she was married to another man."

For all Zeke's toughness and competence, Dani was struck by how thoughtful and perceptive a man he was. That comforted her. With all her confusion and anger—the mind-numbing mix of emotions brought on by the last few days—she appreciated that gentle side of his spirit. But she didn't want to look to him for answers, for a cure for what she was feeling. And there were the questions about his brother and the gold key, questions about her mother. About her father lying in a Saratoga hospital. She needed to call him, find out how he was doing.

Zeke pointed at her with his fork. "You'd better eat."

She looked at him, suddenly grateful for his solid presence. "Thank you."

He grinned, sexy, irreverent. "I can scramble an edible meal together on short order."

"I'm not thanking you for the cooking," Dani said, "but for talking."

She didn't think it was his long suit, but that was fine. These days, listening didn't seem to be hers.

After dinner Dani popped on *Tiger's Eye,* the movie that had transformed her grandmother from an overnight sensation into a true star. When people thought of her, they tended to think of the woman in *Tiger's Eye,* young and sexy and beautiful—so incredibly beautiful—and still a little vulnerable, a little awed. Dani and anyone else who'd come to know her grandmother in her "retirement" had had to reconcile the eccentric, independent, mature Mattie Witt with this glamorous movie star.

Now Dani had another Mattie Witt to bring into her understanding of her grandmother, the young woman who'd freed herself from her strict, unbending father. She tried to imagine Mattie's childhood in the stifling, repressive household of Jackson Witt, to imagine her leaving behind her eleven-year-old sister. Had that been an act of courage or selfishness—or simple desperation?

Because Mattie had left Cedar Springs, Joe and Zeke Cutler had gone to Saratoga, and now, twenty-five years later, Zeke was back.

Tucking her feet up under her on the big comfy chair, Dani lowered the volume with her remote. Zeke was standing at her living-room window, looking down at the courtyard.

"There's so much I didn't know," she said.

He glanced back, his eyes reaching hers, but he said nothing. In trying to imagine Mattie's life in Cedar Springs, Dani had also tried to imagine his. But she and Zeke were from two different worlds, brought together by the life of a woman Dani loved but no longer was sure she understood. And where did her mother fit in? Where did Zeke's brother?

She had to know.

On the television screen, the Mattie Witt of fifty years ago smiled, the red ostrich plume in her hair.

"Mattie never mentioned the book on your brother to me. It won a Pulitzer, but I'd never read it—I'd never even heard of it."

"You were just a kid when it came out."

"Fifteen. It didn't seem so young then. I don't know, I've always half believed my childhood ended when I was nine. After my mother disappeared, I thought I could take anything. I guess I thought that was what everyone else believed, too. But now I see there were those who tried to protect me. My Chandler grandfather, for one. And Mattie." She pulled her gaze from her young, dazzling grandmother and turned it on Zeke. "Did Nick know you and your brother were in Saratoga?"

"You should talk to him about that."

"It breaks one of your rules?"

"More than one, I imagine."

She dropped her feet to the floor, her impatience instantly reignited. "Zeke, you know more than you're telling me."

He didn't even turn his head from the window.

"I have a right to know—"

He faced her. "It's not a question of rights."

It was as if someone had wiped the humor and fatigue and gentleness from his face, the qualities she'd seen over dinner that drew her to this complex man more than the muscles in his shoulders—which were impressive—and the sexy figure he cut in a pair of jeans. Now he looked distant and professional.

Her muscles tightened against another onslaught of shaking from anger and frustration—and fear.

He didn't react. "Dani, there are just some things you'll have to discuss first with your family."

"Fine, then."

She jumped up, banged off the television, so aggravated she could have pulled books off the shelves and thrown them in handfuls at the too-controlled, too-appealing man who'd invaded her space. "I'll find out the rest on my own. I don't need your help or your cooperation."

She headed for the kitchenette and dumped dishes into the dishwasher, put the cap on the olive oil and tucked it back on the appropriate shelf. Zeke continued to stare out the living-room window. He wasn't like Ira, who talked all the time, or Nick or her father, who'd try to sneak off when she was irritated. He wasn't like any of her male business associates, who treated her with reserve, and he wasn't like the men who worked for her at Pembroke Springs, and he wasn't like—he was nothing like—the men she'd dated over the years, who'd talk her out of feeling miserable and take the credit when she was feeling happy.

They'd just stand there when they knew she was mad.

But Zeke didn't work for her and he wasn't a business associate and he wasn't a relative and he wasn't a date.

So what was he?

A complication, she thought, shutting the dishwasher. A man who scared her just for the very questions he presented and the doubts he created. Not just about her mother, Mattie, what was happening in Saratoga. About herself.

She hit the start switch on the dishwasher and wiped off the counter. She had no intention of letting him clean up after he'd cooked dinner.

"You're welcome to stay." Her tone wasn't exactly invitational. "Talk to the pigeons all night if you want. I'm out of here."

He hadn't moved a millimeter. "Where are you going?"

She made it all the way down the hall to the elevator.

Then he was there beside her, silent and so controlled.

She couldn't not look at him. If the rest of him wasn't giving away a thing, his eyes were. They told her he did care. They told her he, too, was afraid of what he'd stirred up by coming to Saratoga—of what he'd find there.

They were so different, she and this man from Cedar Springs, Tennessee.

"You need to rest," he said. His tone was neither patronizing nor demanding, but simply observational. Probably it didn't take any great insight into her character to notice that she was ready to collapse. She could feel the exhaustion curling up her spine, dragging her down. Only tension kept her on her feet.

She banged the down button. Somewhere within the bowels of the building, she could hear the elevator creak and groan. "It's so frustrating."

"Keep your focus on the present."

"Is that your professional advice?" she asked, not meaning to sound so sarcastic.

"My personal advice. I've had a few extra days to adjust to asking the kinds of questions you're asking."

His eyes had become distant again, a closed window to a part of him she could no longer deny she very much wanted to see and understand. What was he like inside?

"I want answers, Zeke."

"So do I."

"Talk to me."

But he merely stood there.

The elevator clunked to a stop at her floor, and the doors slid open. "I should get back to Saratoga and see my father—and I need to apologize to Mattie. I was pretty hard on her. I've never gotten mad at her like that."

"Maybe she's relieved you finally did. Now she's merely mortal in your eyes."

The elevator doors were closing. Dani reached to stick her arm in and stop them, but Zeke touched her wrist, just below her slowly healing bruise. Awareness sizzled inside her. She forced herself to remember the stolen key, ransacked room 304, her father. They weren't coincidences.

"You wouldn't get to see your father until morning." Zeke's voice was raspy and low; he rubbed the soft, sensitive skin on the inside of her wrist. "Hospitals do have their rules."

She pulled in her lower lip and bit down hard. "Zeke, I wish I knew—"

"I know." His mouth lowered to hers, his lips brushing hers, soft and so damn sweet, promising nothing but the moment. He smiled into her eyes. "Will you stay?"

She tried to laugh. "Another minute and I'll be a pile of warm Jell-O."

The humor returned to his dark eyes. "Not me."

Zeke had intended to read her the riot act about being reckless and hotheaded and thoroughly Pembroke when they got back to her apartment. He'd intended to tell her to let him do the heavy lifting—which would surely set her off—and go tend her mineral water and mud baths. He would be cool, distant, professional. Then he'd get out of there.

But there was no lecture, no getting her steamed and he didn't leave.

At least not so far.

"I'd like to take a shower," she said. "To calm down as much as to get clean. I don't know when I've spent so long on edge."

"Good idea."

She looked at him with those big black eyes, and her skin was so pale, her lower lip pulled in a little under her top teeth, and she said, "You want out of here, don't you? You're getting— we're getting—" She stopped, straightening her spine and going high-minded heiress on him. It was as good a defense as any. "Leave whenever you wish. I'll be fine on my own."

But in her fierceness he saw not only strength and character, but also vestiges of the little girl who'd had no choice but to be fine on her own. He sensed her pride and toughness and the twenty-five years of battles she'd had with herself not to show the parts of her that weren't so proud and weren't so tough. He was from another world, one without trust funds to throw in people's faces when he got mad or prestigious hundred-year-old parties to skip, but he thought he understood. They'd both loved people who in the end had left them to face the world alone.

"Take your shower," he said. "I won't sneak out on you."

While she was in the bathroom, he contemplated his next move, whether he at least should tell her that her father hadn't tripped in the woods, something she already seemed to suspect. Should he tell her he'd posted Sam at her father's hospital room? Those were the kinds of things he could legitimately tell her, if he were in the habit of telling anyone anything. He talked to Sam because they worked together, because they were friends. He didn't know what he and Dani were.

"I forgot my robe," she called.

He fetched it from the bedroom and hung it on one finger through a narrow opening in the doorway. It was a thin little scrap of fabric. She'd have had more covering in a good bath towel.

"Does this make me an official white knight?" he asked.

"It does not," she said, a hint of amusement in her voice as she snatched the robe. "I'm just not used to having someone around when I'm taking a shower."

He only got a glimpse of her dripping hand. Stifling an image of her parading around her claustrophobic apartment stark naked, Zeke noticed one of hundreds of photographs, postcards and posters on the hall wall, which she used like a giant bulletin board. It was of her and her grandmother in the basket of a hot-air balloon. Dani must have been fourteen or fifteen. Her smile reminded him of her mother. It struck him that Dani was older now than Lilli had been when she disappeared. She wasn't a kid anymore. Neither was he. They'd both survived loss.

"We've been on our own for a long time," she said, as if reading his thoughts. She'd come up beside him. He could feel the heat and dampness of her skin. The robe, he observed, was as flimsy as he'd expected. "It's been good for me—I've been happy. I don't want to lose that independence. I don't want anyone to have to feel responsible for me, to hurt because I hurt."

"It's not always possible," he said carefully, aware Dani Pembroke had just exposed a bit of her soul, which had to be a rarity for her, "to tell people what to feel and what not to feel. Someone can hurt for you not out of a sense of responsibility, but out of love."

"Kate keeps telling me the only true love is between independent people. She says intimacy isn't about dependence."

"A smart woman, your friend Kate."

The filmy robe matted to the places where her skin was still damp, outlining the soft shape of her breasts. Water dripped from her tangled hair. Zeke told himself to leave. They'd both said too much, revealed too much. But instead he moved closer to her, close enough that he could smell the fresh scent of soap and see the lines at the corners of her dark eyes, sense the desire that stirred inside her. He damn well knew what was stirring in him.

"Don't leave yet," she whispered.

In her bedroom they opened the window to the breeze and the flutter of pigeons. The tie on her robe had come loose, dangling to the tops of her bare feet, revealing her small breasts and smooth, flat stomach. Zeke inhaled deeply. He wanted to go to her. He wanted to strip off his clothes and make love to her now, here, anywhere. But he waited. She needed to be certain. There were questions yet to be answered—even asked—about the places where their pasts had intersected. They mattered. But they didn't, Zeke understood, determine how much he wanted Dani Pembroke, how much this slim, black-eyed woman had come to mean to him.

She stood next to him at the window as he pulled the shade. One side of her robe had fallen off her shoulder and caught in the crook of her elbow. As small and feminine as she was, she was strong for her size, and athletic. And sexy, Zeke thought. He wondered if she knew how sexy.

Hesitating only slightly, she slipped her hands around his lower back. Her touch was light but not tentative, igniting a desire within him so hot it burned his soul. She pressed her breasts against his chest and tilted her head back, dampening her lips with the tip of her tongue, inviting him.

"Don't hold back," she said. "Not for my sake, anyway."

He kissed her then, a long and searching kiss, not an end, he felt, but a beginning. There was much more yet to come between them.

In the midst of it, her robe fell to the floor. He couldn't have said the precise moment, but became aware that she was naked, that his hands were coursing up her smooth, trim bottom. Their kiss had taken on an urgency and hunger that quickly sensitized and electrified every inch of his body, every fiber of his soul.

He dispensed with his own clothes in a matter of seconds.

While he did, Dani backed up and sat on the edge of the bed, almost primly. Then he saw her black eyes on him—not embarrassed or second-guessing him or herself, but shining with unabashed lust.

"Changed your mind?" he asked, half-serious, half-playful.

She shook her head. There was no hesitation. He went to her, sat beside her, and without touching her anywhere else, ran his palms up her bare arms. He could feel the awareness shooting through her.

Her eyes never leaving him, she smiled and came to him. They fell together onto the cool, soft sheets, with the breeze from the courtyard and a cat yowling. Soon Zeke felt nothing but the passion and the power of the emotions he had for this woman…and heard only the voice inside him—insistent, annoying—warning caution and distance because those were his way.

"Zeke…" Her face was a mask in the shadows as she pulled him deeper into her. "I've never felt this way about anyone. It's a little frightening. I know I shouldn't fall for you…I can't…"

"You don't have to." He could hear the aching in his own voice. "Just love me a little now."

Her mouth found his. "I do, now."

Later she fell asleep with her head against his shoulder. He felt the softness of her still-damp hair on his chin, smelled its freshness. He shut his eyes, letting himself relax in the moment.

Suddenly it was as if Mattie and Nick had met on the Cumberland River all those decades ago not for themselves, but for them, the ex-heiress and security expert, both with too many dead dreams.

And Zeke knew what he had to do.

As he extricated himself from Dani's arms, he could see her long, thick eyelashes against the paleness of her skin and the soft shape of her mouth as she slept. There was no evidence of the tension of the last days. She looked relaxed and at peace with her world, a world so different from his. He imagined her at nine, alone, her mother gone, her father shattered. She must have been a tiny girl, a spitfire determined from day one not to be just a "Chandler heiress" or a "Pembroke scoundrel" but only herself, whoever that might be.

Not making a sound, Zeke gathered up his clothes and dressed in the bathroom, quickly, and he got out of there before he could change his mind.

Ninety minutes later, he was driving a newly rented car—now he'd have two—north on the interstate. He finally had himself under control. He could think, figure out what came next. He'd head to Saratoga, find Sam, lay everything out for him, get his unbiased opinion. There'd be no putting off the tough questions. Joe was dead, and Lilli Chandler Pembroke had been missing for twenty-five years. Maybe they were somehow the cause of the break-ins at Dani's cottage and his room and the attack on her father. Maybe they weren't. But it was time to focus on the present before someone else got hurt.

A centered calm descended over him. He was finished standing back. Dani didn't have to like him. She didn't have to appreciate or understand him or the choices he'd made about his life. She didn't have to want him meddling in her life. She could think whatever she wanted to think. Be who she wanted to be. But he'd quit worrying about treading lightly where Danielle Chandler Pembroke was concerned. He'd just added her to his mission in Saratoga.

And that wasn't her problem. It was his.

In the morning Dani got up much later than usual and microwaved a muffin she had in the freezer and found a note on the table, read the precise no-nonsense handwriting.

I've gone back to Saratoga. I need to do a few things on my own. I'll be in touch. No regrets? None here. Z

No, she thought with a jolt of surprise, she had no regrets.

She'd heard him leave but hadn't stirred. On some level, she'd understood that he'd needed to get out of there, be back on his own. He'd tried to be quiet, but it was her door length of locks that had alerted her. If she'd been clothed, she might not have resisted going after him. But she'd have had to dig out clothes and put them on, and by then he'd have been gone anyway. She'd debated wrapping herself up in her quilt and intercepting him, but that could have led to other things, like making love on the hall floor, because it was getting to be that way between them. She'd imagined them using the quilt as a pad. He was an expert in security and self-protection. There was no telling what ideas he'd come up with.

Then she found a sheet of paper under the note.

It was a photocopy of a blackmail note.

The whole world will know Lilli Chandler Pembroke isn't the perfect heiress she pretends to be....

Dani dropped her muffin and fell back against her chair. Her hands shook. Tears sprang to her eyes.

"Oh, Mother...Mama..."

She moved fast, downing another cup of coffee and cleaning up the kitchen, trying to focus—as Zeke had suggested—on the present. On what she was doing. Not on the questions slicing through her mind.

But where had he gotten that note? When? What did it mean? Did Mattie know—Nick—her father?

"Stop," she said out loud, calmly but forcefully. She needed to be able to function. She couldn't indulge wild thinking or ask questions she knew she couldn't answer.

In ten minutes, she was on Mattie's front stoop, ringing the doorbell.

There was no answer. It was a warm, humid morning, and

Dani tried again, waited and finally let herself in with the key she'd always had. In the quiet town house there was no indication that her grandmother had gone anywhere special or planned to be away for long or knew that her daughter-in-law had been blackmailed twenty-five years ago. Or maybe not twenty-five years ago. Maybe the note had been written more recently.

But your secret is safe with me if you pay up tonight....

Using her cell phone in the kitchen, which overlooked her grandmother's beautiful private garden, Dani called the hospital in Saratoga.

Her father was grumpy but on the mend. "Hey, kid, what's up?"

"I'm at Mattie's. Did she call? Is she on her way to Saratoga?"

"Not that I know of. We talked last night—she didn't mention coming up. Why? Is something wrong?"

It was in her voice. Her father had always been able to tell when she was upset. "She's not here."

"Is there some reason we should worry?"

"No, I just..." She exhaled, not knowing exactly what she "just." Just had good reason to worry these days? Just had made love to Joe Cutler's brother and didn't have her head on straight? Just had read a blackmail note to her missing mother? "Never mind, Pop. How're you feeling?"

"Lousy."

"Take care of yourself, okay?"

"Yeah, sure, kid."

On the surface he was lighthearted, irreverent, confident, every bit the man he'd become since his father-in-law had caught him with many thousands of Chandler Hotels's dollars in his personal account. But underneath, where perhaps only a daughter knew to listen, Dani heard his fear.

"Pop, what's going on?"

"I've got to go—the vampires are coming to suck my blood. You should see my day nurse."

"Pop—"

"Talk to you later, kid." He sighed. "Just listen to Zeke, okay?"

"Then you trust him," she said.

But he'd hung up.

Dani left a note for Mattie, and feeling uneasy but at least reasonably rested, fought her way onto the subway and to an Amtrak train heading north.

Fifteen

❧⦿⦿❧

Nick's stamina wasn't what it used to be. The long flight from Los Angeles to New York had worn him out. The young man who'd taken Hollywood by storm seemed to have been another man altogether, someone Nick didn't even know.

Mattie didn't help him feel any less old and useless.

"Good heavens, Nick," she said when she greeted him at LaGuardia. "You look older'n dirt, as we used to say down home."

He grunted at her. "I am older than dirt."

She smiled that still-dazzling smile of hers, ever the dark-eyed eighteen-year-old girl he'd found staring at the Cumberland River. She kissed him on the cheek. "I've a car waiting."

Using his cane, he followed slowly behind her. They didn't speak until they were in the cab, on their way into the city. Mattie placed a wrinkled hand gently on Nick's wrist. She smiled. Two smiles in the same hour. He really must look awful. "We have time," she said. "We'll clean up and have something to eat and catch our breath. Then we'll go to Saratoga."

Leaning back against the seat, Nick nodded and watched out his window as they moved toward a city he no longer knew.

* * *

Sam Lincoln Jones stood outside John Pembroke's hospital room in jeans, a bright orange polo shirt, running shoes and military sunglasses. He wore a shoulder holster that held his Smith & Wesson .38.

"Subtle," Zeke said.

"Subtlety doesn't work with these people."

"Then I take it you've met our patient."

Sam's mouth twitched in what passed for a smile when he was working. When he wasn't working, he'd put on jazz and his half-moon glasses and read thick tomes on criminological theory, and sometimes he'd laugh out loud. "He mistook me for a lawyer."

Zeke laughed, not sure if Sam was kidding.

"I had on a jacket," Sam said. "Got hot in here and figured maybe the gun might impress him."

"Did it?"

Sam just looked at him.

"Anything interesting happen?"

"Roger and Sara Stone showed up a little while ago. They were all real polite and cool to each other. Roger and Sara talked about how worried they were about their niece."

Zeke nodded. "I just stopped at their place here in town. Roger tried to hire me again."

"Bet the pay's good." Sam drank some gray take-out coffee. "But you don't need money to make you keep an eye on this lady, do you?"

"No."

"She blew in here, too. Left about twenty minutes ago. Nurses gave her daddy something to calm him down after she got through with him."

Zeke had second-guessed his decision to leave her a copy of the blackmail note. But it was done. "You listen in?" he asked.

"Part of the job, isn't it?" Sam spoke without relish or distaste; he was just stating the facts. "From what I gather, Dani Pembroke (a) hates anyone taking her for granted, (b) hates anyone short of the CIA deliberately keeping her in the dark about anything, and (c) hates anyone feeling responsible for her happiness and well-being, which is tied up with (a) and (b). I could give you some technical mumbo jumbo analyzing her behavior and attitude, but you get the idea." Sam's eyes were unreadable behind his dark glasses. "She's intense."

"And John?"

"Threatened to pour a pitcher of ice water on her head or hire you if she didn't back off. A real pair. Devoted to each other under it all." Sam was silent a moment. "I debated following her."

"Any particular reason?"

"Bad vibes."

Reason enough.

Even with the sunglasses, Sam's gaze penetrated. "You holding back on her?"

"Not as much as she thinks."

"You've always liked to take your life into your hands in the most peculiar ways," Sam said, not as lightly as Zeke would have wished. "I assume you know Mattie Witt and Nick Pembroke are on their way."

"To Saratoga?"

"Ah. I see you did not know."

Without a word Sam handed over his gun. Zeke took it. Knowing Sam as he did, he'd probably hauled an arsenal east with him. Yet he seldom resorted to violence, even in their sometimes violent profession. He just liked to be prepared.

"Hope you don't need it," Sam said.

"So do I."

* * *

It was quiet and cool in the woods, with almost no breeze. Dani followed the narrow path from the bottling plant. She'd let her staff there know she was on the grounds. The receptionist, a sixty-year-old woman from Saratoga, had reported that Ira was looking for Dani. "He said it was important but not urgent." Meaning whatever he wanted probably didn't involve a burglary or a ransacked room.

Mosquitoes buzzed around her head in the stillness. She'd checked the spot where her father had claimed to trip. It might have happened as he'd said. But she didn't think so, no matter how stubbornly he clung to his story.

Despite the warm air, she shivered, feeling incredibly alone. Her father had said the man posted outside her room—Sam Jones—was Zeke's doing, a partner or friend or both. Jones didn't say a word to her, but had looked as if he was considering stuffing her in a closet until his pal returned. Dani hadn't introduced herself.

She slapped at a mosquito on her leg. She had folded Zeke's copied blackmail letter into a small square and shoved it in her shorts pocket. Its words were seared into her memory.

She went around the hemlock at the top of the cliffs and down the steep incline to the boulder above the narrow ledge where she'd found the gold key her mother had been wearing the night she disappeared. Her heart raced. She felt light-headed. She'd come here straight from the hospital. She needed to eat, rest, think.

A woodpecker drummed nearby.

Did her mother drop the key off the ledge that night? Or was it put there or dropped there sometime between that night and when Dani found it a few weeks ago?

Did it have anything to do with the blackmail note?

Was it here—on the spot where she was standing now—that her mother had met and paid off her blackmailer?

Dani smelled the pungent odor of evergreen needles and heard the faint hum of traffic on the interstate in the distance.

There was a movement behind her, above her, in the woods. A rustling wind in the trees or a crunching of dried leaves. She went absolutely still and listened.

Nothing.

Ordinarily she wouldn't have noticed such a sound. Now, however, following her visit to her father in the hospital, seeing his battered head, feeling her own fading bruises, she was on heightened alert. Her senses picked up every nuance of sight, sound, smell.

"Damn mosquitoes," Ira Bernstein grumbled.

In her immediate, overwhelming relief, Dani almost lost her balance on the rock. She could hear Ira thrashing along the narrow path that spidered out from the old logging road that led through the woods to the Pembroke's main grounds.

"Over here, Ira."

"Yeah, yeah, I'm coming. You know, I've about decided I'm a city person. Think I'll look up your grandpa and see if he doesn't have a new job for me in some decent city in— Hey, who are you?"

Dani tensed at the change in Ira's voice. The sudden fear mixed with indignation. She looked around for a stick or a loose rock, anything she could use as a weapon.

"Dani, run!"

Without thinking, she scrambled up the steep incline, pausing just to uproot a rock about the size of a football and twice as heavy, scraping her fingertips as she dug it free. She ducked under the low branches of the hemlock.

She heard sounds of grunting and choking.

"Ira! Ira—what's happening? Talk to me!"

He didn't answer. Stemming a surge of panic, Dani plunged through the undergrowth of ferns and brush onto the narrow path.

She swallowed a scream and almost dropped her rock.

A tall, muscular, red-faced man had Ira pinned by his throat to the thick trunk of an oak tree. Ira's face had turned purple. He wasn't making a sound.

Dani raised her rock shoulder-high and quickly debated heaving it down on the side of the attacker's head. But she said, "Let him go."

The man had his back to her and couldn't see whether she had a gun or a pitchfork or just a stupid rock. But he released Ira, who immediately sagged to the ground, clutching his throat and gasping for air.

His attacker turned to Dani.

"Get off my property," she said, surprising herself with her quiet determination.

He grinned. "Who's going to make me?"

He sounded like a fourth-grader, only deadlier. The bastard had just tried to kill Ira or at least put him out of commission for a long time. Dani made a quick assessment. The attacker was bigger, stronger and obviously more accustomed to beating up on people in the woods than she was. But if he had a weapon, at least it wasn't pointed at her.

If she was lucky, she'd have one good chance with her rock. Then that would be that.

Not very promising.

"If you leave now," she said, "you'll be long gone by the time I tend to Ira and have a chance to call the police."

He laughed. "Do I look worried?"

That he didn't.

But he added, by way of explanation, "I don't react well to people sneaking up on me."

He blew her a kiss—insultingly, cockily—and trotted off into the woods, not making a sound.

Dani ran to Ira, on his hands and knees, vomiting. "Ira, are you all right? Should I get an ambulance?"

He turned his pale, purplish face toward her. "I'm moving back to Istanbul."

Sinking back against the tree, he coughed and rubbed his neck where there were red fingerprints and broken blood vessels. He winced in pain, growing even paler.

"Ira, I'm getting help."

He held up a hand. "Wait."

"You're hurt—"

"I'll be okay." His voice was raspy, and he was clearly hurting, but he was dead serious. "The Pembroke doesn't need any more bad PR right now."

"I don't care. We can ride this out and—"

"Dani, listen to me. A reporter found out Zeke's been staying at the Pembroke. Figures something's afoot and wants to talk to you."

Dani knelt beside him as his words sank in. Everything was coming apart so fast. She was falling in love with the wrong man, her father was in the hospital, she'd been abrupt with Mattie and Nick, rumors were flying about her and her companies and Ira had just been attacked on his way to find her.

"Did you recognize that thug?" she asked.

Ira shook his head. "You?"

"No. Ira, we can talk about this later. You need to take it easy."

"Dani, one more thing. Mattie called. She and Nick are on their way—they want you to pick them up at the train station."

Just what she needed. Her famous grandparents wouldn't exactly slip into town unnoticed. First, it wasn't in their natures. Second, it was impossible. Somebody would recognize them. "I'll take care of it. Right now I just want to get you out of here."

There was a crunching sound behind them in the woods. Dani whirled around with her rock, which Zeke quickly snatched from her hand, ever the professional. "Good thing your pal didn't test your arm," he said mildly.

Dani felt relief at his presence even as she digested his words. "You saw him?"

"Watched from behind that pine back there. I got here too late to keep him from nailing Ira. You already had the situation in hand." Despite his sardonic tone, his eyes were flat and dark, without humor. He squatted and quickly examined Ira's bruised neck. "Ribs okay?"

"Sore, but I don't think he broke any."

"Throat, neck?"

"They hurt."

His eyes narrowed, Zeke lightly touched the red fingerprints and nodded, as if reassured Ira's injuries weren't more serious. "If it's any consolation, he wasn't trying to kill you. You'd have been dead before Dani or I could have done a thing."

Ira licked his lips. "I suppose I had to know that."

"More to the point," Zeke said, rising, "Dani had to know."

She felt her stomach twist.

"You don't go after a man like that with a rock."

Zeke spoke without apology or arrogance. They were on his turf now, and he knew it.

"Well, if I'd had a gun, I'd have gone after him with that, but I didn't and I wasn't going to run while Ira—" She stopped mid-sentence, seeing the gun tucked into a small holster on Zeke's waist.

He followed her gaze. "Just a precaution."

For the first time she thought she really understood what he did for a living. How little she knew about this man who just hours ago had been so gentle and loving and passionate in bed with her.

"Why didn't you follow him?" she asked hollowly.

"I tried. Got as far as the pavilion. A few of your people were out there on break. I decided not to push it and came back here."

And she hadn't heard a thing. Not a breaking of a twig—until he'd wanted her to hear him. His tone was mild and objective, but Dani felt a chill go through her. Was her situation putting Ira and her people at Pembroke Springs in danger?

Ira, his color returning, pulled himself to his feet. "I'd never make it in the cloak-and-dagger business. Excuse my saying so, Dani dear, but you and our friend Cutler deserve each other. A pity you didn't meet under normal circumstances."

But despite his wry humor, Dani could see he'd had a bad scare. She started toward him but felt Zeke's gaze on her. He hadn't moved. "Zeke?"

"I know who he is, Dani," he said in a low voice. "And I know where to find him."

Ira groaned. "That's enough for me. I'm out of here."

"I'll help you get back to the inn," Dani offered.

"Thanks, but I believe I'm safer on my own, less likely to stumble on big mean guys spying on my boss. I'll have someone at the bottling plant run me back."

Threatening again to return to Istanbul, he staggered off toward the path.

Zeke touched Dani's shoulder. "I'll make sure he gets there safely."

But she insisted on going with them. It wasn't far to the pine-shaded grounds of the bottling plant, where one of the office workers was on break at the pavilion and volunteered to drive Ira back. He assured Dani and Zeke he'd be fine. "I'll get a full explanation another time."

When he'd gone, Dani sank onto a stone bench inside the pavilion, leaving the gate open. Across the shaded lawn she could see the evergreen-colored clapboards of the Pembroke Springs

bottling plant, its old-fashioned look belying the state-of-the-
art equipment inside.

"Better crank yourself down a few notches, Dani," Zeke
said, sitting beside her. He looked hot and unbearably mascu-
line, as if he came upon people being attacked in the woods all
the time. Maybe he did. "If you don't, soon you won't need a
balloon to get you off the ground."

She could feel the rising level of oxygen in her blood. All
she needed now was to hyperventilate. She'd collapse, and Zeke
would scoop her up and carry her off to safety. With his arms
secure around her, she'd just give up. She'd let him find the answers to all her questions, she'd let him solve all her problems.
She'd just snuggle up under a soft, warm quilt and lose herself,
her independence, her defiant nature.

"I'm not going to turn my problems over to you to solve for
me," she told him quietly.

"Didn't ask you to."

"And I want to know where you got that blackmail note."

"Naomi gave it to me," he said simply. "Joe sent it to her in
a separate, sealed envelope. She didn't open it until she saw you
wearing the gold key in the paper."

"So you only just saw it yourself?"

"Yes."

She didn't look at him but could sense his presence beside
her. She couldn't deny the current of excitement running through
her. He was, at the very least, a difficult man with whom to remain neutral.

"And that man who attacked Ira?" she asked.

"Quint Skinner."

She swung around on the cool marble bench even as the
shock sliced through her. "What?"

"Quint's been in Saratoga at least as long as I have. I don't
know what he's after, if anything."

"But why would he attack—"

"I don't know."

Zeke's gaze was unrelenting, but he seemed pensive, even remote. Dani concentrated for a moment on the scent of the roses and morning glories that were tangled together on the wrought-iron fence, on the chipped, worn Spanish tiles of the old fountain. Their familiarity and charm helped soothe her taut nerves.

"Tell me about Pembroke Springs," he said, conversational.

"Zeke…"

He plucked a tiny, wilted pink rose blossom and held it delicately between his thumb and forefinger. Again the incongruities of the man struck her. "Is there much to bottling water?" he asked.

She reined in her frustration and impatience. Perhaps to know more about him—to earn his trust—she needed to let him know more about her. So she said, "It all depends."

"On what?"

"First of all, we're not as precise in this country as we could be about the distinction between mineral water and springwater. Whether a bottled water is called 'mineral water' or 'springwater' is often just a marketing decision as to which would sell better. Still, there are generally recognized criteria that distinguish mineral water. They have to do with what we call TDS—total dissolved solvents per liter."

"Sounds like something you'd use to wash a car." Zeke rested one foot on the opposite knee; he looked relaxed and at least marginally interested.

"TDS are what's left after a liter of water has evaporated. What solvents are present is determined by the rock strata where the springs are located. The water picks up minerals from the rocks it's filtered through. It's really quite logical."

"Examples?"

Dani eyed him, and she could easily imagine him off to slay dragons and rescue fair damsels. He was an intense and capable man. Before he acted, he would want to know everything. And people would tell him, just as she was. Her one consolation was that she wasn't really telling him about herself. And yet she wanted to. That scared her.

"Limestone adds calcium," she told him, "dolomite adds magnesium, igneous rocks add sodium. All kinds of dissolved minerals can be present in any particular water. It's the combination and level of these various minerals that determine the taste, quality and possible therapeutic benefits of any given water. Saratoga's lucky in that regard. I'm not a geologist, but it's believed that this entire region—from Lake George south to Albany—was once under an ocean. Salt water was trapped in limestone, dolomite and sandstone and then sealed underground by shale, which is critical because shale's impervious to water. So any surface water couldn't contaminate the water trapped by the shale."

"Aha," Zeke said.

She smiled. "Am I getting carried away?"

"No. I'm beginning to get a picture of why you can charge what you charge for a glass of water. So if this fancy water's trapped underground, how did anybody find out about it?"

"Fault lines in the shale. They allowed water to escape in aboveground springs and geysers. The Mohawk knew about the springs around here for centuries—they considered them sacred for their curative powers. The properties of the different springs vary widely. Some are alkaline, some saline, some mild, some strong. Different springs were used to treat different ailments, everything from gout and constipation to heart disease."

Zeke pulled his foot off his knee and stretched out both legs, his feet on the brick walk. "And I always thought water was water."

"It is and it isn't."

He tossed his rose blossom into the fountain, where it floated in the clear water. He pointed to it. "Is that springwater?"

"No, it's just water we use for the fountain. There used to be a fountain that tapped Pembroke Springs directly, but we capped it and dug a borehole directly into the aquifer."

"That's not as romantic."

"It's more hygienic—there's less opportunity for surface contaminants to get into the water."

"What's your water good for?"

"The soul," she said and saw Zeke's eyes narrow for a moment, as if he couldn't tell whether or not she was serious—a nice switch. "Actually we just guarantee that our water will do no harm. That's one of the differences between springwater and mineral water. We can't make any therapeutic claims for springwater. But we rarely do for mineral water, either."

Zeke leaned back, looking relaxed yet alert. An intriguing combination.

"End of lecture," she said, figuring he'd had enough.

But he asked, "What about carbonation?"

"What about how your brother got that blackmail note and why you're here?" she snapped back.

"You can't stop a lecture midstream." His lips twitched, and he almost smiled. "No pun intended."

So she explained about carbonation. "Water—whether spring or mineral—can be still or carbonated. Still water is just that—flat. Most of the bottled water sold in Europe is still. I didn't know that until I got into this business. Naturally carbonated water, which Pembroke Springs is, means that as the water comes from the ground it has enough carbon dioxide already in it to make it bubbly—or effervescent or sparkling, which all mean the same thing. We draw off the carbonic gas and reinject it during the bottling process to maintain quality control. If the bottle doesn't say 'naturally carbonated,' that means ordinary carbon dioxide has been added. Frankly, I think it's the quality of the water that matters most."

"Must be a tough business," Zeke said.

"It's intensely competitive. Pembroke Springs is tiny in comparison to the big guns. Brand awareness, marketing costs, distribution costs—they all mount up and make it difficult for the little guy to compete. In New York State, water's the most highly regulated beverage product. We try to use those regulations to our advantage by not just meeting them, but exceeding them. We do microbiological and radiological testing, we test color, turbidity, odor. We test for inorganics—lead, mercury, cyanide and such—and organics, like pesticides and herbicides. Any contaminant or unacceptable level of anything can kill a water's reputation. We're well aware people can just turn on the faucet."

Zeke looked around at the pretty Victorian pavilion and the pine-shaded grounds. "This place is so different from when Joe and I camped here." A curious softness, a melancholy tone, had crept into his voice, and Dani wondered if he didn't have his own dreams of what might have been. "Everything was so overgrown and shabby then—the bottling plant was just a collapsing, empty building. You care about this place, don't you?"

Her mouth had gone dry, and her heartbeat had quickened. "Yes, I do. As far as I'm concerned, making a profit and caring for the land go hand in hand in this business. If I don't make money, no one gets to drink what I consider one of the best mineral waters in the world. If I'm too greedy, I squander a natural resource, the springs dry up and there's nothing left for future generations. That's what happened to a lot of springs around here in the late nineteenth century, until the state finally stepped in."

"And you did it all without help from your mother's family?"

"In spite of them might be more accurate. My grandfather

couldn't see anyone but 'lunatic Greenwich Village types' wanting to buy mineral water. That was before Perrier made its big push in the American market and mineral water became the rage. Which isn't to say I didn't have help."

"Mattie?"

"And Nick." She felt a stab of guilt; she had to make things right with them somehow. "We worked out a deal when he needed money and I needed collateral. I gave him what I could up front, and he waited for the rest. When I could swing it, I bought the entire property from him. I admit I've had days when I wished I hadn't flown off the handle and disinherited myself. My Chandler trust could have come in handy on a number of occasions. But I'm doing okay. The Pembroke's a risk, but not as big a risk as some people would like to think."

"Rumors aside?"

She winced, hating to think about that bit of unpleasantness right now. "The Pembroke and Pembroke Springs are separate entities, although the Springs owns stock in the inn. But if it should go belly up, the stock would be gone, but creditors wouldn't be able to come after any springs assets. Not," she added pointedly, "that the inn will fail."

Zeke laughed. "Spoken like a true Pembroke."

She could see the humor in his eyes and once more was intrigued by his capacity for gentleness. A man in his particular profession, with his particular memories. She remembered his mouth on hers last night, the soft caresses of his hands, the way he'd made love to her, with her. Then she saw the two of them in a moonlit courtyard, with candles and music and the fragrance of camellias all around, and the image surprised her, not because it was so contrary to this hard, silent man, but because, inexplicably, it wasn't.

"I'd like you to come with me a second," she said, climbing

unsteadily to her feet, not sure what she was doing was right. Yet knowing it was necessary.

Zeke followed her back along the narrow path out to the cliffs, where she took him around the hemlock and down the steep incline. He moved with that peculiar combination of grace and assurance. She walked out to the end of the boulder above the narrow ledge.

"I found the gold key down there," she said, pointing. "I was rock climbing, just messing around, trying to calm my nerves about the Pembroke's opening. The key was wedged under a protruding rock. It could have been there for twenty-five minutes or twenty-five years."

Zeke peered down, squinting in the bright sun, but he made no comment, asked no questions.

Dani slapped at a mosquito on her bruised arm and missed. "For years after my mother disappeared, my grandfather hired a series of private investigators to follow up on any leads on her whereabouts. None ever had the slightest success. When I was about sixteen, one of them came to me. He was a burly, pragmatic guy with a strong Brooklyn accent—he seemed nice. He was just getting background from me, he said. He asked me what my favorite dream of my mother was." She looked at Zeke. "Isn't that strange?"

"Sometimes," he said, "a strange question can lead to clarity in other areas. What was your answer?"

"That she was living a wonderful life on a South Seas island. That she was happy, really happy. She'd never come home because she'd somehow lost her memory on her way back after her balloon ride with Mattie. I could actually see her drinking from coconuts and walking on sandy beaches, unaware she even had a daughter."

"It's a nice dream," Zeke said.

Dani felt the warm afternoon breeze. "It's a compromise

between death and abandonment. I get everything—a mother who's alive and happy, who didn't leave me behind on purpose."

"What did the detective say?"

"'Far-fetched, kid,'" she repeated, imitating his Brooklyn accent. "'Better get used to the idea that your mother's dead.'"

Zeke looked thoughtful, neither condemning nor endorsing that advice. "That isn't easy, either."

"Is your mother…"

"They're all dead. My mother, my father, my brother." He kicked a small, loose pebble off the boulder. "We might as well head back."

But Dani didn't move.

Zeke's eyes were completely lost in the flickering shade as the wind picked up. He stood very still, very close to her. She could sense the tension in him. And the resolve. He was just as determined and stubborn as she was, only his manner was calmer.

"There's more," he said, not making it a question.

Dani could feel the ache of fatigue, and she had to force herself not to change her mind. Finally she said, "Zeke, your brother was here after my mother's disappearance. Four years later."

He was silent a moment. "You're sure—"

"I've thought about it ever since I realized who he was, and yes, I'm sure. Everything was blowing up over my father's embezzling, and Mattie grabbed me one day and headed up here."

"What month?"

"August. I remember racing season had started."

"How do you know it was Joe?"

"I recognized his picture in the book. Not at first—it took a while. But it was the same person."

"Where did you see him?" Zeke asked, his tone businesslike.

"Right here on this rock. I used to love taking off in the

woods on my own, and I'd come out here and sit and swing my legs over the edge. That was before I took up rock climbing. That day I found a man standing out here."

"Joe," Zeke said.

She nodded, feeling the wind on her back. Clouds were billowing up, and the humidity had increased, making her shirt cling.

"Did the two of you talk?"

"I think I told him who I was. I was a little nervous about meeting a stranger in the middle of nowhere. He didn't say much that I can recall, just that he'd heard about me and was glad to have met me. That wasn't all that unusual a comment in those days, with the publicity about my mother and grandparents and Pop getting nailed to the wall for his light fingers."

She paused, but Zeke said nothing. She had no idea what he was thinking. A mosquito was on his dark hair. She brushed it away, feeling awkward and nervous, even cruel. He couldn't have a favorite dream about his brother drinking from coconuts on a South Seas island. Joe Cutler was dead. The whole world knew it.

"We talked about the cliffs and the view," she went on. "He didn't say why he was here. That much I can remember, because I'd wondered. He left before I did. On my way back to the cottage, I saw him at the pavilion, just sitting among the weeds. I didn't call or wave to him—I didn't want him to see me, try to follow me home, something like that."

"Do you know if he saw Mattie while he was here?"

Dani shook her head. "I don't know. Not that she'd have told me if he had. Did you know he'd come back to Saratoga?"

"No."

The humidity was bringing out the mosquitoes. They were buzzing all around now, but Zeke ignored them. Dani tried to, but she was tired and confused, and everything seemed to irritate her.

"Zeke, it's your turn," she finally said.

He turned away from the edge of the boulder, his back to her.

She didn't relent. "Why would Quint Skinner be here?"

He was walking away from her, up the steep incline.

"Zeke—"

Looking back at her, he said quietly, "I don't know."

She watched him climb up to the hemlock but didn't hear him as he vanished into the woods, leaving her standing alone in the wind.

Sixteen

⸻⸙⸻

Mattie sat in the window seat on the train, Nick dozing beside her. The peaceful, scenic ride along the Hudson River had always brought her comfort. Looking at her former husband, she ached for him, for he did indeed look every second of his ninety years. The physical signs of age didn't sadden her—the thinning white hair, the protruding veins, the brown spots, the wrinkles and sags—as much as the knowledge that he wasn't always going to be around. Likely enough, the bold, charming man who'd captivated her on the Cumberland River more than sixty years ago would die before she did.

And she wasn't ready. She'd never be ready.

He stirred. "What're you staring at?" he asked, sounding cranky.

"You. How long has it been since I told you I love you?"

"Decades."

She smiled. "Well, I do, you know. I always have."

"Fine way of showing it." But he patted her hand. "I'm cold as a fish. Circulation stinks." He sighed and settled into his seat, hardly moving. He seemed utterly spent after his long—and so far insufficiently explained—cross-country flight. "Don't you wish we had the sense fifty years ago that we have now?"

"What makes you think we have any more sense now? Nick, you haven't changed. If you had the energy, you'd still be chasing women."

"No." His watery eyes fastened on her, as searching and intense as they'd been when she'd stood with her valise on the riverbank so long ago, aching for him to take her with him. "I'd know I had the only woman I ever wanted, and fidelity wasn't too great a price to pay for her."

· Mattie was touched. Nick had never been particularly sentimental. "Oh, Nick, we've had a life together the only way we could. We were never meant to live all this time together under the same roof. It never would have worked. If you hadn't been anyone but who you are, I doubt I'd have kept you a part of my life all this time. And, you know, it wasn't all you."

"You don't say."

But Mattie was serious. "If you hadn't gambled and chased women, I'd have picked something else to gripe about, because I was meant to live on my own the way I have. I went from my father's house to yours…it was important to me to have a house of my own."

Nick nodded, but she wasn't sure, in his exhaustion, he'd absorbed all she'd said. "Have you been happy?"

"For the most part, yes. Very much. I've come to rather enjoy being a screen legend of sorts. It would be ungrateful of me to complain."

She held his hand; it was, indeed, awfully cold. She remembered well how warm he'd been in bed. They'd made love since their divorce. Even since his affair with her sister. Not often, but they'd accepted long ago that whatever bond existed between them—however else anyone might define or judge it—it was one that suited them, and would endure.

"And you, Nick?" she asked. "Have you been happy?"

He averted his gaze. "I've had some grand times—no question of it. But at what cost? Mattie, Mattie." He coughed, looking pale and beyond tired. "I've made so many mistakes. I have so many regrets. Too many."

"Nick, don't."

"Oh, I know. I've done some memorable films. I don't deny that's important and satisfying. I've given some good times to people who needed a break from reality. But when it's all done, Mattie, when you're an old man and the Great Beyond is beckoning, what's any of that matter? I was—am—a poor father to my only son. My only grandchild doesn't trust me, with good reason."

Mattie hated to see her devil-may-care ex-husband so tortured. "But they both accept you. Nick, of course we have regrets. Those who don't never stretched themselves, never took risks."

He nodded, his eyes closed, the once-dark lashes almost nonexistent. "I'd planned a very different life for myself, Mattie," he said in his sandpapery voice. "I didn't expect to end up an old man living on the largesse of my granddaughter."

"Now, don't start being hard on yourself after all these years. You're too old for that. You can't change the past."

"I should never have gone back to Cedar Springs."

"Where would Naomi be if you hadn't? At the bottom of the Cumberland River, likely enough. Would your staying away have stopped Joe Cutler from heading north to tell me my father was dying? Where does the blame begin—or stop? I can blame my father for my repressive childhood, but how did he become such a difficult man? We can keep digging into the past for explanations and excuses, even understanding. You could blame your flaws on a murdered, legendary grandfather who remained an elusive fantasy to you. You re-created him in two of your greatest films, made him both real and unreal. But Nick, ultimately we each have to take responsibility for our own choices and actions."

He looked half-asleep, but instinctively Mattie knew he was listening. "Nick," she went on softly, "if you're going to assign blame, assign some to me as well. I can't get off scot-free. If I'd never left home—"

His eyes opened. "You had no choice."

"Of course I did. Darling, if that day we met on the Cumberland was meant, then so was the rest of it."

"Joe Cutler and Lilli?"

Mattie sank back and stared out the window, the sun glittering on the wide, still Hudson. Joe had died in battle. Lilli—who knew? Still facing the window, she said, "You can't think Joe was responsible for Lilli."

Nick made no comment.

Her heart thumped, spreading pain through her chest; all she needed now was to drop dead of a heart attack. "Nick?"

"Someone knew about her role in *Casino,* Mattie. I was being blackmailed over it."

Mattie felt as if she'd been stabbed. Turning to Nick, she saw he was deathly pale.

"I paid up to keep whoever it was quiet. Lilli couldn't stand the thought of her family finding out about her role in one of my pictures—about her dream of becoming a movie star. Amazing, isn't it? Hundreds of women would have done anything to get that role, and Lilli wanted to keep it secret, at least until she'd figured out if acting was really what she wanted in life. I guess when you think about it, hundreds of women would have liked to have been a Chandler heiress, too. The blackmail was amateurish—demands to have envelopes of cash left in Congress Park, that sort of thing. It just didn't seem dangerous, or I'd have insisted we go to the police."

"You never told me."

"I didn't think it was that significant."

The train rocked slightly as it moved steadily north, and

Mattie felt her stomach turn over as she realized she hadn't been the only one with secrets. "Did you tell Lilli?"

"No. She had enough on her mind."

"Do you think—could it have been Joe?"

Nick's shoulders slumped. "I don't know."

Lilli had always been compassionate and generous, Mattie thought, if sometimes dangerously blind to other people's faults. If she'd suspected Joe Cutler of blackmailing Nick, she'd have tried to help him—to save him from himself. He could simply have gotten in over his head, engaging in a harebrained blackmail scheme before he really got to know her. Mattie was sure his friendship with her daughter-in-law had been genuine.

Nick had closed his eyes, pretending to sleep. Mattie sat back, annoyed. From long years of experience she knew he was holding back on her. There was more he could tell her. She also knew, however, she couldn't torture from Nicholas Ulysses Pembroke one word he didn't want to tell her. Men, she thought, disgusted. They always spared women the wrong things. The truth she could handle. It was deceit she loathed.

But hadn't she deceived her own granddaughter?

"I suppose it would be convenient to blame everything on Joe since he's dead," Mattie said, trying to control her impatience with Nick, with herself. "But would that account for why we're on this train heading for Saratoga right now?"

Nick answered with a badly faked snore.

"If you weren't so bloody old," she said, "I'd give you a good kick."

One eye opened. "You know, Matt, you always have been a hard-hearted old bat."

"A good thing, or living with you would have killed me a half century ago."

The train rocked and pressed on, and Nick settled back in his seat, and in a few more minutes his snores were no longer faked.

Mattie sighed, wide awake. She wished she, too, could sleep. But that was impossible when all she could do—had done for the past few days—was to relive those days twenty-five years ago when she learned her father was dying and her daughter-in-law had disappeared.

"You got it bad, my friend."

"Shut up, Sam."

Sam grinned across from Zeke at a small table at a café on Broadway, drinking cappuccino. Zeke had ordered black coffee. "I only speak the truth."

"Doesn't matter."

"She's only half Chandler," Sam said.

"Half is enough." *We're from different worlds,* Joe had said about Sara Chandler. Zeke understood what he'd meant. "But that's not even the point. Dani is a distraction I don't need at the moment."

"No doubt."

"And she doesn't trust me," Zeke added quietly, almost to himself. "She doesn't trust anyone right now but herself."

"Can you blame her?"

Zeke checked his irritation, which was mostly with himself. After leaving Dani at Pembroke Springs, he'd worked hard to get his rage under control. What had Joe been doing in Saratoga four years *after* Lilli's disappearance? Why hadn't Zeke known? He was tangled up in a thousand threads with nothing to hold them together, nothing to make any sense or order out of them.

"Where is she now?" Sam asked.

"At the train station picking up Mattie and Nick."

"Just what we need, a couple of old Hollywood types underfoot. Know why they're here?"

"No," Zeke said. He had to get himself back on an even keel.

But finding Dani taking on Quint with a rock had thrown him off balance. And Ira. The poor guy had been in the wrong place at the wrong time. Quint could have taken them both out without working up a sweat. Of course, Dani's aim was pretty good....

Zeke pushed back his chair and stood up. "Quint's staying in a rented house not far from here. I went by earlier, but he wasn't home."

"You leave a calling card?"

"I broke in and had a look around. He'll know."

Zeke had considered tossing the place, but he'd found bunk beds in one bedroom and dinosaur sheets in the linen closet. The owners probably thought they'd been fortunate to rent to a Pulitzer Prize–winning writer.

"I'll find him," Sam said.

"Thanks."

"What about John Pembroke?"

Zeke threw a few dollars onto the table in the sunny restaurant, its festive atmosphere so different from his own mood. "I think he's relatively safe in the hospital. My bet is Quint took him out of the picture when he had the chance, or just didn't want Pembroke to see him up at the springs."

Sam's eyes were hidden behind his sunglasses. "And Dani?"

"All my years in this business, Sam, and I've never met anyone—man or woman—so determined to get things done on her own, in her own way."

"She's a Pembroke. She courts disaster."

"Yeah, well, she can wait until I'm back in San Diego fishing."

Sam scooped up Zeke's dollar bills. "Does that mean she's on her own?"

"No," Zeke said, "it does not."

As he left he heard Sam laughing.

* * *

John felt like a little kid when his parents walked into his hospital room, both looking rumpled and exhausted. But nobody pretended they'd gone to all the trouble of getting to Saratoga just for his sake.

"You look awful," Nick said.

"It's all the dope they keep feeding me."

Nick didn't look convinced. Mattie kissed her only child on the forehead. He might have been nine, except his mother had never been one to hover. "How are you, darling?"

"Getting there." He nodded to his father. "I thought you said the trip east would kill you."

"Almost did."

Mattie scowled at him. "You're not ready for the glue factory yet, Nicholas Pembroke." She straightened, effortlessly transforming herself from a solicitous mother into the independent, eccentric, tough woman who'd walked away from a stunningly successful Hollywood career. Her dark, still-beautiful eyes narrowed on her ex-husband. "Tell him, Nick. Tell him everything."

Then she retreated to the waiting room, where Dani, discreet for once in her life, was keeping her distance.

Nick grumbled something about Mattie being more like her father than she'd ever admit.

"Tell me what?" John asked.

Sighing, Nick sat on the edge of his son's bed and told him that he was being blackmailed over Lilli's role in *Casino* when she disappeared.

John listened without interruption. It was just one more thing his wife and father had shared that he hadn't. Shut up in his office in New York, trying to do the right thing, giving Lilli the space to pull herself out of her grief, John had been of no use to her or anyone else. Lilli must have thought him a bore who just didn't give a damn about her. Nick, on the other hand, could never be faulted for lacking interest in a woman's troubles.

But it was far, far too late to condemn Nick for being who he was, and there was time yet to go on condemning himself.

"Mattie knew?" he asked.

Nick grunted. "Not until I told her on the train."

"I'm surprised she didn't throw you off. Maybe she's mellowing."

"Don't count on it. Next she's going to make me tell Dani."

John's head vibrated with pain that zigzagged right down to his broken ribs. "She's right, Nick."

"I know it." He coughed, a wet, sloppy cough the by-product of which ended up in John's wastebasket. His father was clearly exhausted but insisted on getting to his feet. "There's something I neglected to tell even Mattie—I'll be damned if I know why. Not to spare her, for sure. I guess I just don't know what to make of it myself."

"What?" John prodded.

"Joe Cutler came to see me shortly before he was killed. He was on his way home via California and stopped in."

"What for?"

His father's eyes were watery, with spots of yellow clouding the whites, but utterly sane. "He wanted to know if I'd ever figured out who was blackmailing me."

"You didn't, did you?"

"Hell, I thought it was Joe."

John sat up, pain shooting through him. "Nick—"

"But it wasn't. And now I keep wondering if maybe he figured out who it was—or something. I don't know."

"I'll talk to Zeke Cutler," John said.

"Yeah. One other thing, John. There was never anything between me and Lilli. Not even a glimmer. I know it's been on your mind. She treated me like a father-in-law."

"Whom she adored and respected."

"She came to me because she wanted to try something new—to stretch herself. That's all. When she turned up missing, she hadn't made up her mind, as far as I know, about what she was willing to sacrifice to realize her dreams. John—I swear, I just wanted to make her happy."

John reached for his father's bony hand. "I know, Pop. We all did."

Dani flopped down onto a chair at the umbrella table in her cottage garden, kicked off her sneakers and put her feet up. Ira had reported that Pembroke security was on the alert; they'd already escorted several uninvited reporters off the premises.

She unscrewed the top off a bottle of lime-flavored mineral water she'd grabbed ice cold from her refrigerator. Nothing made any sense. Her mother, her father, Mattie, Nick, Joe Cutler, Zeke, movies, Tennessee, blackmail—how could she ever hope to put all the pieces together?

It was hot and sticky even in her garden. She rolled up the hem of her shorts, noticing the grass and dirt stains. She must look terrible. She ought to turn Magda loose on her.

Ira, semirecovered from his encounter with Quint Skinner in the woods, had insisted on greeting the two film legends like royalty when Dani arrived at the inn with Mattie and Nick. If Ira hadn't had such a rotten day, he'd probably have drummed up a red carpet and a couple of crowns. As it was, he'd waltzed them off to the former ballroom—where Nick's grandfather was so famously born—for a candlelight dinner and oohing and aahing by the guests.

Mattie and Nick pretended not to be fazed, but Dani wasn't fooled. They loved every minute of the attention they received.

Nick had called her "urchin" when Dani had picked them up at the train station and acted as if she'd never yelled at him on the phone. Mattie had repressed her earlier hurt and decided Dani's anger had been all to the good. "It's wonderful that we can disagree and disappoint and still be friends. I never could with my father. We never even argued. When I told him I was going to California, he only said, 'If you do, there's no turning back. I'll disown you.' And he meant it."

So even if all wasn't forgiven, Dani and her grandparents accepted the reality of being stuck—and more often than not blessed—with each other for family.

None of which explained anything. The past and the present were intertwined, inseparable. Answers were elusive, she knew, if not nonexistent.

Zeke walked out of her kitchen onto the terrace carrying a tall glass of iced tea. He must have gotten in through the front. Dani hadn't even heard him. "Iced tea's probably a sacrilege around here," he said, "but one more bottle of mineral water or natural soda and I'm likely to effervesce right into space."

"How'd you get into my cottage? I've been locking my doors."

"Locked doors are a specialty of mine." He sat beside her, and she saw him take in her bare feet and everything else about her appearance. "I just left the inn. Your Pembroke grandparents are holding court, enjoying their decorative, healthy meal from what I could see."

"They are a pair."

"Imperfect but, to you, wonderful."

She smiled. "My definition of a family. I've been pretty hard on them—"

"You're hard on everybody," Zeke said without condemnation. "Especially yourself."

"If something had happened to either of them before I could make things right…" She shook her head and drank some of her flavored mineral water. "I don't know."

"They know how you feel. It's obvious that you know they can do wrong and don't care." He looked at her, the lines at the corners of his eyes more prominent against the background of the increasingly gloomy sky. The air was pregnant with impending storms, heavy and still. "And you can't make everything right, Dani. No one can."

"I thought a white knight's mission was to right all wrongs."

He sipped his iced tea, looking distant. "I gave up on that a long time ago. Maybe when I started I wanted to make up for what Joe did—not just for my sake, but for his. What he became wasn't what he was, Dani. I can't explain. Anyway, I came to understand I can't change the past."

"So you live in the present. You isolate yourself from other people."

His dark eyes penetrated her. "So do you."

"Me? I have tons of friends—"

"What about marriage, children?"

His voice was soft and rhythmic, filled with challenge. Dani set down her bottle of mineral water. She could hear Kate—as she had a thousand times—telling her that she needed a man who wouldn't be afraid to ask the tough questions. "I've been busy. You're older than I am. What about marriage and children for you?"

He shrugged and said without self-pity, "They were what another Zeke Cutler used to dream about."

"And now you make the world safe and secure for other people and let them dream your dreams for you."

"You really have to get together with my friend Sam," he said, amused. "The way I see it, I'm just earning a living the best way I know how."

"Does that mean you've ruled out marriage and children?"

"Have you?"

"I know I can be happy without them. If they happen, they happen."

The humor, always so unexpected, sparkled in his whole face, not just his eyes. "That's awfully fatalistic for a woman who's half Pembroke. Aren't Pembrokes all about risk and adventure and taking chances?"

"I don't take many chances with people."

"You take chances with people all the time. The people you employ, the people who buy a Pembroke Springs product, the people who stay at the Pembroke or even stop at your rose gardens—they're all in one way or another risks."

"That's different," she said airily. She wasn't going to lose this one. "It's not like I sleep with them or brought them into the world."

Zeke smiled, smug, as if he had her. "They're still people and they're still risks. So I rest my case."

"You can't just declare victory. You know it's different. Okay, okay. Never mind. Let's look at you. You take physical risks, but I don't see you running around with a toddler on your shoulders."

She stopped right there, her throat constricted as she imagined it. Zeke's dark hair blowing in the wind and his laughter mingling with the squeals of the black-eyed baby riding on his shoulders. It was so vivid and real in her mind that she knew it was possible.

He put down his iced tea and got to his feet and lifted her into his arms. "No more talk."

Her attraction to him, percolating under the surface all day, erupted. The man looked at her—talked to her—as if he knew her. What she was thinking and feeling. She was accustomed to keeping her inner workings to herself, unavailable, even undetectable, to others, but Zeke had worn down all her defenses. Or maybe it was just the timing. She was confused and frustrated and scared, and he happened to have shown up when she didn't want to be alone. She didn't know. She wasn't even sure right now that she cared.

"Let's go upstairs," he said.

"Mattie and Nick should be making their entrance any minute."

Zeke shook his head. "I had Ira give them my room."

"Since when do you have Ira do anything? And those two have been divorced for almost fifty years—they'll start fighting and wreck the place."

"Oh, I think they'll manage." His arms tightened around her, so that she could feel the strength of him, and sense his own ambivalence. He lived in the present. Well, for now so could she. "Let's go, Dani."

She looked at him. "Don't you want to hear about Nick's being blackmailed during the filming of *Casino?*"

A muscle tensed in his jaw. "Upstairs."

Although it wasn't yet dark, Nick collapsed onto the brass bed in the small, attractive room on the third floor of the house his grandfather had built. He couldn't have stayed on his feet if he'd wanted to. He was just too tired. It seemed as if answers, or perhaps just the right questions, were all around him, teasing him, eluding him, and if he could just be still and think, they'd come to him.

He could hear Mattie in the bathroom, washing up, brushing her hair, performing the nightly routine she'd had since she was a girl in Cedar Springs. Nick had never thought he'd live to see her grow old.

She came out, a towel draped around her neck, looking radiant. "You're so quiet. Don't you dare die on me."

"Wouldn't want to annoy you."

Regret washed over her face, and she sat on the edge of the bed. "I'm sorry—staying here must be strange for you."

Ever since turning up the driveway to the Pembroke, Nick had felt as if he was touching the past. Everything triggered a memory. But memories did him no good, and he tried to repress them. His were all so old, back to a time even before Mattie. Most of the people he'd known in those days were gone. Yet, strangely, the beauty and possibilities Dani had discovered in the once-neglected property comforted him, and so did the memories that lurked always in his mind. In his granddaughter's restorations he saw not just her stubborn, risk-taking nature, but also a bit of Pembroke determination. They'd been dreamers and survivors. His grandmother, too. Ulysses's widow, a woman who'd chosen happiness over regret and despair.

Mattie slid under the crazy quilt with him, her body slim and small. "Stop thinking, darling," she said, snuggling beside him. He felt like a pack of toothpicks. "Let's just lie here a while and listen to the rain."

Zeke fingered the Cedar Springs Woolen Mill label on one of Dani's old blankets. "This was made when the mill first opened, I'd say." He was sitting up, the muscles of his bare chest taut, his skin looking almost golden in the evening gloom. "That's well before Joe worked there, or even my mother."

Dani detected a note of nostalgia in his controlled voice. Lying alongside him, she asked, "Did you ever work there?"

He let go of the blanket. "No."

A summer Adirondack thunderstorm was crashing around them. They'd left the windows open, the curtains billowing in the strong, suddenly cool breeze. Lightning flashed and cracked, followed almost immediately by an enormous clap of thunder that seemed to shake the entire cottage. The storm had to be directly overhead. Dani couldn't think of a better time to make love. And she and Zeke had already, explosively. But that didn't stop her from wanting to again. Her life, she decided, had become very complicated.

Outside there was a hissing sound that grew louder and

louder, and then the hard, driving rain came, pounding and drenching the cottage. The wind was still blowing hard into the bedroom, bringing with it sprays of rain. Zeke jumped lightly off the bed and banged the window shut.

Watching him, Dani was struck again by how unbelievably sexy Zeke was. He looked so hard and capable, and she'd given up hope her attraction to him would ever wane. If he walked out of her life now and turned up again in another fifty years, it would still be there, one of those givens in life. Dani Pembroke would always want to make love to Zeke Cutler.

He caught her staring and smiled. "Like the view?"

"I didn't realize white knights could be so sexy."

He laughed. "And I didn't realize hotheaded heiress entrepreneurs who like to climb rocks could be so sexy."

"Ex-heiress," she corrected.

"Once an heiress, always an heiress. It's a matter of attitude, not money."

She didn't argue the point. Instead she enjoyed the idea of being sexy—of his thinking and saying she was sexy. To have him respond to her that way—even if just for now—felt good.

"Are there any other windows that need to be shut?" he asked.

She shook her head.

"Good," he said and came back to bed with her.

The rain crashed against the window, and there was another flash of lightning, then the rumbling roar of more thunder. The storm was moving fast.

Zeke slipped his arms around her, hooking one leg into hers. He was slippery and wet from the rain that had blown onto him, his skin cool to the touch of her fingertips, her lips. They kissed for a long time, slowly, tongues exploring. They paid no attention to the storm. The lights flickered. He cupped her bottom with his hands, then, in the same slow rhythm as their kiss, moved them up her sides, and she wondered what she felt like, tasted like, to him. Was she as new and exciting and different to him as he was to her? Was he as amazed and absorbed by what they were becoming to each other? She didn't want the answers. Not now.

She pulled away from their kiss and lay back on the bed, and he moved his hands over her breasts, watching her as, with one finger, he traced a circle, so slowly, so erotically, around each nipple, not touching it. Then his tongue touched where his finger hadn't. He dragged his hand down her abdomen, to her inner thighs, between her legs. Suddenly she was as out of control as the weather, until she couldn't stand it anymore and pulled him against her, felt the strength of him, and the state of his arousal.

"I'm not holding back," she whispered. "I want you to know that."

He smiled. "I know."

"Are you as afraid as I am?"

"Yes."

His answer reassured her, although she didn't know exactly why. She supposed it was because he shouldn't have all the answers any more than she should, because she wanted him to feel the mystery and uncertainty she was feeling. Falling in love shouldn't be simple and predictable. But was that what was happening to them? Dani felt a shiver of panic. Was she falling in love with this man?

But the storm was howling, and finally he was inside her once more, whispering words against sounds of the rain and the wind.

"I can't hear you," she said.

He brought his mouth close to hers. "It doesn't matter."

And it didn't, she realized. For now, their bodies were doing all the communicating that, at the moment, needed to be done.

Later, when the skies were quiet and the rain had died to a

gentle drizzle and Dani knew she wouldn't sleep, she crept out of bed, wonderfully stiff. She raised the window, feeling the cool air on her overheated skin. She could hear water dripping into puddles in her garden. Chickadees played in her marble bird-bath. She watched them for a few minutes, knowing her life would never be as it had been. Everything had changed, and not just because of the gold key and her mother. Because of Zeke, too, and the capacity for love she'd discovered in herself. She cared about him. What was more, she wanted him to care about her.

When she turned around, her bed was empty. She might have imagined their lovemaking, made up a white knight to carry her off into the sunset.

"Zeke?"

There was no answer. She wasn't sure she'd expected one.

Pulling on her robe, she went back downstairs. No Zeke whipping up something in the kitchen. No note stuck to the re-frigerator. How far could he have gotten without clothes? She took her stairs two steps at a time and checked the bedroom. He'd sneaked out with his clothes. With her right there in the room with him. Had she been catatonic?

"The bastard," she muttered with a small laugh.

She should have waited until after they'd made love to tell him about Nick's being blackmailed.

But she suspected his departure was his way of telling her exactly what she'd been thinking as she'd stared down at her rain-drenched garden—that what they had together was a wonderful dream. It just might not be real.

Seventeen

In the morning Dani made herself get dressed and walk over to her office at the main house. Ira came in to show her his bruised neck. "And you know what kind of sympathy I get around here? None. People say they wish they'd done it. Some friends I have. Rejoicing that I'm almost choked to death by some psychopath."

"Ira, you're exaggerating."

"My own friends telling me that's the way I'll die, with someone's hands around my throat."

Dani tried not to laugh because, of course, she didn't believe a word. "Not if I'm around with my trusty rock."

"Or Zeke with his gun. I think our friend spotted the guy lurking in the woods, and that's why he ran off."

"Women never get credit for anything," Dani said, propping her feet up on her art deco–style coffee table.

Ira scoffed. "Your problem is you want credit for everything. Comes from being the only child of an only child. You don't even have cousins. The rest of us learned what it's like to be shoved out of a tree house by a brother or sister, but not Dani Pembroke. She expects people to behave. Why would some goon want to spy on her in the woods?"

She wiggled her toes, feeling remarkably refreshed given her current state of confusion and sporadic sleep. "Don't inflict your stereotypes on me, Ira. Do you want the day off?"

"No, you'd never manage to run this place and skulk about in the woods for desperadoes. Dani—" He sighed and ran a hand through his corkscrew curls, calming down. "Thanks for letting me vent. I'm worried, that's all. About you, if you want the truth. I know it annoys you to have anyone worry about you, but there it is."

Her eyes misted. "Thanks. If anything had happened to you yesterday—"

"You'd have named some stupid garden after me—The Ira Bernstein Memorial Blackberry Patch." He grinned then, irreverent as ever. "I'll run along and let you pretend to work."

When he'd gone, one of her consultants in New York called. Dani acted glad to hear from him. "What's going on up there? Rumors are flying."

"Such as?"

"Such as an internationally known security expert who happened to have grown up in the same hometown as your grandmother is at the Pembroke."

"Zeke Cutler. Yes, he's here. What else?"

She could almost hear her very professional, very good marketing consultant gritting his teeth. "That Mattie Witt and Nick Pembroke are there."

"Also true."

"What about your wearing the dress your mother wore in *Casino* to the track on Saturday?"

"Not true," Dani said steadily.

"And your having decided to sell the Pembroke because you can't stand the memories?"

"You know that's not true."

He sighed. "Just like to be sure. Is there anything going on that hasn't hit the rumor mill?"

"A lot, but let's talk later."

"Dani…just be careful. Please."

"I will. Thanks for the call."

She hung up before she ended up saying more than she should and someone overheard her in the hall and got another rumor started.

Zeke had returned to her cottage after midnight and stayed until just after dawn. When he left, he didn't say where he'd been or where he was going.

"I'm doing what I know how to do," he'd told her.

"And shutting me out."

He'd smiled in that deliberate, cocky way of his that said he just might know her better than she knew herself. She wondered if he knew how irritating that was. "I wouldn't presume to tell you about total dissolved solvents."

She was smiling, thinking of him, when Eugene Chandler walked into her office. "Hello, Danielle," he said as he looked around, her unconventional work space a contrast to the elegant offices at the Chandler Hotels headquarters in New York. He cleared his throat and added, "I apologize for not calling ahead."

"That's okay. Have a seat. Can I get you anything?"

"No, thank you."

He didn't sit down, but walked into the middle of the sun-washed room, rubbing one finger across the top of her old player piano. She'd opened the windows to let in a cool, fresh morning breeze, filled with the scent of flowers and grass. She could hear guests outside enjoying themselves. Her grandfather peered out the leaded-glass window.

"Is something the matter?" she asked.

"I'd forgotten how quite extraordinary this property is," he said pensively, still staring out the window. "It always was impractical as a private home. Of course, Ulysses Pembroke never concerned himself with practicalities. I understand that but for you, Danielle, this property would be a shopping mall by now."

"I'll take that as a compliment."

"Many people are grateful you stuck to your guns when I told you this scheme of yours would never work. Don't get me wrong. I admire what you've accomplished. I didn't come here to criticize."

His quiet words, the concern in his cool blue eyes, made Dani wonder if she might have unfairly pigeonholed her grandfather, damned him forever for the occasional insensitive remark, failed to understand him as badly as he'd failed to understand her. Failed to forgive. Perhaps, she thought, his rigidness and uncompromising attitude weren't as rigid and uncompromising as she'd always believed. Learning more about Jackson Witt allowed her to look at her disagreements with Eugene Chandler—and there undeniably were many—with a new perspective. If nothing else, she had to give her grandfather credit for always being forthright with her in his own exasperating way.

"I understand Mattie and Nick are in town," he said.

Dani wasn't surprised. That kind of news would travel fast. "They arrived yesterday afternoon."

"And they're already up to their old antics. I was with a friend at his stables this morning, and who should float overhead in a bright yellow balloon but those two. Mattie still has that orange flight suit of hers, I see. I should have thought by now they were too old for ballooning."

"Not according to Mattie. Nick I don't know about—she probably had to browbeat him into going. It's fairly calm out. They shouldn't have run into any problems."

He didn't seem reassured. "Danielle—why are they here? Why is your father here? And what really happened to him?"

It went against every fiber of her being to confide in him.

Dani dropped her feet to the floor and jumped up, wishing for an interruption. A fax, another call from New York, papers to sign. But she walked over to the window and stood beside her tall and very dignified grandfather. She inhaled, suddenly sympathetic to this old man who'd lost so much. But how could she explain questions she barely understood herself—never mind their possible answers?

"I don't know exactly why Mattie, Nick and Pop are here, except that some things have been going on...." But her nature, years of mistrust and miscommunication, and maybe a touch of concern for him, stopped her from going further. She added gently, "I'm sure it's all a tempest in a teapot."

He turned to her, and she could see where he'd nicked his chin shaving, where the dark, puffy circles had formed under his eyes. "There's something I think you should know. Zeke Cutler and his older brother, Joe, were in Saratoga the week your mother disappeared. I didn't know it at the time—no one thought to tell me."

"How did you find out?"

He smiled thinly. "It was the one reasonably interesting detail my private investigators managed to produce. Oh, I had both Cutler brothers checked out. Joe was in the army then, Zeke was in high school in Tennessee. Apparently they came north to inform Mattie that her father was dying of cancer."

"Zeke told me—"

"But did he tell you his brother had decided while he was up here that he was in love with your aunt Sara?"

Dani felt a rush of cold. Sara? And Joe Cutler? Zeke had to know. And he'd chosen not to tell her. She didn't feel betrayed, only a tug of hopelessness. She was falling in love with Zeke—no use pretending she wasn't—but how could they ever really work together? The past seemed destined to extinguish the possibilities that had sparked between them.

"Of course," her grandfather went on, "Sara's heart already lay with Roger. It was right around that time that they began seeing each other."

"Did he know about Joe?"

"I don't think so. I believe Joe knew more about Roger than Roger knew about Joe."

"Then Sara dumped Joe?"

Her grandfather wrinkled up his face in distaste. "I don't think their relationship ever progressed to the point that she needed to be that direct. I'm sure she discouraged him as sensitively as she could."

Dani sank onto the piano bench, remembering her aunt at twenty. She'd been pretty and rebellious, still shattered by her mother's death. Having two men as different as Roger Stone and Joe Cutler falling for her must have been a welcome distraction. But how different was the Sara Chandler Stone of today. "Does Sara realize you know this?" Dani asked.

He shook his head. "There would be no point. She's had enough to endure without another reminder of that terrible summer. Joe Cutler…" He hesitated, turning from the window. "It's too late now, I suppose, but I've often wondered if he might have known something…" He trailed off. "But there's never been any evidence to suggest his involvement with your mother's disappearance."

"Could Roger and Sara know anything and just not realize it?"

"It's possible. I intend to ask." His eyes clouded. "Danielle—I brought you something. I don't know if it will make any difference to you, but—" Stopping midsentence, he reached into his coat pocket and withdrew a small, black leather volume; it looked old. "This is one of my mother's journals. Her last, actually. The entries stop right as her three oldest children became ill with diphtheria and died. Lilli and Sara both read it when they were younger—I'd have given it to you sooner to read if I'd thought you were interested."

Dani felt a stab of guilt. "Grandfather, I had no idea…"

He held up a hand. "I'm not criticizing. I'm merely explaining why I've waited until now to give this to you. Danielle, my mother and your great-great-grandmother—Ulysses's wife—maintained a quiet, almost secret friendship." Handing Dani the diary, he went on. "I've marked an entry I think might interest you right now, given what's been going on in your life."

Dani opened up to the marked page. Her great-grandmother's handwriting was delicate and clear, faded with time. She looked up at her grandfather, but he waved her on. She read:

I saw Louisa today. Despite her tremendous financial woes, she has finally decided not to sell the gold key that Ulysses made to match the gate key to the pavilion at Pembroke Springs, where they met in a more optimistic time. However, neither can she bear to keep it. Ulysses caused her so much joy, and yet brought her so much suffering. She has chosen instead to bury it in the fountain inside the pavilion, as a testament to what I frankly do not know. Her ambivalence about her late husband, perhaps? At least she has made her decision, however little I understand it. I have promised to go with her tomorrow morning to help her dislodge the fountain tiles. Naturally I have told my husband none of this….

Dani pictured the two refined women smashing up the fountain in their ruffled tea dresses. She shut the volume. "Did Nick know about this?" she asked her grandfather.

"Not unless Lilli told him. I'm quite sure his grandmother never told him about having buried a large twenty-four-karat gold key. Otherwise he would have…" He deliberately didn't finish.

But Dani did. "He'd have hocked it first chance he got."

Eugene Chandler let her have the last word on that one. "I only wish Lilli had left us with a similar insight into her character as my mother did." He became strangely quiet, his shoulders slumped. "It would be a blessing to know what happened to her before I pass on. I've always thought I wouldn't have to die with her disappearance still unresolved."

"I hope you won't," Dani said.

"But," he went on awkwardly, "I would rather leave the past alone and not know than to see anything happen to you." He kissed her lightly on the forehead. "It's always a pleasure to see you, Danielle."

She was too stunned to say goodbye. As she watched him leave, it struck her that despite his inability to know what to say to her—his seeming lack of emotion—her grandfather had suffered and had been changed by the long years of not knowing what had happened to his firstborn daughter. His inability to know what to say to Dani—his seeming lack of emotion—didn't mean he didn't care.

She remembered the day he'd marched down to her Greenwich Village apartment for the first and only time, not long after she'd gone into business for herself. He had demanded to know why, if she insisted on a career, didn't she take a position with Chandler Hotels? She'd been mystified. Not only did he disapprove of Chandler women taking careers, and generally disapproved of her choice, but her father had embezzled from Chandler Hotels, betrayed his father-in-law's trust. Betrayed his coworkers. How could her grandfather expect her to work with the same people her father had robbed?

"I'm a Pembroke, Grandfather," she'd told him.

And he'd looked at her with his grave steel-blue eyes. "You don't have to be."

"What?"

"Drop the Pembroke from your name. In time people will forget who your father was. At least they'll know you want no part of him—that you're different."

She'd thrown him out and had called a lawyer to begin the proceedings to disinherit herself. "Not a nickel!" she'd told him. "Not a nickel of his money do I want crossing my palm!"

And not a nickel had.

Quint Skinner handed John his pants. "Get dressed."

John clutched the pants and tried not to look scared out of his wits.

"I'm not kidnapping you." Skinner's eyes were hard, his voice absolutely calm. "You're coming of your own free will."

"Now, why would I do that?"

"Because," Skinner said with no small touch of drama, "I know where your daughter is."

John felt a stab of fear. *Dani.* He swung his legs off the edge of his bed. A hell of a lot of help he'd been since coming to Saratoga. So far he'd had his head knocked in, and now he was getting himself snatched right out of his hospital bed. Where were Sam Jones and Zeke Cutler when he needed them?

"What do you want from me?" he asked the big red-faced man.

"Get dressed first."

Swallowing groans of pain and refusing to whine, John pulled on his pants, which hung even more than usual. He'd lost weight in the past couple of days. Skinner thrust his shirt and sneakers at him. "No socks?" John asked cheekily.

He didn't get even a glimmer of a smile from the stinking thug.

When he finished dressing, he and Skinner headed down the hospital corridor. "What if I faint?" John asked.

"Your daughter lives in a purple cottage on the Pembroke estate. Has a statue of Artemis in the garden."

John felt his knees wobble under him.

Outside, Saratoga was enjoying beautiful weather, last night's storms having washed out the clouds and humidity. Skinner shoved John into the front seat of a dark blue BMW. "Mind the noggin," John said. "I presume it was your doing?"

Quint ignored him.

John sat very still, trying to hold off a wave of dizziness. He'd talked the doctors into springing him today. He wanted desperately to do something to get to the bottom of whatever was going on in Saratoga. He hadn't had being kidnapped in mind. He looked at the solid man beside him. "I know who you are, you know."

Quint nodded. "That stupid book on Joe Cutler fixed that for me. There's no going back once you've lost your anonymity."

Despite his appearance and manner, the man wasn't stupid. John vowed to keep that in mind. "At least you had it to lose. I never did myself. Anyway, I don't recognize you from your book. You tried to interview me in New York before I was nailed for embezzlement. Remember?"

The placid expression didn't change. "I remember."

"You were fresh out of the military, trying to launch a journalism career by digging out a story on my mother. Your angle was unusual. You'd served with Joe Cutler and figured you'd compare the Witts and the Cutlers of Cedar Springs, their different destinies. Only you never wrote the piece."

"You wouldn't talk to me."

John grinned. "I was still noble in those days."

They'd come to a light on Broadway. Quint was a careful driver, confident. He reached over and popped open the glove compartment, pulled out a wrinkled paper bag. He dropped it onto John's lap. "Take a look inside."

He did so. The dizziness from his head injury came in waves. As he stared into the bag, it threatened to inundate him.

Inside the bag were two gate keys, one brass, one gold.

"You took these from my daughter," John said hoarsely.

"Yep. And I didn't hurt her as much as she keeps making out." He shrugged, matter-of-fact. "Not as much as I could have, anyway."

John clutched the bag. "You son of a bitch."

"Save it. I'm not in this to get you people to like me."

No kidding, John thought, annoyed now as much as afraid.

Skinner glanced at him and grinned. "You'd like to smack me one, wouldn't you?"

"I'd like to do more than that."

"Well, you'll just have to wait. Joe found the gold key when he was up here when your wife disappeared. He told me. We were pals, you know?"

He waited, seeming to want John to respond. So he did. "Fine way you had of showing it."

"People read the book wrong. I wasn't condemning him. I was just—never mind."

His knuckles turned white as he gripped the steering wheel; the man, John thought, definitely had his own agenda. But what was it? He asked again, "What do you want from me?"

"There are a ton of gates on your little girl's property. I checked."

His little girl. John shut his eyes, fighting nausea and dizziness and the feeling—the horrible dread—that he was about to fail his daughter again.

"I can't risk making a mistake. So you're going to show me which gate those keys unlock." Quint spoke as if he had no doubt that was exactly what John would do.

"And if I don't?"

"I'll make your daughter show me."

Zeke had too many theories.

He walked through the elegant gaming room on the second floor of the Canfield Casino Museum in Congress Park. The decor was high Victorian, lavish, heavy, dark. The thick, pat-terned carpet absorbed his footsteps as he checked out the faro table, which looked relatively innocuous under an ornate chan-delier. He tried to imagine Dani's two great-great-grandfa-thers—robber baron Ambrose Chandler and gambler Ulysses Pembroke—placing their bets. Maybe it was Jackson Witt's in-fluence on the culture of Cedar Springs, but Zeke had never seen the attraction of gambling.

On his way out he stopped at the glass-fronted display case in the hall.

Beatrix Chandler smiled at him from the grainy photograph taken a few days after her marriage to hotel magnate Ambrose Chandler. She was fair and pretty and just nineteen. She and Ambrose would have four children. Three would die of diph-theria. Money or no money, it wasn't as if the Chandlers hadn't faced tragedy in their lives.

Squinting, blocking out all sound around him, Zeke studied another photograph, this one of Ulysses and Louisa Pembroke in the pavilion at Pembroke Springs just before his bottling plant had gone bust. In small print the caption stated that the shy judge's daughter and the notorious rake had first met in the pavilion. Was that why, of all the gold keys legend says she sold, Louisa Cald-well Pembroke hadn't sold the gold key to that particular pavilion? How had it ended up back there for Joe to find decades later? And then end up on the cliffs for Dani to find twenty-five years after that?

Too many theories to fit too many facts, Zeke thought.

He'd hooked up with Sam in his nondescript car outside Quint Skinner's little rented house last night and discussed the possibilities.

"What about your ex-heiress?" Sam had asked.

"You ever call her 'my' anything within her earshot, be pre-pared to duck. She's her own woman."

"It's just an expression."

"She doesn't have a sense of humor about that sort of thing."

Sam nodded thoughtfully. "I can understand that. So did you leave her to her own devices?"

"Ira Bernstein has the grounds crawling with security people. They're very low-key."

"Any good?"

"I think so."

"What about our boy Quint?"

"Sleeping at the moment."

Zeke had looked out at the small Cape Cod house. "We're missing something, Sam."

"Either that," Sam said, "or we've got all the pieces sitting right in front of us and are too damn blind or stupid to put them together."

After the storms the night air was cool and still, with neighborhood cats on the prowl. "Who stands to gain?" Zeke had asked rhetorically.

"Gain what?"

It was a good point. "The gold key would be worth a hefty sum—not just because it's gold, but also because of its historical and romantic significance."

"The profit motive," Sam said. "Our Pulitzer Prize winner could use money. Think he knows its connection to Lilli?"

"Yes, I do. Joe could have shown him the photograph of her and Lilli in the balloon—or Quint could have just come across it while they served together—and he recognized the key in Dani's picture in the paper, just like Naomi did."

"Would you remember what kind of necklace a woman was wearing in a photograph you saw twenty years ago?"

Zeke gave that some thought. "Maybe if the woman was a missing heiress and the other woman she was with was a legendary actress and I was looking for a way to the top."

"Or maybe if your army buddy pointed the key out to you for some reason." Sam stretched and added quietly, "The Pembrokes could use money, too. John, Nick, even Dani. But it doesn't fit the facts for one of them to be after the gold key for profit."

"No," Zeke said.

"And I gather the Chandlers don't need money. So what if this thing's not about profit? What are the other possibilities?"

A yellow cat had crossed in front of Sam's car and scampered up a maple. "Lilli Chandler Pembroke."

Sam hadn't said anything for a moment. "There are two angles to consider. One, someone doesn't want the truth about what happened to her to come out. Two, someone's after the truth."

So they considered both angles for a while, tossing ideas back and forth in the quiet night.

"One thing we know for sure," Sam said. "Joe's dead. Whoever's doing what around here, it can't be him."

Zeke had spelled him for a while, then headed back to Dani's Hansel and Gretel cottage. Her tale of Nick's blackmail was just another fact to fit into his host of theories.

On his way out of the casino museum, he stopped at the gift shop. Reproductions of the newspaper headline announcing Ulysses Pembroke's horse as the winner of the first Chandler Stakes were almost sold out.

Zeke bought one, just for the hell of it.

Nick and Mattie were at the teak table in Dani's cottage garden when she returned with Beatrix Chandler's diary.

"I'll never do that again," Nick said.

Mattie scoffed. "I still don't believe that was your first time in a balloon. I could swear I took you up once years ago."

"You did not. I must be senile to have let you whisk me off

like that. No wonder people think you're eccentric. If I'd known you were this crazy—hell, I'd have shot you off your moral high horse years ago. You've got no room to talk about me being reckless."

"Now, Nick, it wasn't so bad." Mattie stirred a spoonful of sugar into a mug of coffee; she and Nick had helped themselves to Dani's pantry. "When I die, I'd love to have my ashes sprinkled over the Adirondacks from the basket of a beautiful hot-air balloon."

Nick grunted. "Do that to me, and I'll come back and haunt you. I swear I will. I'm going into the ground in a pine box, not dumped from the sky like an ashtray."

"You two are morbid," Dani said.

Her grandfather grinned at her. "Wait till you're my age, urchin. You'll find the prospect of living forever's a good deal more frightening than that of dying. I know more people in the Great Beyond than I do here."

Mattie handed him the sugared coffee. "That's because you've lived so bloody long."

"To harangue you, my dear."

Dani had had enough. Grabbing a handful of wild blueberries from a basket Mattie had brought down from the main house, she jumped up and started inside.

"Off somewhere?" Mattie asked.

"The springs. I won't be gone long."

Concern darkened her grandmother's face. "But if you were attacked there—"

"I wasn't. Ira was."

"Still, don't you think you should wait for Zeke?"

The suggestion made her raise her eyebrows, and she grinned at Mattie. "What for?"

"He's a trained professional. If someone out there wants to hurt you—"

"Given her gene pool, Mattie," Nick said, "Dani's not likely to appreciate anyone swooping in to her rescue." His black eyes focused on Dani with a measure of amusement. "Are you, urchin?"

What he was saying, she knew, was that she had a tendency to be defiant and independent to a fault. That she was reluctant to trust anyone, including Zeke Cutler.

"I'll be back," she said.

"Is there any particular reason you're going out there?" Mattie asked. She had her mug to her lips and was blowing on the hot coffee.

"Just checking on a couple of things."

One thing in particular. According to Zeke, his brother had found the gold key at the pavilion at Pembroke Springs, no doubt right where Louisa Caldwell Pembroke and Beatrix Chandler had buried it. In Beatrix's diary, she stated that she and Louisa had carefully replaced the tiles they'd dislodged. Decades later, however, again according to Zeke, the fountain had been a mess, with broken and missing tiles, the area overgrown and dug up in places. Fountains and pavilions throughout the old estate had been vandalized over the years. But when Dani had begun her restoration of the grounds after Pembroke Springs was on solid financial footing, she'd been surprised at what good shape the pavilion near the bottling plant was in.

Who, in the years between her mother's disappearance and then, had cleaned up the place? And why?

She asked Mattie, "Did you have any work done out at the springs before I took over?"

"No—why?"

"I'm not sure, but it's not important right now. I'll be back in a little while." She smiled. "You two, behave yourselves."

Zeke headed to Quint's rented house to check with Sam once more before making his way back to the Pembroke. He'd lay out all his theories for Dani, Nick, Mattie, John if he was out of the hospital. They'd put their heads together. See what they came up with.

Sam had moved across the street, down from the cute yellow house. Zeke pulled up behind Sam's car. There was no sign of his friend, but Zeke wasn't concerned. For all he knew, Sam was perched on Quint's rooftop, peering down his chimney.

As Zeke approached Sam's car, the driver's-side door swung open, and Sam fell out onto the street.

Zeke took out his gun and ran to him.

Sam reached for the door handle, grunting with pain and effort as he tried to pull himself up. Zeke got to him. He took Sam's weight and saw the grayish cast to his skin and the blood soaked into his tangerine polo shirt and the leg of his sand-colored jeans. Around them, kids skidded by on bicycles. A mother yelled.

"Looks worse than it is," Sam said, sweating.

"What happened?"

"Shot."

"Quint?"

They were already moving toward Zeke's car. Sam was not a light man. He shook his head, shuddering. Zeke could almost see his friend's pain. "I didn't see who did it. Came up from behind." He grimaced as Zeke held him against his car, opening the back door. "Thought I was dead this time."

"Did you see Quint?"

"No."

"I'll check on him after I get you to the hospital."

As always, Sam's professionalism was in full gear. "I can wait."

But Zeke got him into the backseat and checked his wound. A clean shot to the shoulder and one to the thigh. Blood everywhere. Sam couldn't wait. Slamming the door, Zeke climbed into the front seat. The hospital wasn't far.

In the backseat Sam didn't make a sound.

"Just keep your mouth shut," Quint ordered.

Stretched out on the stone bench inside the pavilion, John watched his kidnapper loosen another section of Spanish tile with his crowbar. He'd decided Quint was mostly a lot of hot air. Oh, he could kill John. Just like he could have killed Dani when he'd had the chance. One whack with the crowbar would do the job. But John didn't think he'd do it. Whatever Skinner was up to, it wasn't about profit and murder. At least not entirely.

"Louisa Pembroke sold off all the other gold keys," John pointed out. He was uncomfortable—his head throbbed—but the scent of roses and morning glories, of the hemlocks and pines, helped. "She probably hung on to the one that matched the key to this gate because she met Ulysses here. Buried it in a fit of pique. From what I hear, she was something of a hothead herself—a lot like my daughter."

Quint smashed two chunks of no-doubt pricey antique tiles into bits, an act of frustration more than purpose. "I don't care about finding more gold keys."

Precisely what John had expected he'd say. "And what do you care about?"

Quint looked around at him, sweat pouring down his unhandsome face. "Justice."

Spoken like a Pulitzer Prize winner, John thought, wondering if he was delirious. Quint had kidnapped him. Why wasn't he more terrified? Because being only slightly terrified is all I can manage right now.

And because he thought Quint Skinner just might be telling the truth.

"What're you going to do with me when you're finished here?" he asked.

"Don't know yet."

John wasn't encouraged. "My daughter has security guards on the property. Aren't you worried someone's going to come out here and ask what you're doing?"

"Nope."

"Why not?"

"Because I'm armed," Quint said, then paused a half beat. "And I have you."

There was that, John thought. He cleared his throat and decided to keep quiet. He had never been a terribly good judge of character, and Skinner might yet prove to be a killer.

But what was he after?

Dani ducked into the bottling plant through the rear entrance. The walk through the woods had helped clear her head, and she wanted to let the security guard know she was on the grounds. She debated having him go over to the springs with her, just in case Quint Skinner was lurking about, ready to pin someone against a tree.

She heard a moan a few feet away, under a wild-looking juniper near the entrance to the shipping office in the old part of the building.

The security guard was slumped under the tree, gagged and bleeding from an ugly gash on the right side of his head. His hands and feet were bound with an extension cord. One extension cord. That, Dani thought, must have required a certain proficiency.

"Russ, are you all right? Here—hold on." Her hands shaking, she pulled out the gag, a simple bandanna. Russ was a skinny guy, about her father's age. No match for the likes of Quint Skinner. "I'll call the police."

"No time," he choked out.

Dani worked on freeing his hands and feet. The cord was hard to work with. "Just take it easy."

She got the cord off, freeing him, and staved off a surge of panic as she dabbed at his gash with the bandanna. He went completely white and swore. The gash looked horrible: bloody, purple, swollen. Dani got out her cell phone. Her entire body was shaking.

Russ was trying to struggle to his feet. "I screwed up, Miss Pembroke."

"No, you didn't. Guarding a mineral-water plant wasn't supposed to be your dangerous sort of security job."

He collapsed back onto the grass, even whiter now. "He's got your father."

She couldn't move. "Skinner?"

"I don't know his name. Big guy." Russ winced in agony. "Said your father's in the car with him. I don't think your father knew he coldcocked me."

"I'll call the police—"

"Get me my gun," Russ said. "Dani—I can't let your father…"

She found the gun under the juniper. "Tell me how to use it," she said, kneeling back down next to him. "I'll go. You wait for the police."

Russ took the gun from her, released the safety and handed it back to her. "Point and pull the trigger. Keep your elbows bent." He coughed, his eyes squinted against the pain. "Be ready for the kick. Small as you are, you'll feel it."

She thrust her cell phone at him. "You're sure—"

"Go," he said.

She was off, keeping the gun pointed at the ground. She concentrated on where her feet touched the brick path, the rhythm of her movements, the weight of the gun in her hand, her breathing.

Pop…

She cut off the thought before it could blossom and over-whelm her. Her father had to be all right. She wasn't ready to lose him.

If she could simply distract Skinner until the police go there…

Listening hard, she heard nothing but birds and the sough of the wind in the trees. She ran through a small grove of pines, feeling the soft grass underfoot, slowing as she came up behind the pavilion where she suspected Quint had taken her father.

Suddenly she heard her father's voice, and the rush of adrenaline was so enormous she thought her chest would burst.

He's alive.

"You should see your face," he was saying to Skinner. "It's about the color of a good roasted red pepper. Keep this up, you're going to have a stroke."

Peering from behind thick branches of a pine tree, Dani saw Quint rising, a crowbar in one hand. "I ought to hit you over the head just for driving me crazy. You're worse than the mosquitoes."

No one, Dani thought, could be more maddening than her father.

She edged forward to the wrought-iron fence. The gate was on the opposite side, which helped give her the advantage of surprise. Skinner would be unlikely to expect an approach from that direction. But it didn't permit her to cut off his exit. The gate had been left wide open.

Ducking under one more branch, she came out within a foot of the gate. She raised Russ's gun. Elbows bent…be ready for the kick…point and pull the trigger…

Her father spotted her. She knew because he looked as if he was going to throw up.

"Keep your hands where I can see them," she said.

Skinner looked around at her, then laid his crowbar onto a massive shoulder like a fishing pole and laughed at her.

"I wouldn't annoy her if I were you," John said. He didn't sound particularly terrified, but that was her father. Bravado in the face of any problem, no matter how serious.

"I don't care what you're doing here," Dani said to Skinner. "Just let my father go."

"You're welcome to him." He slung the crowbar off his shoulder and held it easily in one hand at his side. The amusement left his expression. He nodded to the fountain. "I found what I came to find."

He turned his back to her and her gun and sauntered off toward the gate.

"Hey," she said. "I have a gun pointed at you."

He glanced back at her, his face red and dirty. "So?"

"So you nearly killed my hotel manager and then my security guard. And I'll bet you landed my father here in the hospital."

"Nope," he said. "I didn't do that one. The others—what can I say? Sometimes you gotta do what you gotta do."

"I'm not going to let you just walk out of here."

"Dani," her father said.

"Stay out of this, Pop."

"Sweetheart," Quint said, "you fire that thing, the only one who's going to get hurt is you. It's a forty-four. It'll knock you on your pretty little ass."

He continued through the gate.

Her father jumped between her and Skinner. "Dani, just let the bastard go."

"Relax, Pop. I'm not going to do anything crazy."

"You're damn right you're not," Zeke said from behind her.

She swung around, and he snatched her gun before she could accidentally—or on purpose—shoot him, then caught her by the shoulder, steadying her. She didn't protest. "Where did you come from?" she asked.

"The inn. Mattie and Nick heard from the hospital that John was gone—they're frantic. Ira's got someone with them. He's ready to call out the National Guard."

"What happened to your friend?" John asked, still on the bench on the other side of the fence. "I kept expecting him to swoop to my rescue at any moment. Unlike other members of my family, I'd happily turn my safety over to either one of you."

"Sam was shot," Zeke said, grim-faced.

Dani grabbed his wrist. "Will he be okay? What happened?"

"He's fine, but later," he said. "The police are on the way. Since this isn't my show, I'd prefer not to stick around." He pulled his wrist free and started around the pavilion. "By the way, Quint was bluffing. Your gun's a thirty-eight. It has a kick, but it wouldn't have knocked you on your pretty little ass. I would have. You don't take on killers when you don't have to."

"I did have to."

"Do you ever not argue back?"

She managed a smile. "Never."

He grinned. "Good."

Then he was gone.

"My, my," her father said, eyeing her.

She frowned at him. "It's not what you think."

"Oh, I'm afraid it is."

She would stand for no more of this. "What was Skinner after?"

"I haven't the foggiest. He made a damn mess of your fountain, though." He climbed unsteadily to his feet and walked to the edge of the circular brick path inside the pavilion and examined the area where Quint had been digging. "Oh, hell."

"Pop?"

She lunged for the gate. Her father tried to stop her. But he was too weak, too shocked himself, and she pushed past him.

She saw the twisted, crumpled mess that was still recognizable as the straw hat her mother had had with her the night she disappeared twenty-five years ago.

Eighteen

The cream-colored Chandler house on North Broadway stood silent in the bright afternoon sun. With the watchman's gun heavy in her hand, Dani stopped on the wide sidewalk and looked up at the sky, almost as if there should be a hot-air balloon floating overhead, carrying her smiling mother back to her, just like in *The Wizard of Oz*.

"Oh, Mama," she whispered, fighting back tears.

She'd dragged her father from the pavilion back to the bottling plant, where Russ was holding his bandanna to his wounded head. By then, the police sirens were close. Russ had promised to see to her father and let her borrow his car. She'd driven straight to Millionaires' Row.

Her aunt was in a wicker chair on the front porch, stroking a long-haired white cat in her lap. A pile of crumpled pink petunia blossoms lay scattered on the floor beside her. She wore one of her feminine, flowery dresses and smiled as Dani climbed the steps onto the wide, curving porch. "Hello, Danielle. What a pleasant surprise. Won't you sit down."

"Sure."

But she sat not on a wicker chair next to her aunt, but on the railing, under a hanging basket of petunias.

"Is something wrong, Danielle? You look— My goodness, is that blood on your shirt?"

Russ's blood. And maybe her father's. She hadn't noticed it until that moment. Zeke, too, had had bloodstains on his shirt. That hadn't penetrated until he'd vanished into the woods.

"Sara, we need to talk."

"Of course. You know I'm always here for you."

"Grandfather stopped by today. He showed me the passage in Beatrix Chandler's diary about the gold key and her friendship with Louisa Pembroke."

"Yes, I know. He told me." The corners of her pink-stained mouth twitched in a small smile. "The more you abuse him, the more he seems to appreciate you."

Dani tried to keep her thoughts focused, on course. "Did you show Joe Cutler that passage when he was here?"

"Now, how would I remember something like that?" She faltered, pulling in her lower lip. "Danielle, exactly what are you trying to get at?"

"Is Roger home?"

"No."

"Grandfather?"

"He's not here. Danielle—"

"You know," she said, "I've been looking at this thing all wrong, trying to blame everything on Joe Cutler and Quint Skinner. The blackmail—"

"What blackmail?" Sara seemed genuinely shocked. She shoved the cat off her lap but didn't get up. "You've been under tremendous strain lately, Danielle. Perhaps you've—"

"Gone off the deep end? Started to self-destruct like Nick and my father? Right now I almost wish I had. Sara, Mother and Nick both were being blackmailed over her role in *Casino*. Someone knew she'd have done just about anything to keep it a secret."

"Well, it certainly wasn't me. Lilli never told me a thing about her acting."

The undertone of jealousy and bitterness was hard to miss. But Dani didn't let it deter her. "Joe knew about the blackmail."

"Knew about it," Sara said, her incisive eyes on Dani, "or committed it?"

"For a while I believed he might have committed it." She kept her voice steady and calm, despite the raging inside her. "But it doesn't make any sense. Nick says the blackmailer never asked for much money, a hundred here and there. Joe could have made more than that by selling off the gold key he found. Instead he gave it to Mother."

"She trusted him. Joe certainly had us all fooled. Look what he did in combat." Sara rose gracefully, ladylike. But her skin was a little pale, and she teetered on her high heels. "I don't believe I care to continue this conversation. You understand. It's just too painful."

Dani didn't move from the porch railing. "Joe had a copy of one of the blackmail letters. If he wasn't the blackmailer, how did he get it?"

"I wouldn't know."

"Why did he see Nick a few years later when he was on leave and then come here to Saratoga?"

Sara walked all the way to the ornate front door but stopped there, her back to Dani.

"Did he see you then?" she asked softly.

"Danielle, please don't."

"I'm not trying to upset you, Sara. But I need to know."

"Why?" She spun around at Dani, tears shining in her vivid blue eyes. "Why do you need to know?"

"Too much has been happening. It needs to stop. We need to know the truth about the past."

"Joe is dead. Lilli's never coming back. What possible good

can come of knowing who was blackmailing whom twenty-five years ago?"

Dani persisted. "Did Joe come to see you, Sara?"

Sara sank against the door, slipping her hands behind her and holding on to the polished brass handle. She nodded. "I—I'd caught him blackmailing Lilli. He wanted money to send his brother to Vanderbilt University. I... I made him give Lilli the gold key or I'd tell on him. I saw him that evening—"

"The night Mother disappeared?"

"Yes, but earlier. It's why I was late to help you get dressed. You remember?"

Dani remembered. She'd hated the white chiffon dress and especially the new patent-leather shoes, and Sara had been in such a state she'd almost let Dani wear her shorts.

"I broke off our...relationship. I hadn't been sure how I felt about him—I suppose I was attracted to him for all the wrong reasons. When I caught him at blackmail, I told him to leave Saratoga or I'd report him to the police."

A squirrel ran up a maple in the front yard and out to the end of a branch near the porch and chattered at them. "What made you think Joe was the blackmailer?" Dani asked.

"Oh, that wasn't difficult to figure out," Sara said vaguely.

"Did Mother know?"

"I'm not sure. I never saw her again to ask. Of course, she'd have wanted to save Joe from himself. You remember how she was, especially that summer after our mother died."

The tears glistened on Sara's pale cheeks now, although she wasn't sobbing. Dani made herself press on. "Why did Joe come back four years later?"

She pulled away from the door and sniffled, regaining some composure. The bodice on her dress was cut low, and her breasts heaved with her rapid, shallow breathing. But she tilted up her chin, looking regal. "I wouldn't know. I refused to see him."

Dani didn't believe her, but she decided not to push the point, not yet. She jumped down from the porch railing. "I think he was trying to figure out what happened to Mother."

"What business was Lilli of his?" she demanded, combative.

"She was his friend."

Sara's eyes flashed. "She was my sister!"

As if that gave her prerogatives. Dani moved in closer to her aunt. "Sara, what happened that night?"

She pushed back her hair, maintaining her composure.

"You and Roger went out to look for Mother after the lawn party. Did you find her?"

Even as she stood as still and sleek as a mannequin, tears spilled once more down her porcelain cheeks. Dani felt her own composure starting to give way. She made herself go to her aunt. "Sara," she said, touching her rounded shoulder. "What happened?"

"I killed her," Sara whispered.

Dani shut her eyes, and her aunt fell onto her shoulder, sobbing, quaking with guilt and relief, and Dani had to hold her, had to stand firm, or they both would have collapsed.

"God help me," Sara said over and over. "I killed my own sister."

Zeke got to the little yellow house with the welcome goose on the front door too late.

Quint was sprawled on the living-room floor, dying. Forcing back any emotion, Zeke called the police and found a towel in the downstairs bathroom. He pressed the towel to Quint's abdomen. The wound was bad. Quint's face was gray from the loss of blood.

"Hang on," Zeke said.

"It's too late."

Zeke knew it was. "We'll just sit here together and wait for help."

"Whole thing was a setup. I thought Joe'd found out what I'd been a part of. Thought he'd turn me in. Hell, we were just kids. I…" He swallowed, panting, still fighting. "I was stupid."

"Save it."

"For what? Think the devil doesn't know what I've done? You gotta know, Zeke. Your brother never broke. He did his job." Quint licked his lips, shuddering with pain. "He was the best."

Your brother never broke…

The land mines of his past, Zeke thought, his arm—his entire body—shaking as he held the towel to Quint's wound.

"I watched the terrorists take him out. He was a hero, Zeke." Quint sobbed hoarsely, without tears or energy. "I lied. I made a name for myself on his back. Him—his men—everybody was dead but me."

Because this man was dying, and Joe was already dead, and he didn't know what else to do, Zeke said, "What's done is done, Quint."

He raised himself up off the floor and gripped Zeke's arm with what must have been all his remaining strength. "Joe was my friend!"

"Let it go," Zeke said gently.

"I only wanted justice."

Zeke could hear the sirens not too far away. "Quint, who did this to you? Who shot you?"

"Didn't mean to hurt anybody," he said weakly, his voice barely audible. "Damn, Zeke…she was there all along."

Quint was fading but still lucid, and Zeke felt himself go so rigid he thought he'd crack into pieces. "Do you mean Lilli?"

"In the fountain…didn't want to say anything with her husband and daughter right there."

"Quint—who shot you?"

His eyes focused on Zeke, clear and alert and dying. "You'll fix it?"

He couldn't fix a wound like the one Quint had. He couldn't fix a mother who had died twenty-five years ago. That kind of knight in shining armor just didn't exist. But he nodded. "I'll do what I can."

The siren was getting louder. Once the police and ambulance arrived it wouldn't be easy to get away. And he had to. There were other lives at stake, and nothing more he could do in the grape-colored dining room.

Quint Skinner was dead.

Dani was on her feet, pacing, forcing herself to concentrate, to hold herself together. There was a breeze against her back, and on North Broadway a couple of little girls walked down the sidewalk dragging a red wagon. Suddenly she wished she could be nine again, hiding from her grandfather, thinking up ways to make her mother happy.

"I ran into her on her way home," Sara said. She'd composed herself and returned to her wicker chair; the cat had climbed back into her lap. "I told her I'd broken off with Joe. She was disappointed—I could tell. She liked him. So I told her he was the one who'd blackmailed her."

"Did Mother believe you?"

"No, of course not. She wanted to hear it directly from Joe. So we walked up to the old bottling plant where he and his brother had pitched their tent, only they were already gone."

To tell Mattie that her father in Cedar Springs was dying.

Dani crossed her arms over her chest, hugging herself, trying not to think about herself, her own shattered dreams. No more amnesia scenario. *Oh, Mama...*

"What about Roger?" she asked.

Sara's blue, crystal, tearless eyes focused on Dani. "Roger?"

"You two left the party together."

"Oh, yes. He was there. I mean, he walked up to the springs

with us. He stayed at the pavilion while Lilli and I headed over to the cliffs so we could talk in private." She swallowed, stroking the cat. A part of her seemed relieved finally to talk. "We argued, Lilli and I. We so seldom did. My parents discouraged open disagreement, and there was such a big age difference between us."

"What did you argue about?"

"Everything," Sara said.

Dani fought back her impatience, controlled her grief. "You saw her wearing the key?"

"Yes, it—she said it proved Joe didn't want money, because he'd given it to her. I was upset that he had. He'd found it for me, not her. It shouldn't have mattered that I'd just ended our relationship." She checked her anger, her mascara smudged under her eyes, her normally perfect makeup looking garish against her pale skin. "It was just one more thing we argued about. Lilli got very frustrated with me—she just couldn't bear to hear the truth about Joe."

"Did she say who she thought was blackmailing her and Nick?"

Sara shook her head. "She refused to. She said we should just go on back, and I should let her take care of everything."

"Then she was trying to protect you—"

"No!" She dumped the cat off her lap. "She was protecting herself! I knew she was sneaking around behind Father's back, performing in *Casino*. Why Nick picked her I'll never understand, but I don't care."

Dani stood in front of Sara and touched her hand, the nails perfectly manicured, a pale pink. "Sara, what happened to Mother?"

"She fell."

"On the rocks?"

"Yes!" Fat tears rolled down her cheeks, but she remained

eerily still. "I was so upset. I must have backed her up too close to the edge of the rocks, and then when she tried to tell me what to do—I shoved her. I didn't mean anything by it. It was just a reaction." Tears continued to drop down her cheeks, mingling with the others, dripping off her chin. She didn't seem to notice. "It was an accident…it was so dark out there…"

Dani held back her own tears. "Then what happened?"

"Well, I…I buried her, of course."

"Where?"

"At the pavilion." The whites of her eyes were red, the eyelids swollen, and her speech was slurred. "I thought I'd get the courage to confess everything, but Father—he already despised me. I was too wild, I wasn't his perfect Lilli. And Mother had just died, and I needed him, and then I thought, would it be exciting for Lilli just to have disappeared?"

Dani didn't argue with her. It was far, far too late for what Sara Chandler should have done the night her sister fell.

"She'd be a mystery instead of just another dead heiress." She smiled at Dani. "Do you think people would have made such a big deal about her role in *Casino* if she hadn't been a missing heiress? You see, I gave Lilli what she really wanted. Because of me, she got her fame, her mystique."

"But, Sara—"

"No, it's true. Don't you see? Without me, Lilli wouldn't have achieved the status she has."

Dani took her aunt's hands into hers and held on tight. "I'm not disagreeing with you, Sara, but I need you to listen just a moment. Okay? Just listen."

Her aunt didn't seem to hear her. "And Father didn't suffer. Not really. I became his Lilli for him. She wouldn't have done half of what I've done for him. Look at what she did the first time she was to serve as hostess for the Chandler lawn party. She went hot-air ballooning with Mattie Witt! Left me to dress her only daughter! She didn't even show up." Sara looked at Dani, smiled sadly. "My only failing, of course, was that I could never be your mother."

Hanging on to the shreds of her own self-control, Dani fought an urge to tear at her hair and scream at the sky, to let out everything that was raging inside her. "Sara, what did Joe want when he came back here?"

She bit her lip. "He… I'd confessed to him. I got his address from Quint Skinner when he tried to interview your father, and—and I asked him to come see me when he got out or came home on leave. I suppose I shouldn't have."

"You told him everything that happened that night?"

"Oh, yes."

And there you have it, Dani thought, feeling no sense of victory, only a crushing emptiness. But now, at least, the pieces fit together. She touched her aunt's arm. "Sara, did you look over the rocks and actually see where Mother fell?"

"Wh-what?"

"Could you see her from where you were standing?"

"No, I… It was dark."

"But you buried her yourself."

Sara didn't respond.

"I need to ask you one more question," Dani said softly. "Sara, you're not as tall as Mother was—you've always weighed less. How did you get her back up the rocks to the pavilion?"

Sara's eyes narrowed in confusion. "What?"

"It's a tough, steep climb. I've done it."

"I don't know what you mean—"

"You couldn't have carried her by yourself. Sara, Roger knew what had happened, didn't he? You said he was there with you at the springs."

"He… It was dark…he knew it was an accident…" She cleared her throat, struggling to reassert the cool heiress who would know what to do, what to say, in any awkward situation. "He said I should leave and he'd take care of everything. Dani, please—please don't say anything. You have to understand! Roger's protected me all these years. He can't be a part of this."

Dani felt a surge of warmth and pity toward her aunt, even as the sure, inescapable agony of loss swept through her. "Sara, I met Joe on the rocks," she said carefully. How could she go on? How could she explain? "He asked me if there was any way up from the bottom, any path. I told him there's one that winds around and hooks up with one of the old carriage roads, which branches out into various narrow paths, one of which leads back around to the top of the cliffs. It's the long way around—well over a mile. The only other route is straight up the rocks."

Sara frowned. "I don't see your point."

"I found the gold key Mother was wearing on a ledge about fifteen feet below where you said she'd fallen."

"So? Danielle," she said, reverting to Chandler formality, "what are you trying to say?"

"I'm saying no one would drag a dead body—" *ah, no* "—a mile or more or straight up a sheer rock cliff to bury her at the pavilion. Why not bury her where she fell? I'm saying," she went on hoarsely, "that you don't have that kind of strength. Neither does Roger."

"Joe wasn't there—"

Dani shook her head, cutting her off. "Mother only fell fifteen feet. She landed on the ledge."

Her eyes widening, Sara gripped Dani's arm, digging her fingers into the bruised flesh from where she'd landed on her bureau drawer in what seemed like another lifetime.

"You didn't kill her, Sara."

Her aunt's grip was unrelenting.

"She wasn't dead when you left that night."

* * *

John had been fighting with medical types since they'd strapped him to a stretcher and stuffed him into the ambulance like a loaf of bread. Now he was fighting with an emergency-room doctor. "Get me the police," he said.

"Mr. Pembroke, you can speak to the police when we're finished here. Your health—"

"Now!"

The doctor removed his stethoscope from his ears. A nurse was sticking an IV into John's arm, and someone in the background was denying she'd had anything to do with his premature departure from his hospital bed.

He'd already heard snatches of conversation that told him Quint's body had arrived.

"I can have you sedated," the doctor said.

John was suddenly dead calm. "Try that, and I'll rip your head off. Get the police in here. Now. Some rich snot's trying to get away with murder. I'd like to see him in handcuffs before more corpses come streaming in here. My daughter's in particular."

The doctor sighed, as if he dealt with this kind of lunatic patient every day, and looked at the nurse. "The patient isn't in any immediate danger. There are several police officers in the waiting room. Get them in here, please."

Zeke caught up with Sam just as he was going in for surgery to remove the bullet that had gone through his side and lodged in his thigh. He was sedated but alert enough. Zeke figured he had less than a minute before the doctors noticed and kicked him out.

"Sam, think back. When you were on Quint, did he ever bump into, meet or any way hook up with Roger Stone? He's tall, white, fair and rich."

"Dani's uncle, right? Yeah—yeah, Quint talked to him in Congress Park. Not for long. A minute or two. I should have been paying closer attention."

Zeke shook his head. "I should have given you a rundown on all the players. Get well, my friend."

He turned to go, but Sam stopped him. "Dani'll try to solve this on her own. She's the type, and it's her mother."

"I know."

Sam managed a weak grin. "Guess you'd better get busy."

"How dramatic," Roger Stone said, walking onto his father-in-law's front porch.

Dani tensed every muscle in her body to keep herself from shaking. Sara wasn't going to be any help. Sitting primly in her wicker chair, she gently stroked her cat. She didn't even seem to see her husband.

"You killed my mother," Dani said.

He shrugged. "A sin more of omission than commission."

She noticed he had a gun. Well, so did she. When she'd seen him pull up to the curb, she'd judiciously collected it off the porch railing. "She was still alive when you found her on the ledge."

"Alive and alert." Roger leaned against a thick column; he wouldn't be visible from the street. "But not well, I'm afraid. She had a nasty bump on her head. Proved to be far more significant than I'd anticipated. If I'd gone straight to the hospital...but I didn't." His pale blue eyes narrowed on Dani, focused on her with a mix of despair and hatred that was almost palpable. "You're far more like her than you'd ever care to admit."

"She knew you were blackmailing her and Nick."

"It was just for fun. Nothing serious. But you Chandler women—" He shook his head, sighing. "No sense of fun."

Dani wasn't about to argue with him. "So you killed her?"

"She insisted I confess."

"If the blackmail was just for fun, why didn't you?"

Roger laughed derisively. "You aren't as smart as you think you are. If I'd confessed, I'd have lost my shot at everything I'd ever wanted, including your pretty aunt. You see, I'd told her Joe Cutler was her sister's and Nick's blackmailer, that he'd come to Saratoga for whatever he could get—her, money, anything. Only Saint Joe really wasn't interested in any of it. He gave that damn gold key to your mother—do you see what I was up against? He cared about Lilli, really respected her. And he loved Sara."

In the wicker chair Sara cried softly, stroking the white cat.

"I persuaded her to dump him," Roger said. "It was in Sara's best interest."

"Yours, too."

He smiled. "Of course."

"Did Mother threaten to tell the police?"

"No, no, not our holier-than-thou Lilli. She wanted to help me. At that point I hadn't done anything really awful, just extorted a few hundred dollars from her and Nick and lied to Sara, set Joe up for a broken heart and an abrupt departure from Saratoga. Still, I tried to talk your mother out of her point of view." He paused, his lips drawn together in a straight, unreadable line. "While I was talking, I began to notice she'd stopped arguing."

Dani clutched the handle of her gun; she wasn't sure Roger had even seen it. Her heart was racing along at an alarming rate, but there was a part of her that was utterly calm.

"She was lapsing in and out of consciousness," Roger said. "I knew I should have gone for help at once, but I didn't. I just sat there and waited and—well, she died in my arms. I've read up on head injuries in the years since. You can be fine one minute and dead the next, that's why they watch you. If I'd gotten her to the hospital, she probably would have been fine. But the longer she sat there, the more the pressure built up inside her head…" He trailed off, letting Dani fill in the rest.

"So you buried her," Dani said.

"Yes. I neatened up the area as best I could to make a nice grave for her. Sara came back and planted the roses and morning glories—it was a dangerous gamble on her part."

"You let Sara believe she'd killed her own sister."

He laughed, incredulous. "What else would you have had me do? I certainly wasn't the one who'd pushed her off the cliff to begin with."

"That was an accident. Not taking her to the hospital was deliberate."

"Well, you can't honestly expect me to have told Sara what really happened. I'd have been drummed right out of the family."

It was so important to him to be a Chandler. "You're telling me now," Dani pointed out.

"It no longer matters what you know."

Dani grew very still. "You're going to kill me. Sara, too."

He smirked and neither confirmed nor denied her statement.

"You'll blame my death on Sara, saying she killed me because I'd found out she'd killed her sister. You'll say you tried to stop her, but you were too late."

"No one's ever accused you of being stupid, Danielle."

"And you just had to kill your own crazy wife in self-defense. Everyone would believe you because you're Roger Stone of Chandler Hotels."

"I feel no remorse, Danielle. Everything would have been fine if you hadn't found that key." His eyes pinned her. "Let's get moving."

She tried to keep him talking. "Joe was onto you. Sara had confessed to him, but like me, he couldn't put it all together—"

But Roger wasn't biting. "We have to go now. Drop your

gun, please, Danielle. It's not going to do you any good. I'm an excellent shot. I've already shot two men today, and if I have to, I'll shoot you right here on your grandfather's front porch. I'll get away with it, Danielle. You know I will."

He was supremely confident. Her eyes on him, Dani squatted to lay her gun on the floor. Zeke couldn't be hurt. He couldn't be dead. She needed him right now and he...

He was on the porch steps behind Roger.

Dani only barely glanced at him, not wanting to give away his presence. She'd never met anyone so tough who could move so gracefully and silently. Was it his shoes?

I'm losing it.

Oh, Mama, Mama...

"Sara," Roger said gently, "put the cat down, dear. We need to go. I'm taking you to the springs, to Lilli."

Dani still had one hand on her gun. If she let go, she'd have no chance to stop Roger, to protect herself.

He pointed his own gun at her. It looked expensive and bigger than hers. "Nice and slow, Danielle."

Zeke was on the top step, not two feet behind Roger.

His dark eyes held hers.

She knew what he wanted her to do. Not to give up. Not to turn her life over to him.

To trust him.

As he, now, was trusting her.

She let go of her gun so that Roger would think, for a split second, that he had her completely under his control.

It was all Zeke needed.

He grabbed Roger's gun hand and jerked it up and to the side, away from Dani and Sara. The gun clattered to the porch floor. Dani dived for it, but there was no need. When she scrambled to her feet, Zeke had Roger pinned face-first to the porch column, his arm twisted behind him at a painful angle.

"You had Quint kill my brother," Zeke said in a low, hard voice.

"No! Quint didn't kill him—"

"He set him up. Amounts to the same thing."

"What would you have done in my place? Joe gave me a month to come clean about Lilli. He left me no choice! Don't you understand? I would have lost everything."

Zeke was eerily calm. "Quint knew about the picture Joe took. He recognized the key Dani found and came to Saratoga, stole it, started to look at things in a new light and figured you'd used him. So he decided to try to make things right. You found out and you killed him."

"I offered him a fortune—"

"He only wanted justice."

At that moment the police arrived, followed by a taxi that barely came to a stop before Dani saw her father leap out, gauze and adhesive tape trailing from his head. Then the Chandler limousine slid up to the curb.

Sara calmly pushed the cat off her lap, demurely picked a few white hairs off her skirt, leaned over and stretched so that she could reach the Pembroke Springs security guard's gun.

Dani got to her before her aunt could shoot her husband dead.

Nineteen

Dani joined her grandmother in the garden behind her cottage. It was dusk. The questioning by police, the media, was over. Mattie had found an old kite and spread it out on the teak table, with scissors, a stapler, a jackknife and some twisted nylon line. She had on her orange flight suit, and Dani smiled at this woman she had always adored. "You've always been good with your hands," she said.

"My mother's doing. She taught me how to knit, crochet, tat, quilt, do cutwork. All those ladylike skills. I was supposed to teach Naomi after Mother died, only I never did."

Dani sank into a chair. She was barefoot, exhausted but not so overwhelmed anymore. Just damn tired. "Sara said that the afternoon and evening Mother spent with you had made her realize that we were all a part of who she was and that she could never give us up. Nick had let her go after a dream. You helped her to discover for herself whether or not it was a dream she wanted to make come real."

Mattie had tears in her eyes; it occurred to Dani that she'd almost never seen her grandmother cry. "So did Joe Cutler."

"He was a survivor, too. You have an ability to carry on, Mattie, that I..." She shut her eyes a moment, pulling herself together. It would be ridiculous to fall apart now. "That I hope to discover in myself."

"You will," her grandmother said with confidence.

Dani opened a bottle of Pembroke Springs Mineral Water, now tangibly and forever linked with her mother, as the Chandler Stakes had been. She wondered if she finally understood what her mother's dream of singing and dancing had been about. Her frustration and searching in the months after her own mother's death. Had Lilli simply been discovering her own ability to carry on?

"What about Zeke?" Mattie asked softly.

"I've known him such a short time—it's been a whirlwind." Dani tucked her knees up under her chin; she rarely discussed her love life with anyone, even this knowing, kind woman who'd helped raise her. "I never thought I'd fall for someone the way I have him."

Mattie smiled. "I felt the same way about myself some sixty years ago."

Zeke had been through so much in his life. At the police station, trying to explain the past days, Dani had felt his strength of character, even as the sorrow seeped into her until she physically ached. There was no middle ground now between death and abandonment. Her mother was gone forever. But Zeke had lost a father and a mother and a brother and had worked in a field of loss and danger. He'd suffered and struggled and become strong.

"Where is he now?" Mattie asked.

"At the hospital with Sam Jones."

"Are you going to go to him?"

Dani hesitated. If she asked him, Zeke would suffer for her. It would be so easy to let him. To lose herself. "No," she said, but added, "not yet."

Before Mattie could argue, Nick burst into the garden from

the kitchen. He looked scrawny and ancient and very full of himself. Mattie asked him if he'd hunted up a poker game.

"Nope," he said. "Hamburgers."

"Hamburgers?"

"I have eaten enough nuts, seeds, pasta, grains, fruits and vegetables to last me the rest of my life, be that two more hours or another century. Found a place that makes hundred-percent-beef hamburgers and delivers. They'll be here in ten minutes. With french fries and chocolate shakes. And pickles," he said. "Salty pickles."

Mattie was incensed. "If you drop dead on me—"

Nick grinned. "At least it'll be with meat in my stomach."

Zeke paid the tab for his room at the Pembroke and cleared out. He thought Ira looked glad to have him on his way. But before he left the grounds, he stopped at the rose garden. It was almost dark. A small sign warned him not to pick any roses. He did anyway, using his jackknife. Six in six different colors.

"The thing about my daughter is this," John Pembroke had told him from his hospital bed when Zeke had stopped in after visiting Sam, who'd emerged from surgery in good shape. "She likes to have a challenge. Something comes to her on a silver platter, she doesn't know what to do. Doesn't trust herself with anything easy."

An unusual woman, Danielle Chandler Pembroke.

Zeke would never forget how courageous and gentle she'd been with her aunt and Eugene Chandler. Before anyone—him, the police, her father—could react, Dani had quietly taken the gun from Sara's hand. Later, she'd stayed close to her shattered grandfather.

"I need you, Grandfather," she'd told him, and it was what he'd needed, just to hang on.

Apparently Roger had planned to take Sara and Dani back up to Pembroke Springs to kill them, blaming what he could on

Quint and what he couldn't on his wife. Accepting his own cul-
pability wasn't something of which Roger Stone was even re-
motely capable. Quint had robbed Dani, attacked Ira, snatched
John. But it was Roger who'd stumbled on John in the woods
and nailed him, Roger who'd tried everything he could to keep
tabs on Quint and find out what he was doing in Saratoga, to
stop him from uncovering the truth about Lilli and Joe. Roger
had used Quint, and in the end had killed him.

"I should have guessed years ago," John said, shaking his
head with regret. "The connection between Skinner and Roger
was under my nose, and I missed it."

"How could you have known?"

John looked pained. "Quint tried to interview me. Roger
found out. He must have worried about what else Joe could have
told Skinner. Roger used him," John said. "Not long after I turned
Quint down for an interview, I was framed for embezzling."

"Framed? Why didn't you fight?"

He shrugged. "It was airtight. I didn't have the foggiest idea
who'd done it to me—or even if it might have been just some
god-awful mistake someone made. But Roger and Eugene con-
demned me right off the bat. I knew I couldn't win. I thought—
hell, I don't know. I guess I thought Lilli might come back to
me if I became a good Pembroke scoundrel." He was silent a
moment. "But she was already dead."

Walking back to his car, Zeke stopped a delivery van with
the name of some Saratoga hamburger joint emblazoned on its
side. He got the guy to take his six roses and give them to Dani
Pembroke. "Tell her that if she wants to shoot me out of the saddle, she'll have to find me first."

He'd give her a month to track him down. It'd be a challenge for her.

The woman had to figure out for herself that he didn't come
on any silver platter.

Twenty

‐❦❧❦❧❦‐

The temperature had dropped to a tolerable one hundred degrees when John arrived back in Tucson.

His apartment, shut up for two weeks, was sweltering and smelled bad. His ungodly spider had taken over his bathroom. His living area was scattered with the pages of a manuscript he knew now he'd never finish. The historians could have the last word on Ulysses Pembroke's life.

John would write his memoirs of growing up as the only child of his lunatic, famous, impossible mother and father.

His trip to Saratoga had cleaned him out. There was a letter from the IRS in his mailbox. He needed money, fast.

Looking at the squalid conditions of his life, he wondered why he hadn't taken his father-in-law's offer to return to Chandler Hotels. The job would have meant moving back to New York. He'd be closer to Dani and Mattie. His daughter certainly could use all the moral support she could get. After giving her mother a proper burial next to Claire Chandler in the family plot, Dani had rolled up her sleeves and tackled the problems endemic to the kind of publicity she, the Pembroke and Pembroke Springs had received in the past days. On top of having her mother's body turn up after twenty-five years on her property and a murderer in the family, it turned out Roger Stone had hated her guts and floated rumors of her impending self-destruction. Apparently he'd been terrified Eugene would succeed in bringing Dani back into the fold, make her head of Chandler Hotels. Roger had never felt secure; he could never really be a Chandler himself.

John thought it'd be nice to be close to his mother and daughter.

Dani hadn't asked him to stick around, but she'd kissed him at the airport, slipped him a couple hundred bucks and told him she loved him—she who'd never been open about such feelings. That was enough. More than he deserved, for certain.

And he'd already told Eugene no. Even now he couldn't explain why.

He turned up the air conditioners as high as they'd go, opened a Dos Equis and cleaned out his refrigerator. Then he got down on his hands and knees and gathered up the scattered fragments of his manuscript.

Opening another beer, he sank into his lumpy couch and opened up an old photo album. Right there on the front page was his favorite picture, of the five of them together: Nick, Mattie, Lilli, Dani, himself. They looked happy.

They'd *been* happy.

He was still staring at the picture when someone pounded on his front door. "Yeah, coming."

A troop of neighborhood kids trailed into his apartment. They carried fresh tortillas, pots of beans, a big salad and a dozen eggs, all from their mothers, who'd heard he was back in town and were worried he didn't have any food.

He was thanking them profusely when he sensed the foreign presence at his feet. Standing rock-still, he looked down. There was the hairy little bastard. A few of these let loose on the streets of New York City, he thought, and every smarmy New

York cockroach would head for the Hudson River. For a change, he had on shoes. If he moved fast and stomped hard, death would be quick and sure, if not neat.

The spider scampered toward the toilet. John let him go.

The kids howled with laughter. "Hey, Johnny," one impertinent urchin said, "we sure missed you."

He grinned. "I missed you, too, kid."

Twenty-One

~~~ঙ৯৯৯ঙ~~~

Zeke walked down a dirt road to a quiet stretch of the slow-moving, muddy Cumberland River. He went right up to the edge of the water. It was a warm, drizzly afternoon, and he saw two boys out in a canoe in the middle of the river, heard them laughing and fishing, not caring about the weather or, he hoped, anything else.

He remembered Joe taking him out here to show him the spot where Mattie Witt met Nick Pembroke.

"Can't you see it, Zeke? The two of them..."

Joe had howled with glee at the thought. That story was just the greatest thing to him.

Zeke lifted his pack off his shoulders and got out the simple container that held his brother's ashes. Joe had loved the river. He'd loved Tennessee and the people of their small town.

Stepping just into the water, Zeke lifted the top off the container. There were no accusations or excuses within his brother's ashes. No tales of heroics or cowardice. Just the remains of a man who'd died far from home.

Who'd died a hero to his men.

Zeke knew what he had to do.

Maybe people's ideas about his brother would change now

that the truth was out, but maybe they wouldn't. Quint Skinner was dead, and Joe had been dead for a long time.

Zeke didn't care about what other people thought. He only cared about what his brother had been.

He took out a folded bandanna and wiped the rain from his forehead and the tears from his eyes, and then he wiped his fingers until they were perfectly dry.

And as the boys in the canoe disappeared around the bend, Zeke laid his brother to rest in the river he'd loved.

Twenty-Two

"A kite," Mattie Witt explained to her sister a week after she'd come home to Cedar Springs, "is a heavier-than-air object that requires lift—wind—for it to defy the forces of gravity. Now, contrary to popular opinion, there doesn't need to be a great deal of wind, as there isn't today. Here, I'll show you."

With her back to the wind, she held the simple nylon kite up by its bridle. It immediately snapped into a flying position.

Mattie was delighted. "There, you see? Enough wind."

Naomi dubiously eyed the kite and her sister. "Then we're in business?"

"You bet."

They walked down West Main to the field behind the old military academy. Jackson Witt had forbidden them to play there when they were children. It was a perfect place to fly a kite. Naomi had taken a bit of convincing. She worried about catching a chill and old Doc Hiram coming by and thinking they'd lost their minds. Mattie had been her most persuasive. When Naomi came downstairs in a skirt and pumps and one of those plastic rain bonnets over her neatly coiffed hair, Mattie had withheld comment. She herself had on her favorite orange flight suit. Naomi said she looked like an escaped lunatic.

"It's rather cool out here," Naomi said.

Mattie was sweltering. She gestured to the sweater she'd brought along and tossed onto the grass; it was one of Nick's castoffs. "Put that on."

"Oh, Mattie, I couldn't. It's a man's sweater—"

"Then catch a cold."

Clucking to herself, Naomi scooped up the sweater and picked off bits of grass before she put it on. It was even bigger on her than it would be on Mattie. She neatly turned up the sleeves. "I suppose it won't look too tacky from a distance."

Mattie was getting the biggest kick out of her sister. They'd been together for a week, and Mattie felt as if they were kids again; and yet their relationship felt new at the same time. She couldn't explain it. They would fuss at each other and giggle and cry and argue about anything. That morning they'd gone all through breakfast debating whether Billy Cook and Pearl Butterfield had married, though Billy and Pearl both were dead now. Every night, Naomi dragged out scrapbooks and photo albums and told her sister about virtually every birth, death, marriage and divorce that had occurred in Cedar Springs since Mattie had left.

"Let's get this kite into the air," Mattie said.

"Now, Mattie, you can't be running across this field as if you were ten years old. If you trip, you're likely to break a hip. At your age your bones must be brittle."

Mattie loved the way Naomi said "your" age, as if she weren't in her seventies herself. "I'm not going to run. That's not an effective way to launch a kite."

"Oh?"

She had Naomi's interest now. She came in closer. "If there's enough wind," Mattie explained, "you can launch a kite from your hand. It's just a question of getting it above the ground-air turbulence until it soars. But there's not quite enough wind for that today."

"So what do we do?"

"Well, you take the kite and walk downwind about fifty feet. I'll hold on to the line. When a gust hits the kite—you'll feel it—you let go. I do the rest."

"I think I can do that."

This was false modesty, Mattie knew. In her own way, Naomi was one of the most self-confident people Mattie had ever known. She took the kite and walked gingerly across the field, Nick's pilled sweater hanging loosely from her tiny frame.

"If the kite spins and dives," Mattie yelled, "it's too light for the wind conditions. But I don't think that'll be the case."

"We'll soon find out, won't we?"

Naomi stood on her tiptoes and held the kite up as high as she could, and when the gust came, she released it fast—as fast as Mattie would have—and her sister pulled the line. Naomi squealed and ran back to her. "Mattie, it's working! It's working!"

"Yes, yes!"

Mattie could feel the Tennessee wind at her back, Naomi laughing at her side, clapping her hands, as their kite rode the wind, and finally—just a speck of bright yellow in a clear blue sky—soared high above Cedar Springs.

Twenty-Three

~∽⤬∾~

On a blustery afternoon in late September, when the trees were tinged with bright reds and oranges, Dani eased herself into the hot, bubbling, slightly smelly mineral water in a deep tub in Ulysses's elegantly renovated bathhouse. Thousands of tiny bubbles clung to her skin. The feeling was downright erotic. Her body was buoyant in the highly mineralized naturally carbonated water, totally relaxed.

And yet her mind was spinning.

"Step one," Kate had told her, "is to figure out what you want."

That wasn't step one. She already knew what she wanted. She'd known from the moment she'd tried to bonk Zeke on the head with a Pembroke Springs Mineral Water bottle in her garden.

Step one was finding him.

She closed her eyes, trying to abandon herself to the soothing powers of the water. There was nothing to keep her at the Pembroke. The worst of the summer crisis had passed, and with it the rumors, the horror, the blazing headlines, the pity. Tactless as ever, Ira had claimed to be up to the challenge of having a body discovered on the premises of a luxury spa-inn of which he was manager. "It'll lend a certain cachet and naughtiness to the place," he'd said. "As if it needs more."

But he'd done his job, and the frantic phone calls from her marketing consultants and her bean counters had dropped off, not because of any dramatic improvement in her cash flow, but because Eugene Chandler had offered to have a look at her setup and she'd agreed. Her bean counters had had him over to their office—"A man of his bearing shouldn't have to endure your office, Dani"—and they'd gone over her companies top to bottom, inside and out. Her grandfather hadn't found anything he'd change from a purely business if not a personal stand-point. Personally he'd change a lot. But Dani wouldn't self-destruct anytime soon. Even Ira had been annoyingly reassured.

"I've been telling you that for months," she argued.

"Yes, but you're half Pembroke. He's not."

Her professional life remained full, busy and satisfying. It was her personal life that needed work. Living alone had lost its charm. Before Zeke, she'd been fine. Now, although she didn't feel incomplete and wasn't afraid or bored or unfulfilled, she would sit in her garden and wonder where he was, what he was doing, if he still cared. She'd think of how much she loved about him and imagine the possibilities of a life together with him. Was he, too, figuring out new meanings for the past? Trying to let his brother's life teach him something that he could take with him into his own life?

Suddenly Magda burst into the private, all-white salon room. "Up, up," she said in her Russian accent, shaking out a heated white sheet.

"What's the matter? Have I been in here too long, am I going to shrivel up? Magda—"

"No need to panic. You have a visitor, that's all."

Zeke.

Dani jumped out of the tub and into the towel, but Magda, tiny as she was, pushed her toward the cot and made her lie down, at least for a few minutes. Her skin was too overheated. She didn't want to faint, did she?

"Magda, who's out there panting to see me?"

"Well," Ira said, "I wouldn't say I was panting."

If she'd been in more than just a sheet, Dani would have strangled him. "This is not funny, Ira."

He waved her quiet. "Sam Lincoln Jones is waiting at your cottage—says you may be a budding tycoon, but you make a rotten detective. First, however, I need to give you something."

"Ira…"

"So impatient." He handed over an envelope. "It's a plane ticket. We all pitched in here and over at the bottling plant to send you to California. You know, after a crisis it's sometimes polite of an owner to take a damn vacation and let people adjust."

"You're a fine one to talk about what's 'polite,'" Dani said, but she took the envelope. Indeed, inside was an airline ticket. "Ira, I can't let you guys pay for my airfare— Hey, it's to San Diego. Are you nuts? I can't—"

"Isn't San Diego Zeke's home base?"

"Yes, that's my point!"

"Mine, too. Sam will give you directions from the airport to wherever the hell Cutler's got himself squirreled away. The rest is up to you."

"I smell a conspiracy."

"You're the boss, kid, but you're also our friend." Ira smiled at her, unrepentant. "We just want you to be happy."

For the first time in twenty years Zeke had a dream.

He settled back in the pilot's chair of his boat and indulged himself.

Dani would bounce up onto his flybridge with her dark hair and dark eyes and sparkling smile. She'd be wearing one of her little dresses, maybe have her hair pulled back. She'd laugh when she saw him. He'd scoop her up and carry her down to his bunk where they'd make love until dawn.

It was a hell of a dream.

"Zeke?"

Her voice was always a part of it—the things she would say to him, the things he would say to her.

"You can put down the machine gun. It's me, Dani."

He opened his eyes, and she was there on his flybridge, in a short fuchsia dress and fuchsia sandals. His imagination?

"There you are," she said.

"Hello, Dani," he answered, just in case she wasn't a mirage.

"No machine gun?"

"Nope. I'm retired. Out of the business. Think I'll spend the foreseeable future fishing." Or carrying toddlers on his shoulders. Maybe both. But that was a part of his dream.

She shrugged. "Oh, you'll find something to do. White knights always do. I was afraid for a minute I had the wrong boat. Sam said to look for the oldest, ugliest boat out here—"

"Sam?"

"Well, yes. How else did you think I'd ever find you?"

Zeke sighed. "You weren't supposed to find me so easily."

"It wasn't easy. By the way, Sam's a very nice man. He fell in love with Saratoga while he was recovering in the hospital."

Zeke squinted, wondering if he'd had too much sun or too much George Dickel. Was he hallucinating? "What're you doing here?"

She squinted right back at him, as if wondering if he was the same man she'd met in Saratoga a month ago, had slept with and loved and cried with. She wrinkled up her nose, uncharacteristically unsure of herself. "I need a date."

He started off his chair. A date? "Choking's too good for you. I think I'll just throw you into the bay—"

"No, I'm serious."

He looked at her. How could he have fallen in love with such an exasperating woman? "So am I."

Then she laughed that laugh of his dreams. How could she be real?

"Dani—"

"There's going to be a big gala celebration of Nick's nineti-eth birthday in Beverly Hills on Saturday. It's being televised. Mattie's coming. It'll be her first public appearance in a mil-lion years. Pop's flying in from Tucson—well, you can imag-ine all the hoopla."

Zeke just stared at her. She had to have been born to legends and scoundrels. An anonymous upbringing like his wouldn't have made her who she was. She'd have been someone else al-together, and he didn't want that. He wanted her.

"I dragged Kate to New York, and she helped me pick out a dress," she chattered on. "It's by some fancy designer. Cost more than I've spent on clothes in the last ten years. No lie. Grandfa-ther's picking up the bill. My Chandler grandfather. Nick's as broke as ever. Anyway, Grandfather said if I turned up in some-thing out of a catalog, he'd disown me, not that he can, and Kate agreed that if I tried to use the money for a new roof on the bot-tling plant—"

"Dani," Zeke said again.

She snapped her mouth shut. "What?"

"Why me?"

Brushing her hair back with one hand, she didn't answer right away. He knew then, with certainty, that he was asking her to take the biggest risk of all, one that had nothing to do with money or total dissolved solvents or proprietary bottles. One that had only to do with herself. And him.

"Because I love you."

He slid off his chair and went to her, held her in his arms, felt the tension slide out of her. "Oh, Dani," he whispered, "one day you'll know how much I love you."

Because the bourbon hadn't conjured her up, and neither had the sun. She wasn't even a dream.

Dani—what they had together, what they could be together—was real.

* * * * *

Turn the page for an exciting sneak peek at
COLD PURSUIT
by Carla Neggers,
available November 2008
from MIRA Books.

Prologue

Drew Cameron slipped and went down on one knee in the heavy, wet spring snow, but he forced himself back up again, propelled by a sense of urgency he had never known before.

Not Elijah.

Please, God. Not my son...

Drew took another step, then another, pushing against the fierce wind. Sleet cut into his face and pelted the snow-covered trees and juts of granite on the steep terrain. The mid-April storm was worse than he'd anticipated. In the valley, daffodils were starting to pop up out of the ground. It was mud season in Vermont. If anything, he'd worried about causing more erosion on the trails, still wet from the melting winter snows.

He hadn't bothered strapping a pair of snowshoes onto his pack in case conditions changed—a mistake, he realized now.

But he refused to turn back.

He had gone off the main trail hours ago, but he knew every inch of Cameron Mountain. By now, the snow would have covered any footprints he'd left. If anything happened to him, he'd be lucky if searchers found his body for his family to bury.

"I don't care." He spoke in a ragged whisper. "Take me."

Take me instead of my son.

How many fathers through the millennia had cried out those same words?

Drew coughed and spat, catching his breath as he came to a lull in the upward sweep of the mountain. The summit was another thousand feet up, but he had no intention of going that far. In all his seventy-seven years he had never operated on such blind instinct. He couldn't stop himself—he had to be here, now, at this moment, asking questions, searching for answers.

He wasn't an emotional man, but he couldn't shake the fear that had gripped him since dawn.

He couldn't shake the images.

The certainty.

I'm an old man.

Let me die in my son's place.

As he eased into a dense grove of tall spruce trees, their branches drooping under the weight of the clinging wet snow, he saw young men huddled, battling an unseen enemy.

He saw their blood oozing into the ground of the faraway land where they fought.

He heard their moans of pain amid the rapid, nonstop gunfire.

An ambush...

The vision wasn't born of books and movies, and it wasn't a nightmare to be chased off with daylight and coffee. It was real. Every second of it. Drew didn't understand how the vision of his son in battle had come to him, but he trusted it—believed it.

It wasn't a premonition. The attack on Elijah's position wasn't imminent—it was happening now.

Drew stood up straight, out of the worst of the wind. The ice had abruptly changed back to snow. Fat flakes fell silently in the white landscape, but he saw, as clearly as if he were there, the bright stars of the moonless Afghan night. Elijah never talked about his secret missions. He had joined the army at nineteen, without discussing his decision with anyone—not his two brothers, his sister, or his friends.

Definitely not his father.

But there were reasons for that.

"Dear God," Drew whispered, "let me make up for what I did to him. Please. Give me that chance."

For fifteen years he had convinced himself he had done the right thing when he had kicked Elijah out of the house and sent Jo Harper back to her family. Even now, Drew accepted that he'd had no other choice.

That didn't mean he didn't have regrets.

A.J., Sean and Rose would forgive him if he died on the mountain he loved, but they'd never forgive him if their brother was killed. That Elijah had chosen to become a soldier and accepted the risks that came with it wouldn't soften his siblings from holding their father responsible for driving him from the only place he had ever truly wanted to be.

Drew scooped up snow into his waterproof glove and formed it into a smooth ball. Two weeks ago he had held in his palms a dozen fragrant pink blossoms that had fallen from Washington's famous cherry trees, even as Jo Harper, in her early thirties now, had scrutinized him, obviously wondering if he was half out of his mind.

He hadn't told her everything about his reasons for being in Washington, but he hadn't told anyone, not even his own children.

Maybe he *was* half out of his mind.

He dropped the snowball into a drift and noticed footprints—fresh ones—slowly disappearing in the falling snow. He went very still. He wasn't so disoriented and preoccupied that he'd gone in circles.

No, he thought. They weren't his prints.

Someone was up here with him.

He crept past the spruce and, just ahead, saw the little house he had spent most of last fall building. He hadn't bothered with permits—he figured he'd get slapped with a fine one of these days, but didn't care. He hadn't meant the project to get away from him the way it had. After years of searching, he had finally found the cellar hole of the original Cameron house on Cameron Mountain. He had started by fixing up the rock foundation, and next thing, he was drawing up plans for a simple post-and-beam structure, more shed than house, really. When he finished it, he meant to present it as a surprise to his family, perhaps their last surprise from him.

The closest trail was up the remote northwest side of the mountain from a seldom-used old logging road. His great-great-grandfather would have taken that route two hundred years ago. Few even knew about it anymore.

Drew stopped, held his breath.

There…voices.

"We have to think through every detail of every assignment." A man's voice. Arrogant, deliberate. "We can't go off half-cocked. We have to plan."

"You plan." It was a woman this time, impatient. "I'll take action."

"This is a business. We're being paid to do a job. It's not some adventure to keep you in adrenaline rushes. Just because you don't need the money—"

"I *want* the money. That's enough for me."

"You've never killed anyone," the man said quietly.

A slight pause. "How do you know?"

The door to Drew's little house opened, but he didn't look at who stood on the threshold. Instead he gazed up into the falling snow, letting one flake after another melt on his face. Now he understood the vision. He understood why he was here.

It was meant to be. He was a father who would get his wish. His son would live.

Elijah will come home.

The third novel in The Last Stand series

BRENDA NOVAK

Teenagers Sheridan and Jason were parked at the lake when a stranger shot them both. Sheridan lived, but Jason died—and the stranger was never caught. Even though Sheridan's family moved afterward, she's never been able to put the crime behind her.

Because of a new development in the case, Sheridan returns home. But when she's attacked a second time, it's only because of Jason's stepbrother, Cain, that she survives. Cain knows that whoever killed his brother probably isn't a stranger. But figuring out that person's identity is easier said than done—especially since the killer seems to be taunting them both: Watch me.

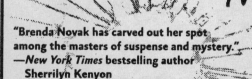

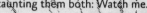

"Brenda Novak has carved out her spot among the masters of suspense and mystery."
—*New York Times* bestselling author
   Sherrilyn Kenyon

Available the first week
of August 2008
wherever books are sold!

New York Times **Bestselling Author**

STELLA CAMERON

Roche is a talented psychiatrist with a life-shattering secret: his sexuality is over-the-top. He's avoided gentle women, but he can't seem to stop thinking about Bleu, a teacher who has come to work in St. Cecil's parish.

And then a man is killed in St. Cecil's church. More murders follow, and the victims are all significant contributors to the church.

Roche and Bleu race to unravel the mystery. But when it is revealed that all the victims are former patients of Roche, Bleu realizes she may not be looking for a stranger....

Cypress Nights

"If you're looking for chilling suspense and red-hot romance, look no farther than Stella Cameron!"
—Tess Gerritsen

REQUEST YOUR
FREE BOOKS!

2 FREE NOVELS
FROM THE ROMANCE/SUSPENSE
COLLECTION PLUS 2 FREE GIFTS!

YES! Please send me 2 FREE novels from the Romance/Suspense Collection and my 2 FREE gifts (gifts are worth about $10). After receiving them, if I don't wish to receive any more books, I can return the shipping statement marked "cancel." If I don't cancel, I will receive 4 brand-new novels every month and be billed just $5.49 per book in the U.S. or $5.99 per book in Canada, plus 25¢ shipping and handling per book plus applicable taxes, if any*. That's a savings of at least 20% off the cover price! I understand that accepting the 2 free books and gifts places me under no obligation to buy anything. I can always return a shipment and cancel at any time. Even if I never buy another book from the Reader Service, the two free books and gifts are mine to keep forever.

185 MDN EF5Y   385 MDN EF6C

Name _____ (PLEASE PRINT) _____

Address _____ Apt. # _____

City _____ State/Prov. _____ Zip/Postal Code _____

Signature (if under 18, a parent or guardian must sign)

Mail to The Reader Service:
IN U.S.A.: P.O. Box 1867, Buffalo, NY 14240-1867
IN CANADA: P.O. Box 609, Fort Erie, Ontario L2A 5X3

Not valid to current subscribers to the Romance Collection,
the Suspense Collection or the Romance/Suspense Collection.

Want to try two free books from another line?
Call 1-800-873-8635 or visit www.morefreebooks.com.

* Terms and prices subject to change without notice. N.Y. residents add applicable sales tax. Canadian residents will be charged applicable provincial taxes and GST. Offer not valid in Quebec. This offer is limited to one order per household. All orders subject to approval. Credit or debit balances in a customer's account(s) may be offset by any other outstanding balance owed by or to the customer. Please allow 4 to 6 weeks for delivery. Offer available while quantities last.

Your Privacy: Harlequin is committed to protecting your privacy. Our Privacy Policy is available online at www.eHarlequin.com or upon request from the Reader Service. From time to time we make our lists of customers available to reputable third parties who may have a product or service of interest to you. If you would prefer we not share your name and address, please check here. ☐

BOB08R